CORNWALL COU

3 8009 034

CW01514203

The Gypsy's Son

Other novels by Theresa Le Flem:

THE SEA INSIDE HIS HEAD

THE FORGIVING SAND

The Gypsy's Son

Theresa Le Flem

Published worldwide 2015 by Theresa Le Flem.

Copyright © Theresa Le Flem 2015

All rights reserved in all media. No part of this book may be reproduced or transmitted in any form without prior permission of the author in writing except in the case of brief quotations within critical essays or reviews.

This book is a work of fiction.
Any resemblance to persons living or dead is purely coincidental.

The author Theresa Le Flem has asserted her right under the Copyright, Designs and Patents Act 1988
284694159

ISBN – 13: 978 – 1514604939

A CIP catalogue record for this book is available
from the British Library.

Cover design by the author.
Photograph of Romany gypsy caravan,
by courtesy of Lynda Collins.
All other photographs © Theresa Le Flem

www.theresaleflem.wordpress.com

One

Cornwall 1953

Finn went to the window, pressed his face against the glass and peered out into the darkness. It was pouring with rain. Bryony, his baby sister, began to grizzle. 'Sshh,' he said, returning to her pram and rocking it gently. But her cries rose into a wail. Picking her up, he carried her into the kitchen. There with relief he discovered her feeding bottle still containing a little milk. Sitting down with her on his lap, he put the rubber teat to her lips and she started to suck. Listening to the rain, and wondering how much longer their mother would be, his eyes came to rest on the shopping bags she had abandoned on the floor. Discovering her purse was missing she had fled back to the shops. 'Oh, I wish Mum would come home!' he muttered.

Within minutes the milk was gone and her crying started again. 'Come on, Bryony,' he said, 'go back to sleep now, eh?' However, her cries grew more desperate and not knowing what else to do, he made a decision. 'Look, we're goin' out to meet Mummy now, alright?' She was too tiny to understand but Finn's activity quietened her for a moment as he wrapped the pink blanket around her. Tucking it in and fixing the hood up on the pram, he put on his jacket and opened the front door. The wind and rain swept in.

It wasn't easy for a boy of eight to manoeuvre the pram out onto into the street, but having tackled the step he finally set off down the steep hill towards the town. The driving rain stung his face. He squinted up his eyes but he was determined to keep going. At any moment he expected to see their mum coming up from the town towards them.

The night air and the motion of the pram had distracted Bryony at first but her cries became louder. As they progressed, the weight of the pram began to pull him down the hill. Faster and faster they went. Blinded by the rain, and with his grasp slipping on the wet handle, it became difficult to hold on as the pram gained momentum. Soon Finn found himself literally being pulled down the incline at a terrifying speed until he was running to keep up with it. Then he tripped and fell.

The pram went hurtling on out of control. Finn jumped to his feet and went chasing after it. But a car, with its headlights blazing, sped past him and in its beam he caught sight of the pram leaving the pavement and lurching into the road. The car swerved to avoid it, its brakes squealed but it hit the pram and sent it careering off sideways.

Finn stopped running. He stared ahead as the initial shock gave way to disbelief. Then a terrible weakness came over him and he bent over, fighting for breath. His hands shook. His knees buckled as the rain beat down on him. Desperately he tried to see, but there was no sign of it. He ran a little further. Then, about thirty feet ahead, suddenly he saw it. The pram was lying dented on its side, its wheels spinning. All was quiet. He shouted. 'Bryony! Bryony?' Now he would have given anything to hear her cry.

Fear, like a thick glove, stole his breath away. Nausea rose in his throat and retreating behind a wall, the shock and revulsion at what he had done overcame him. Trembling he began to weep and then he vomited helplessly. 'I've gone an' killed her,' he whimpered, as he found himself crouching in a clump of wet undergrowth and stinging nettles. Hugging himself, oblivious of any pain, the fear of what he had done hit him with such force he clutched his face in horror. He buried his nose and mouth in his hands, too afraid to breathe. Holding his breath until his lungs were bursting, his heart pounded. It was so loud it filled his ears with a high pitched ringing. Unable to hold it any longer, he gulped for air and fell back into the undergrowth with a long sigh of despair.

However, within minutes he heard shouting. Sitting up, he saw torchlights in the distance and heard women screaming. Fired with a new found energy, Finn sprang to his feet in fear, scrambled out of the shrubbery and ran for his life.

Two

Cornwall's the place to lose yourself if you've a
mind to forget who you are and where you're
going. Gideon Tremayne, a Romany gypsy, was
lost in the past. His mind wandered as he drove his
horse and caravan along the coastal road between
Portreath and Gwithian. Although the sea wasn't
visible from the road, he knew it was high tide because
he could hear the waves lashing the rocks below. The
rugged Cornish landscape around him was high and
level like a plateau, before the sheer drop to the beach
below and the wind cut across from the Atlantic Ocean
mercilessly. Feeling the chill evening air more than he
used to, Gideon lifted his collar and grumbled to
himself. The road was bleak and offered no shelter
except for low Cornish hedges and the occasional
outbuilding. On each side of the caravan he had hung
lanterns but there was little else to light his path under
that dark moonless night. His complexion was like a
windfall apple and his arthritic body was thin and wiry,
revealing that he had seen hard times. Even so, he was
as strong and bold as a terrier, having travelled the
roads of the British Isles all his life.

'Why be I keep thinkin' all these memories?' he
asked himself as he flicked the reins restlessly, causing
his mare to break into a trot. His spaniel, Brannon,
riding at his feet on the driver's board, looked up and

wagged his stump of a tail. Gideon, who was clad in a well-worn jacket, corduroy trousers and strong riding-boots, was not an educated man. He was middle-aged, although what age exactly was unclear. He was poor and he made no claim on the riches of the world, having always supported himself – legally, he would be at pains to point out – entirely from foraging for food from the countryside and making pegs and baskets to sell or barter. With his knowledge of berries and mushrooms, and his skills of hunting and fishing, he survived with no desire for anything more comfortable than a warm bed and a fire. Money made a rare appearance in his hard-working hands but when it did, he handled it with respect. Whatever he did, he was proud of the fact that he always behaved as a gentleman should. In fact, this was his only rule, handed down to him from his beloved grandfather.

The gypsy was inclined to forget about basic things like the time or the date. In spite of this Gideon couldn't help noticing that today, all around him, the granite rocks and the standing stones seemed to be speaking to him. The cliffs, akin to his own resilience, faced the sea with a strength borne out of hardship and self-reliance, just like himself.

Gideon's lifestyle provided him with no more than the bare necessities, but he had no desire for luxury. At times he would take to his trestle-bed in the caravan without supper but in the morning, being woken by the dawn chorus and the light of the rising sun was enough to restore his good spirits. The landscape spoke to him of its history and he took comfort from its endurance. The Cornish cliffs told him of their ancient formation: how they stored evidence of the creation of the world. He remembered when he was a boy, how his grandfather had split rocks on the beach to reveal a surprise: rose quartz, jade or amethyst inside, and sometimes the fossil of a lizard or an insect. His grandfather had taught him how the cliffs keep traces of the past pressed between their pages of quartz, mica and feldspar like an ancient stone scrapbook. The cliffs hoard the earth's treasures in silence, broken only by the tide and the calling of seagulls.

Driving the mare onward, Gideon couldn't help thinking about his youth. He remembered when he had first met his young wife, Sonya, the girl who had come between him and his parents. He had been born into a true gypsy family who adhered to the strict Romany tradition. The rules dictated that they couldn't, or wouldn't accept Sonya into the family because she was a gadje, a non-gypsy. They had refused to allow the marriage. But Gideon was in love. Laws like that seemed ridiculous to him as a young man. He was rebellious and proud, and she was wild and beautiful.

On Easter Saturday it was as hot as a hay-making day. Gideon was twenty-four years of age. He was with his friends, all travelling people, as they set-up the fun-fair which journeyed between Penzance and Plymouth all summer long. They were just beginning a new season. His father had given him sole charge of running the children's carousel rides for the first time and he was pleased with the responsibility and trust his father had shown him. That was the time when the girl, Sonya, had come. The fairground was beginning to fill with crowds. Carousel lights swirled prettily as the music thundered across the sheep-cropped fields to the

6

granite strewn moorland beyond. That was when she asked him for a ride. She wore a thin muslin shirt, the type of cloth he remembered his mother using to strain the goat's cheese. When she came up close he could smell lavender and soap. 'Gimme a ride then, mister?' she said, holding out a sixpence.

'How old are yer?' he asked. 'You ain't allowed on if you're over sixteen.'

'I'm not!' she replied, glancing at him flirtatiously out of the corner of her eye. 'Go on, let me have a go!'

He looked at her doubtfully. 'Nah! You're a lot older than that, my girl, or I be a fool,' he replied.

'OK, so what if I am!' she challenged, standing defiantly with her hands on her hips. 'You wouldn't tell on me would yer?'

'What's yer name?' he asked, smiling. As he spoke he took in her shapely figure and full red lips.

'Sonya!' she cried, pouting, and with a toss of her head she hurled her sixpence at him and mounted one of the brightly coloured horses.

He went after her. 'Hey! Look here Sonya; get off afore I call my dad!' In his haste he let go of the brake-lever and the carousel started up, immediately gaining speed. Several children on the ride began to scream with excitement. Sonya rode like a wild thing, kicking the horse on as though it was real. There was little he could do once the carousel had started and round and round they went. The parents standing below were oblivious and began waving at their children in delight. Eventually it came to a halt and the children started to climb down. Sonya was the last to dismount.

'So?' she said haughtily. 'What's your name then, gypsy boy?'

'Gideon; though some call me Rabbiter.'

'Rabbiter? What kind of a name's that?'

He ignored her and began counting his change. But when she started to walk away, he called after her.

'Want me to bring you a real horse to ride tomorrow?'

'A flea-bitten old donkey more like,' she shouted, throwing her hair back in disgust.

'You'll see,' he said. 'Be here about six, Sonya, an' I'll show you a real horse, the best there is.'

'Might do. Don't forget you owe me a tanner, Gideon!'

'How d'you make that out?'

'You didn't let me have a go, remember? See yer!'

When he led his spirited stallion into the fairground the following evening she was waiting for him. 'Easy now!' he whispered, breathing into the horse's ear. 'She's a wild one this girl, Samson, don't let no harm come to her.' The horse whinnied, stamped his foot impatiently and arched his gleaming black neck.

'You weren't kiddin' were yer!' she cried, her eyes growing wide in astonishment. 'He's really somethin' ain't he!'

Gideon smiled, bursting with pride. 'Give me a minute to saddle him up and you can have a –'

'Oh, to hell with saddles,' she said. 'We don't need 'em, do we boy!' In an instant she had swung herself up on the horse's back and was off.

'Hey! Wait a minute!' he shouted, but his voice was snatched up by the wind. He watched her gallop away and with one magnificent leap, Samson took the far

8

fence and made off across the rough terrain of Trelloweth Tor. Within minutes they were out of sight.

A rumble of thunder brought old Gideon back to the present with a jolt. Another soaking would be enough to bring him down with a chill. The caravan bumped and swayed as the wind caught it and though his old bones were accustomed to the hard wooden seat he felt cold, sore and ill at ease. As though to confirm his fears he shivered. 'Whoa there!' he called and drove the mare gently off the road onto a piece of scrubland. It was too late to look for anywhere more sheltered to spend the night – it was time to stop.

Three

The cast of the Theatre Royale in Tollwithen were in rehearsal for Shakespeare's play, *Twelfth Night*. A storm raged outside. Todd, a young actor who the cast considered to be of only moderate talent, was playing the part of Malvolio. In the lead, Olivia's role was taken by a professional actress called Bianca Tabora. She was in her late thirties; her dark eyes, olive complexion and black hair were Mediterranean in origin and she was, by all accounts, beautiful. Round her slim waist dangled a medley of beads and chains which rattled as she moved. She always dressed flamboyantly in rich colours, clothes she made herself of silk and satin, and an aura of perfume surrounded her. Attractive as she was, she remained unmarried and took life rather more seriously than her appearance might suggest.

On the other hand Todd was a bit of a clown. Todd bore some resemblance to his role character Malvolio, the Shakespearean fool. He was wearing jeans and chewing gum as they rehearsed their lines.

"I told him you were asleep," he began, reciting his lines with a cheeky glance at Bianca over his shoulder. *"He seems to have foreknowledge of that too, and therefore comes to speak with you."* At this point Todd pretended to spit on the floor, before adding: *"What is to be said to him, my lady?"*

Bianca wrinkled her nose in disgust. *"Tell him he shall not speak with me,"* and she turned her back on him. There was a loud sarcastic cough from the director.

'Bianca, darling,' Seamus complained. 'Can we give Olivia just a little more gusto when she makes that remark?'

Bianca raised her eyebrows at Seamus. 'Is it worth it?' she asked. 'Oh, whatever you say.' Todd waited for a moment to see if Bianca was going to repeat her line, but she didn't so he looked at Seamus for a moment and then continued:

"Has been told so, my lady.
He says he'll stand at your door like a sheriff's post..."

He stopped, 'What the hell's a sheriff's post, boss?'

Seamus was annoyed. 'If you're going to keep questioning every turn of phrase, Todd, we'll be here all night! I can't start explaining why Shakespeare chose to...'

Obliterating the director's voice, a loud screech of brakes outside stole their attention.

'Blimey!' shouted Todd 'That sounded close!'

Bianca caught her breath. 'Oh, my goodness,' she cried. 'There must have been an accident!' Flinging down her script she gathered up her long skirt and descended the stage steps. Seamus called after her.

'Bee! Come back here! Bianca! I expect it was nothing!' Dropping his voice to address those remaining on stage he muttered miserably, 'Oh, for Pete's sake! It's like Piccadilly Circus around here sometimes!'

Bianca was already stepping through the stage door and running out into the rain. Arriving in the dark windy street, she stood still for a moment straining to see. Out of nowhere a young boy came running past and bumped straight into her. She cried out and shouted after him but he fled and disappeared. It was pouring with rain and the wind caught her long skirt and sent her hair flying across her face. But she was oblivious to this; her attention was drawn to the crowd which had gathered. Several people, who had evidently also heard the noise, were gathered there. 'What's happened?' she shouted, pulling her long scarf up over her head to cover her hair.

'We don't know, love,' replied a woman. 'It seems a car came hurtling down the hill at full speed and ran right into that pram! It never stopped, never even slowed down! Bloomin' maniac!'

'Oh how terrible! There's not a baby inside is there?' cried Bianca, seeing the pram, badly dented, tipped on its side in the road, its wheels still spinning.

'Hate to say it, love, but I think there is. I heard a baby screamin' only just before. Poor little mite – didn't stand a chance! No sign of its mother though. Funny that! My hubby's phoned for the ambulance. Don't you go and look love, bound to be upsettin'. They'll be here in a minute, let them deal with it.'

But Bianca couldn't wait. Stealing herself, she stepped towards the pram with her heart pounding. Peering inside she saw what looked like a pink shawl. But at that moment the spluttering cry of a baby was heard coming from several yards away.

'Hey! Look over here everyone!' A man's voice came out of the darkness. 'There's a baby's here – it's alive! Over here!'

'Let me see!' pleaded Bianca, hurrying towards him. She shuddered as the cold wet struggling bundle was placed into her arms. The strength of the baby's body as it kicked and cried amazed her. She looked for its little face, fearful of what injuries she might see. Finding no sign of blood she began talking gently and rocking the baby in her arms. Gradually the infant relaxed and quietened. 'It must be a little girl,' she told the crowd. 'Look at her pink bonnet and booties.'

'Ah! Bless her heart! Be careful though. She's bound to be hurt love, go easy; they'll be on their way now. Hear that?' They all listened and true enough, they could hear the ringing of an ambulance approaching in the distance.

'She seems fine,' said Bianca. 'Not a scratch on her!'

'Perhaps she was thrown clear,' suggested another onlooker. 'That bit o' grass would've softened her fall. Lucky to be alive, ain't she.'

The baby stopped crying and her tiny face peered up at them curiously. Her big brown eyes fixed on Bianca with an expression of wonder and trust.

First the ambulance, and then the police arrived. A nurse took the baby up the steps into the foyer, examined her thoroughly and finding no injuries, she wrapped her in a thick blanket and handed her back to Bianca. There was a bustle of activity, with people giving their account of the event and speculating as to how the pram came to be in the road. Satisfied that the baby wasn't hurt, Bianca sat cradling her while gradually the noise, the questions and the attention of the onlookers faded away and the crowd dispersed into the stormy night.

Retreating from all the attention, Bianca carried her into her dressing-room while she waited for another policeman to arrive at any moment who, she had been told, was coming to take the baby since no-one had come forward to claim her. She cherished the last few minutes she had left with her and gazed into the baby's face seeking clues to her identity.

'You're the lucky one, aren't you!' she whispered. The baby's tiny hand grabbed her finger in response and she inhaled excitedly. 'Ga ga!' she said, kicking her strong little legs. 'Who would have believed it?' she asked herself. 'A baby almost crushed to death in a pram and no-one there with her? It doesn't make sense.'

A sharp knock came on the door and a policeman entered. 'Excuse me, miss. Let's have a look at it then.' He looked down his nose at the infant without stooping, his back straight and his helmet shading his eyes. 'Do we know whose child it is then? I gather you're not its mother?' He had his notebook at the ready and looked at her expectantly.

'No, she's not mine. I've no idea who she is, officer. It was a miracle she wasn't killed.'

'Most certainly was, miss. Can I take your name please?'

'That's my name there!' Bianca nodded towards a poster on the dressing-room wall. She was still rocking the baby in her arms.

The officer cleared his throat. 'Yes, of course; Miss Tabora.'

Bianca's attention was solely on the baby. The policeman, asking her a string of questions to which

14

she had no answers, appeared to be losing his patience.

'I'm sorry, officer,' she said, 'but I didn't see it happen. I was inside. We were busy rehearsing. We heard something and I rushed out to look.'

'I see.' He nodded while apparently writing this in his notebook. 'What did you observe when you arrived on the scene?' Bianca told him about the noise, the crowd, the young boy who nearly knocked her over, and the fearful possibility of discovering the baby horribly injured inside the pram.

After a while he seemed satisfied. 'Well, no-one's claimed it so far, to my knowledge. It's a bit of a mystery I don't mind telling you, miss. We'll continue with our investigations and make house-to-house enquiries, but these things often take time. It could have been abandoned by someone off the London train or anything like that. We have hundreds of cases like this y'know – babies dumped on doorsteps, in phone-boxes, and the like.' He straightened his shoulders. 'Right! I'll send the district-nurse up for it, miss, to take it off your hands.'

'Thank you, officer, but there's no need, really. She's quite content to stay with me as you can see. I have a large apartment and I would willingly take care of her until her mother comes forward.'

'Very kind of you, miss, I'm sure, but it's regulations. We have to go by the book you understand.'

'Yes, of course, officer.' She turned once again to the baby and holding her up towards him, she said playfully, 'Say: "thank you" to the kind policeman.'

A pink flush spread across the officer's face as if he had just become a grandfather. 'Ah, just look at her!' he said, removing his helmet and tickling the baby's chin. Off-duty for a moment, he seemed to come to a sudden change of heart when he said, 'If you'd like to look after her yourself, miss, it could be arranged I suppose.' He scratched his balding head. 'Think you can manage her then?' Bianca assured him that she could and after replacing his helmet and resuming his professional stature, he added: 'Well, she seems happy enough. Can I have your address? I'll tell Sergeant but I can't make any guarantees mind. Rules are rules after all.'

When he had left, Bianca carried her through to the theatre's kitchen, where she laid her in the laundry basket which could double as a temporary cradle. This contained remnants of material, velvet and taffeta, which had been discarded after the recent bout of costume making. The kitchen served a lot of purposes. On the table stood a Singer hand-sewing machine and a heap of sequins, lace, and ribbons. An ironing-board was in the corner near the sink, a dress draped across it and beside this a garment rail with coat-hangers bulging with costumes of every shape and size. Next to this there was a fridge on top of which were stacked numerous packets of breakfast cereals, the staple diet of a dedicated theatrical company. There was also a neglected cooker with fat burnt into black and brown stains on the top. It was a busy room with actors constantly popping in and out, making coffee or re-touching their make-up. It was a place familiar to her, and was effectively her second home.

Finding an unopened pint of fresh milk in the fridge, she set about making a feed and five minutes later she was spooning warm milk into the baby's mouth. 'Is that nice?' she asked, and began to worry as the baby started fretting, used to suckling no doubt and frustrated by the hard metallic spoon. But soon hunger overcame her confusion and she began swallowing eagerly with her brown eyes flitting about as each new mouthful touched her lips.

The new role excited Bianca like no other. Feeding the baby, seeing her respond to her, was something which had always been denied her. Marriage and a family were things of the imagination, roles she could play on stage but never in reality. At her age she was unlikely now to bear a child. Love was never as strong and passionate as it was in plays like *Romeo and Juliet*. In relationships, she always ended up feeling she had gone from being the leading-lady to the understudy. Love! What was it about love that meant it never lasted? Perhaps it's easier on the stage to play a person who is always attractive, whose words are eloquent, and whose face is always beautiful. It's easier to act out someone else's life rather than your own. In looking at things that way, Bianca knew she could keep her sadness at arm's length, never having to admit to herself how empty her life really was.

A shopping list was forming itself in her mind. She would need a feeding bottle, nappies, clothes and blankets...it was all new. Could she afford it? If she was honest, she hardly knew anything about looking after babies. But her anxiety evaporated as soon as the baby girl clutched her finger and opened her tiny mouth for more milk. 'We'll manage somehow,' she whispered, 'won't we little one?'

Whereas some directors have a clear idea of what the tone of a production should be: how much realism to portray and where to inject humour, Seamus muddled through. He made it up as he went along. This was infuriating to some members of the cast.

'Never mind the audience,' he would say. 'Only we need to know what goes on this side of the curtain!'

Some of the cast loved him for his easy going approach. Others were frustrated by his lack of discipline and tendency to move the boundaries. However, on opening night the whole company trusted that he would bring the show together, and he usually did. As Seamus sat on a box at the back of the stage sipping his tea, he thought about Bianca taking charge of "that baby" with a mixture of disbelief and irritation. He waited for her to return to rehearsals and wondered why other people's needs always took precedence over his own. She would never, and had never, taken him seriously. He knew there had been some sort of road accident but he had no intention of getting involved. The last thing he wanted was to be called as a witness. If people were injured he would rather not see them, and if they were dead there was nothing he could do. So he sat listening to the ambulance bells and the police cars, wishing he lived in Shakespeare's time when folks sat around reciting poetry and playing the lute. It was so much more civilised then, he thought, even if they didn't wash too often. Grudgingly, he stood up and shouted. 'Todd? Toddy, where the hell are you?' Almost immediately the young man appeared. 'Oh, there you are! Can you call everyone together please? We'll be taking Act One from the beginning of Scene Two.'

However, Bianca had no intention of returning to rehearsals. Having fed the baby, she gathered a few things together and telephoned for a taxi. 'Come on, little one,' she said. 'We're going home.' Lifting her up, she found the baby's natural scent so sweet, and the touch of her firm round head against her cheek so comforting that only then did she realise how attached to her she had already become. A pang of regret gripped her. 'Poor darling!' she whispered. 'If they come to take you away, please don't let it be tonight. Let me have you for a little while!' Minutes later, swallowing her tears, she swept out of the theatre door with the baby in her arms.

Todd was standing in the doorway smoking. 'Not another puppy, Bee!' he said. 'Look what happened last time, remember? You nearly broke your heart with that stray!'

'It's not a dog, Toddy, it's a baby! Look at her, such a sweet little face too!' Bianca pulled the blanket back and showed him.

'Ugh! They all look the same to me! Not yours is it? Blimey, you kept that quiet!'

'Honestly!' Bianca sighed. 'Can't you be serious for once in your life?'

'Nope', he replied. 'Don't do serious!'

'Todd! It's a miracle she's still alive.'

'Yeh, right.'

Bianca appealed for some compassion. 'She must be from a poor family, look, her clothes are worn thin.'

'Some woman's probably abandoned her on purpose,' ventured Todd. 'You know, some young girl who's got herself into trouble, got fed-up and couldn't cope. Chances are she knew a softie like you would come along and take pity on it.' He looked at the baby in a bored fashion. 'So, are you keeping it then?'

'Don't be silly Todd. You can't just keep lost babies! They belong to someone. And even if they don't – you have to go through the adoptive process properly.' The baby started whimpering. 'It's alright, darling, you must be tired; of course you are.'

'Well? Will you then?' he persisted.

'What?'

'Keep it. You know, adopt it like.'

'I don't know, do I? I've only had her five minutes, give me a chance! Go and tell the others to carry on rehearsals without me. Her parents are probably going frantic trying to find her at this very moment. I bet that policeman will be back before long with some desperate woman running behind him crying her eyes out.'

'So – if she cared about it that much, where is she? Bet you she doesn't give a damn. Bet you she's abandoned it! She's probably got ten kids at home already an' can't handle any more.'

'Oh, get lost! You don't know the first thing about babies!' snapped Bianca.

'Well anyway,' he retorted. 'Seamus said to hurry up; you're on in the next scene and they're all waiting.'

'Tell him I'm busy!' she exclaimed. 'Men!' she added, turning to the baby. 'They always expect women to drop everything to suit themselves, don't they darling!'

'Why don't you go and tell him then?' demanded Todd. 'Why should I do your dirty work?'

'Look! The taxi's waiting; I've got to go. Tell him I'll be back first thing in the morning, I promise.'

'So, what do you expect us to do without you tonight?' he asked, folding his arms and leaning against the door-frame.

'Oh, for goodness sake, Toddy, improvise!'

Four

Having spent a few days trading his baskets in and around Newquay, Gideon was pleased to have left the town behind. He drove his mare down the quiet country lanes towards Kestle Mill. It was good farming country and in the near distance he could glimpse the magnificent rooftops of a manor house. It would be a braver man than he, thought Gideon, who would dare to knock on that door and try selling his wares. It would take a fair number of baskets to impress the gentry who lived in that grand house. However, when he stopped to rest his horse, workers in the fields told him the old place was undergoing restoration and they kindly volunteered some useful information: some new tenants had recently moved in. They might have need of some practical items. He was dwelling on the possibility of doing some trade with the kitchen staff but he wasn't sure he should venture up that long drive for fear of being accused of trespassing. He thanked them anyway, told them he would think about it and urged his horse forward.

Driving on, he had covered another few miles when suddenly he spotted something moving in the hedgerow.

'Whoa there, Belle…Whoa!' he called. Was it his imagination or had he just seen a small nut brown head of hair? Yes, there it was again! A little head bobbing up and down, and two badly-scratched knees. It was a boy, he figured, a small boy trying to hide under the hedge. He reined in and stopped.

'You alright down there?' he called, hooking the reins over his knee and resting his arms. He had no intention of passing on by until he could discover who the head and knees belonged to. He asked again until at last the timid response came.

'Yeh, I'm OK.' Two brown eyes gazed up at him. It was a boy, aged about seven; and he looked petrified.

The mare, sensing an opportunity to snack, lowered her head and snatched a few mouthfuls of grass from the roadside. Gideon climbed down from the caravan, and taking off his hat found a fallen branch to sit on.

'So why aren't yer runnin' around playin' like other kids?' he asked gently. 'What yer be doin' hidin' there in the bushes, lad?'

'Just leave me alone will you!' the boy shouted, hiding his face behind his thin arms.

Gideon was never a man to hurry things. He drew a tin of liquorice from his waistcoat pocket and taking one himself, held the tin out towards the boy and rattled it. 'Want one?' he asked. 'There's only a few left but yer welcome.'

'No, go away an' I wish I was dead!'

'Well, I'm right pleased yer ain't. It wouldn't be nice at all comin' across a dead body stuck under the hedge. What do yer want to spoil a nice evenin' by bein' dead for?'

As he said this, a faint smile crossed Gideon's weather-worn face and he sat chewing, while the dying sun caught the gold earring in his ear and sent a flash of

23

light into the dark woods beyond. The mare moved on a few feet to reach more succulent grass, drawing the caravan with it. Seeing her, Gideon shot a loud warning and got to his feet. 'Don't yer dare move!'

The boy jumped in fright, but realizing the reprimand was directed towards the horse, he relaxed again. Standing up, Gideon applied the brake, took hold of the reins and tied them to the bar below the driver's board before sitting down on the branch again.

'So, what's yer name then, lad?' he asked. 'I'm Gideon, an' that there dog o' mine's called Brannon.'

The boy looked up curiously, and following the gypsy's gaze saw the sleeping spaniel's head lolling half-in, half-out of the front canopy of the caravan. Brannon was liver and white, with a patch over one eye.

'Are yer in a spot o' trouble then, lad?'

The boy sniffed and a sob escaped from his throat. 'I dunno how it could have 'appened?' he said, and crawling out of his hiding-place, he began to unload his problems. It seemed he couldn't help himself. Once he started he couldn't stop. 'If only time would wind back a bit,' he sobbed. 'I shouldn't have gone out after me mum at all but I thought she'd be comin up the hill. She said she must've left her purse down the shop so she went back to find it. But she was gone ages an' she didn't come home.'

'Oh?' He scratched his head. 'But she did come back eventually like, eh?' he asked good-naturedly. He always enjoyed a good story.

'No, she never. I kept thinkin' when me mum's home it'd be alright. But my baby sister kept cryin' an' screamin' an' I didn't know what to do. She were

24

hungry so I gave her the bit of milk left in her bottle but she wanted more an' it were all gone. I couldn't stop 'er cryin'.' He sniffed and wiped his nose on his sleeve. 'I picked her up and cuddled her but she just kept screamin' an' screamin'.'

Glancing at Gideon uncertainly, he continued: 'I thought: I know, I'll take her out in the pram an' go an' look for Mum. I thought she'd be just comin' up the hill.' He broke off, realizing now he had trapped himself into carrying on with his story. 'It's not fair,' he complained. 'I'm only eight an' I don't know about babies.'

Gideon shook his head. 'No, I ain't no good wi' kids neither,' he said, as though confiding in an old friend. 'What happened then?'

The boy continued breathlessly, mesmerized by his recollection. 'I wrapped her up in her blanket an' put her in her pram an' pushed her out into the street.'

The gypsy nodded wisely. 'Good idea, lad,' he commented, but he was watching him now, under his whiskery eyebrows, wondering at the source of the boy's distress and where it was all leading.

'It were rainin' out there though,' he continued. 'It were freezin', but I put the cover over her an' tucked her in. There was no sign o' me mum, so I carried on. It's heck of a steep down the hill an' it started to pull me, the weight o' the pram I mean.' He shuddered, struggling now to remain calm. 'It pulled me, faster an' faster, an' the wind was blowin' and then suddenly I tripped and fell over!'

'Flamin' Charlie! Did yer hurt yourself, lad?'

Ignoring him, the boy continued re-living his terror: 'I went straight over, flat on me face an' I'd let

25

go of the handle o' the pram hadn't I – I didn't mean to!'

'Yeh?' prompted Gideon. 'Go on, lad! An' then what happened?'

'When I looked up I could see the pram runnin' down the hill an' I could hear Bryony still bawlin' her head off inside. I got up an' raced after it. I ran as fast as I could, mister, but I couldn't catch up with it.' At this, the boy put his head in his hands and spoke through his fingers. 'Then I saw it run all wobbly like into the road an' a car come, an' I heard the brakes screech!' He dropped his hands and stared at the ground, deathly pale. 'An' then I knew she was gone.'

'Gone, yer say? What, killed yer mean?' asked Gideon, and shook his head solemnly. The boy nodded; his face was ashen grey. 'An' the car didn't stop,' he added miserably.

'Poor little blighter!' exclaimed Gideon and breathed out a deep sigh. 'You did yer best, lad. It can't be helped. Things happen what can't be explained, lots o' things, some's good but some's really bad.' He stopped speaking for a moment, contemplating the baby's fate.

Finn began to babble now through his tears, unable to hold back. 'I couldn't run no more, mister. My legs went all watery an' I don't know why but I just went an' hid behind a wall!'

Gideon nodded and reaching out, picked a blade of grass and began chewing the end thoughtfully. After a moment or two of silence he glanced across at Finn. 'And when did this 'ere happen, lad? Were it yesterday or what?'

The boy eyed him suspiciously and shook his

head. 'Dunno how long ago,' he replied. 'It were cold then, freezin', an' it's warmer now. I've been runnin' an' hidin' since then. I found a farm an' I were sleepin' up on top o' the straw bales in a barn,' he sniffed, 'till the cowman saw me an' chased me off. I don't want no-one catchin' me an' lockin' me up in prison 'cos I didn't mean to kill her.'

Gideon's curiosity caused him to pause a moment while he took in the boy's grimy complexion, his torn soiled clothes and wild hungry eyes. He figured he must have been on the run for weeks. A feeling of great compassion came over him. 'Of course yer didn't mean her no harm, lad. Any fool can see that. Never mind,' he murmured. 'You're only a young pup an' all.'

Encouraged by this comment, the boy sniffed again and rubbed his nose.

'What have yer been livin' on then? What have yer been eatin', lad?' asked the gypsy, seeing the boy's wan face and thin little legs.

'I...' His voice shuddered. 'I pinched some o' the cow's food an' a bit o' the milk sometimes when the cowman weren't looking.'

'Yer ain't been livin' just on that though, have yer lad?'

'Sometimes I found some stuff, in sheds an' that. There were some chickens so I got some eggs as well sometimes, ugh! I had to eat 'em raw. I liked the chickens. They were nestin' in the straw an' I used to cuddle up with 'em 'cos they were nice an' warm. There was a lady in one house – she used to chuck some bread an' scraps out for 'em every mornin' an' I had some o' that.'

'But why didn't yer go home, lad? Yer could've

starved to death out here on yer own.'

'I can't go home again, not without me baby sister.' He sniffed and sighed as though relieved he had finished his confession. 'Anyway, me mum was bound to have seen the baby all killed an' all the blood an' everythin' an' the pram all smashed up. I couldn't face tellin' her what I'd done.' He began crying again, distraught by grief and guilt. 'I didn't mean to kill her, honest. I'd never 'ave hurt her on purpose.'

'Of course yer wouldn't, lad!' exclaimed Gideon. 'What about yer dad though? Where was he? He would be worried about yer both wouldn't he, an' come lookin' for yer?'

'I ain't got no dad,' replied the boy bluntly. 'Me dad went sea-fishin' an' didn't come back. Anyway, one day me mum said he'd got drowned an' he wouldn't be comin' home no more. When I asked her about him she used to shout at me an' start cryin' and then she said I shouldn't talk about him 'cos it only upset her.'

Gideon could hardly conceal his sadness at the boy's story. He thought for a moment, and scratched his head philosophically. 'Yer don't want to go blamin' yerself for an accident like that, lad. An' yer baby sister wouldn't have felt a thing. Bang! And that's it – no sufferin'. That's just how I despatch rabbits, so they don't feel no pain. I wouldn't want to hurt no livin' creature neither. Here!' he said, and he held out a grass-stained hand. 'Shake old Gideon's hand now, because I be a gentleman, an' you, my young fella, you be a gentleman too in my opinion!'

The anxiety and fear melted away in the boy's eyes. He stretched out his arm and the old gypsy took

28

the small hand in his and shook it firmly.

'Gideon – Gideon Tremayne, though I be known to some folks by the name o' Rabbiter. Pleased to meet yer, lad! An' what's your name?'

'Finbarr McKinney. Finn they call me.'

'Where is it yer hail from then, Finn? Round these parts? I don't recollect hearin' any tales o' that nature in the news hereabouts. Where did it happen, did yer say?' But Finn was reluctant to own up to where he came from; he looked away, his face pinched with worry. 'It don't matter where it were.' Nodding, Gideon agreed they had dwelt long enough on the tragedy and his thoughts turned to more practical matters.

'Well Finn,' he said. 'I think after that I'm ready for my supper, how about you?'

The boy nodded. 'I'm starvin' - I ain't got none though.'

'That makes two of us, but we'll soon sort that out!' He cast a critical eye up into the evening sky, and declared: 'This place is as good as any to pitch camp I suppose, an' I think the horse has had enough for one day. Looks like yer need a hot supper inside yer an' a good night's sleep. How about joinin' me? We'll set up camp over there an' we'll worry about tomorrow when tomorrow comes, eh?'

'Thanks mister,' replied the boy, wiping his nose on his sleeve. Gideon led the mare off the road and the caravan went bumping and swaying over the rough ground. He unbuckled her harness, tethered her to a tree and gave her some oats before setting about making a fire. 'Come an' sit yerself down here lad, while I sort out a few things.

Finn did as he was told and sat on the rough blanket Gideon had spread on the ground. Although it wasn't that cold, he sat hugging his knees shivering while he watched the gypsy gather sticks and dried grass. But however much he rammed his jaws together, he couldn't stop his teeth from chattering or his limbs from trembling. Night was descending fast as Gideon crouched down over the pile of fuel he had gathered and started to light the fire. Strange bird-song seemed to echo Finn's feeling of alienation. He was far away from home and from the day the accident happened, his life was irreversibly changed. There was no question of him going back; he had made up his mind about that. It was as though he could cancel out of his mind the memory of his experience with the pram, the loss of Bryony, even the existence of his mother. It was like he was another boy altogether, with another life, because his old life had gone so horribly wrong. He was going to begin his life anew. He took a deep shuddering breath and sighed, as though he was tearing a page out of his school-book and starting again.

'All yer need to do to make a fire, lad,' came the gypsy's voice, breaking into Finn's thoughts. 'All yer need is two bits o' wood, bit o' dry grass an' a bit o' patience,' he said, blowing through his gnarled hands. 'Come on, yer beauty!' he said, purring softly over the bunch of hay as smoke began to filter out through his fingers. Like a firefly, a tiny burning ember opened its wings and fluttered into a flame. The first crackle of life caught the dry grass and the gypsy released the smouldering bundle onto the collection of twigs and leaves. Within minutes, flames leapt up into the evening air. 'Right, Finn, sit yerself down here, lad,

30

near the fire and keep feedin' in bits of twigs – don't let it die down too much – an' I'll be back in two secs with somethin' to cook.'

Finn did as he was told, glad of the warmth from the fire which had the effect of easing the tremble in his limbs, and melting the tension in his shoulders. His back relaxed and as the heat toasted his face and knees, he huddled closer to the fire and fed into it twig after twig, watching the flames dance and the shadows lengthen. Beside him, the spaniel lay panting and watching for his master's return with anticipation.

Gideon soon re-appeared with a dead rabbit strung over his shoulder. 'Soon have this skinned an' roasted, lad. They don't call me Rabbiter for nothin'. Find us a good stout bit o' branch will yer?' While Finn watched in astonishment, the gypsy took out his pocket-knife and skinned and gutted the rabbit in a matter of minutes. Squatting down by the fire, he drove a stick lengthwise through the body and strung it up above the flames. Soon the meat was sizzling and giving off an appetising aroma. 'Smell's good, don't it, my 'andsome! Ever had rabbit afore?'

Finn nodded. 'I've seen 'em hangin' up in the butcher's shop in Tollwithen. Me mum makes a lovely pie with it.' He caught a sudden image of his mother in his mind's eye. He could see her as clear as day standing at the kitchen table rolling pastry, her hair done up in a red scarf round the top of her head and her cheeks rosy from the heat of the oven. She was happy then.

'Mother's generally do,' replied Gideon, 'but I prefer it as it is – can't see the point myself in wrappin'

31

it all up in dough. All goes down the same way don't it eh?' He cast Finn a sideways glance. 'Tollwithen yer say? Be that yer home town then, Finn? That be a long trek from here, up Bodmin way.'

Realizing he had said too much, Finn stared hard at the fire.

'You thirsty?' Gideon asked, changing the subject.

'Yeh,' he replied. So tired now, he hardly cared that Gideon had discovered his origins so easily.

'Here,' said Gideon, and he went to the back of the caravan and filled him a tin can full of cold water. 'Plenty more where that came from. Drink all yer like and help yerself to more if yer want it.' The water tasted as cool as melted snow, like rainwater on apples. It had a rusty, slightly sweet flavour.

'What did the cow's food taste like eh, Finn?' asked Gideon, his eyes twinkling with curiosity.'

The boy sniffed. 'A bit like Weetabix I suppose...an' a bit hard.'

Gideon chuckled. 'I might 'ave to try some o' that! Mind the meat for me a sec, will yer? I'll just go and unharness Belle. She'll be wantin' her oats. I've got her bag ready in the back.' When Gideon had gone and his gentle voice could be heard crooning away to the horse in the background, Finn started to feel better. He turned the meat on the branch that was lodged in a crook over the fire and the smell was delicious. He could hardly wait to taste it.

When the rabbit was cooked, Gideon fetched him a tin bowl from the back of the caravan. 'Here yer are lad,' he said, tearing him off a good portion of meat and handing it to him. 'Get stuck into that. I'll manage without my bowl tonight. Tastes just as good, if not better I'd say, straight off the bone!' Blissfully the boy sank his teeth into the moist joint. The spaniel lay fully alert, his tongue lolling from his mouth as he watched them eat.

'Here, fella!' said Gideon, tossing a morsel of meat towards him. After eating their fill, water was boiled in a kettle hanging over the fire. While they were drinking tea, the gypsy asked:

'So, have yer ever camped out afore?'

'Only since I ran away,' replied Finn, 'an' I never had no fire.'

Gideon straightened his cap. 'Well look, lad. If yer mum's anythin' like mine were, she'll be pinin' for yer. Got any brothers at home?'

He shook his head.

'Nor sisters, Finn?'

'Not now,' he replied glumly.

'So yer live in Tollwithen, right?'

Finn nodded reluctantly, not taking his eyes from the fire. He wanted a new life. He didn't want the old life back where it had all gone wrong. He didn't want to think about that. 'It's nice here. I ain't goin' back, never.'

'But what if your mother's frettin' about yer? It's only right yer tells her where yer are.'

Finn was mute. He began to feel afraid again.

'Tell yer what: yer can stay wi' me tonight an' tomorrow, we'll see if we can't start makin' our way back, eh? It'll take us a day or two at least to get there. You've covered a good stretch. Belle's a faithful old girl an' she'll get us there so long as I give her plenty of oats and see her feet are OK. Yer poor mother must have been out of her head with worry – when she came back, I mean, and found yer gone,' he added, glancing at Finn. 'It's one thing losin' a baby, but losin' yer son as well – that's just plain tragic that is – lookin' at it from her point of view.'

Finn turned his face away and refused to comment until eventually the gypsy began to move about carrying blankets and cushions as though sorting out where he could sleep. He wondered if he should creep away and run off but he hated the thought of being alone again, of having to leave the fire and losing the gypsy's company, even if he was asking a lot of questions. He felt safer than he had done in a long time. At least if he stopped one night it would give him some time to think. But he might have to make his escape and move on again before the gypsy woke in the morning. There was no way he was going to let him take him home.

Gideon climbed up the steps into the caravan. Moments later he came back carrying a violin case. 'Know what this is?' he asked, undoing the clasps and opening the lid with a look of rapture on his face. 'Ever seen a fiddle like this afore, Finn?'

Finn squinted at it in the smoky darkness. 'I ain't never seen one o' them close to,' he replied. 'Some kids at school played 'em. I asked me Mum if I could learn, but she said lessons cost money and that sort o' money we ain't got, so I never done it.'

Holding it up proudly, Gideon polished the back of it with his sleeve. The wooden body of the violin glowed in the firelight.

'How come you've got somethin' nice like that?' asked Finn, looking at the gypsy sideways. 'Did you

34

nick it?'

Gideon threw back his head and laughed. 'Yer think old Gideon's a thievin' tinker, do yer? No, it's my family heirloom, Finn. It's been handed down to me from my gran'father. But yer right about it lookin' like it would be worth stealin'. Listen, I don't believe in stealin' stuff. Folks as can't be content without eyein' up what others have got, an' takin' what don't belong to them, well, they ain't worth knowin' in my opinion.'

Finn hung his head, looking awkward. 'Sorry,' he mumbled.

'We'll get to know each other, Finn, happen as time goes by. But you're right, there's them as would steal it from under my nose and sell it. Some folks don't know the real value of a beautiful thing like this. My gran'father told me it be worth somethin' but he didn't judge the value of it in money. It's worth more to me than that. There's folks would like nothin' better than to get their hands on it and not for makin' music with neither.' Saying this, Gideon sighed and plucked the strings one by one with grimy fingers. 'It's bound to me by blood, this fiddle, Finn, an' I always keep it by me. They might call some of us "common gypsies". They might say we'd steal the coat off yer back. But they don't have no respect for a thing of real beauty. There be things that go beyond the weight of coins in a man's pocket.'

Finn was quite in awe of this serious tone and sat listening in silence.

'I wish I still had the art o' playin' it though, lad,' continued Gideon. 'My gran'father learned me when I were your age. He could play all them classicals an' that. But look at my hands now. Reckon too much hard work has taken all the music playin' out of 'em.' He held out his hands for inspection. Sure enough, they were as gnarled and knobbly as old tree roots. 'Now my gran'father, he had the hands of a woman he did, long an' graceful fingers, nice fingernails not all broken an' stuck wi' dirt. Let's have a look at yours then, lad?'

Finn held out his small hands shyly and Gideon studied them, seriously contemplating whether they were fit for purpose. 'Them hands o' yours look promisin' lad. Yer could 'ave a bit o' fiddle playin' in them hands. We'll need to tune it up a bit. I ain't played it for ages.' Having said this he produced a tuning fork from his waistcoat pocket and while Finn watched, the gypsy went through the ritual of striking the metal on the side of his boot, plucking each string and turning the wooden pegs on the violin. 'There yer are, Finn,' he said finally. 'It be tuned up as best I can. Here,' he said, and passed it across to him. Finn began trying to play and Gideon sat back watching him, thinking about what his grandfather had told him about some people who had the gift, who could pick up the spirit of a fiddle and just play it. It's an instinctive thing, he'd been told, which no amount of explaining could ever describe. You either had it or you didn't – that's what his grandfather believed.

What happened next made Gideon gasp in surprise. Finn, who had been running the bow across the strings tunelessly, suddenly picked up a melody. The soulful sound of Greensleeves rose up into the night sky. As he played, Finn's eyes closed and his forehead creased in concentration. He played on, for five, ten, fifteen minutes before finally bringing the music to a finish. Lowering the violin, he sighed and gazed at Gideon as though a spell had descended on him. They were both silent for several moments. Somewhere in the distance an owl hooted, and nearby, the horse shifted her feet and neighed. The dog stood up, shook himself and whined.

'You said yer ain't never played a fiddle afore today?' asked Gideon. 'You sure you ain't? You didn't forget yer might 'ave learned it once, by accident like?' He studied Finn's face as though the question was a matter of life or death. 'You sure lad? Are yer absolutely sure?'

Finn nodded. He seemed as surprised as Gideon was.

'Sit down here again, lad,' said Gideon in a hushed voice.

'It were like magic,' Finn explained. 'Like it were playin' itself. Honest it were! It weren't me, I mean...'

Gideon smiled. 'Magic?' he sighed. 'In a way it were magic, Finn. Don't yer worry lad. You've got the gift. Ah, it were just like my old gran'father had come alive again. You've got the gift that no-one's had since my gran'father 'ad an' he's been dead and gone long since.' The gypsy pursed his lips and thought deeply. Presently he seemed to come to a decision. 'Tell yer what, my handsome, that fiddle can stay wi' you tonight an' tomorrow we'll start us back on a journey towards yer home town. See if we can't speak to yer poor mother an' tell her all that's happened an' see what she says. I'll speak to her an' back yer up, Finn. She'll be so pleased to see yer she's bound to forgive yer, lad, you're only a kid an' all. She'll still love yer as sure as any mother loves her son, eh?'

37

Finn nodded solemnly and watched as Gideon fetched some blankets and made him up a bed by the fire. Feeling very tired, he thanked him, sat down to remove his broken shoes and stretched out gratefully. The dog, sensing it was time for bed, settled himself down beside Finn and curled up. Collecting some more sticks, Gideon made up the fire, then brought what he called his "best winter coat" and spread it on top of the boy before warning him not to get too close to the flames. Finally he bade him goodnight.

Finn lay on his back in his makeshift bed by the fire but sleep wouldn't come. The fabric of Gideon's thick coat smelled musty, of horses, old sacks and hay and he found the smell comforting. He lay still for a long time and stared up at the stars, feeling happier and more secure than he had for many weeks. Amazed at how Gideon had looked after him, and how he had trusted him with his violin, he tried to imagine what would happen the next day when he went home. The ordeal seemed too much to face. Deciding to get up very early and make his escape while the gypsy was still sleeping, he closed his eyes. He didn't want to hurt the gypsy's feelings but no way was he was going back.

As Gideon took to his own bed in the caravan, he couldn't get Finn's predicament out of his mind. What would his poor mother be thinking? Losing her children like that and not knowing how or why. It would surely be enough to break the woman's heart. Remembering him curled up by the fire, his pale face just visible above the covers, Gideon resolved to put things right between Finn and his mother as soon as he could.

38

Five

The sun was just rising when Gideon woke the next morning. He dressed, washed and shaved with cold water but when he was finished he saw that Finn was still sleeping with the dog beside him. As he left them and went to feed the mare, Brannon raised his head, whined, but didn't jump up and follow him as he would normally do. Gideon nodded, understanding the instinct a dog has to protect any vulnerable human being and he went to start his chores alone. Finn's predicament reminded him of the fledgling he had picked up from the roadside, that had fallen from its nest. It had the first growth of stubby feathers but nothing to protect it from the cold. He'd kept it tucked inside his shirt and dug worms to feed it. He could almost smell the musky odour of the baby bird again and feel its rubbery beak nudging hungrily against his hand. But the boy's future wasn't as simple as the choices the bird had – eat and learn to fly, or die.

Gideon's heart grew heavy at the prospect of the day ahead. If the little fella had run away from home, he knew there wasn't much he could do to stop the authorities taking him back. If Finn was in real trouble with the law he'd be 'taken into care' or some other such phrase they use for locking kids up. Words from the old family Bible his grandfather used to read to him popped into his head. '*Foxes 'ave holes*,' he murmured aloud to himself as he began clearing the ashes from the fire. '*Birds of the air 'ave nests. But the Son o' Man has nowhere to lay his head.* I ain't what you'd call a religious man, but that good book do come out wi' some comfortin' words sometimes, don't it.' Shaking his head thoughtfully, he gathered a clump of dry grass and twigs. After feeding and rubbing down the horse he found Finn still hadn't stirred so he set about lighting the fire and went off to gather more sticks.

As far as Gideon could tell, Finn must have covered many miles since he had been on the run. His shoes were worn to pieces with half of one sole hanging clean off. Deciding he would have to fix them up, he started rooting around in the back of the caravan for a strip of rubber bicycle tubing and some glue which he kept in a biscuit tin under the driver's board. As he did so he reflected on Finn's dilemma. 'Seein' his baby sister killed?' he said to himself. 'What a flippin' horrible thing to happen to a poor kid. It would have been in all the newspapers at the time. But I ain't heard talk of any such accident. Them I pass along the road, they ain't heard no talk about a kid gone missin'. But even if Gideon had seen the odd newspaper blowing around his feet on market days, he wouldn't have been able to read it. Not having attended school, the skills of reading and writing had escaped him. His parents always said there were more important things to learn, like reading the signs in the sky for changes in the weather, taking notice of the wind direction, discerning which wild fruits and fungi were safe to eat. He was too busy following his father out hunting and acquiring the skills essential to someone dependent on nature for his livelihood. He didn't have time for school.

Gideon's thoughts turned to breakfast. Keen to give the boy something nourishing before they set off, he took a basket and went about under the trees collecting mushrooms where the air was heavy with leaf mould and the fragrance of wild garlic. When he returned, Finn was still asleep so taking the frying pan from its hook, he began frying and soon had the mushrooms sizzling away, producing an appetising aroma. This time the temptation was too strong for Brannon who stood up, shook himself and went to nuzzle his master's hand.

Finn sat up looking dazed. 'Where am I?' Coming to his senses, perhaps he realized he was too late to make his escape. A kind of panic drained the flush of sleep from his face.

'Come on lad, want some breakfast? Wake up an' fetch yer bowl, tis nigh on ready. Yer need to build up yer strength, my handsome. We've got a full-day's travellin' ahead of us. Grab yerself some bread from that tin there. It's a bit dry but it ain't too bad.'

'Thanks,' mumbled Finn and went round the back of the caravan to relieve himself.

When he returned a few minutes later, Gideon asked:

'Where's yer bowl then?'

'I dunno.'

'It'll be where yer left it last night, Finn, if yer didn't wash it and put it away.'

Finn looked around on the ground miserably and found the bowl in the grass. A slug had crawled into it. 'Ugh!' he cried, flicking it out with his finger. Gideon chuckled but said nothing. The bowl was rinsed and filled with sizzling hot mushrooms straight from the pan. Finn began devouring them with relish and it wasn't until he had finished that he looked up sheepishly and said, 'Thanks, Mister.'

'No need to keep callin' me *Mister*! Plain old Gideon I be; ain't nothin' grand about me.'

Finn nodded and smiled shyly. 'Gideon? Are you really takin' me back home though?' he asked pensively.

The gypsy put down his breakfast and straightened up. 'Now Finn,' he replied. 'We can't call ourselves honest folk if we can't face up to our wrong-doings now can we?' With this reply he fixed him with a serious stare, and then winked at him, throwing the boy into a state of confusion.

'But what if…?' Finn began. 'What if me mum's there an' she hates me 'cos of what I've done an' she calls the police and they come an' lock me up an' everythin'.'

The gypsy took his pocket-knife and began paring a stick thoughtfully. Finn watched his face anxiously, waiting for his answer. The gleaming white wood began to appear with a silvery sheen to it as the fronds of bark were stripped away. 'See this willow,' said Gideon. 'Under all that rough green skin there be a beautiful bit o' new wood. That's just like you, Finn. Under all that worryin' and bad feelin' there be a good well-meanin' young gentleman – of that I'm heartily sure.' He turned towards the boy and put down his knife. 'If yer mother don't mean yer no good, we'll know about it soon enough. We'll stay a while an' talk to her. You'd be best explainin' what happened and

42

sayin' yer sorry. Then if she don't forgive yer, we won't tally too long in her company. We'll be takin' our leave, me an' you, 'cos I've seen enough of how folks have wronged people an' put the fear o' hell in 'em for no reason.'

'Will you really? Will you let me come along with you if she don't understand it were all a horrible accident?'

'Aye, lad, I will, an' yer can shake my hand on it 'cos I'm a man o' my word.' The gypsy held out his weathered hand. As Finn took it in his own, he thought to himself that it was the first time in his life someone had ever spoken to him with respect.

When the fire was doused, the horse harnessed and everything packed away, they set off for Tollwithen. Finn rode next to Gideon on the driver's board. Sheep gazed at them over Cornish hedges. People working in the fields stopped and stared as the horse-drawn caravan passed by. Skylarks soared overhead and seagulls gave their raucous cries. Cow parsley, speedwell and wood-sorrel were growing high from the banks on each side of the road, their musky fragrance rising in the damp morning air. It was peaceful everywhere; there was no outward sign of the turmoil going on in Finn's head. Often he glanced at the gypsy as though to satisfy himself that his intentions were good but each time his anxiety was driven away by an encouraging word. They often stopped to brew tea or cut willows and reeds. Sometimes they pulled up by the cliff edge, letting the horse crop the coarse salt-laden grass while they watched fishing-boats out at sea. They had made good progress but by nightfall it was getting too dark to continue into Tollwithen so they stopped and set up camp. It was a relief to Finn that he had escaped facing his mother for another day. The gypsy drew water from a nearby stream. He came back carrying a full bucket of water saying:

'Get yerself out' o' them clothes, Finn, and scrub up a bit. Here's soap, and there's a towel of sorts. See if yer can't wash yer clothes too an' while yer doin' that I'll be sortin' out a few bits inside. I've left some old things o' mine there for yer – make do with 'em for now, eh?'

Finn thanked him and sat staring at the bucket of water and the soap for several minutes. The gypsy paid him no further attention and disappeared into the caravan so he had no option but to do what was required. When Gideon emerged some time later, bearing a large travelling trunk, Finn was sitting by the fire wearing a motley assortment of clothes, socks so big for him they came half-way up to his knees and a green jumper that hung over his hands. His pale face peered out of a rough cotton shirt that was too big for him too. This was tucked into trousers rolled up to shorten them. Finn's own clothes, ragged and torn though they were, now dripped from a rope strung between two trees.

'Ah! Yer scrubbed up well!' said Gideon. 'Here, try these on for size.' He handed him a pair of blue lace-up shoes. 'Happen them clothes'll be dry come tomorrow. I've had a sort out – I'm thinkin' I might do a bit of tradin' when we get to Tollwithen.' Finn tried one of the shoes on but his foot was encased in a thick sock. He pulled the sock off and tried again, but without success. 'They won't fit,' he said, pulling a

44

face.

'Won't fit, eh?' replied Gideon, studying the shoes and the feet with a serious expression. 'Want me to cut 'em a bit so yer can get 'em on? I don't like to cut 'em but I will if they'll do for yer.'

Finn shook his head. 'No, thanks; they're just too tight.'

The gypsy looked relieved. 'They are small,' he said. 'Them belonged to my young wife, Sonya. I ain't had 'em out in the light o' day for, let me see...' He scratched his head, 'must be near on twenty years.' He took up the little shoes in his grimy hands. 'Sure you don't want me to cut 'em for yer?' he asked again. Finn nodded solemnly and without another word Gideon retreated to the back of the caravan and put them away, re-appearing with Finn's own shoes. He had bound them up with rubber and insulation tape; they looked rather odd but Finn agreed they were wearable and thanked him.

'Happen if yer gets home tomorrow you'll have some better shoes there to put on, eh?'

Finn shook his head. He watched the gypsy rummaging again inside the caravan, and bringing out creaking baskets, armfuls of boxes, trinkets, knives and bundles of wooden pegs. These he laid out on the grass as though he was summing-up their total value. Finally he came and sat down near Finn and said. 'I'll have to make a few more o' them baskets afore I go round tellin' folks I got all shapes an' sizes. I could get a few done tonight, lad, if you'll give me a hand.'

Finn looked at him. 'Doin' what?' he asked.

'Collectin' some sticks an' withies,' said Gideon, 'an' weavin' 'em up. There ain't no work a little fella

45

can't do if he puts his mind to it.'

'But I don't know what to do or where to get 'em from,' he protested.

'Nor did I when I were your age, but seein' is learnin', lad. It'll warm us up if we get workin'. Come on, we'll fetch in a few afore we have our supper, eh? Then we can get on an' make 'em by the fire afore we take to our beds.'

Finn followed him to the stream where reeds moved in the evening breeze. They had a green sheen on them, and when the breeze caught them they were as smooth as a wave on the ocean. Suddenly there was a flash of blue as a kingfisher dived into the water. The gypsy took a knife from his belt and began to cut some reeds. 'Mind yer hands Finn. Hold 'em by the end like this or they'll be through yer skin like butter. Better still, yer see to them willows – a few of 'em low hangin' branches what's young an' pliable. Here, take this knife, it ain't so sharp.'

By the stream, the willow trees were trailing leafy branches into the water. Finn struggled with the blunt knife, bending the young branches this way and that but still failing to break them off. He uttered a cry of frustration.

'Oh! I can't do it!' he complained. 'You do it!'

'I'll eat yer supper for yer too if I hear any more o' that. Workin is all about tryin' hard. Nothin's easy in this world, Finn. Thought yer would 'ave found that out for yerself afore now.' The boy looked ashamed and continued wrestling with the branches in silence until he saw, with a measure of pride, that his pile of willows was growing.

46

The next morning Finn's clothes had dried so he could put them on. They reached the town of Tollwithen soon after nine. Cottages huddled down the narrow twisting streets leading to the River Fowey. Level crossing lights signalled that a train was due and as the barriers came down Gideon pulled the horse to a halt and rested his arms on his knees to wait. Several pedestrians gathered at the gates anticipating the arrival of the train. Passengers, waiting on the platform with their luggage beside them, were enveloped in a cloud of steam and smoke as it roared into the station, heaving and sighing as impatiently as a shire-horse on a cold misty morning. Then, as visibility returned, the train collected up its passengers, obeyed the guard's shrill whistle and took off again, heavy and clumsy and magnificent.

When they came to the cattle market, it was noisy with sheep bleating, pigs squealing, and market traders shouting. Cages housing chickens, rabbits and plump pigeons were stacked waiting to be auctioned; stalls selling fruit and vegetables were already busy while farmers stood leaning on the railings talking and smoking. Finn sat on the driver's board nervously hoping no-one would notice him while Gideon went to barter with the baker for some fresh bread in exchange for a basket. He soon returned, pleased with his purchase and they left the market and went on up through the town. Its narrow streets of terraced houses were chilly in the shade. Suddenly a familiar sight came into view: the Theatre Royale. It was showing posters of the summer variety show which gave a splash of colour to the grey street but as they turned uphill, Finn's heart began to race – he was nearly home.

'Is this the right way, lad?' asked Gideon, flicking the reins to give Belle a bit of encouragement up the steep incline. 'Yeh, suppose so,' he replied. The mare began to strain on her harness, dutifully pressing her great chest against the bar to pull the weight of the swaying caravan up the hill. Froth began to foam on her mouth and her breath caused clouds of mist to billow about her. Gideon gazed unconcerned over her ears, murmuring commands to her while Finn held on grimly, afraid at any moment he might fall as the caravan lurched this way and that. In the exertion, the horse snorted and sweat broke out on her grey flank. The caravan creaked and groaned and from within Finn could hear the pots and pans rattling. Each step of their ascent was so traumatic that they had reached the row of stone cottages which were so familiar to him before he realized they were there. Fear gripped him. He was home.

'Whoa, whoa there!' called Gideon, casting an interested eye on Finn. 'This'll be it then, eh?'

The boy nodded, looking pale and mute.

'Right,' he said. Tying the reins up and applying the brake. He jumped down and from the back of the caravan brought out a block of wood which he slipped under one of the wheels to stop it rolling back. 'Come on lad, two heads are better than one when it comes to sortin' out a matter o' life an' death.' Finn looked at him quickly and gasped.

They stood on the doorstep together and Gideon knocked loudly. Finn kept whispering things like, 'She won't believe me!' and 'What shall I say?' But there wasn't a sound from within. Gideon knocked again, while Finn's eyes darted about like a frightened stoat. It

48

was then the gypsy's gaze fell on the windowsill; it was as dirty as the window itself and the ornaments within smothered in dust. 'Looks like no-one's had a mind to clean this house in a long while, don't it, Finn? Yer got a front-door key, lad? Don't think yer mother's at home.'

Finn shook his head and stood on a flower-pot to stretch up and peer into the room. He rubbed the glass with his sleeve and squinted up his eyes. Suddenly he felt he had been hurled back in time. The sight gave him such a jolt it made him tremble. Stowed away in the shadows was his baby sister's cot. The table was set for tea, and there was his mother's armchair with her knitting beside it. The room looked brown, drab and deserted but it was exactly how he remembered it. He found himself staring into a pocket of memory where pain and hurt lay frozen and undisturbed. Questions lay unanswered and the explanation he had practised was rendered useless. His mother wasn't there. All his feelings of regret and sorrow came back at him like a slap round the face. He could see his own reflection in the dark window, that of a weak frightened boy. In his mind's eye he saw his baby sister too and almost heard her crying again. How he longed for his mother's forgiveness. But all that met his stare was a cold uninviting room.

'We could try round the back,' suggested Gideon. At that moment a woman appeared next-door, holding a dust-pan and brush.

'What are you two up to?' she demanded harshly. 'There's no-one there so there's no use banging on that door. If you're looking to sell stuff you can be on your way. I don't want pedlars hanging round here!'

49

Gideon looked at her steadily. 'Excuse me missus, we won't cause yer no trouble. Beggin' yer pardon but we be lookin' for the lady o' the house. Do yer happen to know where she be?'

'There ain't been no-one livin' there since I moved in a few weeks back. Folks say she left her kids for dead an' ran off. I don't know about that, but I can tell you one thing though – there's been enough people bangin' on that door to give an old soul a headache. I've lost count of how many. People askin' for money I don't doubt. I bet she owed lots of money, that's what I think anyhow. Folks say her husband left her destitute.' The woman stared at them both after giving this speech as though challenging them to dare linger any longer.

'Thanks, missus,' said Gideon and touched his cap. 'I think we must've got the address wrong, 'cos the lady we're seekin' ain't owin' nothin' to no-one.' He turned to Finn. 'Right then, lad, let's be on our way.'

Finn, rubbing his fists into his eye-sockets, fought back the tears and hid his face. Gideon pressed his shoulder and steered him back to the caravan. 'Let's get goin' my 'andsome. Our business is all done here. Up you get! That's it!' Picking up the block of wood from the wheel, Gideon jumped up after him and flicked the reins. 'Gee up there, Belle,' he announced firmly, as though making certain they both knew their attempt at reconciliation was over. Instead of taking the same route back through the town and doing some trading as he had intended, Gideon drove the caravan on, over the brow of the hill until they had left the houses way behind. Ahead of them lay the open countryside.

'We'll put a few miles between us an' this ole

place an' then we'll pitch camp,' he said. 'I'm just about ready for a cup o' tea, ain't you lad?' Finn nodded but he couldn't find a voice to reply.

Six

1958 Five years later

Finn became accustomed to the travelling way of life. Spending his days working alongside Gideon, he had grown tall and strong and his voice was breaking into a husky drawl. One misty morning early in October they were camped on some rough grassland near Redruth, within sight of Carn Brae, when a visitor arrived. Winter was approaching and they were busy chopping logs to keep their wood-burning-stove well supplied.

The stranger parked his car in front of their caravan. Gideon straightened up and stared at him as though wondering if the man was deliberately blocking their exit. He was always wary of strangers, having been told to "move on" so many times. People on the whole didn't make him welcome.

The driver of the vehicle approached them boldly, wearing smart city clothes. 'Good morning, sir!' he said, greeting Gideon while his eyes flicked across to Finn suspiciously. 'Staying long in these parts are you?'

Gideon didn't speak at first. He had met people like this before and heard about their ways. Chances are he was a plain-clothed policeman or a tax-inspector. They were camped on common land – they had as much right to be there as anyone else.

'Could be,' he replied, watching him. 'Why? Who wants to know?'

'I'd like a word, sir, if you don't mind,' said the visitor, 'in private.'

Gideon didn't like the sound of this at all. He glanced across at Finn, his eyes clouding evasively. 'Whatever yer be goin' to say to me, yer can be sayin' the same to us both, or yer needn't bother. My boy here, he's as much right to be a listenin' in on what it is yer have to say – so what is it?'

The man coughed and looked slightly taken aback. 'Right! Can we, er, sit down? Inside maybe?'

'No. If it's all the same to you, I'd rather speak here.'

'Well, er, the thing is… I've come on behalf of Her Majesty's Inspector of Schools, sir. There's the matter of the boy's education.' The man turned to Finn. 'How old are you, young man?'

Finn looked hard at him but didn't answer.

'He be near on fourteen years old,' said Gideon guardedly. 'Why?'

'Ah! And he does attend school regularly, I presume?'

'No,' replied Gideon quickly. 'He don't attend no school. I be learnin' him all he needs to know – how to get by an' feed himself an' keep himself out o' trouble. There ain't no schoolin' can teach him that.'

'But my dear sir!' said the inspector. 'That's exactly what school is all about. At school he will be taught how to make a living, get himself a job and earn a decent wage!' The man's chest seemed to inflate with pride at the apparent generosity of these advantages.

53

'No need,' said Gideon. 'He be doin' that already, here wi' me. He don't need to go to no school to learn that.'

'But are you teaching him to read? To do arithmetic? Are you teaching him algebra, geometry? What about the sciences? How can you, if you don't mind me saying so – a poor travelling man like yourself – how can you be expected to teach your son all these things?'

Gideon looked up in surprise at the word "son" and seemed about to correct him but instantly changed his mind. 'We manage,' he replied. 'Now, I don't know about you but the weather's not lookin' good an' we be havin' work to do, so if yer don't mind…'

'Yes, sir, well – I'll leave you to think on what I've said. I'll be along again tomorrow and I'll bring some forms with me. I can see you're doing your best for him and I must say; he looks well! Your son's a credit to you, sir, a credit!' The man's attempt to cajole the gypsy was accompanied by an inflamed rash that spread up his neck making his collar look tight and uncomfortable. 'There's no need to worry about anything, sir, like a uniform or books and pencils. We'll see to it all, fit him up and sort out the practicalities. We'll soon get him into a nice class. There's a splendid local school near here. There will be boys of his own age there he can play with.' Turning to Finn he added, 'That'll be fun, won't it lad? Have a game of football? Find some playmates of your own age?'

Finn's expression remained solemn and unyielding. 'Well? What do you say, lad?' he persisted. 'You'd like that, wouldn't you?'

'I'm alright here, mister,' said Finn, staring at him. The blood had drained from his face. Words like "school" reared up like ghosts from the past.

'Say thankee kindly,' suggested Gideon. 'The good man only be doin' his job, ain't that right?'

The inspector looked back at Gideon in surprise. 'Why, thank you, sir! That's right. I am only doing my job!' He paused as though wondering whether this softening of the gypsy's attitude might bring instant results. 'Well, I can see you're busy,' he conceded. 'I'll be on my way then.' He stepped forward to shake hands and then, curiously, withdrew his hand again almost as quickly.

As he walked away, they both stood watching him in silence. Neither of them looked at each other until he had started the car, reversed back onto the road and driven out of sight.

Immediately Gideon shot a command. 'Let's finish an' start loadin' up the caravan, Finn. We be packin' up an' leavin' tonight afore it gets dark. He'll be back tomorrow I don't doubt it, an' he won't be so courteous next time.'

With a rush of affection for Gideon, Finn laughed and swung an arm round his shoulder, hugging him affectionately. 'Hey, Dad! I thought he was goin' to take me away!'

'Over my dead body,' replied Gideon glumly.

'I wish you were my dad though!'

Gideon stopped and looked at him, and the trace of a smile lit up his eyes. 'Happen we're alright as we are, son. Now let's finish sawin' this lot an' get on the road.'

Back in Tollwithen, the cast at the Theatre Royale were hard at work preparing for the Christmas pantomime. However, Bianca Tabora had been unimpressed by the choice Seamus, the director, had made – it was Cinderella. She was even more annoyed when he didn't offer her the leading role. But she swallowed her pride. While Seamus was willing to pay her she was content to stay on. Colette was now five and half years old and had just started at the local school.

Colette Tabora, now Bianca's legally adopted daughter, had grown into a clever, somewhat serious and thoughtful child. Like any mother, Bianca's life revolved around her daughter. So much so that Seamus once accused her of letting the Theatre Royale take second place. This was true; the actress was devoted to Colette. She would be the first to admit she had become disenchanted by the theatre and that her acting career was just cruising along. The excitement had gone out of it. Perhaps partly to blame was Seamus' lack of drive. His attitude had dampened her spirits and turned her vocation into a mere job. But being realistic, she knew at her age a big break was becoming unlikely. Serious attempts to further her career would have meant auditioning for a leading role in London's West End. The experience didn't appeal to her. She craved a stable and secure environment for Colette to grow up in. She even dreamed about her daughter's career more than her own.

Not long before Christmas, during a break in rehearsals, Bianca found Colette backstage. She was crying.

'Darling! Whatever's the matter? What's

happened?'

'It's that horrible school!' shouted Colette, jumping up and stamping her foot.

'But I thought you loved going to school! What's happened to upset you? Tell Mummy, darling, what is it?'

Colette sat down again sulkily. She sniffed and recovered herself a bit, while her hair clung to her tear-stained cheeks. 'They're being really horrible to me and I hate them! They're pigs!'

Bianca was amazed. 'Who? But you've made some lovely friends there, darling! Wendy, Mary and Alice... they're all sweet girls in your class!' At this, Colette's tears resumed but she was defiant. 'It's those beastly boys! They said I'd been dumped in the street like a puppy in a bag! They said when you found me you must've felt sorry for me being such a dirty baby in the gutter an' probably the gypsies chucked me out 'cos I'm so ugly and they left me there to die!'

'But that's not true at all! Who are they, these boys? They've no right to say things like that and upset you. It just goes to show what silly boys they are, darling, and such cowards for picking on a little girl, don't you think? Now, listen, Colette. There's not an ounce of truth in what they're saying, honestly.'

Colette snorted, took a deep breath and let out a shuddering sigh. Her tiny shoulders relaxed a bit but she was watching Bianca's face as though the truth, whatever it was, lay there for her to discover.

'Mummy?' she began. 'I don't know where I came from though and who my real mummy is, do I? I don't know anything!' Her tears threatened to return again but Bianca enveloped her in her arms.

'Darling!' she exclaimed, hugging her close. 'You're my little girl! I adopted you because I loved you from the minute I found you.' She kissed her tear-soaked cheek. 'Colette, now listen! Look at me? I'm your mummy and if anyone says anything else take no notice, alright? They don't know anything about your parents, any more than I do. I expect they're jealous that's all – because you're so pretty and your mother's a famous actress!' She stroked her hair and smiled. 'And look at us two – aren't we lucky! I bet they wish they could be backstage in this wonderful theatre and meet all the stars! Look, if they talk like that again, just laugh at them for being so childish. I'll have a word with the headmistress tomorrow and ask her to keep an eye on those naughty boys.'

Later, when she was alone, Bianca puzzled over her daughter's trouble at school. Children can be so cruel sometimes, she thought. But I wish I could find out who her natural mother was – it would lay to rest some old ghosts and it would settle once and for all this mystery about how I found her. Before she fell asleep, she determined to do something about it. There was nothing to be afraid of, she told herself. No-one can take her away from me now, she's mine, legally. But the fear was always there, that the natural mother would re-appear and lay claim to her. Even as she fell asleep, she found herself hoping the poor woman, whoever she was, was dead. 'Forgive me!' she whispered, 'I didn't mean to wish for that... it's just, I can't bear to think of losing my darling Colette.'

Autumn turned to winter and the threat from the school inspector was always in the back of their minds.

Gideon knew from what he had heard among the Romanies that the authorities don't give up easily. Wherever they went, the same situation arose. Gideon always talked his way out of it, broke camp, loaded the caravan and moved on. Finn was now fifteen years of age. He had grown in height like a young silver birch sapling, as tall and athletic as a greyhound. His education had grown with him. He had picked up the knowledge of nature without any need to attend school or read books.

Many times they would encounter a gypsy camp settled by the roadside, its presence made known long before they saw it by a wisp of smoke from the fire, the barking of dogs and the playful screams of children playing. When they met these friends on the road, Finn was indistinguishable from any other gypsy boy. His quick mind and good humour helped him make friends easily although he also got into a few fights and tussles as any lad his age would. Gideon judged each new combat with the silent wisdom of experience, and let Finn fight his own battles, knowing all the time he was growing in knowledge. Skills like carpentry, in regard to essential repairs to the caravan, were handed down to Finn not only from Gideon but from many other travellers who were generous in sharing their talents. It was the education of the road – and all directed towards one essential task – self-sufficiency and survival. Finn was able to tackle basic mechanical repairs to the caravan with ease. He learned horse-management, foraging food from the wild, hunting, cooking and vehicle maintenance as well as the finer skills of basketry. It was a good all round education, even covering etiquette, of sorts. Politeness, Gideon believed, was essential to the manners of a gentleman like himself. "Kids can't learn how to live from no book-reading" was a phrase he often repeated on his frequent encounters with school inspectors. In carrying out manual tasks, Finn had developed more physical strength than Gideon now, whose ageing arthritic joints had begun to cause him pain.

*

The following spring, Gideon and Finn were on their way to Wadebridge for the County Show when a shout went up which neither of them could fail to notice.

'Hey! Be that you, Rabbiter?'

Gideon eased back on the reins, squinting against the harsh sunlight to try and identify the voice. 'Who be callin' me like that? I ain't been called by that name for years!' he muttered. Bringing Belle to a halt and shielding his eyes, he exclaimed: 'Well, I'll be jiggered if it ain't my cousin, Albert!' he cried. 'Look there, Finn! We'll pull in and see what he's at.' He hailed the man with a hearty greeting: 'Hey there, Bert! How yer be doin', my old codger?'

Albert, a lean and gangly gypsy hobbled down from the steps of his mud-spattered vehicle waving his arms in a parallel fashion as though directing a plane into land. 'Come in here alongside my trailer, brother! ' he shouted.

Several cars were parked there, with caravans or trailers linked behind. Many of the gypsy travellers were now using motorised vehicles rather than horses. There were a few horses there, tethered by long chains, grazing the fresh spring grass. Three small stick-fires, each with a family clustered round it and dogs and children playing close-by, made a welcoming sight. Here and there a hen strutted, clucking and scratching at the loose soil in the shade.

As soon as they were parked satisfactorily, Gideon jumped down and shook the old gypsy's hand vigorously. 'Well, I'll be!' he cried. 'Must be years! Look here, Bert – this be young Finn.'

'Right pleased to meet you, Finn,' said Albert warmly, shaking his hand and looking him straight in the eye. 'This be a new family member then, brother?' he asked. The question was directed towards Gideon although he still gazed at Finn curiously.

'He be all the family I got Bert, an' ever will have, an' that's how things are. Yer know I lost my darlin' Sonya?'

Albert scratched his head, looking embarrassed. 'Yeh, yeh, sorry, brother. Too bad, that business weren't it, eh?' he said, but immediately cheering-up he cried: 'Hey, what am I thinkin' of? I'm forgettin' me manners! Come over an' we'll brew yer a cup o' tea. Do yer take tea Finn or will yer be drinkin' that coffee? The youngsters like the coffee these days apparently. Can't say I do, but times yer have to modernise, don't yer brother?'

Finn, recognising the easy-going family resemblance between the two men, instantly felt relaxed. 'Tea's fine for me, thanks,' he replied and followed the two of them, listening to them chattering together. How many times they might have run into each other but hadn't, they exclaimed. All the fairs they had each been to – presumably missing each other by no more than a wisp of straw.

'Must be fate brought us together today, eh Rabbiter?' concluded Albert, giving Gideon an affectionate slap on the back.

'Want me to see to Belle afore I have my tea?' asked Finn.

'Ah, yer be a good lad, thanks,' said Gideon. 'I was fair forgettin' about the poor old mare, talkin' with my cousin here!'

Finn left them and headed back to unharness the horse. He couldn't help noticing the litter strewn about between the odd piles of scrap-metal and was curious to see so many rusting exhaust-pipes and bicycle wheels. There were a few youths hanging about. They were eying him suspiciously, he thought, and decided it was best to carry on seeing to the horse and ignore them. He unbuckled the straps and led Belle gently out of the shafts, fastening a lead rope to a nearby fence where she would enjoy the new growth of grass and be sheltered from the sun. Taking a handful of straw from their caravan, he proceeded to rub her down and he was just lifting her front hoof to clean the shoe with his pocket-knife when one of the youths strolled up to him.

He was older than Finn and dark, with black deep-set eyes and a cloth cap balanced on the back of his head. Chewing gum, he said casually,

'You stoppin' long?'

Finn shrugged, continuing with his work on the hooves. 'Don't know, mate,' he replied. 'We're on our way up to the County Show. You goin' that way?'

'Could be,' said the youth, staring at him. Finn turned and looked at him briefly and then continued, moving round to do Belle's other side. He felt the

62

youth was eyeing his pocket-knife – perhaps with admiration – and he was pleased he had oiled and sharpened it the night before.

'Are you tradin' up there then?' asked the youth.

Finn straightened up and looked him straight in the eye. 'Could be,' he replied, imitating the other's voice and giving him the slightest hint of a smile. It wasn't much, but it was enough to break the ice.

The youth looked at him twice, grinned and held out a grubby hand. 'I'm Danny,' he said. 'Any time you want some help wi' that old critter, give us a shout.'

'Thanks, mate. I'm Finn.' He shook Danny's hand firmly. This was almost an imitation of Gideon's gentlemanly gesture and it served him well.

The youth seemed impressed with this response. He nodded, indicating Belle, and added: 'Is she alright? I don't have much to do wi' horses now. We're haulin' our trailer wi' the motor yonder. Some's say they be poisonin' us folks wi' all their fumes, but I like 'em.'

Finn nodded. 'Belle's gettin' on a bit now, but she's fine. Which one o' them motors is yours then?'

Danny indicated a shiny grey and white trailer and the mud-caked Land Rover it was attached to. 'Looks grand,' Finn replied. 'I think you'd have a job persuadin' Gideon though. Can't see him tradin' in our old Belle for one o' them.'

'He might change his mind when the bad weather comes,' said Danny, stepping forward to stroke the mare's nose. He took something from his trouser pocket and fed it to her by laying it on the flat palm of his hand. Belle took it delicately with her lips as though accustomed to such delicacies.

63

'What was that?' asked Finn.

'A Polo mint. They like 'em, don't you old girl! Ain't you never seen 'em before?' The mare nuzzled the boy's hand looking for another.

'No. Don't think she's used to treats like that. She has to put up with what we give her, don't you old thing! Hay, oats an' not much else.'

Danny wasn't interested in horses any longer. 'Want to have a look at the motor?' he suggested. 'I'm gonna strip down the engine later.'

Finn responded to Danny's invitation with genuine curiosity and followed him to where it was parked. Motors were fascinating to him, with their noise, vibration and strong smell of petrol. He couldn't disguise the admiration in his eyes when Danny began to explain the mechanics of this powerful machine and before long, the two of them had their heads under the bonnet and their hands smeared with oil.

*

Albert added a few sticks to the fire and checked the weight of the kettle before placing it on the steel cradle over the heat.

'Be there any family news?' asked Gideon. 'Times I've thought on you and Dulcie,' he said and sighed, taking in the group who were huddled near him including Dulcie, Albert's wife, who sat beside him. She was a heavy woman of sixty or so. Her solid black hair was cut straight across in a formidable fringe and her throat was bejewelled with numerous gold chains. Her eyes were quick and her rather harsh mouth was softened by a generous application of lipstick.

At the mention of her name she appeared to warm to Gideon, leaning towards him; so much so her weight pressed heavily against him. She whispered, 'He won't tell ye,' she said, indicating her husband who had just risen to his feet to pick up a log, 'but he ain't been the same since he heard about his younger brother.' With this comment she inclined her head to confirm that it was her husband, Albert, she was talking about. A confidential shake of her head suggested that he wasn't altogether aware of everything that was going on either.

Gideon frowned. 'Yer ain't gonna tell me Jack's passed on? But he weren't no more than forty-five, surely?'

Without speaking, Albert reached for a tin of Golden Virginia in his waistcoat pocket and proceeded to roll up a cigarette thoughtfully. 'Might 'ave been better if he had,' he said quietly. Dulcie caught Gideon's eye and shook her head vigorously. Presently, Albert ran his tongue along the Rizla paper, sealed it and put the finished article between his lips. He lit it using a flaming twig from the fire but in doing so he appeared not to notice he had burned away half the scantily filled paper. 'Yer didn't stop by to see me just to hear all the bad news, did yer brother?' he asked. 'Let's leave it a while eh? Ain't anything gonna change history now is there? No point in dwellin' on the past.'

'Huh!' exclaimed Dulcie loudly. 'Try tellin' yourself that next time, darlin', when you're sittin' around with a face like a cow's backside.' She glanced at Gideon. 'It were Jack's choice,' she added. 'We don't need to tell you what our family say when a poor soul loves the wrong women. They told Jack if he went against the family an' married a gadje it would be the death of him – an' it has been, almost. He only has himself to blame though, in my opinion.'

Gideon waited. He knew, sooner or later, Albert would tell him the full story in his own time.

'Look 'ere, woman,' said Albert, suddenly agitated. 'Go an' fetch our visitors somethin' to eat. Can't I stop yer gossipin' for a minute? Mind I don't fasten yer mouth up with a bit o' stickin' plaster.'

'Oh, get away with you, husband o' mine!' complained Dulcie, rising from the fire and gathering up her full satin skirts which had, even by Gideon's standards, seen better days. 'Come on you lot!' she called to the various young women who had gathered to hear what the stranger had to say. 'Come an' give yer auntie a hand in the van – see what we can muster up for these folks.'

As soon as the family were out of earshot, Albert appeared to relax. Flicking the ash from his cigarette, he began: 'It were a few years ago I heard about our Jack takin' to the drink. He'd 'ave sold our own mother to buy a bottle o' Scotch. Goes to show I ain't seen yer to speak to must be seven year or more. He were deep sea-fishin' but seems he got the alcohol to 'is brain. He got into a fight, well he were always gettin' into fights when he were on onshore, but one night he went a bit too far.' Albert turned away, his jaw working involuntarily as though the words were beyond his reasoning. 'Them said he knocked a fella down with his fists an' finished him off with his boots – smashed his head in an' killed 'im, so's I've heard. The cops took him away an' locked him up. Good job an' all. He were no good, brother, no good at all. He thought the whole world owed him a favour an' when things didn't go his way he took it out on his poor wife, so's I've heard.' Here, the old gypsy spat into the grass as though to be rid of the memory of it.

Gideon was chewing a blade of grass thoughtfully. 'Where be his wife livin' now?'

'Don't know, brother. She never got in touch when he were put inside. If Jack ever gets out he ain't better cross my path. I'll not offer him so much as a cup o' water so he'd best stay away.'

In the silence that followed, Albert seemed to see it as an invitation to explain more. 'I think she were Irish – his wife – took off after Jack was thrown in prison an' disappeared off the face of the Earth. 'She were left penniless, folks say, with a young boy an' pregnant too. I would've helped her if I'd known at the time. I ain't one to bear a grudge – whether she were gypsy or not – times 'ave moved on since then. After she'd taken up livin' somewhere else, there were an accident apparently.' He paused, glanced over his shoulder and lowered his voice even further. 'Her boy and the new baby were run down an' murdered in cold blood by a motor-car. She must've lost her marbles over that 'cos she ran off an' left 'em dead in the road. No-one got to hear of her ever again. Just think! Poor little blighters.'

Gideon, who was chewing a grass-stalk methodically, slowly took it from his mouth and felt the pulse quicken in his temple. Surely it couldn't be the same…? He took a deep breath, trying not to show any reaction while his head spun with the similarity to Finn's own story.

'Tragic that,' he commented finally. 'How long did Jack get then, Bert?' he asked and glanced across to where Finn was still engrossed in the Land Rover.

'Search me, brother. Paid for his evil ways though, didn't he! I hope they keep him inside till he rots. I wouldn't want to see his face round 'ere again, that's for sure.'

'You're not likely to, are yer Bert? He won't be let out for a long time; not after murderin' someone.'

Albert didn't say anything. He dragged on his cigarette and stared into space. But the silence seemed to gnaw away at Gideon and he became tense and awkward.

'Bit hard on his wife an' family, lockin' him up for life.'

Albert refused to sympathise: 'Tis one of them things, brother. Them as does wrong shall reap their reward. Ain't that what the good book says?'

Gideon didn't reply.

Albert shrugged and said: 'Ain't surprisin' road accidents like that happen. That's why I don't like them new-fangled motors that folks are takin' a shine to nowadays. Bloody dangerous machines! I'd sooner have an 'orse any day.'

Gideon responded quickly, 'You can't talk! Ain't that your motor an' trailer?' he protested.

'I only bought one 'cos my missus insisted. Never get no peace otherwise!' Albert spat into the grass. 'No, brother, yer be much better off with an 'orse. So,' he added, peering at Gideon thoughtfully. 'Who be this lad tallying along o' ye?'

It was no use. Gideon knew he would have to explain sooner or later. 'Goes back years, Bert. I were travellin' along the lane one evenin' an' I sees somethin' in the hedge. I says to myself, that looks like a boy hidin' in there. So I reins in Belle an' pulls up an' I looks. He were as frit as a jack-rabbit, he were, as wild as a stoat an' starvin' half to death. I says to him he should be out playin' with other boys not hidin' there in the hedge.' Remembering that evening with fondness, Gideon smiled to himself. 'He's been wi' me ever since. He don't go to no school or such. I've learned him all he needs to know. He's a good lad, as good as a son to me, he is.'

Albert inhaled the cigarette thoughtfully. 'Where had he run away from then, did yer say?'

'He wouldn't tell me at first, but I caught the name o' Tollwithen. That's where he be from.'

'Tollwithen yer say?' Albert scratched his head. 'Funny that!' He looked across at Gideon thoughtfully. 'That ain't so far from Fowey.' He sighed and looked puzzled. 'He has a look about him, brother. I can't be sure but he has a look that makes me think he be our own kith an' kin. Know what I mean?'

Gideon was slow to reply. Albert's story, about his brother Jack, about the woman, the boy and the baby being killed – it was the same story that had troubled him ever since the night he had discovered the boy in the hedgerow. He couldn't deny it could be the same boy, but he needed time to digest this strange coincidence – if it was merely a coincidence. If it was, it would be a mighty fine thing and something belonging to a far greater plan than he himself could ever have dreamed of. Fate doesn't strike very often, he knew, but when it did Gideon had the greatest respect for it. Destiny goes far deeper than coincidence; in fact he believed it reaches into the soul. To save those greater thoughts for when he was alone and able to think, he gave a quick jerk of his head and said:

'Finn be no relation to us, brother. Many is the time folks have said the same, but there be no truth in it.'

But Albert wouldn't let it go. 'Tell yer what I think, brother. I think he has the look of our Jack about him. Take a look at him now,' and he gestured over to where Finn was bending over the bonnet of the Land Rover inspecting the engine 'If I didn't know different, I'd say he were my brother's son. I bet yer that woman he married spread rumours about her kids bein' killed so she could run off wi' some fancy man. Maybe they weren't killed at all. Know what I mean?' He touched the side of his nose with a crooked nicotine-stained finger.

Gideon made a sound like a growl that seemed to suggest that it was a ridiculous idea. 'Yer be thinkin' too hard for yer own good, Bert. Seems that brain o' yours has gone soft – too much baccy, that be yer trouble.'

'You please yourself, brother, but think on it. If that boy were my kith an' kin, I wouldn't rest till I'd sorted it.' Turning towards the trailer he bawled at the top of his voice: 'Where are yer, woman? Can't yer get us poor folks a bite to eat? We're all dyin' of famine here!'

Glad of the distraction, Gideon withdrew into his own thoughts. He had experienced what he could only describe as a huge turning of the Great Wheel. He was a strong believer in chance and circumstance, and he knew months, even years could pass without any interference from the searching fingers of fate. But the tide is always turning; the waves that thunder towards

70

us will soon turn away and gently make their retreat. What his cousin had told him had caused a sense of inevitability to rise up in his bones. Some things are meant to be. He turned and looked at Finn. Was there "a look" about him? Yes, it was unmistakable – how could he not have seen it before?

It grew dark. Finn and Danny joined them round the fire and while Albert applied himself to toasting bread and chunks of cheese on a toasting fork by the fire, Dulcie and several other women soon came bearing various cooking pots including a steaming pan of stew which tempted them with its appetising aroma.

As Dulcie ladled the stew into their bowls, the company fell quiet. Sounds of the night permeated their gathering: the hoot of an owl; the rustling of hedgehogs and the contented snuffling of the horses. Interspersed with these sounds was the slurping of hot gravy, munching, and the sighing of several weary travellers. After a short while the conversation started up again. Having taken the edge off their appetites, they were able to enjoy their meal at a more leisurely pace.

'More stew anyone?' asked Dulcie and her heavy gold necklaces and bracelets rattled as she delved into the pan with her ladle and scraped the sides to share out the last of it.

'Tradin' alright these days?' asked Gideon. He hadn't failed to notice the woman's adornment of jewellery.

'We get by,' replied Albert. 'Fair bit o' scrap we get, an' we sold a good 'orse or two when we had the chance o' buyin' a motor. Been fruit-pickin' and doin' a bit o' casual labour, ain't we? Not afeared o' hard work, are we, girl?'

71

Dulcie's chest appeared to swell with pride as her husband uttered these words and she said: 'Born an' bred for workin' we are; you won't see us in no dole queue. I like to live I do. Mother says to me once if you get to a certain age an' you ain't got a bit o' gypsy gold to show for all your blood an' sweat you'd best dig yourself an hole and jump in it for their won't be nowt else to give you no reward.'

Gideon had to think about this philosophy for several minutes before he could respond. He wasn't a man who expected or even desired anything in return for his labours, other than a hot meal and a bed for the night. The delay could have been offensive so he muttered an agreeable, 'Too right, Dulcie. My feelin' is – an' it's only what my dear gran'father handed down to me – it be what's in the soul that counts. What be treasured close to the heart gives a person more satisfaction than all the riches in the world. That be right, ain't it Finn?'

Finn nodded, 'Like your gran'father's fiddle, eh?' he suggested.

Gideon agreed. 'Ah, that be a fine thing. Go fetch it, lad, an' let's be having' a tune to help our supper go down.' Turning to Albert he said, 'Plays just like my gran'father, he do.'

Finn rose to get it and while he was away, Albert began to look interested.

'So yer still be carryin' that old fiddle all these years, brother?' he asked. 'I heard tell apparently that be a valuable instrument.' He pronounced the word *instrument* very carefully, as though it held special significance.

Gideon nodded. 'So's I believe, Bert. Yer wait till

72

yer hears how my Finn plays it. He has the gift yer know, better than I could ever play it. I tell yer he could play it from the first – like he was born to it. Yer don't get them real fiddle playin' hands every day. You wait till yer hear.'

When Finn began to play it immediately dissipated all the tension. Dulcie clapped her hands and though still seated, swayed her body in time to the music. Albert's hob-nailed boots began tapping on the ground.

'Yer right, brother, he do play with a bit o' spirit, don't he!' he exclaimed.

It was a cheerful gathering and Gideon couldn't help feeling proud. 'Can't put a price on talent like that, can yer Bert?' he said. 'Who would've known the lad could play like that?'

Gideon sensed danger as Albert asked: 'Had it valued, have yer? I wouldn't mind havin' a closer look at that *instrument* later; could be worth summat to folks as knows about such things.'

'It is worth somethin',' said Gideon sternly, 'to me, that is. I ain't sellin' it, not for any colour o' money, so don't yer get any ideas.'

Albert shifted awkwardly. 'It be a family heirloom, that's what I've heard. That means it belongs to all of us, all our family, an' we should all have a share. We could do with some saving's for our old age, ain't that right Dulcie, love?'

'Leave your cousin alone, man. Can't you keep your greedy hands off anythin'?' She winked at Gideon. 'He'd have the gold off my neck an' melt it down if he had half a chance. Take no notice of him, my darlin'. He don't know what folks mean by

73

sentimental value – he's only interested in the cost o' summat! Hard as granite he be.'

At these words, Albert grumbled, making a sound like a low growl and kicked the ashes of the fire spitefully.

'See? Look at him!' she said, confiding in Gideon as though Albert couldn't hear. 'He be like a spoilt kid who can't have his comforter.'

Turning back to her husband she shouted above the music: 'What's up with you? Can't you count the money in your own pocket afore addin' up what other folks have in theirs?'

Finn stopped playing abruptly and looked at them curiously, wondering why there were raised voices. 'What's going on?' he asked. Gideon was swift to reply. 'Just remindin' people that some things are worth more than the money yer can get for 'em, ain't that right Dulcie?'

'That's it,' she replied. 'You can't put a price on everythin' an' you shouldn't try to, that's my belief anyhow. That fiddle is like your flesh an' blood, any fool can see that. And yer can shut-up too!' she added, turning to her husband who was already beginning to argue.

'What's all this about the fiddle?' asked Finn.

'We're just sayin': Be on yer guard,' said Gideon. 'Yer never knows the likes o' some people who only think o' their own good fortune an' don't give no regard to others.' He looked across at Albert but Albert had already backed-down under his wife's critical eye. 'Yer can't trust some folks, that's all I'm saying.'

'What sort of people?' asked Finn curiously, who

74

had never heard Gideon speak a word against anyone before.

'Yer will know 'em when yer sees 'em. I could tell yer a pretty story or two about some people in the past an' the greed that drives 'em to do hurtful things. That fiddle that you've learned yerself to play so beautifully, Finn, it be somethin' people like to put a price on – an' they'll be of a mind to sell it to profit 'emselves.' He turned his head briefly in Albert's direction. 'So like I say – be on yer guard. There be folks who can't look at a beautiful thing without thinkin' how much it'll fetch. They don't know the meanin' o' real beauty – they never did an' they never will. They're greedy an' they'll steal it an' make off wi' the money if they have half a chance.'

Finn looked at Gideon anxiously. He had never seen him that angry before in his life.

Gideon removed his cap, scratched his head, replaced his cap and began a story.

'Years ago, when I were a boy, Finn, people wouldn't let us gypsies alone. They was always accusin' us of stuff an' movin' us on. If you've lived all yer life a Romany, then it don't come as no surprise there be some folks out there in the world who'd sooner turn his back on a gypsy than shake his hand. That's what I mean, Finn, there ain't no explainin' it when it comes to people an' politics. I'll tell yer: Somethin' happened one night that finished us, just about – finished our family I mean.'

Albert nodded. 'Ah, too right, brother,' he murmured.

Finn was intrigued. 'What happened?'

'I'll tell yer. It were when I were a lad about the

75

age yer be yerself now, Finn. My gran'father passed away an' he were buried in the churchyard. It were all dignified Finn an' we was all mournin' his passin'. We was all that fond of him, ain't that right Bert?'

Albert nodded while mumbling something else to himself.

'There was the matter o' the burnin' Finn. It be our Romany custom to burn all the possessions – so we 'ad to burn 'is caravan an' everythin' else like his clothes an' his fiddle. We burn everythin' apart from jewellery an' such as' won't burn. Things like pots an' pans.' Gideon sniffed as though reluctant to face the next part of his story. 'We was all mournin' his passin' till the early hours. We was a big family community in them days an' we weren't afeared of partyin' to mark us bein' born or bein' wed or passin' on. We had a few good deaths in them days, eh Bert?' Gideon's face crinkled into a smile at the recollection.

'Go on then Gideon! On with the story!' cried Dulcie impatiently.

'I'm just sayin',' continued Gideon. 'We had good weddings too. Us boys always married a gypsy gal – it were expected of us. There be no way anyone would be allowed to marry outside o' the gypsy community.' He paused and lowered his voice. 'Happen it weren't for me, that rule,' he sniffed, 'but that were later. There were a lot of us travellin' together in them days, Finn. Maybe seven or eight caravans, a dozen or so horses, an' all of us kids were like brothers an' sisters playin' and growin' up together.'

'Blimey, old gran'father; he'll turn in his grave if you don't get on with it!' Dulcie complained. 'Well, it grew late,' Gideon continued. 'And 'cos I was still young I was sent to bed. I couldn't sleep, could I. Not when I were layin' in bed listenin' to all the singin' an' dancin' an' fiddle playin' round the stick-fire. My pa, he were playin' the fiddle and they was all clappin' their hands and tappin' their feet. Grand it were! I must have dropped off to sleep 'cos durin' the night summat woke me. Suppose it weren't till gone midnight. They must've started burnin' my gran'father's caravan an' all his stuff. There were a bright light shinin' on the far wall of our caravan an' a roarin' noise an' I could hear folks screamin'. Not nice screamin', like they was enjoyin' themselves, but screamin' like somethin' was wrong. Strange it were, an' I jumped up an' peeped outside. It weren't just one caravan burnin' – there were three of ' em on fire! I could smell burnin' an' then I saw smoke curling up through the floor under my bunk too. 'I jumped out o' bed. I was gettin' out, lad, I weren't waitin' to be roasted alive!

I found my ma an' pa an' the others standin' outside. Ma hugged me an' kissed me like she thought she was never goin' to see me again. The fire had spread to the other vans, yer see, Finn. They must've put it too close. Someone must've called the fire brigade 'cos we heard the fire-engines comin' an' then my pa suddenly said he weren't goin' to let the fiddle burn an' he were goin' back in for it. He were goin' into the burnin' caravan wi' all the flames roarin' up an' no-one could stop him. My ma was shoutin' an' carryin' on – in Romany as well. She always started talkin' half in Romany when she were excited about summat an' us kids never knew what she were sayin'. She were shoutin' things like: "*Have yer gone off yer*

77

bloomin' head?" Yer won't believe this, Finn, but my pa comes back out the fire wi' that fiddle in 'is hands! He were a darin' man, he were.'

Dulcie was nodding with a mixture of pride and rapture on her face. Albert, however, swearing under his breath, said: 'Riskin' yer life all for a bloody stupid fiddle!' He took out his tobacco tin and began rolling a cigarette.

'So he was alright then?' asked Finn. 'An' the fiddle too?'

'Yep, it weren't even scorched. Well yer can see that for yerself.' And he nodded at the violin in Finn's hands.

Finn gazed at the instrument with renewed respect. 'He must have been brave, your father.'

'He were Finn. But it were a bad omen to some folks – takin' summat out the fire that should've burnt. It be like stealin' from the dead. Doin' somethin' like that – it were looked down upon, like it were evil. My ma an' pa were never treated the same after that. The others wouldn't speak to us, nor share their food wi' us. After a while they told us to get out the camp. All us family had to go. We had to leave the travellin' gypsy community an' strike out on our own.'

'What, all because he wouldn't let them burn that fiddle?'

'Yep. It's tradition yer see, Finn. There ain't no accountin' for tradition. But my pa kept that fiddle by him till the day he died an' he told me not to burn it till it were my time. He says to me it's got to go wi' me when I go. He said we'll be cursed else. An' so it must be thrown in the fire next time – I owes it to him to keep my word – it's only fair.'

He were lucky he weren't killed, goin' back into the fire for it,' said Finn.

Gideon nodded. 'Must be somethin' up there what's got our lives planned out for us, Finn. Happen fate steps in to help us sometimes, eh? Ain't that right, Dulcie?'

'I'd bet my life on it, Gideon,' she replied while her husband grunted in disgust and put the cigarette to his lips.

'So you really believe somethin' powerful works everythin' out for us in the end?'

'I hope so, Finn. I flippin' well hope so. Sometimes yer have to believe there's more to this old life than you can understand what's logical. Don't yer agree, Albert?'

'Huh!' grunted the wily old gypsy. Dulcie nudged him hard in the ribs. 'Of course you do!' She winked and said, 'Take no notice of him, Finn; he's too old and set in his ways.'

Seeing his young troubled face, Gideon wondered if Finn was thinking about his own destiny. Why hadn't fate intervened to save his baby sister that dreadful night? But these questions were too great to deal with, especially when folks' stomachs were full and their eyes were heavy with sleep.

'Think I be ready for my bed,' said Gideon. 'Yer won't mind us stoppin' here a while wi' you, eh Bert?'

'Stop as long as yer like, brother,' replied Albert, 'but there ain't no sleep to be got, not yet. We've got a lot o' catchin' up to do, ain't we? So long as yer don't go on about that bloody fiddle. Fetch us another cup o' tea, Dulcie love, I'm fair parched wi' all this talkin' – don't know about you.'

Taking the violin back to the caravan and putting it away safely, Finn left the company of the fire and went over to Danny. They began tinkering about with the Land Rover's engine again. They had the moonlight and the light from torches to assist them as it had already been dark for some time. Finn had quickly formed the opinion that his new friend had a fair amount of knowledge about mechanics. This was new to him, and he was happy to watch in admiration and help occasionally as spanners and screwdrivers were applied, oil administered, and various nuts and bolts removed and replaced. Looking across at Gideon and the group still huddled round the fire, he saw there was no sign of it breaking up. Part of him wished he could have stayed listening to the stories of the old days. He felt a kind of comfortable security in being one of them.

Finally the bonnet was slammed down and Danny climbed into the driver's seat. 'Jump in, mate! We'll give her a spin down the lane.' Without any hesitation, he started the engine. The headlights cast a strong beam of light, picking out the flanks of the horses and stretching further to the open road, and into the darkness beyond. Finn climbed in, and releasing the hand-brake, Danny revved it up and steered it across the grass verge yelling, 'Here she goes!'

Finn, looking over his shoulder, was half-expecting to see the trailer following and bumping along behind them, but it was still in its place – no more than a shadow now in the gloom. The various huddles of gypsies around the fires, the darkness and the smoke slowly obscured any traces of the camp as the Land Rover raced up the road. Danny was no more than seventeen years old, but in Finn's eyes he was very capable and an expert when it came to motors – he was already a man, in fact. Finn began to wish that he himself knew more about cars, and life, and women, like Danny obviously did. He made up his mind to be smarter, like Danny, from that day on.

*

Gideon was up at dawn. It was light by five o'clock and he was anxious to be off. It had been a good evening, but he was still wary of Albert's ideas. He saw to the horse, and called Brannon to heel as he went off in search of some dry wood to light the fire but the spaniel stayed where he was beside Finn. The dog was showing his age now; his eyes showed signs of cataracts and he was greying around the muzzle.

Gideon needed time to mull over all that had occurred between them and as ever, he was cautious and protective of his free and simple way of life. He didn't want family intervening, changing things or coming between him and Finn. He was keen to get back on the open road and find himself again. They had a long day ahead of them if they were going to make it to the fair as they had planned. Judging by the sound of snoring as he passed the trailers, the occupants were still sleeping. It had been a long night; they had sat up talking until gone midnight – much later than he was used to. But he hadn't wanted to miss the conversation, especially when he still needed to learn all he could about the family history, now he had a special interest. It was when it was least expected, he knew, that fate intervenes – and last night had seen one of those

81

unexpected revelations. He felt troubled, and still needed time to digest the information he had been given.

Being with family members again was difficult in a way. It was drawing on memories and stirring painful feelings he had left undisturbed for a long time. His dear wife Sonya, who had been so strong and defiant, was beaten by the simplest and most natural thing in the world – giving birth to their child.

Instantly, the burden of his grief became raw again. Yesterday the tide had turned. The news about Finn's father being non-other than their own Jack, Albert's younger brother, if it was true, would take a lot of thinking about. There was the question of Finn's baby sister; what if the girl was still alive?

He decided he wasn't ready to tell Finn the extraordinary news about his parents and how such an uncanny coincidence had come to pass. How many times had he just missed his cousin Albert? And yet yesterday was the day when their paths collided. So it had to be – and so it was.

*

By the time Gideon and Finn had finished breakfast, seen to the horse and packed up their belongings most of the family were up and about. It was a noisy, cheerful but emotional parting as they made ready to leave. Many shook them both firmly by the hand, and when Gideon wasn't looking, Albert slapped Finn on the back in genuine affection saying:

'Look after the old boy, Finn. Rabbiter's knockin'on a bit now y'know, gettin'a bit long in the tooth.' Finn smiled and nodded, feeling slightly anxious at the suggestion that Gideon wasn't perhaps quite as strong as he believed him to be. Danny was ready to wish him well too. He stood to mock attention and saluted Finn, army style, before discreetly pressing half-a-crown into his hand and saying under his breath, 'Here, buy yourself a beer or summat. And take no notice o' that old git. Gideon will go on another hundred years at least!'

With one last farewell they both climbed up into the caravan and with a flick of the wrist, Gideon said: 'Get up there, Belle!' They moved off at a gentle pace, giving a final wave as they left the roadside and headed east.

Finn was excited and wanted to share his new found knowledge about engines but he sensed Gideon was reluctant to talk. Every question was answered by a quick 'yes' or 'no' until finally he just had to ask him if anything was wrong. 'Are you wishing you hadn't left 'em so soon, is that it?' he asked.

'Nah! I've got me a lot o' thinkin' to do, that's all, my 'ansome. No, I ain't wantin' to stop there, not while we got the fair to go to. Anyhow, they'll be doin' their own thing. It's good to meet the old folks once in a while, but we don't want to dally too long.' With this he closed his mouth firmly and again resorted to silence while he held the reins tightly and kept the mare going at a lively trot.

'They'd got some stuff there hadn't they?' ventured Finn. 'The vans and cars an' all them dogs – must be hard keeping all that lot. Least there's only you an' me to feed.' Gideon merely grunted in response. He tried again. 'Danny took me for a ride in the Land

Rover – did you see me? Wish I could drive!'

'Huh!' grunted Gideon, with his eyes firmly fixed on the road ahead.

Just as Finn had decided it wasn't worth even trying to talk to him when he was in this mood, the gypsy himself broke the silence:

'Tell yer anythin' did he, that Danny?'

'Yeh, he was tellin' me about engines an' how they work. He made it sound really easy. I think I could pick it up if I could've stayed a bit longer.'

'Huh!' growled Gideon again. 'Tell yer anythin' else, did he?'

'No, nothin', why?'

Gideon nodded as though this satisfied him and without answering him continued to brood thoughtfully all the way to the fair.

The few parting words that Albert had said came into Finn's mind: *"Look after the old boy..."* and with that he studied Gideon's face. He saw his gnarled hands, his stooped back and he began to worry that perhaps he was indeed becoming too old to be travelling the open road much longer. With Danny as a measure of how he himself was doing, he began to realise that it was time he grew up a bit, that he should be a bit more like Danny and not dependent on Gideon for everything. It was time he learned to become a man. If only he could see Danny and talk to him again! Sadly he realized he probably wouldn't see him again for months or even years – or perhaps ever. That was the way of the road, he knew that. Gideon had told him often enough to take each day as it is comes, and be grateful for what it offered them.

But if Gideon had voiced his thoughts aloud

instead of quietly mulling them over, Finn would have heard him say, 'Until the Wheel of Life intervenes, lad, then it knocks yer for six for yer never knows the meanin' of it all.'

Seven

In her Victorian apartment, Bianca Tabora switched on the lamp, paused from her cooking and looked at the clock. Everything was ready but Seamus, the director, was late. She lit the candle on her dining table and threw herself down in the arm-chair restlessly. Now they would have to eat in a rush if they were going to get to the theatre in time for their late-night rehearsals.

With the performance only days away, and last minute run-throughs likely to go on until midnight, she began to think it had been a bad idea inviting Seamus in the first place. Bianca and Colette lived on the ground-floor of a large house in Tollwithen. She and Seamus were old friends and although she always denied it, he evidently considered they were more than just friends. Others in the company often speculated that they were lovers and she preferred to keep them guessing. Rising from the chair, she went to the mirror to check her make-up and she was pleased to see that the candlelight concealed the odd strands of grey in her black hair. Years were passing, and with them the possibility of ever meeting the right man – someone really special to share her life with. However, she wasn't prepared to sacrifice her happiness and independence for just anyone. Ever since Colette had come into her life she had put any romantic thoughts aside in favour of caring for her daughter. Colette was sixteen now, and might very well soon leave home and find a young man of her own but even then, Bianca still felt disinclined to promise herself to a man, least of all someone like Seamus. 'So why am I trying to impress him with a quiet candlelit meal at home?' she asked herself somewhat guiltily. Almost as though someone else had posed the question, she shrugged her shoulders and brushed it off. She had no idea! Perhaps, she was leading him on, she admitted with a mischievous smile. Poor Seamus! Examining her face in the mirror once more, she was satisfied that the shadows under her dark eyes enhanced her mystery. Smoothing her skirt over her hips, she turned and admired her figure. Not bad for a woman of fifty, she thought. It wasn't easy to keep slim when so much time was spent hanging around in dressing-rooms waiting to be called on stage.

Colette was out for the evening and Bianca had made an extra effort to entertain her old friend and lavish him with a bit of luxury. Her Italian mahogany table was laid with her finest linen cloth and the candlesticks glowed in the candlelight casting gentle shadows across the walls where her watercolours hung in their gilt frames. Having high ceilings, the lounge was furnished with the full-length curtains she had sewn herself years before, purchasing the plum coloured velvet in London. They were old and faded, and although dust often covered much of her furniture – housework was not one of her strong points – she was satisfied with the over-all effect. Was she excited about having Seamus all to herself? In a way, yes! Usually the whole theatre company lounged about her living room in the evenings, reciting their lines, dripping coffee on the manuscripts, or re-telling stories she had heard many times before. It was a casual, sleepy after-hours existence. As the years passed, her girlhood dreams of one day becoming rich and famous had been swept away as unceremoniously as the glitter from last night's performance. But when she had a new leading role to play, when she stepped onto the stage and the curtain went up, then she came alive! The roar of applause, the lights and the music would rouse new energy in her and suddenly she wasn't Bianca Tabora, the second-rate middle-aged actress in an out-of-town theatre, she was Olivia! Or Titania! For two or three brilliant hours she was transformed out of her own skin. She could forget how lonely she was and exchange her ordinary life for that of a star!

Bianca's landlord evidently spent very little on maintaining the apartment. The gutters leaked, the paintwork was peeling and damp crept up the walls but she daren't ask him to do repairs in case he increased her rent. She loved the place – the high ceilings and huge fireplace, and the large though draughty windows. There was a terrace at the back, a sun-trap in summer, cluttered with pots where Bianca grew geraniums and sometimes, strawberries. At the end of the garden there was a horse-chestnut tree; it was heaven for her to sit in the shade under its vast canopy and read through her scripts.

    A smile lit up her face as she thought how Seamus was as devoted to her as a faithful old spaniel. He was a decent honest enough man, and if she had agreed to marry him all those years ago, they might have had a family of their own by now. Now age was catching up with her she felt her quality of life was becoming shallow and losing its charm. However, with a wave of her hand she dismissed these negative thoughts. 'Just look at the time,' she said, 'and still he's not here!' At this rate Colette will be home before we've even started our meal.

Bianca and Seamus had shared many seasons at the theatre, from summer shows to Christmas pantomimes, Shakespearian tragedies to bedroom farces, they had done them all. If he once had ambitious ideas, he now seemingly accepted his lot. He never made any attempt to pursue a more lucrative position in the West End. The box-office takings at the small repertory theatre were poor, but no amount of cajoling from Bianca or from other members of the company could persuade him to take on something more daring, a production which might give them the publicity and crowds which the theatre so needed. Sadly, Bianca had come to accept that he was not a man to move with the times. Having apparently resigned himself to the routine of the theatre without much attention to his personal life, a somewhat bleak bachelor existence replaced the home comforts that others enjoyed. If she had stopped to think for a moment she might have begun to feel sorry for him again. In actual fact, she realised, she knew surprisingly little about him. However at that moment the doorbell rang and taking a deep breath she went to let him in.

A gust of cold wind rushed in ahead of him and she closed the door after him quickly. 'I didn't realize the weather had turned so bad!'

'It's blowing a gale out there,' he said, giving her a kiss on each cheek and handing her a bottle of wine.

'Thank you! You feel so cold, darling. Come in

and make yourself at home.' She took his jacket and offered him a glass of red wine.

'Cabernet Sauvignon?' she asked, adding tactfully, 'Dinner's almost ready.'

'I'll have a dry sherry first if you don't mind. It's better for my digestion.' Seeing the dining table, he looked a little sheepish. 'You needn't have gone to a lot of trouble, Bee, not on my account,' he said.

'Oh, that's alright! We don't often get the time to have a quiet meal together, just the two of us, do we?' She smiled, meaning it sincerely. He was adorable in a comfortable sort of way. A tall man, he had a loose way of walking as though being operated by a puppeteer. At times this quality suggested more of a feeble, lazy way of moving which was partially true. But he was a good director, if somewhat unadventurous. No-one would ever find him showing any interest in the avant-garde.

Surveying the room where Seamus now sat holding a glass of sherry, Bianca realized that something, or rather someone, jarred. Seamus was looking far from relaxed. He sat on the edge of the sofa self-consciously as though expecting to be called in to a doctor's surgery. She knew he wasn't a man who would set out to impress, but she immediately began to feel her efforts were unrewarded and couldn't help feeling disappointed by his failure to smarten his appearance. All old cardigans take on the shape of the wearer but she wished he had made an effort for once. Brushing aside her misgivings, she bid Seamus to sit at the table. After testing the vegetables, she took the roast pork from the oven. While Seamus poured the wine, she brought the hot food to the table and when she sat down opposite him her eyes were shining with a mixture of excitement, and fatigue.

He raised his glass. 'Here's to the most beautiful star of the show!'

'Oh, not quite, darling, but thank you! Cheers!'

'Well, this is very nice, Bee,' he said, eyeing her curiously as though beginning some kind of guessing game. 'Perhaps you sensed it was going to be a special occasion tonight?'

'Special occasion?' she asked. 'Why special, Seamus? Don't tell me – have the Arts Council changed their minds about the grant? That's fantastic! We'd better invite the others round and celebrate!'

He shook his head quickly. 'No Bee, nothing to do with the theatre.'

Sensing danger, she exclaimed: 'Oh, I see! Shall we make a start then? We don't want to be late for rehearsals.'

'This is about you and me, darling,' he said, taking a tiny box from his pocket and opening it. Bianca caught her breath.

'Bee, my dearest, I know you've been reluctant before, but I've waited so long...' In the white satin lining, which was stained with a kind of rust, nestled a small gold and diamond sapphire ring. She heard him take a quick nervous breath. 'This was my mother's engagement ring,' he said. 'I want you to wear it for me, Bianca, darling! You and I, we go together so well, don't we? Just like this ring – you, the precious gemstone and me - the plain old gold. We belong together, Bee.' He gazed up at her adoringly. 'My love! Please! What do you say? Will you marry me?'

'But I...' She struggled to remain calm and

stupidly was worrying about the vegetables getting cold. 'I'm not the marrying kind, Seamus! I thought you understood that. We've worked together for years now, we're like a pair of old slippers aren't we! We just shuffle along side-by-side!' She sang this last phrase like the old song, and tried to make a joke of it but nothing would penetrate the seriousness in his face. 'Come on, Seamus! Me and you, married? It wouldn't work, darling, you know it wouldn't! Haven't I said so, so many times? Come on now,' she pleaded. And with a gentle touch of his hand she urged him to put the ring away. 'Come on, love, let's eat now, before it gets spoiled.'

A shadow came down over his face and he bent his head over his dinner plate in silence. Anxious now to fill the void between them she carved him some meat and spooned potatoes and carrots onto his plate. Was she so wrong in dismissing his proposal a second time? Bianca stared at the candle flame, watched it jump and dance in the draught and tried not to cry. The silence was unbearable. Hadn't she just been thinking how empty her life had become?

'I'm sorry, Bee,' he said eventually. 'I didn't mean to embarrass you. It was a ridiculous idea. You're much too good for me anyway. What would a beautiful woman like you be doing, marrying a silly old fool like me?' He raised his eyebrows and attempted a smile, put down his knife and fork and surveyed the room with an expression of genuine humility. 'I don't know what you'd think of where I live. It's not stylish like this, Bee, honestly. I haven't got any of this finery. It's a bachelor pad, that's all, an ordinary bachelor pad with plastic flowers on the table and not much else.' He smiled sadly. 'You think I'm joking? I'm not y'know. That's why I've never asked you round to my place.'

Now Bianca was embarrassed. The effort she had gone to, to give their evening a bit of class had all back-fired. Her cheeks flamed.

'Most of this "finery" as you call it belonged to my parents,' she admitted. 'I only rent this place, Seamus. I don't get paid a fortune as you know, and anyway, life isn't about things, it's about what we do and feel. I care about you a lot, you know I do, but if we thought about getting married, well, it would complicate everything. It would spoil our friendship. I'm so independent and you're so...so...' She was running out of excuses.

'Ordinary? I'm sorry, Bee. Let's forget I said anything.' He put the small box back in his pocket and took up his knife and fork again.

Bianca tried desperately to make amends. 'You're not ordinary, Seamus! I would never say that. It's just that I don't think it would work. We've both been on our own for too long, we're set in our ways, aren't we?'

He nodded, gave her a sad smile and reaching for her hand, kissed it tenderly. 'We'd better eat,' he said. But by then neither of them was hungry.

After drinking too much wine and papering over the cracks which had opened up between them, they finally left the house together and walked the short distance to the Theatre Royale. They only talked about the performance, having left all their personal feelings to grow cold with the rest of the dinner. It was a chilly night and Bianca, wrapping her coat tightly around herself, hoped the awkwardness would dispel once they started work. They knew each other too well to bear grudges. In a day or two they would probably laugh about it together and sigh in relief.

Within half-an-hour, they were hard at work in rehearsals.

Eight

It was a Sunday evening and a thunderstorm was rumbling in the distance. Colette was sitting by the fire with her mother who was repairing costumes. Bianca was playing the role of Titania at the Theatre Royale and it was in its final week. Her dress lay in a heap of shimmering purple on the floor in front of them. The coal fire burned merrily in the grate and occasionally it sent up a shower of sparks.

'Seems funny,' said Colette, 'staging *A Midsummer Night's Dream* on a dull wintery day like this.'

'Yes, trust old Seamus to get his timing wrong!' Bianca replied.

Colette wrinkled her nose. 'Still, we can pretend it's summer I suppose.'

'You're right, darling. Theatre's all about pretending and convincing the audience they're in a different time or place.'

'Yes,' she replied, dreamily. 'That's why I love it, Mum. I can just sit down, watch it unfold and escape into another world.' Her face was transformed as her imagination took over. Bianca smiled. 'Why don't you change your mind and have a go at acting yourself? We could try to get you into Drama College for next year, since you haven't set your heart on anything else. What do you say?'

'No way, that's entirely your domain!' she replied haughtily. 'I don't see myself as an actress and never have. Something will come along, you'll see.'

'You'll have to support yourself sooner or later though, darling. I won't be able to keep you forever. The theatre scene's changing – in London at least – they're bringing in all this modern stuff. It's not my cup-of-tea at all. I don't understand its popularity.'

'Nor does Seamus probably,' chuckled Colette. 'I can't see old Seamus directing a modern production; imagine him taking on something like Samuel Beckett's *Waiting for Godot!*'

They both laughed at the idea and although a pang of anxiety crossed Bianca's brow, neither of them spoke any more about it. The rain was pouring down and an occasional gust of wind brought a clatter of heavy raindrops against the window. Time had given Bianca's hair a tinge of silver. She was well aware that her future in the theatre was limited. A frown of regret creased her brow as she pondered on their sometimes precarious means of income. Why hadn't she agreed to marry Seamus? Their lives might have been more secure. He was, after all, a harmless enough chap and she was very fond of him. But even before she had finished asking herself that question, the answer came flying back to her: Why hadn't she fallen in love with him? With anyone? How had love escaped her? Colette was sitting perched on the edge of the sofa unpicking the stitches in a seam. Scripts for *Oliver Twist*, their next scheduled production for the weeks leading up to Christmas, were left scattered around from the previous evening. Seamus and the company of actors had stayed there until late the night before, reading through their parts. Colette had gone to bed after a while, but the sound of their laughter had kept her awake for hours.

Seeing her poring over one of the scripts, Bianca said, 'You're miles away. What's so puzzling about *Oliver Twist* all of a sudden?'

'I was just wondering what a foundling was,' she replied, resting her blunt chin on her hands and looking at her mother with a frown.

'You're such a serious girl sometimes, aren't you,' she replied. 'It's an orphan; you know the story – a foundling school was where they looked after Oliver along with the other poor children. It was a long time ago, and quite harsh treatment they had there too, by all accounts.'

Colette put the script down, still looking worried. 'They didn't send me to a place like that though, did they?'

Bianca gazed at her. 'Poor darling! No, they didn't have to! I looked after you from the first day I found you. Then after a while, when no-one came forward, I applied to adopt you. It wasn't easy. In those days they preferred a woman to be married, and an upright respectable member of society.' She pronounced this description with exaggerated primness. 'And as I've told you, they couldn't find any trace of your natural mother, nor your father. I must say the authorities tried their best. But finally the court made you my adopted daughter legally and that's what you are now and always will be.'

Colette sighed. 'If you hadn't found me though, Mum, I could have been like Oliver, all ragged and starving and shoved into one of those horrible places.'

'I suppose you might have been, but it is more

civilised now than it was in Oliver's time. In Victorian times, I mean, life was very harsh.'

'Mum, why do you think that woman – my natural mother I mean – why do you think she dumped me in the street like a bag of rubbish?'

Bianca laid down her sewing and thought her reply through carefully. 'As far as we can tell she didn't just dump you, and certainly not like a "bag of rubbish"! There was the car accident. She must have had her reasons – it's possible she was injured. We don't know darling.' Bianca paused and thought for a moment. 'Colette, you mustn't think too badly of her. No-one who's given birth to a baby would deliberately choose to be parted from her so cruelly would they? Whatever the reason, I believe she loved you – dressed as you were in your little pink booties and your hand-knitted jacket. Poor woman,' she added, shaking her head. 'It must have broken her heart.'

However, Colette was still dissatisfied. It wasn't that she felt neglected, but she felt deprived of something – her birth-right, she supposed. One day, she resolved, she would find out for herself what really happened. Suddenly she burst out: 'Oh Mum! I'm so glad you found me!' she cried, hugging her for reassurance as though thoughts about her natural mother had somehow come between them.

'So am I, darling!'

'I wonder what she was like though,' mused Colette, 'and I wonder if I ever had a real father.' She stood up to look out of the window at the rain-soaked streets. The road was empty. In the gathering darkness, street-lighting sent fragments of light dancing on the uneven pavements.

Bianca put down her sewing. 'Everyone has a father of some sort. Some people don't know who their father is – or they prefer to keep it a secret, but ... all I can say is, whoever your poor mother was, she must have been in deep trouble and very unhappy to have abandoned you like that. If you take after her, with your big brown eyes, then I expect she was very pretty, just like you.'

'Thanks, Mum,' she said, smiling. They had been through this conversation before, and although it never seemed to lead anywhere, it always pacified her a little.

'Perhaps one day you might like to try and trace your natural parents?' Bianca asked.

Colette's smile faded and she looked puzzled. 'I don't know. It seems weird, the idea that I could have had another life and never known you! If whatever happened to me hadn't happened, I might have been someone else entirely.'

'I don't know what my life would have been like either, darling, if you hadn't come along.'

Sighing they both put the subject aside, but this wasn't the last of it. The mystery returned to puzzle Colette time and again, especially at night when she often found it difficult to sleep.

*

Gideon pulled up in a clearing by a dark wooded area and he sent Finn off to catch their supper. Soon they would find somewhere to set up camp but Gideon was looking for an excuse to be alone and think. At the sound of Finn returning, Gideon came to with a start.

He had been lost in his thoughts and whether he was any closer to a decision wasn't clear. Finn had a couple of rabbits slung across his shoulder when he came up saying, 'We could do some tradin' if you like, call at a few houses on the way.' Finn had learned all the secrets of an itinerant-trader's skill of knocking on doors.

'Another mile or so an' we'll be there, lad, if you're up to goin' on a bit further,' Gideon replied. 'We'll find a good stoppin' place when we get there, eh?'

Finn agreed. 'After we've eaten we'll make a few extra baskets to sell then, eh?' He climbed up beside Gideon and rolled up his sleeves, revealing his strong sunburned arms, and took the reins. 'Get up there, Belle!' he called gently: As the horse moved off, he began crooning almost inaudibly in the unique horse-language he had picked up from Gideon. The quiet clip-clop of the horse's hooves rang out in the hollows of the road which were sheltered on each side by larch trees. It was as though they were entering a tunnel. The horse waggled an ear occasionally as if she was listening.

'Y'know, I seem to recognise this place,' said Finn suddenly and he shouted, 'Whoa there!' He secured the reins and stood up to see into the far distance where the roofs of houses and a church tower rose above the trees. 'We ain't been here in a long while, have we?' He looked at Gideon and met his gaze. 'You knew we were heading here, didn't you,' he said, and a kind of nervousness gripped him. 'Oh no, it's my home town ain't it,' he groaned. 'We're not stoppin' here are we? Can't we take the other road and go on to Fowey? We don't need to stop here.'

100

When Gideon finally took the grass straw from his mouth to speak his eyelids were lowered. 'You've no need to be afeared of this place, Finn. Mistakes of a boy don't follow 'im into manhood. A young lad's allowed to make mistakes – stands to reason you'll be afeared o' what 'appened in the past, but you've a lot more life under yer belt now. Whatever's there, you must be a man now an' face up to it. You ain't still as timid as one o' them rabbits, are yer Finn?'

'No, but there ain't no need for me to go back there, any more than any other place.'

'Don't bother me wi' whinin' like a young pup. Let's be stoppin' an' havin' supper afore it gets dark.'

Finbarr, now a young man of twenty-four, was sitting by the camp-fire playing the violin. The rabbits he had caught earlier were roasting on a stick over the fire, the horse was munching contentedly on bag of hay, but Gideon was restless. He got up, stretched and said, 'Just see if I can't find some mushrooms for our breakfast.' Taking his old basket he walked some distance away from the camp, sat down on a log and stared back in the direction of Finn's fiddle playing which could still be heard. It rang clearly, penetrating the woodland and rising above the bird-song with a melancholy that only contributed to the sadness Gideon was feeling.

'Look at 'im,' he mumbled to himself, 'just a scrap of a young man and no flesh on 'im. He should have a proper home, not be stuck out 'ere on the road with an old gypsy traveller like me. He should be makin' his own way in the world, findin' himself a wife, marryin' an' having a family afore it's too late.

101

What's he doin' still hangin' round wi' old Gideon?'
He was choked with emotion and struggled to speak.
'I've got to tell 'im to go. He's got to get a job an'
somewhere proper to live, plough his own furrow in the
world. It's no good, I'd best tell 'im tonight while my
mind's set. He'll not want to be turnin' into an old
drop-out like me.' He shook his head as though the
home-truths he was telling himself were news to him
too and it pained him deeply. 'I've grown so fond o'
the lad, I'll be sorry to see 'im go, but I can't keep 'im
travellin' on wi' me – not for my own company like,
just for myself. No, that wouldn't be right at all.'

He stood up stiffly and walked on a bit further.
Here and there, mushrooms poked their pale faces up
through the leaf mould and he gathered a few for their
breakfast, dropping each one into his basket. The
pungent smell of their dark woody stems, which he
normally savoured, was lost on him. He stopped and sat
down on a fallen tree. 'I've done a good job o' trainin'
him, can't say I haven't,' he mumbled and scratched
his head. 'But what can I give him to set him up with? I
ain't put anythin' in store for him, nothin' put by to
help 'im make a life for 'imself. That were plain stupid
o' me, never seein' he'd have to go his own way one
day. I'll have to give him somethin'. I can't send him
on 'is way wi' nought an' I ain't got no money to speak
of. All I've got is a few baskets an' a bit o' food for the
road. Oh, I don't know. After all these years! No good
givin' the lad a basket that's worth nothin' more than a
few shillin's. He'll need more than that to keep 'im on
the straight an' narrow. I could give 'im my best
pocket-knife but I need that myself. There's no more
than tuppence ha'penny in my pocket at the moment,

things being the way they are. No money about, that's what folks say an' it be true. Oh, I'm gonna miss the young fella though, I know I am.' Gideon stood up decisively and then sat down again.

'Listen to 'im playin' that fiddle now,' he continued, staring up into the cloudy evening sky. 'I've never heard the likes of it. I must tell 'im he's got to go afore I lose my nerve. There's nothin' for it – I'll have to lend 'im that fiddle. He's learned himself to play it so well an' it's not goin' to do me no good stuck in the back of the caravan. I'll ask him to take care of it for me, he can do a bit o' buskin' an' earn a few bob an' it'll see he's all right. He'll have to look after it, mind, or my gran'father will turn in his grave, but it'll make him a livin' sure enough, when folks do hear 'im. It's only fair an' natural to let him 'ave it till my time comes. I'll tell 'im tonight that I'm givin' him the fiddle for safe-keepin'. He's a good lad, my Finn. My ma an' pa, if they'd been alive to see him, they'd have wanted him to play it – not see it hidden away in the caravan wi' no good comin' out of it an' the damp seepin' through the wood. I'll give him one o' my best baskets too an' I'll put in some o' my...' Gideon broke down, coughed and stood up. The tears were streaming down his cheeks. He rubbed his eyes with his grimy fists and muttered, 'Silly old fool!'

*

When he arrived back at the camp, Finbarr had stopped playing.

'Got some mushrooms then did you?'

Gideon nodded. He felt choked with the decision

103

he had made. 'Yeh, plenty of 'em,' he replied, and lay down his basket brimming with the delicate fungi. 'Are the rabbits done?' he asked. 'They'll be grand, Finn, washed down with a can of ale.'

'The horse is a bit spirited tonight, Gideon,' Finn observed. 'Real spooked she is. I don't know that she'll settle. Do you think there's a storm brewing?'

'Aye, I shouldn't wonder, but it'll pass,' he replied, thinking to himself how even Belle knew something was in the air. 'Come an' bring yer dish an' we'll get stuck in.' Gideon tore a leg from the pheasant and handed it to Finn. It was well-roasted now and came away from the bone easily. It smelled delicious. 'Help yourself then lad, an' if yer want any more there's plenty.' The old gypsy watched Finn tucking into the meat with quiet affection, seeing how it brought the colour to his cheeks. He thought how happy and relaxed he looked and dreaded telling him what lay ahead. I hope he don't mind too much, he thought, when I tell him he's got to go an' strike out on 'is own. It's for the best. I wouldn't tell 'im if it weren't the best thing for him.'

He was just thinking how to approach the subject when Finn said,

'You know what? It's great bein' out here with you an' Belle under the stars. I wouldn't want to change places with no-one else in the whole wide world.'

Gideon swallowed hard and coughed. 'Ah, you're right, lad. There be no better life than this, warm an' dry with a belly full o' supper – what more do we want eh?'

'Nothin' mate,' said Finn. 'Nothin' at all.'

Gideon sighed, cursing himself inwardly for not speaking up when he had the chance. How could he tell him now?

But the next moment they both jumped when a charge of electricity crackled through the air and the first flash of lightning forked across the sky. Finn stood up, left his supper and went to comfort the mare. Gideon, feeling he had been a coward, felt it deep in the pit of his stomach yet he was relieved that the storm had stolen the task away from him. Rumblings of thunder followed. He gathered their things together, kicked out the fire and took their supper into the caravan.

'He's got to learn to stand on his own two feet sometime though,' he told himself. 'Old Gideon won't be around forever.' He stood in the doorway of the caravan, watching Finn putting the rug on the horse. 'It's gettin' late now an' I'm too tired to be thinkin' o' the right words to say to 'im.' A loud crash of thunder seemed to confirm his decision and with one last look up at the stormy sky he muttered, 'I'll be sure an' tell him tomorrow.'

The next day, Finn found Belle was in danger of casting a shoe so their route to Tollwithen would have to take them past the farrier. The branches were bare now and the road was carpeted with a layer of golden brown leaves, muffling the sound of the horse's hooves. Gideon's back was bent and he looked small next to Finn who had grown into a tall strong young man. They travelled in silence, each with their own thoughts, but Finn was concerned about Gideon. He began to understand that as people got older, the freedom of the open road would be less inviting, frightening even. Glancing across he saw Gideon's gnarled hands were worn to a shine across the palms where the horse's reins had rested so easily. His weathered face had lost its rosy glow, his skin was dry and brown and his long hair was thin and almost white.

'It's grand, ain't it,' he said, trying to cheer him up. I mean, bein' out on the open road, free to go where we want an' no danger of bein' robbed.'

'Yer can hope so,' said Gideon flatly.

Finn looked at him quickly, expecting it to be a joke. But the gypsy was serious.

'What d'you mean?' he asked. 'There ain't much chance of anythin' bad happening' to us out here, is there?'

'One thing yer need to know, son,' said Gideon gravely: 'If I ain't around to tell yer, don't trust all o' them yer may meet. Folks ain't always what they seem. If yer happen to see any one hangin' about who looks as though they might be up to no good, don't yer pass the time o' day with 'em, Finn, they be a bad lot.'

'Who? What d'you mean?'

'Here, ease up and let me take the reins now,' said Gideon. 'Climb down, son. I've got somethin' to tell yer.' They changed places and assuming his natural stance driving the horse, Gideon seemed more himself. They set off again at a gentle pace. The landscape opened up before them and the town of Tollwithen became visible in the valley below. But Finn was watching Gideon and waiting.

'My gran'father used to travel the world he did, him an' that fiddle of his. Them were the golden days, them were.'

106

Finn relaxed – so it was just another story after all.

'Yep, he were a proper gentleman, my gran'father. One day, so he told me – an' he's told me this many a time – he were called to play his fiddle at the Russian Embassy in London.' Gideon smacked his lips as though he really enjoyed saying the words "Russian Embassy". 'Really somethin' it were, wi' chandeliers all sparklin' an' carpets on the stairs an' little dogs wi' ribbons round their necks. He'd never seen the like of it. It were a celebration o' some kind, Finn, for them foreign diplomats from all over the world as yer hears of. Gran'father were clever yer know. He were educated, an' he were tall an' andsome in them days, or so's was said. He told us not everyone can speak Russian, but everyone can understand music whatever language they do speak. He told us lots o' them stories.' He turned to look at Finn briefly. 'That's how he came to meet my gran'mother. Time goes on, yer know lad, time goes on.' He stopped talking and his eyes rested on the road ahead as if that was the end of the story.

'What happened then?' prompted Finn. He was sure his tone had indicated something more important. 'Oh, they all sat down on chairs an' played their music,' continued Gideon amicably, 'an' one o' them diplomat's daughters takes a shine to my gran'father. She were Russian an' she had beautiful long black hair all plaited up like a horse's tail. That was the girl who became my gran'mother an' that's how I come to 'ave Russian blood in my veins. That fiddle yer have there, it were her father's, till he died an' she gave it to my gran'father for safe-keepin'. She said it belonged to

107

Nicholas, the Tsar o' Russia. She said he used to play it 'imself – till he was murdered, that is.'

Finn came to with a start: 'Murdered?' he exclaimed. 'How? Why was he murdered?'

'Politics,' replied Gideon, tapping the side of his nose. 'Politics, son. Whoa girl, whoa!' Pulling on the reins he drew the caravan to a halt.

'Listen Finn, I'm tellin' yer this on account o' what yer be goin' to do.'

Finn looked at him curiously.

'Now listen!' continued Gideon, resting his arms on his knees. 'Yer don't have to keep runnin' away, Finn, I've told yer. It's your choice what yer do wi' yer life but old Gideon ain't runnin' away. I ain't got anythin' to run away from anyhow. Well, I don't belong no-where, that be the truth of it. There's more to tell yer. Let's stop off here and brew up some tea, an' I'll tell yer.'

'More about your gran'father is it?' asked Finn, keen to hear more of the story. 'No, it's what I've been meanin' to tell yer for a long while.' They drew into a clearing and Finn unharnessed the horse and gave her some hay. When he had a fire going and the kettle was singing, Gideon called him over.

'Come and sit down, son. I've put off tellin' yer long enough.'

Finn looked at him quickly. 'Are you ill? Bein' out in the cold, on the road all the time, it can't be good for you.' He squatted down by the fire, gazing at him anxiously.

'Good for me?' Gideon chuckled. 'I ain't known no other life. I've been on the road since I was a babe in arms. It ain't no use tellin' a tree it ought to be

108

stayin' indoors in the dry!' The idea amused him briefly and his face creased into a smile. 'Look at my skin, lad; it be as rusted and wrinkled as a windfall apple. No,' he sighed, serious now. 'I've been rollin' around in this world long enough. Comes a time when all us folks have to return.'

Finn stared at him, worried now. 'Return? What do you mean, return? Where to? Are you goin' back to your family?'

Gideon shook his head. 'No, son. I ain't got any flesh an' blood as would care to know me, save old Albert as we see from time to time. Yer ought to know that by now, Finn. My parents an' gran'parents 'ave passed on, God bless 'em. Haven't I learned yer to keep goin' though in spite o' what folks think of yer? I be content enough weavin' baskets o' willow an' gatherin' the reeds an' rushes as I goes along but some folks, Finn, they'd sooner turn their backs on yer. Folks call us gypsies all kind o' hurtful things, an' they don't like us marryin' their women. Happen they don't care to mingle their blood with ours. It be like throwin' water on the fire – each spittin' an' fightin' the other, an' doin' each other no good – best we keep to our own road eh?'

Finn was struggling to make sense of all this and wondered what he was getting at. Gideon often spoke in riddles, but this didn't seem to make any sense at all. The kettle boiled and he made their tea in the chipped enamel teapot they had used for years. After pouring it out and passing a mug to Gideon, he fetched some more wood for the fire.

'Even dyin' has its uses,' broke in Gideon. 'Just like that wood there on the fire. It be keepin' us warm

109

an' lettin' us brew a cup o' tea. Without the tree lettin' go o' that branch we'd have no wood to burn.' He looked up and caught Finn's eye, as if making sure his message had been understood. 'Just like that dead branch, I be a windfall apple, all seasons comin' an' goin' an' I can't hang on no more'. He picked up a stick and placed it firmly in the centre of the fire. 'I've got to let go, son. It's gonna be soon, I can feel it in my old bones….my returnin'. I'll go back into the soil, turn to dust an' the leaves'll come an' cover me over – an' then old Rabbiter can rest. Ain't that right?'

Finn frowned. 'No, not yet you ain't! Don't talk like that!' Gideon smiled sadly and with a new found cheerfulness he took out his pocket-knife and began to whittle a stick. 'There! Now yer knows the ways of old Gideon, an' the road that lies ahead o' me ain't the same one you'll be goin' on. You'll be goin' yer own way, findin' yer own place on the wheel, eh? That'll be grand, an' only right an' natural like.'

'But you ain't dyin' yet!' protested Finn. 'Come on, don't talk as if it's about to happen! None of us know when our time's up.'

'Remember the day I sees yer in the hedge hidin' as frightened as a rabbit, an' I took yer along wi' me?'

Finn stared at him. 'You know I do, I won't forget that day, ever.'

'Well, happen I've heard more about yer mother as what I've chosen to tell yer.' He coughed nervously. 'I should've told yer years ago somethin' I've been ponderin' on as what's hard to explain. But you be a man now. Happen as you'll understand the ways of life, that it ain't always easy for some people. Sometimes it be better not to talk about such things.'

110

'What things? What's happened? You're not ill are you?'

'No, no nothin' like that.'

Finn was so worried he sat waiting on the gypsy's every word.

'Remember when we stayed wi' Albert an' Dulcie them years back? I know we've passed 'em on the road since then – but when we stopped the night wi' them, when they an' I got talkin' while you an' Danny were seein' to the motor?'

'Yeh, of course I remember that night! But what about it? Can't be anything that bad or Danny would've told me afore now!'

'I ain't been honest wi' yer, Finn. All them years yer travelled along o' me on the road, thinkin' yer father were lost at sea an' yer dear mother had left yer. Truth is, yer father: he weren't drowned at all. What happened was – he got the worse for drink one night, got into a fight down the pub an' murdered someone. He were arrested an' charged wi' murder, but he got sent down for manslaughter, so's said. Fifteen years he got. Soon after that, Albert told me, his kids were killed in the road by a motor an' their poor mother went off her head wi' grief an' ran away.' Gideon sniffed loudly and wiped his nose on his sleeve because whatever tears had been stored up, now escaped in a steady stream. Albert says happen you be one of our family, or so he thinks. Well, Finn, I knows yer are. You be like a son to me an' always 'ave been, but he says' yer be our own kith an' kin, our own flesh an' blood. He thinks yer be that boy as was killed. He thinks yer be his brother's son. Yer father's name were Jack, weren't it? Well, he thinks yer be his boy.'

111

Finn was stunned. He took a while to respond. 'If you talked with Albert about all this, all o' them years ago, why didn't you tell me?'

'I'm sorry I never told yer afore, but I ain't sure it be true. I mean I ain't sure whether Jack be the same man an' his name weren't McKinney like yours...' Gideon looked up and held Finn's stare with a steady gaze. 'But it could be him, son,' he added and looked at him steadily. 'I didn't mean to keep it from yer. I didn't know how to tell yer. Truth be, I didn't have no desire to tell yer that yer father's alive 'cos he's a murderin' villain an' he's locked up in Bodmin Jail. Maybe he be as good as dead to yer. Maybe yer be better off not knowin' about him?' Gideon shrugged. 'Anyhow – Albert – he do come out wi' some stories sometimes, an' half of 'em ain't what yer would exactly call true.'

'So...' Finn began, trying to make sense of it all. 'So, Bert says my father might be his brother?' He whistled. 'That's weird!'

Gideon nodded. 'An' I might be yer uncle or cousin or other, eh?' he added, but he wasn't finished. 'Listen Finn,' he replied, putting down his pocket-knife and resting his arms on his knees. 'If that story be true, then chances are yer father's still alive an' he may even be out o' jail by now. Yer ain't a boy no more. Happen it's time yer put things straight wi' him an' yer poor mother, wherever she be. Yer need to sort things out wi' yer family an' when yer can, yer needs to settle down and start a family of yer own. Find a girl an' fall in love. That be the best thing as can happen to a man, Finn, in my opinion. It'll happen – as sure as winter turns to spring. The day I met my Sonya – she were a head-strong filly! She weren't what yer would call

112

perfect, an' my ma an' pa would have none of her, but I loved her, Finn, more than I can say.' He sniffed and again wiped his nose on his sleeve. 'Old times are best left in the past. Happen I've been thinkin' these things too long an' not tellin' yer, but yer should be farin' for yerself like a man an' I can't protect yer no more. It ain't for me to say what yer should be doin'.' A shadow flitted across Gideon's face and he began shifting the embers with a stick before he continued.

'The road I travel on, it's a long aimless road, Finn. Even if I don't return just yet, the nights are dark an' cold an' the caravan's damp as yer well know. No, I don't need to tell yer that.' He mumbled and sniffed, struggling with his thoughts. 'If yer stick along wi' me much longer yer feet'll grow like mine, like twisted old tree roots wi' no soil around 'em. I can't settle down nowhere, see? I don't want yer to grow into a useless nobody like me. I want yer to be like my gran'father – a proper gentleman wi' talents – I were proud of 'im an' I'm gonna be proud of you. You're clever too, an' yer can play that fiddle just like he used to. Yer could do well for yerself – given half a chance.'

'I can't read no books nor nothin'. I ain't got no head for numbers an' stuff. Where am I gonna get to without bein' able to do that?'

'Yer can play, Finn. Yer can play that fiddle like an angel, I've told yer. I never could play so good as that. I ain't got no ear for music but you 'ave. It ain't doin' it no good neither, bein' out in all weathers in the caravan. No, I tell yer what I want yer to do. It's important so listen.' He cleared his throat and spat into the grass. 'In the mornin' you'll need to pack a few things so yer can be on yer way.'

113

Finn looked up. 'On my way?' he asked. 'What, on my own you mean?' In shock, he felt needles shoot to the tips of his fingers and the hairs bristle on the back of his neck. 'Why? Why have I got to go?' he asked. But Gideon refused to look up and meet his gaze. He kept poking the fire and didn't answer.

'Anyway, I ain't got nothin' to pack. What d'you mean, I've got to pack?'

'You've got to take enough to last yer a week or two, till yer get yerself sorted. Till yer find a job, I mean. A proper job wi' money an' that. An' you'll need to find somewhere to live.' He paused, and a flicker of emotion passed across his face. 'I'm sorry, son, but that be for the best. If yer make a start in Tollwithen, where yer lived afore all the upset, then there be half a chance of yer finding where yer are an' pickin' up the reins again where yer left off, ain't that right?'

Finn stared at him. He suddenly felt afraid and nervous. 'What? You mean you really want me to go tomorrow? Why? What 'ave I done though? Tell me!'

'Finn, yer ain't done nothin' wrong at all, son.' A weathered smile creased up the old gypsy's face as he tried to reassure him. 'You've growed up enough to start livin' a bit, that's all. Yer don't want to live like old Gideon all yer life, do yer?' He looked away again into the fire, shaking his head. 'You've got to let me take a different path. I've got history, family history I need to mull over. I've got a lot o' thinkin' to do an' sortin' things out in my head. I'll be alright, an' you've got to get yerself back on the road to somewhere proper, son. You've got to find the life God's given yer an' not leave it to get trod on by the wayside.'

Finn peered at him in alarm. He was speechless.

'It be the Wheel of Life, Finn. I've told yer. It be like the tide, always turnin', an' if yer don't jump on when yer have the chance then you've missed it. It's gone an' then where are yer? Left out in the cold. Left out in the cold like old Rabbiter!'

'But I like bein' on the road!' Finn protested. 'I don't want to go and settle down! I like bein' with you!'

Suddenly Gideon's face changed. His smile disappeared and in its place was a cold stare. The light had gone out of his eyes. The door had closed.

'Finn, listen to me, son,' he said. 'I can see myself in you. You're as good as a son to me, the boy I never had. I'm more fond o' you than I can say. But I was a loser, I don't mind tellin' yer. I wouldn't learn. I couldn't read no books an' all I wanted to do was go fishin' an' larkin' about. When gran'father tried to teach me to play that fiddle I weren't interested. You've got the gift I should've had, Finn. Not many of us 'ave it, but you've got it lad, an' I'm proud of yer. You've got to trust me. Play it in my gran'father's memory, an' for his sake I'm gonna it give yer for safe-keepin'. Treat it as yer own an' look after it for me till my returnin'. Guard it wi' yer life an' when my time comes bring it back for the burnin', so's I can take it wi' me to my grave like I promised.'

It grew dark and the fire was dying down but Finn didn't move. He hardly recognised the old face which spoke to him now with such earnestness. A shiver ran down his spine. He turned up his collar and stared into the dying fire. His breathing became so shallow he felt as though he was without breath, cold and unable to move. 'I don't understand,' he said, and his teeth chattered. 'How will I know when your time comes if I ain't travellin' along with yer no more?'

'You'll know, son. Haven't I learned yer to look at the stars an' read the signs in the sky like the good book do say? Fetch the fiddle now,' he urged, 'an' play for me. It'll cheer us up.'

Reluctantly Finn went to get it and when he came back Gideon was sitting with his eyes closed almost as though he was asleep.

But opening his eyes, he looked directly at him and said loudly: 'Promise me one thing, Finn. Don't ever be tempted to sell it, or give it to no-one, or even lend it to no-one. Will yer promise to keep it by yer side always, until my time comes, and then, at my passin', put it in the great fire?' He waited. 'Well, what do yer say?' he demanded, staring at him as though his life depended on it.

'Alright, I promise,' Finn replied reluctantly and hung his head as the finality of it all hit him. 'I give yer my word,' he replied and with that he reached out to shake his hand, as only a gentleman would.

'Thankee son, I can rest now.' Gideon closed his eyes again; the conversation was finished.

Finn heard the mare shifting uneasily, rattling her bridle. 'I'll see to the horse. I don't feel like playin' the fiddle now,' he said and going to the caravan he pulled down the horse-rug which was a rough bundle of material. Weighing it heavily over his arm he went out to Belle. He stroked her soft nose and she pushed her muzzle into his hand and neighed softly. It was as if she understood. There were so many thoughts spinning around in his head he couldn't think straight. But as he fed her a handful of oats, he heard Gideon climbing the steps into the caravan. It was dark and he could barely see him, but before he disappeared inside Gideon called sternly over his shoulder:

'Be up early, Finn. Hit the road when the birds start, and you'll have the whole day ahead of yer.'

The rejection shot like a bolt through his heart. From where he stood he didn't see Gideon's tragic face nor see his eyes filled with tears and he felt utterly confused and lonely.

Nine

Finn remained sitting by the embers of the fire. He stayed awake for hours feeling restless and agitated as he thought about what lay ahead of him. When he heard the first bird, even before the first glimmer of light, he checked what he had packed in his rucksack. First: an aged white shirt still in its brittle cellophane wrapper which was a present from Gideon; various other articles of clothing; a towel; a small illustrated book on mushrooms; a saucepan; an enamel bowl; some cutlery; a bar of soap and his pocket-knife. Having satisfied himself that all was in order, he set about shaving, as a growing sense of unreality descended on him. He had become used to the morning ritual of shaving outdoors, with cold water, summer and winter alike, but today was different. While packing his razor and a few other items from their storage box, he saw Gideon standing at the door of their caravan looking pale in the blue light of dawn.

'I'll light the fire an' boil the kettle, he said. 'You'll need a can o' tea inside yer to warm yer afore yer go.'

A quickening of his pulse made Finn anxious to leave. 'No thanks,' he replied. 'I'll hit the road now if that's alright. When the sun's up I'll stop an' rest a bit.'

Gideon looked at him steadily. 'Whatever yer think's best, son. I'll make yer a sandwich then. You'll be wantin' somethin' to keep yer strength up.' As he spoke, he took bread, butter and cheese from a tin just inside the caravan door. 'Now listen,' he continued. 'It be Market Day in Tollwithen today if I be right. It'll be a fine time to be playin' the fiddle to the folks there. Happen as you'll earn yourself a few bob. Take the road due east, headin' into the sun, an' you'll be there soon enough.' He paused. 'Finn, I've been thinkin',' he said. 'When the weather's warmer, come Easter Sunday,' he said. 'When the church bells are a ringin' a full peel an' the ladies are walkin' into church, I'll be in Tollwithen to meet yer.' He began spreading a thick slice of bread with butter. 'I'll see yer by the bridge near the railway-station an' you can tell me how you've done.'

A glimmer of hope flitted across Finn's face. 'So you won't be far away?'

'Nah, I won't be far off. Easter mornin' then, Finn? Yer won't forget? Keep a close eye on that fiddle o' mine!' he added and winked.

With a surge of relief Finn's trust in him was renewed. Soon a new feeling took over the anxiety of the night before. He began to feel a sense of excitement. His future was in his own hands and a new awareness of responsibility descended on him. Packing the food, he slung his rucksack over his shoulder and looked Gideon straight in the eye.

'I'll be off then,' he said as the seriousness of the occasion caught him in the throat. 'Thanks, you know, for …well…'

'Yer welcome, Finn.' Gideon's eyes clouded over as he took Finn's hand and shook it firmly. 'Good-luck, son. I won't forget yer. I'll see yer in Tollwithen like I promised – an' don't yer let me down now, eh?'

'I won't! I'll be there!' Stepping forward, he gave the old gypsy a hug. He wanted to say so much more but the words just wouldn't come.

With determination he picked up the rucksack, tucked the violin under his arm, and set off. The sun was just rising, and the morning dew was glistening on cobwebs, decorating the hedges like white lacy handkerchiefs but Finn was blind to its beauty. Parting company with Gideon was more than he could bear. He hadn't walked far when he heard the sound of hooves and, looking back, saw the caravan swaying unsteadily as it took to the road in the opposite direction. Within minutes Gideon's horse and caravan had rounded the bend and disappeared from sight.

A strange feeling came over him. It was years since he, as a frightened young boy had run away from Tollwithen and spent weeks hiding in barns. Gideon had been a father to him, taught him valuable lessons about life, shown him how to feed and clothe himself, how to read the patterns of the weather in the clouds, and how to hunt and gather food. In spite of feeling apprehensive, Finn carried with him the confidence and trust Gideon had in him and this gave his step a sense of purpose. Gradually the rising mist revealed the town of Tollwithen itself. The houses and church were clustered around the river and in the far distance he could see the Fowey estuary. A small flock of sheep grazed in the field behind him and some watched his progress along the road with interest. A new spirit of independence filled him with energy. Confident of the task Gideon had set him, he marched on, daydreaming about what opportunities may lay in store for him.

When Finn arrived in Tollwithen he was hungry and his feet were sore. The market was noisy with traders setting up their stalls, farmers bidding, and stallholders competing with the noise of crates being unloaded, and animals being brought to auction. Feeling pleasantly inconspicuous among the crowd, he sat down on some steps and easing off his boots, inspected a blister on his heel.

'Buy your onions here!' shouted one stallholder. 'Three pounds for one an' nine! Five shillin's for a sack o' spuds!' roared another. He walked on a bit, dropped his cap at his feet and took up his violin. There was no harm in trying, he thought; he could do with a few bob to buy a cup of tea. Tuning up, he began to play a lively Irish jig.

Albert and his friends used to dance and skip to the tune he was playing. He could see them now in his mind's-eye: the skinny figures prancing around the fire and the impish faces of the gypsy children. He was so absorbed he barely noticed the people stopping to watch him, or the coins falling into his cap. He finished one tune and started another: "*The Star of County Down*". He closed his eyes, swaying in time to the music and when he opened his eyes again he saw a crowd had gathered. In the front was a pretty girl who was smiling at him in delight. He liked her innocent expression and her mop of black frizzy hair.

'Blimey, what smashin' music!' he heard her remark. 'He's good ain't he! I could listen to 'im all day if I weren't goin' to work!'

Hearing this, he paused in his playing and called: 'Want me to play somethin' special for you?'

The girl blushed, nearly dropping her purse.

'Who, for me? Any'fin',' she replied, shyly tucking a loose strand of hair behind her ear. 'I can't stop long, I'm late for work already!'

'Do you know this one?' he asked and began to play: *Scarborough Fair.* He had picked this up listening to an old transistor radio Gideon had been given in exchange for a couple of rabbits.

When he finished, a ripple of applause broke out and several people threw more money into his cap. The girl clapped and cried excitedly: 'Oh please! Please don't stop!'

'No more! You'll be even later for work!' he teased. And thanking the crowd he picked up his cap and put the loose change in his pocket. The audience began dispersing, but the girl remained where she was.

'Who learned you to play like that?' she asked, stepping nearer. 'I've never heard nuffin' like it!'

'No-one,' he replied. 'The fiddle sort o' plays itself.'

'I ain't seen you round 'ere before, have I?'

'I only came today. I'm lookin' for a job.'

'Poor you! I work at the Theatre Royale, just up there. George will be moanin' if I ain't there when he opens the box-office. He's always moanin' about me bein' late; I'd better go!'

'What's your name?'

'I'm Mitzi. Play somefin' else,' she pleaded. 'Just a short one. It stops me head achin'. Play like you did just now, go on! I love it.'

Finn took up the violin again. She stood entranced, her pointed chin resting in her hand, her big eyes staring dreamily. When he stopped she looked at her watch, made a face and pointed up the road.

'Suppose I'd better go!' she said. 'See you!' He watched her walk away, until she disappeared from sight, with her cute bob of hair bouncing, her heels clicking and her red handbag swinging from her shoulder.

He bought a cup of tea and a sandwich and still thinking about the girl, he played on for several more hours, pausing only occasionally to rest. He moved to different corners of the market, accepting gifts of tea and fruit from nearby stallholders who were all friendly. The day wore on and all too soon it began to get dark, the stalls and shops were closing and the traders soon forgot about him as they packed up their wares. Animal trucks began reversing into the market-place ready to load up and the traders carried their boxes back to their vans. Gradually the market-place emptied. Exhausted, Finn put the violin away in its case, picked up his cap and was pleased to find it weighty with coins. The weather was changing and a chill breeze drifted across the market. He looked up at the sky and saw a storm was brewing.

Instinctively, like a moth to a candle, he wandered the streets attracted by the lights and warmth of the shop-windows. Pausing outside a rowdy pub, from which the pungent smell of beer, food and cigarette smoke wafted, he glimpsed the rosy faces of people inside, talking and hooting with laughter. Suddenly he felt shut-out and lonely. The gaiety, the rattle of pots and pans and the smell of cooking set his stomach rumbling. Already he felt homesick for the caravan and wondered what Gideon was doing. Imagining him setting up camp, lighting the fire and cooking, he longed for the comfort of the fire. Taking

123

the direction in which the girl had gone, almost immediately he found a fish and chip shop – its delicious aroma was irresistible and he stopped to wait in the queue. When he had a bag of hot chips in his hands he sat on a low wall and ate them hungrily before walking further on. Finding himself outside the Theatre Royale he remembered in fear that it was there, on a dark stormy night all those years ago, that his baby sister's pram had run into the road. His heart pounded in his chest and he looked around, suddenly afraid that people would recognise him. But as he stood there, the lights came on in the theatre's foyer and someone inside came and unlocked the doors. Finn tried to calm himself and took the violin out of its case. Thinking there may be a chance of seeing Mitzi if she worked at the theatre, he began to play "Scarborough Fair" again, hoping she would hear him. While he was playing people began arriving. A taxi drew up and a glamorous lady climbed out wearing a long dress. She was accompanied by a teenage girl who glared at him quite haughtily. Finn played on, changing from the folk tune to a sad melody as the beautiful lady sent the girl on ahead and stopped to listen.

Bianca Tabora hunted for some change to pay the driver. Her daughter was hurrying towards the theatre steps and stood holding the door open for her. Bianca having paid the taxi driver, started towards the entrance but her attention was drawn to the fiddle-player. At that moment Mitzi appeared wearing a Front-of-House uniform.

'Blimey, it's turned cold out here!' she complained. 'Come on inside, Colette, we need to close these doors!'

'Wait, my mum's just coming,' replied the girl.

Seeing Finn outside, Mitzi stopped and looked at him curiously. 'Hey, see that busker?' she whispered in Colette's ear. 'I saw him playin' in the market today. I think he fancies me!'

'Oh! I suppose you think he's standing out here in the cold just for you!' asked Colette. 'You've been watching too many sloppy films! He's after money, that's all he's interested in. They're all the same, those buskers.'

'You never know,' Mitzi replied, pouting. 'He might fancy me!' In spite of her friend's disapproval, she smiled and waved at Finn, who raised his bow in response, causing her to giggle in delight.

'Go on in, you two!' Bianca's reprimand was enough to send both girls inside. When they had gone, she waited while her eyes adjusted to the darkness. To her annoyance she realized she had given the taxi-driver all her change and she had nothing to give the fiddler apart from a pound note. It would be ridiculous to give him so much, she thought, she couldn't afford it. Common-sense told her to ignore him but the music captivated her. Before she realized what she was doing, she took the pound note out of her purse and tucked it carefully into his cap on the ground.

'Thanks, ma'am,' Finn replied, his eyes shining in gratitude.

'Your playing's beautiful!' she said. 'Tell me, young man: why are you out here playing on this awful night? Surely you have a home to go to?' As she spoke, rain began to fall and she hugged herself, waiting for him to answer.

125

He came to the end of a phrase, stopped and replied, 'I ain't got no home, ma'am. I'll get by alright, though, wi' folks like you helpin' me out.' He picked up the pound note and put it into his pocket before continuing to play.

There was something about his manner and his brown eyes which reminded her of her daughter Colette. She couldn't help but persist in her questions even though the rain began to penetrate her thin dress. Wrapping the shawl tighter about herself, she asked. 'So where do you come from then?'

He stopped playing. 'I've been on the road a long time, ma'am. I did a stupid thing once. Then after that, I lost everythin', my home an' my family. It were a long time ago though.' He turned and began putting the violin away because the rain was getting heavier. In one last attempt to reach him, she said: 'Tell me: you look vaguely familiar. Have we met before? What's your name?'

His eyes flashed with sudden fear like a fox in the sights of a gun. He looked stricken, and before she realised what was happening his manner changed and he shouted, 'No, ma'am, you don't know me! I'm just earnin' a bit o' pocket money, that's all. I ain't homeless or nothin' at all really; I just made that up.' He flung the violin down in its case and attempted to close it, but in his haste he failed to close the catch, the bow strings caught on the latch and he struggled with it for several seconds. Another taxi pulled up with its headlights blazing. People began to spill out onto the pavement. They were loud and vivacious, laughing and opening their umbrellas.

Bianca moved away from them, stepping closer

to Finn. 'Just tell me your name young man, please? We might be able to help you. We could get you to play on stage, in a concert or something. I have influence you know. Would you like that?'

'No, it's alright, thanks missus,' he said, fumbling with the case. She was shocked to see how afraid he was of her, how desperate to get away. He gave up trying to close the case and suddenly, to her astonishment, he left it and ran for his life.

'But wait!' Bianca shouted after him. 'Your violin!' But he was away down the street. 'Don't go! Please!' In distress she went after him, but her stiletto heels caught on the uneven pavement and she almost tripped. She had to turn back. Seconds later she found herself at the theatre once more, with the violin abandoned on the pavement. The rain bore down, stabbing through her silk dress and racing down her neck. She had to go in but she couldn't just leave it there, it would be ruined. Quickly she picked it up, case, bow and all, and hurried through the doors. Once in her dressing-room, she peeled off her wet clothes and climbed into a hot bath. It was only after she was bathed and changed into her costume did she come to look at the violin more carefully. It was still spattered with rain and wiping it dry she marvelled at the deep mahogany wood and its wonderful shine. In earnest she began searching for the boy's name. There could be an address or something in the case, she thought. But there was nothing, other than some resin and a dusty cloth. But on a faded label inside the body of the violin, she saw a maker's name – she couldn't quite make it out. 'Oh, my goodness, what if it's valuable!' she asked herself. And then the doubts started to creep in. How did he come by it? Was it stolen? Was that why he looked so guilty and ran off? The horror of what she had done stunned her and she scolded herself for picking it up. Now she was involved, what should she do with it?

Looking at the clock she realized she was due on stage in less than ten minutes. There was no time to think. She knew being in possession of stolen goods, if it was stolen, would be a criminal offence, so she ought to tell the police straight away. Then she hesitated – there was something about him. She couldn't put her finger on it. Those big brown eyes, just like Colette's – she thought – and those long sensitive fingers. He just didn't look like a thief. No, she thought to herself, I won't report it just yet. I need more time. He might come back for it anyway. Fearing someone would come in and find it she pulled back the carpet under her dressing-table and pulled up the loose floorboards. It was where she hid her jewellery while she was on stage. Putting it back in its case and securing the catch, she posted the violin into the dark recess under the floor and replacing the floorboards, sat down just in time to hear a knock.

Sticking his head round the door, Todd shouted: 'Ten minutes to curtain up!' and immediately slammed it shut again. Deciding to put the matter out of her mind until the show was over, she took a deep breath, sat down to compose herself and added the final touches to her make-up. After the performance, if the busker was outside, she would give it back to him. Even if it was stolen it wasn't her responsibility she told herself. And if he wasn't there, she would give it to the Front-of-House staff as Lost Property. She smiled to herself and sighed. There was nothing to worry about after all.

After running a short distance, Finn slowed down and looking over his shoulder, saw with relief that no-one was following. He turned up his collar and, as he did-up his jacket a button came off in his hand. Crouching down with his back against the wall, he closed his eyes against the drops of rainwater that crept through his long hair and ran down his neck. But he found the sudden downpour strangely comforting; the smell of the rain; the way the wind whipped around him. It reminded him of the wildness of the open road. Immediately his thoughts went back to Gideon and he wondered where he was and what he was doing. He recalled images of their stick-fire to comfort himself and decided there was nothing for it but to huddle in a shop doorway for the night. The nights were cold and he knew he must do as Gideon had asked him – find lodging, and a job. But however much he told himself that Gideon was right, the feeling that he belonged nowhere, that he could fall asleep and die right there without anyone knowing or caring made him feel like giving up.

Then he remembered the pound note the lady had given him. The dry rustle of the money in his pocket confirmed that it was true. Instinctively he reached out to pick up the violin, keen to buy something else to eat. But it wasn't there! The shock hit him like a punch in the stomach. 'Oh no!' he exclaimed, and jumping up, he began to run back through the rain. Cursing himself, he arrived at the theatre steps to find no sign of it. 'What have I done?' he asked, unable to believe that on the very first day Gideon had trusted him with it, he had lost it.

Hoping someone might have handed it in, he made his way up the steps and opened the theatre door. Inside, a hush as soft and thick as the carpet under his feet made him feel like an intruder. He made straight for the box-office window but a doorman barred his way. 'Do you have a ticket, young man?' he asked.

'Er... I left my fiddle out there on the steps. D'you know if anyone found it?' His heart pounded.

'No, not that I'm aware,' replied the doorman. 'You left it where, did you say?'

'Just outside, sir, on the steps.'

'No, I would've seen it,' he said dismissively and began to look Finn up and down. The internal door opened and Mitzi appeared, laden with a full tray of confectionery strapped to her shoulders and balanced on her waist. She turned pink when she saw Finn.

'George, I ain't got any float. Is there some change in that other till? It'll be the interval soon an' I'll have a queue of people waitin'.'

The doorman cleared his throat irritably. 'I dare say I have, in there.' He seemed annoyed, or tired, or both. As soon as his back was turned, Mitzi asked Finn: 'You alright?' She was smiling and showing him the whites of her eyes.

Finn shook his head. 'I've gone an' lost my fiddle!'

'How did you do that?' she cried with a giggle, tossing her head and giving Finn a cheeky smile. His expression must have revealed how upset he was because she grimaced, bit her lip and said, 'Sorry! Has he found it for you then?'

The sound of coins being counted suggested the

doorman was occupied for a moment so Mitzi took a few steps towards Finn and whispered,

'Where did you lose it?'

'Out there on the steps; I only left it a minute. Someone must've taken it.' He kept looking back at the door as though contemplating his escape. 'I wondered if that nice lady picked it, the one with the long dress an' all the jewels ...'

'Oh, Bianca Tabora, y'mean? Yeh, she's lovely she is. She's our leadin' lady.'

'What have you got to split, girl, is it a fiver?' asked George loudly through the box-office hatch.

'A tenner, mate. I told you.'

Colour flushed on the doorman's neck and he stared angrily, 'No you didn't, and I'm not your mate!' he hissed before withdrawing and diving into the till again.

Mitzi raised her eyebrows and gesturing to Finn, whispered:

'Go through there while he's busy! I'll ask around for you durin' the interval – see if anyone's found it. Quick, go now!'

Finn slipped in through the swing-doors and found himself cast into darkness. As his eyes adjusted, he saw the stage was lit up like a vision with caverns of blue and luminous green light. He was unsure what to do but a girl came with a torch and indicated an empty seat. Sitting down, he relaxed and let the darkness fold in around him. As though he was in a dream, he saw a woman sleeping in a hammock which was strung between pink and green trees. The sleeping figure stirred and Finn recognised her – it was the beautiful lady. As the spotlight shone on her face she awoke, stretched her arms above her head and asked: *"What angel wakes me from my flowery bed?"*

Someone with a donkey's head appeared and began to sing. The lady left her bed and embraced this strange creature, saying: *"I pray thee, gentle mortal, sing again!"*

A torch-light came towards him. It was Mitzi. 'George can't find it,' she whispered. 'He said you'll have to go an'...'

But at that moment there was a piercing scream and a crash from the stage. Shouts and cries erupted as the audience rushed forward to see what had happened.

'Call an ambulance,' someone ordered, 'quickly!'

Moments later an announcement came over the loud-speaker:

"Ladies and gentlemen! I'm sorry to tell you that our leading lady, Bianca Tabora, has had an unfortunate accident. The performance tonight will have to be postponed. I do apologise most sincerely on behalf of the..."

'Blimey! It's Bianca!' cried Mitzi. 'She's gone an' fallen off the stage! I'd better see if she's alright!' Before Finn knew what was happening she had hurried away. All the house-lights came on and Finn, feeling exposed and conspicuous, didn't know what to do. Seeing a side door as a means of escape, he made his way towards it through the crowds. As he did so he caught a glimpse of the beautiful lady lying lifeless beneath the stage. Her gold dress was spread out around her, crumpled like the wings of a butterfly.

Pushing against the side-door it opened and seconds later he found himself alone in the dark empty street.

Crowds hurried out past him, not seeing him, making their way back to their homes. He shivered as a gust of cold wind blew round the corner. How he longed to be safe with Gideon again, to be sitting by the stick-fire eating their supper. But the fiddle – how could he tell him he'd lost it?

Walking the streets he grew more and more tired and anxious. He felt so alienated and lonely it reminded him of when he was a small boy. Was he really running away again? Had he so easily returned to the same state as before? The rain stopped but a hollow feeling came over him as though everything was unreal, as though he didn't belong anywhere. He felt like a ghost creeping about in a world where no-one could see him. Finally he came to a place which seemed familiar. Leafy evergreen shrubs and the scent of pine needles, moss and lichen mingled with the damp mist rising up from the river. It reminded him of collecting mushrooms with Gideon and it helped him relax. He sank down as exhaustion came upon him like a gentle hand, lifting him effortlessly over fields and hedgerows, leading him through dank sweet-smelling trees to a place which was secluded from the road and sheltered from the wind. There, oblivious to the cold and the wet, he lay down, pulled his jacket tightly around him, pulled his cap over his eyes, and tried not to think about anything at all.

Ten

A few weeks later

Seamus was having a bad day. He was sitting backstage with a pile of unpaid bills in front of him. If it was anything like last time, half the tickets would remain unsold. He scratched his head, stood up and lumbered about thoughtfully, his big feet becoming even clumsier in his anxiety. The costs were mounting, the artistes were asking for their pay, not to mention the technicians and other staff, and to cap it all Bianca's accident had forced him to give her part to her understudy. The girl was fully capable of taking it over, but she wasn't known to the audience and it's difficult to introduce a new face half-way through a run. It doesn't draw the crowds. If Bianca's injuries were purely physical it would have helped. He shrugged his shoulders because he began to feel slightly guilty thinking about the inconvenience her accident had caused. She had suffered a broken collar-bone and two fractured ribs after her fall from the stage but the head injury, followed by the concussion she had suffered, was the main cause for concern. Her memory had been affected. Unless there was an improvement soon, he knew she may never act again. Professionally, it was a worry for him – but of course it was also a personal blow. Now he had to admit that the chance of them ever getting married was more unlikely than ever. Some would say he had had a lucky escape. Suppose she had married him and then lost her marbles! What a burden that would have been! Flushing with sudden embarrassment as though fearing someone may have overheard his thoughts, he glanced about and taking a deep breath, tried to pull himself together.

Without Bianca returning as his leading lady he couldn't imagine the theatre being able to carry on. It was time to face the facts. He must call a meeting of the staff and tell them – the theatre was under serious threat of closure. It would take all his strength to stand up to the company's inevitable protest at this decision and he didn't have the confidence he once had. As it was, these days his judgement was often being questioned – even by Todd. At that moment, Todd himself came swinging through the door. 'I hear you've really put your foot in it this time!' said the blazer-clad comedian, who had a history of superficial relationships and never took anything seriously.

'Why? What have I done now?' asked Seamus miserably.

'I hear you virtually accused Bianca of being no more than a useless stage-hand, that's all. What were you thinking of?'

'What d'you mean?' he demanded. 'Of course I didn't! All I did was ask her to take on a minor role – you know, a non-speaking part – just until she feels better. I don't think that's being unreasonable, do you? I wasn't being patronising or anything. After-all, her understudy has got to know where she stands. Rebecca's the leading lady now – we've got to promote her as our new star, whether we like it or not. Bianca's

135

not going to get better overnight, more's the pity.'

Todd had flung himself down in a chair and was now sitting with his legs stretched out and his feet resting on the edge of the table. He sat twisting his ankles this way and that, admiring his new two-tone Italian shoes. 'So Bianca's going from being the leading lady to a mere servant girl without any script at all! I'm not surprised she took the hump – or at least her daughter did. She said offering her mother that part was an insult! Well, I can't say I blame her!' He stretched up his arms and linking them behind his head, yawned dramatically. 'And it's not often I agree with Colette but honestly!' With this, two of his blazer buttons popped open revealing more of the pink striped shirt.

'I was trying to help her, Todd, believe it or not. Between you and me they're in a bit of a spot financially. Unless Bianca's memory miraculously returns she's got no hope of learning her lines. I don't know what Colette's going to do with her actually. She doesn't even feel it's safe to leave her alone. They've hardly got a penny to their names and they're behind with the rent on their apartment. That's why I offered Bianca a walk-on part – they need the money.'

'Don't we all, darling! Why don't you just give Bianca some cash? You've got a nice little nest-egg stashed away I bet, with no little woman to spend it on. You've always had a soft-spot for Bee, it's no secret. Let's face it, Seamus darling, you should've married her years ago, while you still had some hair on your head.' He glanced at Seamus as though for a second he thought he might have gone a bit too far, but seeing no change in the man's demeanour, he carried on. 'Look, why don't you just hand her over a wad of notes and save us all a load of grief, eh?'

Seamus didn't seem fazed by this remark. 'Todd, I was just trying to be diplomatic to the poor woman,' he replied, sighing. 'I need to cast someone in the servant's role – Bianca needs the work – so I still don't see why I shouldn't have offered her something to do.'

'Are you serious? Do I have to spell it out?' cried Todd, throwing his hands up in mock despair. 'Because you don't give a prize-winning racehorse a bunch of carrots and enter him for the donkey derby, that's why!'

'It's not like that at all! Anyway, if we must have such a crude simile, when racehorses get injured they shoot them. End of story. I'm not being brutal, Todd. I'm giving the woman a second chance. What's wrong with that? Either that or she's off sick for weeks and won't have a part in the play at all. I'd even offer it to that daughter of hers, if she wasn't so offish with me.'

Todd was bored with the conversation now. 'Look Seamus old chap, there might be a reason why you're of a certain age and still living on your own – do you see what I mean? You and women?' He made a balancing gesture with his hand, swung his legs down from the table and stood up.

'Huh! Who are you to talk?' demanded Seamus. 'You're not exactly spoken for yet are you?'

Todd shrugged. 'Women don't appreciate the subtle nuances of my character,' he replied. 'They'll learn! I'm saving myself. One day, the female form of perfection personified will waltz into my life and you won't see me for dust, darling!'

'Call me when it happens then, I'd hate to miss

it,' replied Seamus sinking lower into his chair and contemplating the idiosyncrasies of his job with a dour expression. 'Don't bank on having the theatre to fall back on. The way things are going I can't promise they'll be a theatre here this time next year.'

Todd made a move towards the door. 'Oh, we are down in the dumps aren't we! Well, I've got a life to live even if you haven't. I'll be seeing you – and hey!' He paused in the doorway, 'Watch what you say to that daughter of hers. I've heard women bite when they're annoyed.'

*

Twenty miles away, on the edge of a small spinney bordering a field of freshly ploughed soil, Gideon tossed and turned in his bed. He had been talking to the old farrier and the rumours he had heard stirred a fateful mystery from the past. The story told of a baby found abandoned in the street. Gideon lay awake for hours trying to make sense of it and when he did sleep he began dreaming feverishly. 'Whoa! Whoa, there!' he mumbled, waking as a sharp pain shot across his forehead. He was sweating profusely, his chest ached with a heaviness he couldn't understand and his heart thumped like a leaden bell. In his nightmare, a woman had stepped right out in front of him. The horse had reared up, tipping the caravan over backwards and he had felt himself falling… He had had too many bad dreams lately and he knew that was a bad sign. Trying to grasp a sense of reality, he attempted to sit up and saw, through half-closed eyes, a grey mist hanging like a shroud in the woods beyond and creeping into the caravan. Comforted by the familiar sight of his copper pots and pans hanging from their hooks, the colourful tartan blanket on his bed and the wood-burning stove, he thought about making a cup of tea and began to feel better.

But he had always said a man was a fool if he ignored the warnings of a strong dream. There had been a lady, quite a glamorous lady, in his dream. She was holding a baby in her arms. Oblivious of everything around her, she was engrossed in the baby, singing and talking in the affectionate way people have with infants. He shook his head, trying to shake off the images. 'Ah, I be gettin' too old for these puzzles.' It involved Finn, he had no doubt, and the road was on a hill, similar to where Finn's house in Tollwithen had been situated years ago. A terrifying sense of danger came to him as he recalled the horse rearing up, whinnying in fright, and the woman... Closing his eyes, he must have drifted off again because he returned to the place of the dream. No lady this time, no baby – but he saw his fiddle smashed to pieces in the road. Gideon forced himself awake. Feeling strangely weak and shaky, he climbed out of the caravan, and went to get a drink of water, gulping it down and gasping at the cold shock of it. Shaking off the nightmare, he tried to follow his usual routine. He went to collect some mushrooms and wood to cook his breakfast. But he had no appetite and when the fire wouldn't take, he had a growing sense of foreboding. Something dreadful was about to happen.

*

Where Finn lacked knowledge about reading and arithmetic he made up for in survival skills. Gideon had taught him well. Making the bridge next to the railway station by the River Fowey his temporary home, he was careful to make sure he was up and away at first light. There were early morning trains, some shunting into the station carrying newspapers and deliveries, others speeding through on their way to London. To keep himself clean, a cold wash and shave was essential as part of his daily routine. Before dawn he stripped to the waist and washed himself in the river. Now without the violin, he had no means of earning money, so putting his things away in his rucksack he set off once again to look for a job. He walked around the town all day, asking at various industries and establishments, but without any success and by nightfall he was famished. Passing the pub and feasting his eyes on the company within, sitting at ease by a roaring log fire, hunger pains drove him to stop by the pub door. Suddenly someone came bursting out of the door and virtually knocked him over.

'What the flamin' hell are you doin'? Were you deliberately tryin' to trip me up or what mate?'

Finn defended himself. 'Sorry. I was just goin' to ask inside about…'

'About what? Well, get in there, man! Don't be loiterin' around here like a spare part.' The man took a packet of Woodbines out of his pocket and with a cigarette hanging precariously from his lower lip he said, 'Well?' and stared at Finn in cold expectation. 'Are you goin' in or what?'

'Hey Drew!' someone called, sticking their head out of the door. 'It's your round. You ain't gettin' out

140

of it by hidin' out there, mate!'

'I'll be in when I've had a fag,' he shouted. Turning to Finn again with a menacing scowl he said, 'Well? What are you waitin' for? Get in there man an' get a drink down you. You look half-dead.'

'Are you buyin' then?' Finn asked, determined to play him at his own game.

'No, I bloody well ain't,' replied the man.

Finn thrust the door open. The strain of the song, *Wait a Minute, Mr. Postman* by the Beatles was playing on the juke box. As he stepped inside there was a cascade of giggles from the girl behind the bar. Finn didn't care anymore. The atmosphere obliterated the uncomfortable feeling the encounter outside had given him and its cheerfulness warmed him as rapidly as the heat from the fire. He felt his complexion begin to tingle as the heat took effect on his chilled skin. The close proximity of people, in contrast to his isolation and his empty stomach, made him reel for a moment.

'What can I get you, love?' asked the bar-girl.

After hearing his request for a job, she led him through to the back where the landlord was making sandwiches with his shirt-sleeves rolled up to the elbows and a tea-towel around his waist.

'This fella's askin' if we've got any jobs, boss. I've got to go back, they're waitin' for another round.' She disappeared, involuntarily tugging her mini-skirt down over her thighs as she went.

'What can you do then, lad?' asked the landlord, jutting out his bottom lip with a sneer. He stopped work and began watching Finn as though expecting him to perform a magic trick. Finn listed the things he had thought of, including being able to gut and skin a rabbit in five minutes which he thought might add to his qualifications. The landlord looked less than impressed. As Finn waited for a reply, he cast about, trying to avoid meeting the landlord's pink eyes and sagging bull-dog jaws. Pieces of grated cheese were on the floor; some were already trodden into the tiles. A tea-towel was draped over the door of a cupboard stacked with food.

'Think you can turn your hand to makin' sandwiches?' he asked, gesturing with his thumb to the task in hand. 'We don't do anythin' grand here.'

'I've done plenty. Peanut butter's my favourite,' said Finn, whose stomach was beginning to rumble.

'Right, lad, you ain't got a prior appointment tonight 'ave you? Want to start right now? Get yourself washed through there and the lass will give you a clean shirt to put on. We'll give you a trial run. I can't be havin' sloppiness in the kitchen. I've got my reputation to think of – understand?'

Finn nodded, but he couldn't disguise his surprise. 'Thank you, no, I mean, yes, and thanks.' Without hesitating the landlord put down the buttery knife, washed his hands at the sink and called loudly, 'Deborah! Out here! Get the lad kitted up, he's got work to do.' Turning to Finn once more he asked: 'What's your name then?'

'Finn, short for Finbarr.'

'Right, Finn, let's get sorted then. My name's Fred, that's short for Fred, right? Now, make me up ten rounds o' cheese and onion, white bread, cut diagonal – know what I mean by diagonal?' Finn shook his head.

The bull-dog took up a large knife, and slashed a slice of bread across with a cruel sweep. 'Like that! Got it?' he said, stabbing the knife back in the block.

'Yeh, I've got it, sir,' said Finn.

The landlord looked up at him in surprise. 'Blimey, I ain't been called "sir" in twenty odd years!'

Finn stared at him for a moment. He wasn't used to being spoken to in such an odd way.

Shaking his head in mock despair, the landlord mumbled to himself, 'Right one we've got 'ere.' As he returned to the bar he shouted, 'Deborah, go an' get the lad a clean outfit before I change my mind.'

Finn worked solidly for three and a half hours. He didn't taste even a morsel of the soft delicious bread or nibble a piece of cheese. His heart had left his chest and was beating somewhere in between his ears when Deborah came and perched on a stool beside him showing her laddered tights. She took off her shoes and moaned, 'Oh my feet! They don't belong to me no more. What a night! Can't wait to get into a nice hot bath. Here, no need to make any more. It's nearly closing time.'

Finn began putting the unused bread back in the waxed-paper packet. 'What are you doin' that for?' she asked.

'It'll go dry otherwise. You'll want some for tomorrow.'

'Dry? Who cares! It'll go in the dustbin tonight. We'll have fresh in tomorrow.' She chuckled, 'You're a hard worker; I'll give you that.' Standing up, she picked up the loaf, flipped the pedal-bin open with her toe and was just about to throw it away when Finn stopped her with a firm grip on her bare arm. 'No, wait!' he said. His head rocked at the sudden rush of blood to his head. Taking it from her, he said, 'Sorry,

143

but we can't go wastin' it!'

At that moment the landlord barged through carrying the cash tray from the till. 'Go and fetch them glasses off the table under the window for me, Debs. We ain't finished yet an' I've still got cashing up to do.' He turned his attention to Finn. 'You did well tonight, Finn. I don't mind tellin' you, you surprised me. Never thought you had it in you.'

Deborah loitered by the door. 'He was just moanin' at me for chuckin' the bread away an' wastin' it!' She raised her neat eyebrows and giggled. 'Right old fashioned, he is!'

The landlord eyed Finn curiously. 'Was you now? I ain't complainin' about anyone bein' thrifty.' He looked Finn up and down. 'You look a bit peeky to me, lad. Have you eaten tonight?'

'No, sir, I mean, no, I wouldn't have eaten anythin' unless you said I could. I ain't touched a thing, honest.'

The man shook his head and smiled. 'Blimey, you've been well brought-up. More than I can say about some people round 'ere.' He scratched his head. 'So you've had nothing to eat, did you say?'

Finn's grip on the packet of bread tightened. 'If you don't mind, I mean, if you're just chuckin' it away could I take this wi' me? It'd do me for a bite to eat tonight.' Fred broke out in a roar of laughter and slammed the till-tray loaded with cash on the work-top causing the coins to jangle noisily. Taking a pound note from the tray, he held it out to Finn with a smile. 'Here, son! Come on, take it! That's your wages for tonight. Come back, same time tomorrow an' I'll pay you twice that much if you work as hard as you did tonight.'

Finn took the note and his head spun. 'Thanks,' he said, 'OK, I will.'

'Right! Good! You can go now then an' we'll see you tomorrow.' Finn turned towards the door and saw Deborah flash him a smile as she disappeared back into the bar.

'Hey, hang on!' said Fred. 'Do you want that bread?'

Finn nodded.

'You could've had a pie or somethin' if you'd said. You're entitled to a free meal every day when you work for me, you know. Tell Debs what you want tomorrow and she'll see you're alright. OK?'

Fred took the bread and cheese from the counter and crammed them into Finn's arms. 'Take these with you, lad, an' tomorrow night, before you start, sit down in the bar an' order yourself summat to eat. An' don't wait to be told, mind. Oh, an' anythin' that's left over you can take home and you're welcome to it. Some people round here don't appreciate good food till they trip over it. Hey!' he added. 'Can't have my staff workin' on an empty stomach now, can I?'

When everyone had gone home and the streets were quiet Finn made his way back to the river and slipped in through the shrubbery. He sat on the ground in the dark cold shelter of the bridge. Carefully he removed the packages of food from inside his jacket. The sweet fragrance of the bread filled him with joy. Biting into it, he took a mouthful of cheese and his stomach was hurting in anticipation of the food. It was more delicious than anything he had ever tasted! Even the thought of Gideon's rabbit couldn't detract from his enjoyment. He had his first wages in his pocket, the prospect of a good meal tomorrow, and a job. Sighing with relief and exhaustion he fell asleep, even before he had finished eating.

Over the next few weeks, while working at the pub every evening, Finn was at a loose end during the day. He didn't earn enough to rent a room and concealing his living arrangements was becoming increasingly difficult. Finishing work late at night he would return to the sanctuary of the river, but he had to be up at dawn to wash and shave, and concealing his meagre possessions under the bridge was a problem. He used the launderette in the town to wash his clothes and often smiled at the thought of what Gideon would think of such an establishment. The only person who knew where he was sleeping was his new friend, Mitzi. She often worried about him, he knew, and would bring him little treats like chocolate bought with her own meagre wage.

He grew quite fond of her and loved her china doll face and her simplicity.

One day when they met in the town Mitzi began to tell him more about Bianca Tabora: 'Since havin' her accident she can't act no more and Seamus, he's the director, he said he can't afford to keep her an' she'll have to go.' Mitzi glanced up at Finn's face for a response but finding none she persevered. 'Colette says the theatre's runnin' out of money an' if it shuts down I'll lose me job.' Again she waited, but Finn was preoccupied.

'Where will she go?' he asked suddenly.

'Who?'

'That Bianca whatever her name is – I was

wonderin' if she's got my fiddle.'

Mitzi shook her head, 'I told you! She don't remember nothin'! She must've lost her memory with that bang on her head 'cos Colette said she can't say her lines without makin' a mistake an' Seamus, he's sacked her. So even if she did find your fiddle she probably won't remember. My friend Colette,' continued Mitzi importantly, glancing at Finn for attention., 'she said she was goin' on about somethin' weird in the hospital. It were the fever though an' it didn't make no sense. Even if she did have it once – she ain't got it now 'cos I asked Colette to 'ave a look for you. She said she would've seen it if it were there.' Mitzi paused and seeing Finn still staring at the ground, tried again.

'Colette said she wished she could find it so she could flog it an' get the money 'cos they can't pay the rent. They've had to move into a dingy 'orrible little place the other side of town.'

Suddenly Finn sprang to life. 'She can't sell it! It's mine! I mean it's Gideon's,' he shouted in dismay.

Mitzi looked at him in amazement. 'OK, keep your hair on! She were only jokin'! She ain't got it anyway!' She shrugged her shoulders and began to sulk.

'Yeh, but...' He looked away, embarrassed. 'Sorry, but I don't know what I'm goin' to do if I can't find it... that's all I'm sayin'. It's so important to old Gideon.'

Mitzi recovered quickly and giggled. 'If it's that important you shouldn't have run off an' left it then, should you! Didn't you tell the police you'd lost it? Someone might 'ave handed it in, you know.'

The word "police" sent his pulse racing and he turned away. He had learned from all the gypsies that the police were to be avoided at any cost. 'Yeh, maybe,' he replied. 'Want to come down the pub where I work?' he asked, keen to change the subject. 'It gets right busy down there of a Saturday.'

Mitzi failed to notice his change of tone. She was too pleased to have his attention. 'I ain't got no money to go out.' She peeped up at his face, hoping to catch his eye. 'You offerin' to buy me a drink then?'

'Might be! I'll be in the back workin' but Deborah will talk to you, she's quite friendly.'

'Who's she then?' asked Mitzi. 'Is she your girlfriend?'

'No! She works behind the bar that's all. She ain't my sort anyway.'

'Ooooh! Who is your sort then, Finbarr?' she teased, taking hold of his arm and stepping along with him in mock imitation of a lady. 'Am I your type o' girl then?'

He looked at her out of the corner of his eye. 'You could be, if you grow a bit taller!'

Mitzi pushed him away. 'Cheek of it! I've got me posh red heels to put on if anyone asks me out!' But when he didn't respond she glanced up at him again, more earnestly. 'Is anyone askin' me out then?'

'Could be,' Finn replied, and he looked away from her, up at the clouds passing in the sky, as Gideon used to do when he was making an important decision. 'What are you doin' on Sunday?'

Eleven

Colette and Bianca were moving home. As they opened the door and entered the terraced house, Colette saw the carpet was worn so thin it had taken on the shape of the floorboards it covered. Hauling her suitcase up the steep staircase, she was hoping their new flat was going to look better in daylight. 'Not far now, Mum!' she called. Bianca was lagging behind with more luggage. Although her broken bones had healed, the head injury still affected her, giving her an innocent demeanour. Her face bore an expression of childish wonder as she gazed up at the peeling wallpaper in the hall as though she was entering a palace. She recalled little of the accident or what her life had been like before and, as she climbed the stairs, she began humming a tune.

'What's that you're singing? Is it an old music-hall song?' called Colette.

Bianca smiled happily. 'I don't know.' Both suitcases were heavy, loaded with all the possessions they had left. So much of their stuff had been sold or given away. But there wasn't much that could dampen Bianca's spirits. She had little recollection of their previous home. Sadness misted Colette's eyes. Just this once she wished her mother wouldn't sing. Emotion caught in her throat but she refused to give in to tears. She had to be strong for both of them.

Quickly becoming out of breath, Bianca stopped. 'These stairs are so steep!' she cried.

Colette put down her case at the top and was just about to go down and help her when she heard heavy footsteps descending from the upper floor. A man appeared, short, unshaven, with his shirt open to the waist revealing his hairy chest.

'Here, love, let me take that!' he said, pushing rudely past Colette to assist Bianca and filling the air with the odour of beer and sweat.

'It's okay, we can manage thanks,' said Colette. But already Bianca had relinquished her grasp on the suitcase and was watching him carry it up to the landing in admiration.

'There you are, darlin', no problem!' he declared. 'Anythin' else you want doin' just give old Drew a shout, alright babe?' As he said this, he glanced at Colette and said to Bianca confidentially. 'Bit high an' mighty, aren't we?' The comment was lost on her but it was close enough for Colette to hear. Taking up her suitcase again, she crossed the landing impatiently and thrust the key into the lock. Flinging the door open, she hurried inside.

The man carried on down the stairs. Bianca called after him: 'Would you like to come in for a cup of coffee?'

Colette's head reappeared round the door. 'No, Mum don't!' she cried, rather too loudly.

Immediately he turned back, smiling a toothy smile. 'Thanks love, I will,' he said, grinning with satisfaction.

'No, sorry you can't!' said Colette. 'I mean – we haven't got time. We've only just arrived and nothing's unpacked.'

'Time?' replied the man. 'Now that's somethin' I've got plenty of. Money? No. Time? Yes.'

Feeling slightly guilty, Colette suggested, 'Perhaps you'd like to come another day, when we've settled in a bit?'

He touched his cap and replied, 'Thank you, I'd like that, ladies! Very kind of you I'm sure. Drew's the name, Drew Caudry. Pleased to meet you!' Colette returned the introductions, and he left them and went on down.

'What a nice man!' declared Bianca, when they were inside.

'Yes, Mum, but I wish you hadn't invited him in like that,' said Colette, opening the door a crack to make sure he had gone. In the back of her mind she sensed danger, as though a black spider had just scuttled out of a corner. Undisturbed, Bianca was standing in the middle of the sitting-room looking satisfied and gazing around with bright eyes. 'This is lovely, isn't it!' she said. Anything seemed to please her these days but perhaps it was just as well.

Just inside the flat, opposite their front-door, was an oddly situated wash-basin. It was set into an alcove with a mirror above it; the sink itself was stained. The flat was furnished with an odd assortment of items but it was functional. They were having some of their own furniture brought from the apartment, but the majority of it had been sold. Finding the narrow space restricting, Colette wasn't sure how the removal men were going to manage bringing in their furniture, but she considered it essential to keep some familiar things, especially for her mother's sake, even if they did become overcrowded with them.

Still with an excited flush to her cheek, Bianca went to look out of the window. 'It's a beautiful view from here!' she declared. Colette joined her and had to agree. 'Yes, you can even see the spire of St. Bartholomew's Church in the distance,' she said, 'and look at all those seagulls raiding the bins!'

Entering the first bedroom Bianca exclaimed, 'Ooh, I like this room!' It was as small as the theatre's kitchen and the walls, cupboards and even the cast-iron fireplace were painted egg yellow. But it had a certain charm, Colette had to agree.

Bianca began unpacking her suitcase. She pulled out the most fabulous lilac and purple satin dress which was studded with sequins that sent tiny mirror reflections of light dancing across the wall. 'Look at this!' she squealed. 'Where did this come from?'

Colette bit her lip. There were many incidents like this. 'You wore that when you were playing the leading part in *Scheherazade*, Mum! Don't you remember? Think of all the colourful Arabian costumes, the dancing and those stories!' Bianca, crushing the beautiful dress as she held it against her cheek, was looking troubled and confused. Colette stopped herself and, stepping forward, gave her a hug.

'I'll dig out the photos later to remind you, Mum. One day it will all come flooding back, really it will! Come on, let's leave this and make some tea, shall we?' Disappearing into the kitchen, she found a gas stove and the most meagre of basic essentials supplied. 'We'll soon make it homely, Mum, you'll see,' she said, deciding that she had to make the best of it whatever happened. Filling the kettle, however, she discovered they had no means of lighting the gas.

'No matches! We'll have to wait for our tea,' she called. 'I'll pop out for some in a minute.' And pausing to look out of the kitchen window she added: 'Look, it's quite a nice view from here too.'

Going down the stairs on her way to the shop, Colette found the main front door wide open. A cold breeze was blowing into the hall and to her disgust Drew Caudry was there. He was engrossed in the task of sharpening his cut-throat razor on the stone step.

'Excuse me,' she said, in as business-like a voice as she could muster.

'Off out already are you?' he asked, moving aside.

'Yes, shopping – just to the corner-shop at the end of the road.' She was a few paces away when he shouted:

'Couldn't get me some fags, could you love?' He began delving into his trouser pocket and brought out some change. 'Ten Woodbines, cheers,' he added, holding it out to her. Colette felt she had no choice. She took the money and went on her way, scolding herself for having done so. Now she would have to buy cigarettes for the first time in her life. What was worse, they were for a man she already despised. The coins felt dirty in her hand and she scraped her palm along the side of her skirt, making a mental note to wash her hands as soon as she got back.

When Colette had gone to buy the matches, Bianca stood rubbing her shoulder which was aching after carrying the suitcase. Her memory was returning in bitter snatches like clips from an old film. And similarly, the strange room in which she stood contained fragments of another person's life which could easily be her own. Remnants of other people's attempts to create a home touched her: the poor single bed under the window, the worn red rug, and the tiny fireplace. Remains of pop posters hung from the wall and a child's toy lay abandoned on a faded pink armchair.

Unaware of the poignancy of her situation, she started work on the rusty gas-cooker, scraping away its heavy coating of blackened burnt-on grease. It had been months since her accident but the gaps in her memory were becoming evident and she couldn't bring herself to talk about it with Colette. It was only a bang on the head after all, she told herself, and the doctors reassured her everything would be fine. As she doused the top of the cooker with water and scattered some soap powder, which she found in a damp box in the cupboard, she tried to remember the night she fell from the stage. What were the lines she was reciting? How did it happen? She stopped working and stood at the sink looking out of the window. Beyond the network of yards, fences, garages and washing lines, there lay the intimate inside-story of people's lives; their washing drying, their trips to the dustbin, their scolding of children. Little did they know that she could observe their comings and goings. If only she could look down on her own life like this, turn the pages of a huge scrap book and be reminded. She had some vague memories. They lingered in her mind like bits of a dream without any meaning. Pictures of the apartment they had left behind returned to her in fragments. Their old home

154

had been shrouded at the back by tall trees. Pigeons nested in its branches, flapping their wings and cooing contentedly. It was a peaceful place. She saw faces sometimes, laughing, talking, and a roaring fire. But she didn't know who the people were. She could see, in her mind's eye, large rooms with high-ceilings and long floor-length curtains and tears stung her eyes. Swallowing hard, she turned away from the window and forgetting about cleaning the cooker, she resumed her unpacking. As she did so she began to hum a tune. Then she heard a knock on the door.

Returning from the small corner shop twenty minutes later, Colette found that Drew Caudry was no longer there. With her brown paper carrier bag of groceries in one hand, and the man's cigarettes and change in the other, she was annoyed at having to go up the stairs to the second floor to deliver them. But when she reached their floor, she was surprised to hear voices coming from inside their own flat. As she opened the door with her key, she heard her mother responding with a girlish giggle to whatever Drew was saying.

Colette scowled and greeted him with undisguised hostility. 'I didn't expect to find you here! There's your cigarettes,' she said, thrusting the packet out towards him.

'Only bein' neighbourly,' he remarked. 'Your mother here wanted her case liftin' up onto the wardrobe, didn't you love!'

'He's very kind!' said Bianca, obviously delighted.

'I could have done it, Mum. You could have waited until I got back.'

155

Drew walked towards the door. 'No need to get all stuffy wi' me love,' he said. 'We're all in this dump together, ain't we? Some of us are goin' up in the world.' He looked around the room for a moment as if summing it up. 'And some of us are goin' down. Don't make no difference to the price o' bread do it?'

Colette, taken aback, hastily mumbled an apology, her cheeks burning with embarrassment.

'Right,' he replied, winking at Bianca as he went through the door, 'No hard feelin's. See you, ladies!'

Meanwhile, on the other side of town, Finn's dedication to his work had impressed Fred, the pub landlord. However, Finn noticed Deborah and the other bar staff appeared to regard him with some amusement, so he kept out of their way as much as he could. His greatest fear was that they would discover where he spent the night. The fictional address he had given Fred could easily be disproved. If his home under the bridge was discovered he knew he would become a laughing stock. But something else was worrying him. Easter was approaching and with it, Gideon's return. How he longed to see him again and yet, without the violin, he couldn't face him. But one problem was unexpectedly resolved when Fred surprised him by by offering him staff accommodation at the pub.

Finding himself in a warm room of his own, with a soft bed under a sloping ceiling and a bathroom, was more than he could ever have dreamt of. Outside his bedroom window, the pub's sign hung from a wrought iron bracket. It swung in the breeze and kept creaking during the night in a way that reminded him of the old caravan rocking in the wind. With Mitzi's help, he

156

spent some of his wages buying bedding, towels and soap which she particularly enjoyed choosing for him, wrinkling her pretty snub nose and giggling. It was she alone who knew he had been sleeping under the bridge, she who kept his secret without laughing at him or judging him. Because of this they had become closer. The more he told her of his past, the more he led her into his quiet troubled world. As every day passed, he felt himself falling more and more in love with her. Soon he found himself thinking about Mitzi most of the time and forgetting about Gideon's fiddle altogether.

Twelve

In a rented room over a grocer's shop in Plymouth, Sarah McKinney languished in a stale bed. She was thin. A long illness had left her so weak she could barely look after herself properly. Her complexion was sallow and creased with sleep and she rarely ventured out. No longer did she care what people thought of her, though it wouldn't surprise her to learn that as a stranger arriving in their midst, neighbours and customers to the shop often speculated about her past. She had no intention of volunteering any information. Let them believe what they will; let them keep guessing, she told herself, because who would sympathise with her, or believe her story?

Shortly after taking that small shabby room, one or two locals ventured up the back steps to tap on her door and bid her welcome. But she refused to be drawn on their questions, and never invited them in so after a while people stopped calling. Rumours spread of a prison sentence, or that she had abandoned a religious vocation and left a nunnery. Funny what ideas people will dream up if given the opportunity. It was probably on account of her having next to nothing in the way of possessions when she came, nothing more than the clothes she stood up in. On the rare occasions when she did go out, she left the room early and walked to the Catholic Church where she attended Mass. Sometimes the shopkeeper, her landlord, who had become somewhat protective of her, would tell her what stories were circulating about her when he brought her up some groceries. In response to these wild ideas, she would give a little laugh and shrug her shoulders.

It was to this shop Gideon arrived in his horse-drawn caravan one heavily misted morning. Troubled by haunting dreams and exhausting restlessness, he had travelled all the way to Plymouth to settle a matter close to his heart. He needed to talk to Finn's mother. By putting together the various clues he found among the gypsy community, with his own insights gained through instinct and folklore, he had been able to fit the pieces of Finn's broken childhood back together. All that was needed to fuse them now was the natural love of his estranged mother. When he pulled up outside the shop, the clip-clop of the horse's hooves had already attracted the customers' attention and they stopped talking and stared as he came in through the door. Holding his cap in his hand, Gideon stamped his boots on the mat as though emerging from a snow storm.

'Would there be a Mrs. McKinney livin' here at all?'

'Who wants to know?' asked the shopkeeper.

'My name be Gideon Tremayne. She don't know me but I have important news for her, so's I believe.'

'Important news have you?' repeated the shopkeeper, eyeing him suspiciously. 'What's so important as you can't let a body know before you turns up out of the blue? She didn't say nothin' to me about expectin' a visitor.' As he said this he glanced at his two customers for moral support.

'She be a stranger to me, as yet,' Gideon replied. 'Fact is, she don't know me at all an' I don't know her neither. But it's like this: if she be the person I think she be, I've come with news of her long lost son.'

The shopkeeper regarded Gideon curiously. He looked intrigued, perhaps thinking there might be a chance his poor tenant had come into some money and this possibility kindled his interest.

'Her son? I see!' he replied as though beginning to rub his hands together. 'If that's true, she'll be right pleased to meet you I don't doubt. You'll find her if you go out the back and up the steps. 'Knock loudly, you might have to try more than once. She ain't been well an' she's not much good at answerin' the door.'

The gypsy nodded and thanked him. 'She's as timid as a church mouse,' called the shopkeeper after him. 'Go gentle now!'

'Thankee kindly,' said Gideon and replacing his cap he left the shop, ascended the staircase and tapped on the door. There was shuffle inside but no response. He knocked again. Keys jangled and slowly the door opened to reveal a figure in a dressing-gown. 'I'm right sorry to fetch you from yer bed, ma'am,' he said. 'Be you Mrs. McKinney? If you ain't feelin' well I could come back another day.'

'What is it you want?' asked Sarah. 'If you're selling stuff, I'm not interested. I don't buy anything from people on doorsteps.'

'No, no. I'm not tryin' to sell baskets today. There be more important matters to see to, seein' as I've got some good news to tell yer. Well, I'm thinkin' it be good news. To tell you the truth I've been searchin' for you for, let me see, must be years now. At

160

least, I'm thinkin' it's you I've been lookin' for, but I might be wrong.'

Gideon's explanation produced a confused response. Fear crept up on her face like a shadow and she asked guardedly: 'Why would anyone be looking for me?' Her voice shook and her eyes flitted about nervously. 'Who told you I was here? No-one knows me, apart from my landlord and he doesn't bother me much. What do you want?'

'I don't mean to upset you ma'am. My name be Gideon Tremayne an' I be a gentleman. I wouldn't be here troublin' you at all if it weren't for your son.'

Sarah stared at him in astonishment. Gideon stopped, standing on one foot then the other, like a horse waiting. She appeared to be trying hard to comprehend what he was saying. Her paper-thin complexion crumpled. 'Did... did you say my son?'

He nodded slowly and looked her straight in the eye. 'Can I come in?' he asked. 'It be a long time that I've been thinkin' how I can best say what I be havin' to tell yer.'

Almost in a whisper she replied, 'Yes, please come in.'

As Gideon stepped inside he saw her take a furtive look outside before closing the door. He found himself in a small square room that smelled of soap due to wet washing which was pegged to a piece of string tied between two chair backs.

'Excuse the mess, sir,' she said.

He found it curious that suddenly she had given him a kind of superiority and her self-conscious humility caused him to warm to her. Not only this, but he could see, without any doubt, that she was indeed

161

Finn's mother.

'Take no notice o' me, ma'am,' he said. 'I ain't used to houses at all, never mind houses wi' nice furniture an' pictures.' As he said this his eyes were drawn to a photograph on the sideboard. It was an old sepia photograph in a dark wooden frame of a couple on their wedding day.

'That be you in the picture then?' he asked.

'Yes,' she replied. 'My husband was drowned at sea. It was years ago now.'

'Is that what he told you to say?'

Shocked, she looked as though she was about to cry. Pressing her hands to her face, she repeated, 'Told me to say?'

'I'm sorry, I don't mean to alarm yer, it's just that... happen yer husband told yer it be best not to tell the boy the truth, to save 'im from shame.'

'Who are you? Even if it's true that my Jack's not drowned, how did you know?' A haunted expression drained the colour from her face and she whispered: 'Did he tell you? Is that it? Were you in prison with him?'

'No, no, ma'am!' Gideon chuckled. 'I'm right sorry to 'ave scared yer. It were my cousin Albert what told me about Jack. Yer remember Albert? Bert ain't altogether truthful but he ain't no liar neither. It were 'im do tell me his little brother got 'imself into serious trouble.' Gideon paused, watching Sarah's face keenly. 'It were on account o' family matters, that be why he told me, seein' as we hadn't set eyes on each other for years.' He stopped again before he asked, 'Yer knew Albert, his brother, didn't yer dear?'

She nodded vaguely, as though she had lost all

sense of reality. 'So you're telling me you're related to my Jack?' she asked. 'My husband was a good man once, but then he changed; everything seemed to get him down.' At this she burst into tears and sat on the edge of a chair weeping.

Gideon eased himself onto a seat near her. 'What I've come about, ma'am, Mrs. McKinney,' he said gently. 'The thing is, I've come on account of the fact I found a boy once. It were a long time ago, fifteen year or more in fact, and he be a fine young man now.' He paused to allow this information to register. He wasn't looking at her but staring at the floor and fidgeting with his cap. 'When I came across him hidin' in the hedgerow he were a little skinny lad with no more fat on him than a new-born lamb.' Glancing up for her reaction, he continued, 'He were right afeared he were of what he'd done – an' he'd upped an' run off like the hounds were after him. Poor little beggar!' Gideon stopped talking to gaze at her, watching the truth filter through as naturally as the light crept though the curtains in his caravan at dawn.

Her hand caught at her throat and she gasped. 'What do you mean?' Her face became animated, the bony jaw working as though she was speaking but no sound came. Eventually she asked, 'What are you saying? What had the boy done?' You can't mean it was my Finn!' She watched him as though he held her fragile life dangling between his fingers.

'Finn? Yep, Finbarr! That be his name an' has been since the day I come across him hidin' under the hedge, poor lad!'

'But I lost my boy! I lost my son Finn and my baby daughter – all on that dreadful night! I thought

163

they were both dead!' She collapsed again in uncontrollable tears.

Gideon was more used to dealing with animals than people. He knew when a dog was whimpering and shaking with fear it was only reassurance, a soft voice, and the passage of time that would heal his fright. He knew how to pacify a horse if a bully had whipped him at the horse fair or if a sheet of newspaper had blown into his path. In the same way, his soothing tone gradually put Sarah at her ease. She dried her eyes and her breath shuddered to a slow steady pace.

'I can tell you be his mother alright, my dear. Sure as I can tell a mare an' her foal – you have Finn's look about yer.'

'But I can't believe it…'

'It be a lot to take in after all these years – you believin' all this time he were killed when he's alive – an' his sister too.'

Sarah stared at him as though he was an apparition. 'My baby…' she whispered. 'My little Bryony was crushed to death in her pram…'

Gideon began to wonder if he had gone too far. The poor woman seemed so ill, so fragile he dared not go further and yet now it was too late. He felt he couldn't deny telling her the truth. 'Yer baby, my dear, happen she weren't killed. Finn were that frightened he'd killed her – that's why he ran off like he did.' He paused, wondering what effect the shifting of a person's memory from death to life can have on a woman already weak with illness and grief.

'Thing is, he don't know it but I've been hearin' many things. I've seen what sad stories can come out o' the evil in people's hearts an' I've come to tell yer that yer boy be alive an' yer daughter too; she weren't killed at all.'

'Not dead? How can that be? I don't believe it!'

'Takes a lot o' believin' to undo the wrongs o' people, my dear. Finn didn't mean no harm by what he done, an' him believin' she were dead, he couldn't help bein' scared an' runnin' off since he were only a kid an' not ready for such a big thing to happen.'

He waited for her to come to terms with what he had told her. It was a long complicated tale to unravel. When he had answered as many of her questions as he had the knowledge to answer she recovered enough to make them a cup of tea. As she was bringing the tray from the kitchen, they heard footsteps on the stairs and a loud knock sounded on the door.

'Are you alright in there, Sarah?'

She responded: 'Yes, thank you, everything's fine.' The landlord grunted a reply and the footsteps retreated once more. 'He's very good to me,' she explained. 'He keeps an eye on me, you know.' Soon, sipping her tea, she began to tell her side of the story. 'I hadn't lived in Tollwithen long. I moved away from Penzance when... well... Jack was deep-sea fishing and when he came home he usually got the worse for drink. I wasn't coping well and I was so worried about money all the time. Often I didn't eat, just so that Finbarr could have something. He was such a thin little boy. But Jack didn't care. All he wanted was his drink and his cigarettes. He didn't care about us. The truth is I couldn't wait for him to go back to sea again, so I could have some peace.' Sarah sighed, clutching her handkerchief so tightly her knuckles were white. 'One night he was arrested after being in a fight down the pub by the harbour. I knew who he'd been fighting with; I knew the man's wife and he wasn't a trouble-maker – it was all Jack's fault. He'd pick on anyone. Old Ted was rushed into hospital, critical they said.' She sipped her tea, put it down and sniffed. 'The next day a policeman came to the door. He told me the poor man had died and Jack was on a murder charge.'

'What were the fight about?' asked Gideon.

She shrugged. 'Money. Jack owed people, lots of people.'

Gideon gazed at her sadly. 'Happen it be money at the heart o' most trouble folks get into. Did yer go an' see Jack in prison?'

Sarah shook her head. 'I couldn't face him… and he… he wasn't a loving husband if you understand what I mean. I'd hardly any money and I didn't know what to do. I just stayed indoors, waiting to see what would happen. I wasn't well… I couldn't cope and little Finn, he …' She took a deep breath. After the trial at Truro, Jack was found guilty of manslaughter and locked up for fifteen years. I was five months pregnant with Bryony by then. Finn was at school; I didn't want the other children finding out his dad was in prison. Imagine what they'd say!'

Gideon sat listening, turning his cap round and round in his hand. 'Yer don't have to tell me all of it, my dear. If it be hurtin' yer too much – '

'No I must explain or you won't understand why I had to leave!' she cried. 'You see, I was so ashamed! All the finger-pointing and staring. Finn didn't know where his dad had gone, he thought he was back deep sea-fishing so I lied to him. I told him he'd been drowned at sea. It seemed easier to tell him that. I

166

didn't have enough money to carry on though, for buying food and the rent was in arrears.' She looked at Gideon as though it had all been too much to bear.

'There be no need for yer to go through it all wi' me,' he said. 'I can see yer were meanin' well an' only wantin' the best for him. Don't yer be upsettin' yerself, rakin' it all up again, my dear.'

But Sarah was adamant that she wanted to finish her story. 'I decided to go away and make a new life for me and Finn somewhere else. I pawned my wedding ring. I know it was an awful thing to do but I needed some money. Then I packed a few bags and bought a train ticket for Plymouth. I didn't know what I was going to do when we got there but I just had to get away. But when the train stopped at Tollwithen it looked so nice and quiet and suddenly I said to Finn, "Let's get off here!" so we did.'

'Got off the train wi' no-one there to help yer? What did yer do then?'

'I told Finn it was a game and we had to pretend we were explorers. We walked for a bit and Finn helped me carry the bags. Then after a while we saw the Catholic Church and we went in just to say a prayer and have a rest. The priest...' she faltered '...the priest there he was so kind. He helped us so much. He found us a small house and suggested I could take in people's washing. The house belonged to a parishioner and she told us she wouldn't mind if I didn't pay straight away. I never wrote to Jack or told him where we were... and I made up another name. I told Father O' Leary my name was Mrs. McKinney.'

'Didn't yer tell him about yer husband, dear? Happen he would 'ave asked where yer lived afore surely?'

'I told him what I told Finn – that he was dead, drowned, and I'd not paid the rent and I said the landlord had chucked us out. '

Gideon shook his head in dismay.

'I know it sounds a bit heartless but he was trouble from the start, my Jack, and if he ever got out of prison I didn't want him to come looking for us. I was pregnant and not feeling that well but I took in some washing to earn some money. But when the baby came it was even harder to get by. One night, we'd just got home from the shops, me and Finn and I had Bryony in the pram. I realised I'd lost my purse and all the money we had left was gone!'

Gideon looked up. 'Finn told me about your purse.'

'But I didn't know what to do!' she continued, anxious to explain. 'It was all we had. I should have kept it in the drawer or even put it in the post office instead of carrying it around.'

'I keep mine under the horse's oats,' he added gently, breathing easier. 'So yer left young Finn and the baby and set off to find it then?' he prompted. 'I would've done too, I don't blame yer. Yer purse could've been laying there on the pavement. It could have been stolen out yer pocket even. Yer never knows what thievin' folks are about.'

'It was such an awful night! The rain was pouring down and the wind! I couldn't take the children out again in that so I told Finn to stay and look after the baby while I went back. I told him I wouldn't be long.'

Gideon sat with Sarah in the growing dusk and the

168

story of what happened that night gradually played itself out before them. It grew darker but Sarah didn't switch on the lights.

'I was much longer than I meant to be. When I got to the shop it was already closed and the shopkeeper had locked up and gone home. I knew I wouldn't be able to rest without finding it so I decided to walk to the address which was up in the window. It was pouring, a gale was blowing and I was soaked through, but I had no choice. When I came to the house it was in darkness and the bedroom lights were on. I knocked on the door and after a while he came down. He was very angry. 'What do you want, missus, knocking me up at this time of night?' he said. 'Come back in the morning and when I open up I'll have a look.'

'No, please!' I pleaded with him. 'Could you look now? I must find it tonight. I had all my money in it you see. All I have left in the world!' Anyway, he took me in his car back to the shop but it wasn't there. He wasn't too pleased and he left me there, standing in the rain and drove off. So I started walking home. I'd never left Finn to manage the baby on his own before. He wasn't clever but he was a good boy and Bryony would probably still be asleep. I hoped so anyway. Probably they would both be asleep by the time I got back. Then as I got near the theatre at the bottom of the hill, I saw an old battered pram. It was lying on its side by the kerb, same colour as mine, I thought. The light shining from the theatre cast it into shadow but as I came closer, I couldn't believe it. It was exactly like mine. But I'd left it at home! She can't be here! I thought. How could she be here? What's happened to my baby? And where's Finn? I tried to pull myself together. Of course it's not, I told myself and I went up to it, just to look. And then... I saw her pink blanket and I thought I saw blood... and I just ran.'

'No, my dear, there was no blood. Happen times when a soul has too much to bear it sees things what aren't there and tricks people into thinkin' things what aren't true.' He laid a hand on her arm and tried to comfort her. 'She wasn't killed, Sarah. They're both alive. It were on account o' your illness an' worry what caused yer to believe such things. It ain't easy when yer be on yer own.'

'I told myself I might have imagined it, but...'

'Sarah, my dear, listen. They're both alive.' Gideon sat in silence, waiting for her to comprehend what he had said. 'She wasn't in the pram, Sarah. A car hit the pram but she were thrown clear onto the grass verge. She wasn't even hurt.'

'I can't believe it. Please, sir, if my little Bryony's still alive and you know where my boy is – please tell me where they are!'

Gideon stirred himself. 'Finn ain't left my side these fifteen odd years, my dear. He's a grown man now an' he's not long set himself up with a job in Tollwithen. He's a good kind-hearted fella an' though it pains him inside – you can see that he carries the guilt an' memory o' that night somethin' dreadful.'

'Sarah stood up covering her face with her hands. 'My poor boy,' she sobbed. 'He must have thought I'd deserted him! May God forgive me! That night, I couldn't take any more. I don't know what came over me. I saw the pram all crushed and I saw the blood – I thought he must be dead too. I panicked and I just kept

170

walking in the rain, on and on, and then somehow I found myself back on my own doorstep. I thought then, perhaps I'll open the door and there they'll both be, fallen asleep waiting for me. But the house was dark, empty! I tore through the rooms upstairs and downstairs, calling Finn! Finn! But he wasn't there – and the pram was gone. I never thought he could be out there looking for me.' Her thin legs buckled underneath her and she sat down and started rocking herself, weeping into her hands. 'I thought it was God's judgement on me, for being a wicked mother and leaving them alone. I thought that's why He's taken them. I couldn't look after them properly and I couldn't feed them and He's taken them to heaven.'

Her story was almost too much for Gideon. He hadn't anticipated her being so remorseful, so cruel to herself.

'We all make mistakes and do things we regret, my dear. Listen!' he said firmly. 'Finbarr ran away on account o' what he'd done. He couldn't face seein' yer an' havin' to tell yer he'd killed his sister. He blamed himself for doin' it – he didn't think anythin' more than that. When I found 'im, I took him back home to Tollwithen to see yer to explain it all. I was all for bringin' him back to you. But the house were empty, deserted like, and no-one as knew where you were. A lady next door told us there were no-one livin' there no more – not for weeks. So we went away an' left that place. Young Finn, he were shocked and shakin' wi' fear. It were best we left it all behind an' hit the road. So that's what we done. If there be a God up there, an' he were lookin' down on me an' young Finn, he would 'ave been smilin' to himself an' thinkin' we be a

171

foolish herd o' sheep.'

Sarah looked confused by these words. 'So Finn knows you've come to find me today?' she asked.

'No, my dear, he don't know as I'm here. He don't know nothin' about where you are now or what happened to yer – an' I dare say he'll be real surprised to hear how you've been livin' hereabouts all these years an' he never knew. I can't say I'm likely to tell 'im without him fallin' over in shock.'

Sarah looked up anxiously. 'What will he think of me – his own mother running away an' leaving him?'

'Well, he ain't a boy no more, dear. He be a good strong young man an' yer can be right proud of him. I don't mind tellin' yer I've raised him to be honest and able to look after himself but I ain't showed him how to read an' write 'cos that's summat what I never had. I gets by alright though. Book readin' don't bring in nothin' to eat nor drink do it?'

Sarah stopped crying. She wiped her eyes with a tissue, blew her nose and when she looked up she saw that Gideon was smiling. 'Thank you,' she said, 'for looking after him. I can't believe it! My Finn's alive! And my baby?' she seemed to make a supreme effort to concentrate. 'You said she wasn't dead?'

Gideon reached across and put a hand on her shoulder. 'No, my dear. Bein' as there were no-one around to claim the child, she were adopted by a kind lady from the theatre. Her name be Bianca Tabora an' she be a good woman. She be takin' good care o' yer daughter as if she were her own. I'll tell yer more when I knows more.' He stood up as though he was about to leave and she rose to her feet also. Gideon wasn't a physical person normally but some instinctive reaction

172

made him feel drawn to her as he would to a suffering animal. He made a step towards her and gently he drew her close to his chest and hugged her. It was a simple gesture, as he would take a lost lamb he might have found half-dead and cold on the moor and hold it close. She was such a fragile thing. But as he held her, a feeling of tenderness came over him. It was a feeling he hadn't experienced for many years. His destiny in love, as in life itself, had been overshadowed by feeling he was a man set apart from the crowd, a man on the edge of society. His Romany blood would become fired up in his veins, restless and free, and he knew he always had to keep moving on. But when he released Sarah, it left him feeling sad and inadequate and quite at a loss. His beloved Sonya was long dead and yet the wildness in her still tore at his heart. He was reminded, in an instant, of how lonely he was.

'I'd best get goin' afore the poor old horse thinks I've forgotten 'er.'

Sarah embraced him again and before letting him go, she whispered, 'Thank you, sir, and God bless you.'

'Sir?' he chuckled. 'Come now, call me Gideon – I ain't no "Sir". Wait till Finn hears about that – callin' me "Sir" indeed!' He paused in the door-way, realizing she would need time to absorb what he had said. She wasn't strong, he could see that, but when she was ready, he would reunite them – Sarah and Finn and Colette – and they would be a family again. 'I'll be back afore long, my dear. Happen you'd like to see your children again soon?'

'Oh, I would! I never thought I'd see the day! God bless you!' she cried with a look of sheer wonderment on her face. 'How can I thank you?'

'I'll be back afore yer knows it,' he replied, and he bid her goodbye as he stepped outside. Such a poor woman, he thought. If any poor soul needed a bit of love, she did more than most. He began to descend the steps quietly, not wanting to attract the attention of the shopkeeper. But then he changed his mind and went into the shop to thank him.

'She's had a bit o' good news an' it's shaken her up a bit – but she's alright. If you'd like to look in on 'er I'd be mighty grateful,' he said.

The shopkeeper nodded but looked at him suspiciously. 'Good news did you say? Well if that's good news, pity the poor folks that have bad news eh?'

His attempt at a joke passed Gideon by. The old gypsy touched his cap and retreated back out of the door. 'Thankee kindly,' he said before closing it.

All the way back to the caravan, he couldn't forget the comfort he had felt in the warmth of Sarah's hug and his loneliness returned to him like the presence of a ghost.

Thirteen

Finn had arranged to meet Mitzi in the market place. It was busy and at first he couldn't see her, but hearing raised voices, he saw a crowd had gathered around a stall where people were shouting angrily. Making his way across, he was surprised to see Mitzi herself was the centre of attention. 'No I never!' she cried. 'You can't say them things about me! I ain't' been thievin' none of your rotten apples so there!'

As soon as she saw Finn approaching she shouted across to him: 'Hey, Finn! Tell 'im will you? Tell him I don't go round nickin' things!'

Finn found her standing defiantly, with her hands on her hips, and her lips pouting.

'What's goin' on?' he asked.

'But I saw you, miss,' protested the stallholder. 'I saw you put it in your handbag! You can't say I'm making it up, love, I caught you red-handed. I've got a good mind to call the police. They'll soon sort it out.'

Mitzi, her cheeks flushed and her hair dishevelled, threw her hands up helplessly. 'What's he accusin' you of?' Finn asked her quietly. In fact he had already guessed what the problem might be; he had known her take things before, and had warned her about it more than once.

'He's sayin' I stole his flippin' apple an' I never did,' she cried.

Finn looked at her curiously. She could put on a good performance when the mood took her. He turned to the stallholder. 'How much was it worth?' he asked.

'Nuffin' she interrupted. 'It weren't even ripe!'

'There you are, didn't I tell you? She's admitted it!' roared the stallholder.

Finn glared at Mitzi and said to the man. 'I'll pay for it, twice over. How much?' Delving into his pocket, he gave the man a shilling. 'Sorry, she don't mean no harm by it. She won't trouble you again.' Leaving the stallholder speechless, he took hold of her hand and pulled her away. 'Come on, let's go for a walk.'

Leaving the market-place behind them, they climbed over a stile and took the well-trodden footpath up towards Restormel Castle. It was a bridle path forming a shaded tunnel of trees and rhododendron bushes broken in places by clearings of short cropped grass. Mosquitoes hummed above clusters of cow parsley, bluebells and nettles. Finn was still angry. 'You'll be caught once too often nickin' stuff in that market,' he warned her. 'They'll not let you off another time.'

'They don't scare me,' she replied. 'Stupid greedy pigs! I was starvin' an' they chuck loads o' stuff away. They leave fruit an' veg to get squashed on the flippin' pavement when they're unloadin'. I've seen 'em. I only took one of his stupid apples!'

Finn gave up trying to reason with her. Thunder clouds were gathering in the west and a black hood of cloud was easing its way across the sky. He turned to her and said: 'We'd better find shelter, there's a storm brewin'.' They hurried now, searching for a stable or barn which would offer protection from the rain. As a

176

clap of thunder rumbled in the distance he sighted a building in the clearing. It was an open-ended barn. Weeds and rusted farm machinery half-blocked the entrance but without hesitating he lead Mitzi into the darkened interior as the first rain-drops came pattering through the trees. 'We'll be alright in here,' he said. 'Just till the storm passes.'

But the rain didn't cease. It grew cold and Finn set about making a fire. He cleared a space on the edge of the barn's opening, found some twigs and taking a handful of hay he worked away quietly until a tiny plume of smoke emerged, wafting up into the evening air. The rain drops fizzed as they hit the smouldering twigs but the couple were sheltered by the barn. 'Ain't you clever!' squealed Mitzi, rubbing her palms together and shaking her shoulders as a shiver prompted her to huddle closer.

'It's only what Gideon taught me,' he replied. 'I can look after myself if needs be, an' you too if you like. If you're hungry I could catch a rabbit an' cook it over the fire if you don't mind a bit o' dirt.'

Mitzi's eyes grew wide in admiration. 'Ooh! Like real campin'! I'd love to live out here all the time, wouldn't you Finn? We wouldn't have none o' them 'orrible town folks pickin' on us would we, not out 'ere. Couldn't we get an' orse an' caravan like your Gideon's got?'

Finn laughed and put his arms around her. She was such a sweet innocent thing really, he thought. Nothing seemed to matter to her and when he was alone with her he felt carefree and relaxed. 'You won't go thievin' anymore though, will you?' he asked. 'Promise?' With one arm still around her shoulders, he began poking the small fire with a stick, causing splinters of flame to dart around the twigs. They crackled fiercely and sent up sparks. He was waiting for her reply. She frowned.

'Promise me Mitzi?' he asked again.

'Yeh, but I've done some awful things in the past, Finn,' she said. 'You'd hate me if you knew what I'd done. One thing was really wicked. I don't mean to be bad but my brother, he was always windin' me up at home.'

'Oh yeh?' he asked, not expecting to be impressed. 'We've all done stuff we shouldn't have though.'

Mitzi continued regardless; she seemed determined to tell him. 'I was sick an' off school when I done it. My big brother was always boastin' about his flippin' racin' pigeons. He used to take some of 'em out every Saturday on the train an' set 'em free somewhere, goin' a bit further away every week. He'd bought a really special white one, cost loads o' money she did, an' he called her Pearl. When she was trained up enough he said he was goin' to put her in a show 'cos she was bound to win first prize. I got fed-up with him goin' on an' on about it. I never had nothin' special like that of my own. He always had money to spend 'cos he had a paper-round but he never gave me nothin'.'

Finn watched her, chewing a grass stalk and enjoying the story. 'What did you do that was so bad then?' he asked, laying back and pulling her down with him.

'One day, when he was at work I'd had enough of him bein' so big-headed. I couldn't reach 'em so I

178

climbed up the cages in his pigeon loft – the wire had all poo and stuff on it stickin' on the ledges - and it was all musty and mouldy smellin'.' She wrinkled her nose at the memory. 'Them pigeons kept lookin' at me with their beady eyes, cooin' an' cockin' their heads at me. His new one was there – Pearl. She was pretty too but …Well, I went an' undid all the cages an' let 'em go. You should have seen 'em! They were all flappin' and squawkin' an' then they took off altogether like a huge cloud flyin' round an' round me!'

'But they must've come back? Homin' pigeons always come back, that's why they call 'em that.'

'They did, yeh, or most of 'em, not his new one though. Someone wrote an' said Pearl had been found dead miles away; they sent my brother her ring back in the post an' he was so angry wi' me he wouldn't talk to me for ages. Me mum stopped my pocket-money for a whole month. I was sorry 'cos I didn't mean any of 'em to get killed, but she said I was wicked. She said I was born stupid.' Mitzi turned to see what Finn's response would be, her eyes filling with tears. 'Suppose that's why all I've got is a stupid job sellin' ice-creams.'

'I don't think you're stupid, Mitzi. We've all done bad things.' He kissed her softly on the cheek and asked, 'Do you love me?'

'Loads,' she said, and returned his kiss, this time on the lips. 'Do you love me though? Bet you don't!'

He smiled and kissed her again. 'Bet I do.'

'Wouldn't it be good,' she began, 'if we could always be like this? Stay together an' travel on the road with an 'orse and caravan of our own!'

'Yeh, all we'd have to do is find enough wood for a fire every day, do a bit o' fruit pickin' and potato pickin'. I'd catch us rabbits to eat an' other stuff like berries an' mushrooms.' He kissed her again, smiling.

'Why don't we then, Finn? Let's do it!' she cried, her eyes shining.

'It ain't that easy,' he replied. 'Where would we get a horse an' caravan for a start? We ain't got the money to buy one, and anyway, you'd be happy in the summer but what about when it's cold and freezin'? There would only be a stick-fire an' a wood-stove in the van if we're lucky. You'd have to wash outside in cold water. You wouldn't like it then, I bet!'

'You've done it though, you told me you have!'

'Yep, I've done it. It were the best time ever with old Gideon. He could do anythin'. I learned a lot from him but –'

'Why didn't you stay with him?' she asked. 'Why did you come to Tollwithen when you could've stayed on the road?'

'He said I couldn't stop with 'im no more. He said I had to make my own way in the world, earn myself a livin' an' settle down. He said I'd got to stop runnin' away.'

'You weren't runnin' away though, were you?' she asked. They were lying on the ground with their arms around each other.

Whether it was the falling rain, the camp fire spitting and hissing or whether it was the silence of the woods beyond, something made Finn remember when he had been hiding as a small boy. Ducking under the hedgerows and trying to feed himself, feeling desperately cold and lonely. Without meaning to, he began to tell her his secret.

'Once, when I was a little kid,' he said. 'I did

180

somethin' really terrible. I didn't mean to, but it just happened. It were the worst day o' my life.'

'What? Can't be that bad!' she replied with a giggle.

'It were bad, Mitzi, really bad. I killed my baby sister.'

'You what?' said Mitzi, her brow creasing into a little frown and a smile playing around her mouth. 'You didn't really! Stop muckin' about, Finn!'

He sat up, staring away from her into the distance. 'I did too,' he said. 'I was pushin' her in her pram an' it just took off an' I let go. It went runnin' down the hill an' I couldn't catch up with it and then it ran in the road an' then a car...' He shrugged as though that was end of the story.

She was staring at him open-mouthed. Her teasing was forgotten. 'That's awful!' she whispered. 'But... was she dead then?'

Finn nodded. 'That's why I ran away. I mean, I couldn't go home an' tell me mum what I'd done – I just couldn't. So I ran off, and I was hidin' in the fields, walkin' for miles, I don't know for how long, weeks or months or somethin'. It were horrible and I was starvin' and all my clothes were stinkin' and dirty – an' that's when Gideon found me.'

'Blimey!' cried Mitzi. 'A real murder!'

Immediately he was upset. 'Don't be daft!' he said, turning back to her. 'It weren't like that! It were an accident. Gideon said it weren't my fault. I didn't mean her to get killed.'

'No, 'course yer never. Sorry,' she whispered, kissing him. 'What did your mum say when she found out?'

181

Finn shrugged. 'I don't know. I don't know whether she found out or not. I were gone by then.' A lump came to his throat, his head ached and he almost began to sob. He shuddered and tears welled up in his eyes.

'Don't cry!' she said, kissing his face and his neck and hugging him close. 'You didn't do it deliberately – not like the bad thing I done!' She carried on kissing him and soon the rain was drumming heavily on the tin roof of the barn and Finn put away all thoughts of that dreadful night. He took her in his arms, seeking comfort in her warmth and smothered her in his salt tears. When she yielded to him, he felt as though he was flying and leapt away from his grief as gracefully as a barn owl leaves the dark eaves of a tower and spreads its wings into the night sky. In loving Mitzi, he was free. Nothing existed in his mind anymore except for the soft scent of her bare skin and the comforting feel of her body's response to him. Forgetting everything, he loved her and as dusk fell those two lost people became one.

Fourteen

It was Easter Sunday and the bells of St. Bartholomew's Church were ringing a full peal. But the sight which lay before Finn as he turned the corner sent his heart pumping wildly. True to his word, Gideon, driving his horse and caravan, had just appeared in the distance. What would have been a thrill at seeing that familiar sight was deadened by his guilt. How could he face him now? How could he tell him he'd lost the fiddle? He ducked into a doorway and stood back in the shadows so as not to be seen, his cheeks burning with shame. Excuses poured into his mind but he knew it was pathetic trying to defend himself. He knew Gideon loved it more than anything and he had betrayed his trust. The sound of Belle's hooves came closer and Finn held his breath. But the smart trot came near and passed without slowing down. Giving a cowardly sigh of relief, he peered out as the receding sound had been replaced by the approach of stiletto heels.

'What's up with you?' piped up Mitzi's cheerful voice. 'Someone walked over your grave?'

Finn glanced round furtively. 'Oh, hello,' he said. 'I just saw Gideon go past.'

'And?' she asked, lifting her cheeky face to meet his eyes. 'Why didn't you give him a shout an' run after him? He'll be half way to London by now if you don't hurry.' She reached up and giving him a fleeting kiss, attempted a cuddle, but he shrugged her off.

'What's the matter? Don't you love me anymore?'

'Oh, just go away an' leave me alone. I'm not in the mood.'

'Pardon me for breathin'!' she cried. 'What's eatin' you all of a sudden?' She took a step closer and peered up into his gloomy face with a child-like curiosity. 'Have you lost your job or somethin'? There's always others – don't let 'em get to you; that's what I say! You can have mine if you like! I don't think I can stand that doorman much longer, the toffee-nosed git.'

Finn's mood softened and he began to smile. 'Can't see me carryin' round a tray of ice-creams somehow, can you?' he said, but immediately his smile vanished. 'I was supposed to meet Gideon down by the bridge this mornin'. I can't bring myself to tell 'im I lost his fiddle. He'll think I don't care about it an' I do! It's just other things got in the way of me carin' enough that's all.'

'Do somethin' about it then! It ain't the end of the world. Tell him it's at home an' you'll give it to him next time you see him. It's not a big deal! I'll help you find it if you like or we'll get him another one somehow.'

'It's not as simple as that,' replied Finn sadly. 'I wish it was, but it ain't.'

*

Seeing the railway station at Tollwithen ahead of him, Gideon pulled up in the yard beside the bridge over the

River Fowey. Bringing out a bag of oats, he gave it to the mare, fastening the straps behind her ears. 'There, old girl,' he said, glancing around to see if there was any sign of Finn. A smartly dressed gentleman passed by and Gideon nodded to him obligingly.'

'Good morning and happy Easter to you!' was the response. 'Fine day is it not?'

Gideon agreed and the gentleman paused, regarded the caravan for several moments before asking, 'What brings you to Tollwithen of a Sunday morning? Surely you're not trading here on the Sabbath?'

Gideon smiled. 'No, I'm here to meet a young friend o' mine, name of Finbarr.'

'Young, you say? Then he'll still be lying in his bed, I shouldn't wonder. Youngsters these days don't see this side of noon – not if they can help it. My two grandsons don't know what a morning looks like.'

'He'll be here afore too long,' said Gideon patiently.

'I admire your faith in the boy. You could be waiting a while. Do you want to join us in the service?' He nodded towards the spire of St. Bartholomew's Church. 'You'll be made very welcome.'

Gideon declined the offer but thanked the gentleman and resting his arms on the bridge, he began to watch the river meander gently past. The horse finished her oats and he put the bag away. He was beginning to wonder where Finn had got to when he finally saw him in the distance, with his shoulders hunched and his head down. He seemed in no hurry to meet him. When their eyes finally met, Finn looked away and didn't appear pleased to see him at all.

185

'So you came, like you promised,' said Finn by way of a greeting, but his face was pinched and troubled. 'You been waitin' long? Sorry.'

'Long enough, son,' Gideon replied, watching him carefully. 'Got somethin' to tell me you'd rather not?'

Self-consciously, Finn tried to avoid his gaze. He didn't know where to put his hands and shoved them into his pockets, brought them out again, stretched his fingers and clenched his fists. 'How are you then?' he asked finally.

'I'm here,' Gideon replied. 'That be all yer need to know. Seems yer got somethin' on yer mind as wants warmin' up.' He studied Finn curiously. 'Want me to brew us a cuppa while yer think about it? I've got somethin' to tell you too, as it 'appens. Come on back to the caravan.'

The mare was grazing on the grass that had sprung up under the fence. Finn patted her, saying,

'How are you doin' old girl?' before following him up the steps.

'The kettle's on the hob. Get yer cup an' sit yerself down.'

It was half dark in there and the dank smell, so dear to him, cut Finn to the quick. As soon as they were settled he owned up. 'I'm sorry. I've gone an' done the worst thing I could have,' he admitted and he stared into his tea.

'I can see you 'ave,' said Gideon, 'seein' as yer ain't got the fiddle under yer arm.' The old gypsy turned his face away, his jaw working involuntarily as though he was finding it hard to speak. He was truly upset. 'You ain't sold it, lad, 'ave yer? Yer wouldn't 'ave done that to me surely?'

'No, no, of course not,' replied Finn, shaking his head. 'I wouldn't ever do that. The truth is… I lost it. I left it on the steps o' the theatre – I didn't mean to, an' when I went back for it… it were gone.'

'Stolen was it?' asked Gideon. 'Didn't I tell yer Finbarr? There be some folks that'll take it an' sell it wi' no thought to its real value.'

'I were playin' the fiddle there an' a nice lady come by. She stopped an' give me some money and then she started askin' me lots o' questions an' it scared me. I ran off an' I forgot it – I'd left it on the steps.'

Gideon gave no reaction but his anguish was plain to see. Finn continued, 'I thought she must've picked it up an' kept it for me… I did try an' get it back.'

Still Gideon was silent but after a while he asked, 'Who was the lady? Did yer know her?'

'No, but she were the star o' the show. Her picture were on the posters outside.'

'Then did yer go back an' ask her, son, if she had it or what?'

'I was gonna ask her, honest, straight away! I went into the theatre to ask her but the play had started, an' afore I had a chance she fell off the stage. She were really badly hurt an' all the people were screamin'. I couldn't get nowhere near her. They took her away to hospital. Then after that – she were ill an' couldn't be in the show no more. They said her memory had gone…' Finn gave up and sat fidgeting with his pocket knife. 'So I couldn't find out from 'er where it was.'

They stayed silent, as awkward as strangers. Finn looked around the interior savouring every last memory he had of happier times when he was a boy and the caravan had been his sanctuary. His shame was too much to bear. He thought it might be the last time he would see it.

Gideon coughed, sighing and mumbling to himself. He glanced up at Finn and looked away as though unable to deal with the loss. 'An' when did yer say this all 'appened?'

Finn's misery was complete. 'The first night I come to the town. I were cold an' starvin' an' it were rainin' an' I 'ad nowhere to go.' This statement seemed to be tinged with an appeal for sympathy but Gideon ignored it.

'Well, Finbarr. Happen your news be about as easy as what I have to tell you. It ain't bad news but it ain't easy to tell yer even so.' He coughed again. 'If I were to give yer the bare bones o' what's happened since I saw yer last, I could tell yer it's like this, so listen, son. Yer baby sister, what yer believed to be dead an' killed in the road – well, she ain't dead at all, she be alive an' well.'

Finn stared at Gideon as though he had gone mad. 'What?' he said. 'What do you mean she's alive? She can't be! How can she be?'

'There ain't no other way o' sayin' it, son. It be the truth as sure as I'm sat here. An' there be more to tell yer. I were up country, Plymouth way, these days gone by, to see yer mother.' He looked at Finn steadily for a moment. 'I've talked with her, poor woman, fair broken-hearted an' ill she be.'

'You saw my mother? My sister's alive? Don't be tellin' me that! You know it ain't true an' it ain't fair – sayin' she's alive when she ain't. You be playin'

188

games wi' me just to punish me.' He stared fiercely at Gideon as though he was about to hit him. 'I'm sorry I lost your fiddle, Gideon. I'm that sorry, an' I'll try an' find it, I promise! But please don't say things what ain't true. It ain't right!'

Gideon stood up looking deathly pale and began to leave the caravan. He turned back and looked at Finn sadly. 'Playin' games?' he said. 'Happen that be all life is, son. We tries our best an' we do a lot o' harm tryin', an' in the end happen it all be a game. Gideon don't play games. What I've told yer be the truth. I don't play games wi' folks' lives.' And saying this he went out and down the steps like a broken man.

'Wait!' shouted Finn and hurried after him. 'Gideon!'

'Finbarr,' he said, stopping abruptly. 'Yer be forgettin' me already. There be some things old Gideon knows that need knowin' – them can't be told in no pretty way. What I tells yer be the truth. Yer poor mother is a sick woman but she be a lot better now she knows yer be alive – you an' yer sister – when she believed both of yer were dead an' gone.'

'But how can my sister be alive? What d'you mean?' he pleaded. 'I don't understand!'

As Gideon looked at him, the years between them fell away. He saw Finn not as the strong young man he was, but as the little boy in the hedgerow again, frightened and crying for help.

'Remember I told yer once, son: there be some things yer can't understand. They be bigger an' more mysterious than any of us can reckon on. Let's be goin' an' sit inside again an' drink our tea.' They went and sat down and Gideon poured himself another cup from the old enamel teapot. 'I had dreams, Finn,' he began, slowly stirring his tea. 'Dreams like I've never 'ad afore. They told me many things. It's all bein' on account that I be goin' to return soon.'

'No, not that again!' cried Finn angrily, anxious to do away with such talk. 'Tell me about my mother! Where is she? What happened?' He was bursting with frustration.

'Listen, Finn!' said Gideon firmly and he began to explain the story from the beginning, of how he had gone to find the place where a woman by the name of Sarah McKinney lived and how poor and lonely she was. 'She were over the moon, son, when I told her about you!' The pity and love in his voice couldn't be disguised. His weathered face, dry as leather, became sprinkled with tears. 'Look at me; silly old fool!' he grumbled. 'A man goin' soft in his old age – that ain't a pretty sight.'

'So it's true,' said Finn. 'I ain't learned nothin' since I was a small boy runnin' away… nothin'!' And putting down his cup he left Gideon and went down the steps again and away into the town. He was walking but he didn't know where he was going – anywhere, to get away from himself and his own thoughts.

*

It was a few hours later when he returned to the river and stood far off, looking towards the bridge. He saw with relief that the caravan was still there. A plume of smoke was rising from its chimney and he could see Gideon moving about. He had to make amends. Taking a deep breath and straightening his shoulders, he approached the caravan and found Gideon seated on the steps working on a basket. 'I've been thinkin',' Finn began. 'I'm right sorry I let you down an' lost the fiddle an' all.'

Gideon ignored him.

'I owe you... for doin' all you did for me.' He fidgeted with his cap, turning it inside out and turning it back. 'Will you... will you help me find the fiddle? You know, how you knows about things what ain't real. I mean...' Here he stumbled, afraid he was getting himself into even more trouble. 'You can see things what others don't, an' hear things what others can't, so will you...?'

Gideon raised his head and looked him straight in the eye. 'Happen yer think it takes an olden to sort out the ways o' the world?'

Finn hung his head in shame. 'I just hoped you would...'

'Fact is, son, I knows where that fiddle be. It be in the dark, in the dry, where the mice run an' the boards creak. It sings, Finbarr. It sings to me when I'm a sleepin' in my bed under the stars an' it be a cryin' to me like a lost child.'

'You know? Then why didn't you say? Why haven't you got it back?'

'There'll be the right time, an' when that time comes she'll give it back.'

Finn was mystified. 'Who, Bianca? Oh, you mean my mother's got it?'

'No son, not yer dear mother, bless her.' He shook his head in despair.

'Then who?'

'Time'll come Finn, when yer will play that

fiddle again an' yer heart will burn in yer chest like a ragin' fire.'

'But who's got it? What do you mean?'

'Leave me, Finbarr. There be things I need to think on an' I can't be sayin' no more.'

'But Gideon! You must tell me!' he shouted.

But the gypsy wouldn't say. He just stared at him with the dark midnight sky in his eyes. It was a look that made Finn shiver. Sadly he turned away, glancing back several times as though hoping Gideon would relent and call him back but he was met with the same cold stare.

'I be workin' at the Coach an' Horses, an' livin' there too, if yer want me.'

'I know where yer be livin', son,' came the distant reply.

But as Finn walked away, the things Gideon had told him overcame everything else. He began to feel light-headed. The sorrow he had carried around for years took flight and soared away into the empty sky. 'My mum's been found,' he murmured, 'an' my baby sister didn't die!' Overcome with joy, he began to run.

Fifteen

Colette struggled to sleep. There seemed to be people walking up and down well after midnight, with car doors slamming and raised voices. She got out of bed, went to the window and peered out onto the dimly-lit street. There was a group of youths smoking under a street-lamp. Forcing herself to be more alert, it made her head ache and she returned to her bed anxious and unable to relax. When the youths moved off and passed under her window, she was lying there listening for them to return. Distant pop music made a regular thumping noise as the beat vibrated in the walls around her. She put the pillow over her head but it clamped itself around her nose and mouth and she threw it back, choking. Getting out of bed once more, she fetched a glass of water from the kitchen – tip-toeing so as not to wake her mother who slept lightly since her accident. Moving her bare feet cautiously on the thin carpet, and holding her breath as a floorboard creaked, she stopped and listened. If she woke Bianca there would be no sleep for either of them for the rest of the night. But all was well. Drinking some water, she re-filled the glass and returned to bed. At last she began to feel really tired. She yawned, sighed and closed her eyes.

When the creaking floorboards above her head woke her, she couldn't have been asleep for more than half an hour. It must be the tenant above, that ghastly Drew Caudry, she thought. For several minutes she lay there, hearing him walk across the floor, and then back again. Drawers were opening, a tap running. She lay listening to every movement he made. It was almost as if he was in the same room. But then she heard what must be him unlocking and opening his door. She looked at the clock – it was a quarter to four. Straining to hear more, her guess proved correct. With a rattle of keys she heard him close his door and descend the stairs. Her heart was pounding, but she didn't know why. He might be just going for a walk, she told herself, or even going to work. But when he passed their door and went on down the stairs, she held her breath.

Jerking herself out of bed, she was at the window craning her neck to see his stocky figure walking out into the street and making his way up the road. As he walked away, he seemed to be glancing furtively from the right to the left and then he turned his head and looked back towards the house. She could have sworn he looked directly at her. Where could he be going at this time of night? He was carrying what looked like tools in a soft canvas bag. Returning to bed, she must have drifted off to sleep again because the next thing she knew there was a thump on the ceiling. Someone was moving about in the room upstairs again. He must be back. She looked at her watch: it was five-thirty.

*

Seamus was far from happy. The theatre was struggling even more and Todd was ready to lay the blame on him.

'You keep coming up with the same old stuff!' Todd complained. 'It's all so boring – so old hat! You need to do something modern! You are familiar with that word, are you darling, "modern"? If the theatre offered something new for a change, it might make people sit up and take notice! You can't just sit around sulking about having to replace Bianca – she's not indispensable you know. None of us are, well, most of us aren't anyway. There are plenty of other perfectly talented actors about.' Grabbing a scarf from the back of a chair he threw it about his neck and posed in front of the mirror. 'Me, for instance!' he said. 'When have I ever been offered a serious part?'

'When have you ever been serious enough to deserve one?' asked Seamus.

'I could put my mind to it if you asked me. I do like a challenge, darling! Nothing like a challenge for charging up the spirits. You know what? Sometimes you remind me of a damp flannel.'

'Thanks,' Seamus replied, sinking even deeper into his mood.

'Well, I'm going now. I'll leave you to soak up my suggestions for a while. Try and think "modern" darling. Colour! Vibrancy! Life!'

'Get out and find someone else to annoy, will you?' said Seamus in a tired voice.

'I'm going, darling. Why should I waste my time if you can't appreciate help when it's offered?' And with that he swept out dramatically.

Seamus sighed with relief. Standing up he went to look out of the window and began pondering on what he should do. Perhaps he should chuck it all in and let people like Todd take over. He really didn't have the energy any more.

'Hey, Boss!' Todd was back. 'There's a gypsy hanging around back stage. He's asking for Bianca; shall I tell him where she's moved to?'

'What does he want with her?' demanded Seamus, instantly on the defensive.

'It's about her daughter apparently. He said he's got an important message from a distant relative. He looks a right old weirdo, if you ask me!'

Seamus peered through the door and saw Gideon waiting in the shadows. Pushing Todd aside he stepped forward. 'What can I do for you?'

'It be the good lady Miss Tabora who I be lookin' for, sir,' said Gideon.

'I'm afraid she doesn't work here anymore, well, not at the moment. I can't help you, and we are rather busy.'

This reply was met by the gypsy's penetrating stare. 'I'll find her, if yer be kind enough to direct me to where she be livin'. I have some business with her, which may be to her advantage. I'd be mighty grateful of your kindness, sir, if yer would tell me where she is.'

In spite of his suspicions, Seamus thought that if this gypsy had some fortune to bestow on Bianca it could only be good news for him too. He therefore gave Gideon Bianca's address, though by means of verbal direction since the scrap of paper on which he wrote it meant nothing to the gypsy.

Todd remained quiet for once, but when the visitor had left he gave out a long whistle and exclaimed: 'Poor old Bee! Let's hope he doesn't go up there and murder her in her bed!'

196

'Oh shut-up will you?' shouted Seamus.

'Yes, boss! Look! See?' He mimed zipping up his mouth. 'Here am I, silence personified. I won't say another word... oh, except one!'

'And what's that for Pete's sake?'

'Bye!'

*

After Todd had left, Seamus was worried. Was he really that tactless? How long had he worked with Bianca? How long had he been her close friend? He'd practically become engaged to her! Shouldn't he have shown that gypsy the door and told him to be on his way? What was it about that scruffy character that had made him appear trustworthy? Bianca needed looking after, but she had always refused his help! Was it his fault she had refused to marry him? Why do women – he corrected himself, this was no time for generalities – why does Bianca always have to be so independent? You would think, especially now she wasn't well, that she would accept a bit of help gracefully. But as he pondered this new dilemma he thought to himself: Why don't I try proposing to her again? She's got no-one – apart from that stuck-up daughter of hers – and I've got no-one. She's broke, I've got money. Well, a bit. How can she possibly refuse? So he decided, at the next opportunity, he would try to make amends.

*

It was a chill wind that blew over the fields the morning Gideon determined to put his plan into action.

His latest vivid dream, he believed, had been an omen that signalled the end of his days. Deeds needed to be done or there would be no sleep for him that night. Even so, he drove the caravan at a slow pace, for he was in no particular hurry to carry out the task which lay ahead of him. He began to think about Finn, who he had planned to meet once more in the market-place in Tollwithen. But there was something in the air; he felt the stirrings of something germinating in his soul. He knew, at last, he was at the beginning of the end of his story.

There was an angry sky overhead that billowed stormy clouds. Rain would soon come, flooding streams that were already swollen with silt, clay, weeping willows and tangled reeds. The shady unkempt banks of knotted tree-ivy, honeysuckle and sweetbriar sheltered a dark unspoken world. Gideon knew the footpaths and contours of that rich granite landscape intimately. He had traversed it as a boy with his father, had returned to it faithfully again and again as his journeying took him around the country, and he still found the terrain held a silent reserve. Cornwall would be his final resting place. He loved it in all its mystery, its deep undergrowth and shrub land of gorse, heather and rhododendron. He felt akin to its alienation when the cruel salt wind cut across its moors and its standing-stones stood stark against the skyline, alone and waiting. He loved its history of Celtic saints, its myths and legends but most of all he loved the land in its fertile richness, its wild turbulent seas and windswept moorlands. Each shrub had to fend for itself to survive against the elements just as every person had to, come rain or shine. It was a battle he had fought ever since he was a small boy, a battle perhaps that he was now too weary to fight any longer.

Driving the horse and caravan into the market place he brought it to a halt. 'Easy up, Belle,' he said, sighing, applying the brake and climbing down. His vivid dream was still fresh in his mind. Although now June, it was chilly that morning and he tightened his neckerchief and buttoned up his jacket as he made his way to the back of the caravan. Here, in stacks five or six high, were the willow baskets he had brought to sell.

Usually he made for the smarter houses in town but on this occasion he had something more important than making money on his mind. He scratched his head and looking around, almost tested the air with his nose as a hound does – for there was the scent of old times in the air, echoes lapping the corners of his consciousness. He had tried all night to stave it off – but the feeling was there and he couldn't ignore it any longer. It was a nagging pain, not a physical pain but a need, like a hunger, and without satisfying it he couldn't treat the day as it deserved. It should be a day for selling, for enjoying the fruits of his labour. Because hard labour it was – cutting reeds and willow, drying them out and weaving baskets for folks that can't or won't do it for themselves. No, this other task must be done or he would have no rest. He must speak to the actress, Bianca Tabora, about Finbarr before doing anything else.

Loading himself with some baskets that creaked and groaned in their newness – for the sap was still fresh in some of them, making them feel smooth and flexible in his hands – he set off for that particular area

199

of the town to which Seamus had directed him. It was a place where those who, perhaps through no fault of their own, were living in poor conditions. But Gideon had a task ahead of him, a duty, as he saw it, and nothing would come between him and his duty. The signs had been going on too long, gnawing at him. He turned a corner and looked down a street of terraced houses. They were tall, having three floors or more and quite likely, cellars as well. The bay-windows of each house showed a mixture of curtains of various colours as tenanted houses often do. The small front-gardens, with iron railings, bordered the road. At the first house, a thin tabby cat came out mewing and wrapped itself around his legs. He stooped to stroke its firm head and it pushed its nose against his hand.

Walking half-way down the street, he paused before turning in through a gate. There were three doorbells one under the other, with the occupants' names. Unable to read, he rapped loudly on the door to enquire. As he did so the door, which must have been left ajar, swung open of its own accord. It showed an entrance hall with a worn carpet. As he stepped inside he saw three empty shoe boxes stacked on a table, presumably one for each tenant. Some contained letters. A vague disinfectant type smell wafted down the staircase which Gideon always associated with houses. It wasn't often he stepped into a house, but when he did, they usually smelled of something like this. But Gideon knew where he was going and climbed the stairs slowly and deliberately, like a tired man after a day's work. Coming to the door which had appeared several times in his dreams, he knocked loudly.

'Beggin' yer pardon ma'am,' said Gideon as the

door opened. 'I was wonderin' if you might like a new basket. They be good and strong lady, an' you won't see none others made so well.'

'Thank you sir, but I've no need for one, fine though they look, and no money for buying anything either at the moment. We've just moved in here you see and times are hard for us just now. I'm sorry.'

He regarded Bianca with a long stare. 'Yer think I don't know that ma'am? I knows yer ain't gonna buy no baskets.'

Bianca looked at him in amazement. 'How do you know that? What are you doing here then?' she asked. Gideon stepped back, glanced to his left and right, and then looked at her solemnly. 'People as have to live 'ere don't have no money for new baskets.'

She waited, expecting him to explain why he had come. 'Then what do you want?' she asked. He didn't reply and she was about to close the door in his face when what he said next shocked her.

'I've come about yer daughter what you found, ma'am.'

'What did you say?'

'She be called Colette now I'm thinkin' though she weren't called that once, yer know.'

'How do you know about her? Who are you?'

'I carry the name o' Gideon Tremayne. Most folks call me Gideon, or Rabbiter – happen not often Rabbiter these days but...'

She stepped back and started closing the door on him. 'Well, I'm sorry, Mr. Tremayne or whatever your name is. You'd better be on your way or I'll have to call the police.'

Gideon smiled sadly. 'You've no need to fear old

201

Rabbiter, my dear. I knows about things what others don't, but it ain't of my choosin', it just happens that way.'

'Please go! My daughter will be here in a minute.'

'Ma'am,' he said. 'I don't mean yer no harm. Don't ask me how, but I knows about folks. Where they comes from an' where they goes. I knows about you an' yer daughter who yer found as a little baby. Yer can trust me with yer life an' I won't fail yer, ma'am.'

Shocked, Bianca stood staring at the gypsy as though she could hardly believe what she was hearing.

'Can I come in?' he asked. 'I've got somethin' private to tell yer an' I don't want no other ears takin' it in.'

She hesitated. If Colette was home she knew the gypsy would have been sent packing straight away. But how did he know about her finding the baby? Who was he? In spite of her misgivings, she found herself stepping aside and inviting him in. He came through the door slowly, his stack of baskets creaking in his arms. Quickly she closed it after him and watched as he lowered his load onto the floor, removed his cap and sat down with the ease of a working man who had just arrived home. Turning his cap round between his knobbly hands, he said,

'Let me tell yer why I've come an' I'll be on my way.' He waited for her to sit down but she remained standing, watching him.

'I knows yer have a good heart. I be troubled by dreams, ma'am. Dreams that tell me how yer saved a baby that were nearly killed by a motor in the road.'

202

'Oh my goodness!' she cried, staggering back. She steadied herself, but her eyes were staring wildly at the gypsy. Suddenly she could remember the night she had found Colette vividly. In shock, she sank into a chair, staring into space.

'I knows, my dear, that yer memories be stolen away.' He looked up. 'Yer be sufferin' too much I'm thinkin', since givin' yer money to a poor homeless boy buskin' in the street. He be a young man now an' he's been a rattlin' round in this old life wi' me like a coin without a pocket. He ain't got no-one to call his own, no family to go back to. If he were my son, he would be a good son to me I don't doubt it.'

She was sitting with a handkerchief pressed to her mouth. 'Listen to me, ma'am,' he said. 'If yer want to get well, think on that fiddle the boy were playin' an' what yer did to save it for him.'

'What?' stumbled Bianca. 'What fiddle?' Startled into a new wave of fear, her mind reeled. But almost immediately everything became clear.

'Yes, I remember! There was a young man!' she cried and tears of surprize broke through, choking her. 'He was playing outside the theatre! I said something that scared him and he ran off in the rain... of course!'

Gideon nodded. 'An' that be a very special fiddle. It were my gran'father's, and then it were mine. It be precious yer see, like a family heirloom. It's got history, yer understand. I gave it to Finn for safe-keepin'. He can play that fiddle like my gran'father could – born to it, natural like. I never heard the likes of it. Finn's like family to me – like my own son, he be. But I've got to tell yer, my dear, he be Colette's brother. Now that's somethin' to think on, 'cos neither of 'em do know they have each other.'

He gave a big sigh as though revealing the news had made him feel very tired. 'He was just a boy of eight years old,' he continued wearily, 'an' as green as a branch o' willow he was, the day I found 'im hidin' in the hedge. But he lost that fiddle and he needs it, ma'am, more than any old gypsy like me do need it now.'

There was a torrent of questions pouring into her mind but before she could speak, Gideon laid a weathered hand on her arm. 'Bound to be a storm brewin' in yer head with all the troubles as you've had, ma'am. Don't yer be afeared o' the past all a tumblin' back.'

What a strange language he spoke, thought Bianca, yet she understood him and felt she could trust him. But how could the busker be Colette's brother? Recovering herself slightly, she dried her tears, blew her nose and was just about to ask Gideon something when the door flew open and Colette herself breezed in.

'Oh er... hello!' she said, looking at the gypsy as though he was a mange-ridden dog that had strayed in. She shot a questioning look at her mother and then her eyes travelled back to Gideon, across his thin bony face, his worn clothes and his boots, until finally she met his eyes. Their directness shocked her; they held her in a spell-binding stare.

'Mornin' to yer, miss,' he said, his face breaking into a smile. 'Pleased to meet yer, young lady, an' yer dear mother here'.

Colette looked twice at her mother's tear-stained face. 'Are you alright, Mum? What's going on?'

'Colette darling, this is er... Gideon,' said

204

Bianca. 'He's a… a friend of mine. We've just been talking about your...'

'Yer mother's a good soul,' said Gideon. 'Now, you'll be wantin' to have your dinner so I'll be movin' on.' He rose to leave. 'Gideon Tremayne,' he added, holding out his hand.

'Pleased to meet you,' she replied doubtfully, stretching out a small hand gingerly and resting it momentarily in the gypsy's own before snatching it away. 'Did Mum offer you a cup of tea or anything?'

'I would have done …' interrupted Bianca but Gideon was quick to respond.

'No, no thankee, I'll be off now.' He replaced his cap, and nodding to them both, picked up his baskets. Turning to Bianca and raising his voice he said, 'Remember what I said an' yer will be well again, my dear, in that yer can be sure. I'm tellin' yer this on account of old Gideon knows these things. Them as do good turns have good turns done to them sevenfold. It be all written in the sky, I promise yer.' He gave them a reassuring smile. 'I bid thee well,' he added, and replacing his cap, he left them.

When the gypsy had gone, Bianca's face was flushed with emotion.

'What on earth was all that about?' asked Colette. 'He was weird.'

'Don't be so rude, darling, and don't jump to conclusions about people. We'll have some tea and then I've got things to do.'

Leaving Colette looking incredulous, and feeling more like her old self than she had for months, Bianca went into the kitchen to fill the kettle. She needed time to think while all her memories began to filter through. Like the morning mist lifting, she could picture Finn playing the fiddle outside the theatre. How frightened he had been by something she had said! And then, in a flash, she remembered exactly where she had hidden the violin – and why.

Rehearsals were evidently in full swing for the summer show. Bianca could hear everyone noisily congregated on the stage when she entered the theatre through the backdoor. A dusty silence permeated the corridors backstage, where her old dressing-room was located. Finding the door unlocked she let herself in. There was nothing in there she recognised apart from the dressing-table. She caught a glimpse of her own reflection in the mirror as she bent to lift the edge of the carpet. Relieved to find the floorboards still loose, she had the board up in seconds and felt around in the dark cavity beneath. 'Ah, it's here! Thank Goodness!' she whispered to herself. Hauling it out, she brushed off the dust from the violin-case and opened the lid. There it was: as shiny, undamaged and perfect as when she had hidden it there. Closing the lid again, she picked it up and hastily made for the door.

'Seamus!' she cried as she bumped into him. 'I just came to...'

'Bianca? I haven't seen you here for ages. My life! You've found your old dressing-room too?' His eyes were shining with honest undisclosed joy.

'I just came back to get this.'

'A violin?' He looked puzzled. 'Where did that come from? Is it yours?'

'It belongs to a friend of mine. Well, not exactly

a friend, but I left it here months ago. I had that accident. and forgot all about it so I've got to return it to him. I'm so relieved it's still here!' She was smiling happily. 'Oh, Seamus! My memory's coming back! I can't believe it! An old gypsy came to see me and he told me all these things... oh, you wouldn't believe what he told me!'

'You're right there,' replied Seamus moodily, recalling the scruffy character he had directed to her flat. His bad humour dampened her spirits immediately.

'No honestly, listen! He knew everything about me! He knew about Colette too – the night there was that accident and how I found her as a baby! It's incredible! He was so kind! I'm beginning to feel myself again after all this time – it's like I've been asleep!'

Seamus was watching her now with a resigned expression.

'Well?' she asked, searching his face for any response. 'Aren't you happy for me?'

'You shouldn't be so taken in by people, Bee. Chances are he dumped the wretched baby in the street himself – that's how he knew about it.'

She stared at him in total astonishment. 'What a thing to say! Of course he didn't!' As if she wasn't going to allow anything to spoil her happiness she said,

'Come on, Seamus! Aren't you going to offer me a cuppa? You do still have a kitchen here, don't you?'

'Yes, but that's probably all we will have soon.'

'Oh why's that?'

He didn't answer. She followed him along the corridor and while the kettle was boiling, she rinsed some mugs for him under the tap.

'You're feeling a lot better then, I gather?' he said. 'You're looking better.'

'Yes! My memory's returning in leaps and bounds,' she replied. 'There are still gaps. It's been such a rush, one minute I couldn't remember a thing and the next...' She gazed about the kitchen in rapture. 'It's like I was here only yesterday!'

'So...' said Seamus carefully. 'Perhaps we should get together this evening – have a nice cosy meal somewhere – just you and me, for old time's sake? I've missed you, you know.' He licked his lips and gazed at her.

'I don't know, darling. I've got a lot to think about at the moment. Maybe another time.'

Slightly irritated, he followed her movements suspiciously. 'What's the great mystery with this violin then?' he asked, watching her spoon instant coffee into the mugs. 'I never saw it in there when we cleared your stuff out.'

Letting her eyes travel around the old familiar room, Bianca explained how, on the night of her accident, she had stopped to listen to the young busker playing and how he had run off and abandoned the violin on the pavement. Thinking he might come back for it, she had hidden it under the floorboards ready to return it to him after the performance.

Seamus shrugged. 'Since you've been ill I've let things go a bit,' he admitted. 'The heart's gone out o' the place. I don't know if we can keep going. I don't think my job will be here much longer, Bee. I'm not daft. The owners are planning to sell up. It's not paying its way and the audience figures are so poor I hardly dare send the accounts in.'

208

While he was speaking, Bianca couldn't help noticing that the kitchen was no longer the homely room she had been used to. It was like a storeroom, hardly recognisable among a heap of rubbish and stacks of boxes. 'What's been going on here?' she asked.

Seamus sat down heavily, took his coffee and nursed it between his hands. 'The demand for tickets just isn't there anymore. Audience numbers are dwindling week by week. People are content to stay at home and watch those new video machines. Some want to see the kind of stuff decent people do better not knowing about, if you see what I mean. Attitudes have changed, Bee. It's not enough apparently, for folks to have a good night out at a variety show an' have a laugh. And talk about putting on Shakespeare or George Bernard Shaw! They've started saying it's too flipping highbrow!'

'But surely people still like the classics? We used to play to packed houses!' exclaimed Bianca indignantly.

'It's fashion. It all changes! Stuff like that, it doesn't draw the crowds anymore. What people want these days are cheap thrills and half-dressed women!'

Bianca looked sceptical. 'That can't be true,' she said. 'So what show are you putting on next season?'

'Nothing. After this one there won't be another performance. I've had to cancel the contracts. The box office takings have been so bad I can't afford to stage another show. The owners have told me they won't renew the insurance. No! We're finished. The theatre's beaten me this time, Bee.' With a shake of his head he put down his mug, stood up and put his hands in his pockets. 'It was a piece of cake when you were topping the bill,' he said, turning to face her. 'You're different you see, you've got class. You gave the place a bit of quality, made people feel they were being treated to a real star performance. Not like the artistes I've got now. Half of them can't keep their act decent or their language clean! It cheapens the whole place. I've seen better jokes on a lavatory wall.'

Bianca's heart went out to him; he looked so forlorn. 'You really are down in the dumps!' she said. 'Surely you're exaggerating? It can't be that bad.'

'It's worse than bad,' he replied. 'Shame I've had to tell you it straight like this, when you've just come back.'

'I haven't actually *come back* as such, Seamus. I only came for this,' she said, indicating the violin. 'It's like I've been asleep for years and I've just woken up!' Her face was looking almost young again, as radiant as a girl's and her eyes were shining.

'Bee?' began Seamus, fixing her with an urgent stare. 'Would you help me? I don't want to see the theatre go down the pan and I bet you don't either, do you? I've buried some of my savings in it already but I still can't afford to keep it going. Could you help dig us out of this mess? I wouldn't ask you if I wasn't desperate.'

She thought carefully before replying. 'I can't do anything, Seamus, I'm sorry. I've had to sell most of my jewellery. Poor Colette has had to put up with scrimping and saving and wearing second-hand clothes. You know I couldn't afford to keep the apartment going; we've had to move into a dingy old flat the other side of town. I haven't worked since my accident and now I'm getting older I don't think...'

210

'You'll never be old! You'll never be washed up like some…'

'Be realistic, I am getting old, and I'm rusty. I haven't been able to learn lines for I don't know how long. If Shakespeare's gone out of fashion, what future is there for me? What sort of show would pull in the crowds? What you need is something new, a real live concert – something sensational like The Beatles or the Rolling Stones!'

Seamus sat down and picked at his trouser bottom which was fraying. 'Then there's nothin' for it; we'll have to close. I just dread telling my loyal staff. George on the door, and the front-of-house staff, they'll not thank me for putting them out of work.'

'They'll know it's not your fault. I expect they already know it's coming, if they've got any sense. They'll know how poor the box office figures have been. It won't come as a surprise. They won't blame you.' She patted his arm sympathetically, 'You shouldn't blame yourself.'

But he wasn't comforted. He took a deep breath and made an extra effort to draw her closer. 'Bee? I could have been stronger, more successful, if you… I mean if we…' He stopped himself and bit his lip.

'If I hadn't had my accident you mean? It's nice of you to say so but one actress can't stop fashions changing. It was bound to happen sooner or…'

'No!' he interrupted. 'What I was going to say was: I would have been a more successful director, and more enterprising, if you'd agreed to marry me when I asked you.'

Bianca looked genuinely confused but he appeared not to notice. 'What are you talking about?'

He stared at her. 'I've always loved you, you know. I'd do anything for you – well, you know that.'

'Seamus! You can't blame me for everything!' she cried in alarm. 'How dare you!' she cried and was about to walk out with the violin hugged to her chest protectively when his next comment frightened her.

'Wait a minute! That violin there – let me have a look at it. How much do you think it's worth? We could sell it. There's no need to give it back.'

She felt him bearing down on her as he came towards her and took a step back.

'Sorry, sorry, Bee. I get a bit carried away sometimes. Here, sit down a minute. Look, just suppose it hadn't been there when you came back for it. You could always tell that boy it had gone when you went to get it.' His coaxing was slow, manipulative and deliberate. His breath was warm on her cheek.

Her heart thumped in her chest. 'No Seamus,' she replied. 'I never thought you had it in you to suggest such a thing, you being the director too – a man with responsibility.'

He looked glum. 'Well I won't be for much longer. That would make you happy eh? See me out of a job? Anyway, no matter. You should tell that busker, whoever he is, to look after it, to be more careful with it next time. He could've lost it for good. How was he to know someone like you would pick it up and look after it for him?'

'He didn't… he doesn't know, well, not yet. But his gypsy friend will tell him, if he hasn't already. I'm going to see him right now, to return it. I promised him I would.' She picked up the violin and hastily made for the door.

'Bianca! Wait, please! Look at it from my point of view! We could sell it together! It might be a Stradivarius or something! Open it up and let's have a look at the label? It could be worth loads of money; some of them fetch thousands! Just think!'

He tried to grab the case from her and when she pulled back in alarm, he placed himself between her and the door.

'Get out of my way!' she squealed. 'You never worried about me when I was ill. All you think about is yourself and what you can get out of people. You've never given anything to anybody out of the kindness of your own heart. Oh yes, you're a good director! You're good at telling people what to do – how to feel, when to laugh and when to cry – but you can't be a stage director all the time. Life's not like that, Seamus. Actors might do what you say, but they have their own lives. You can't manipulate everyone you meet – pulling strings here, daubing make-up on there. That's why I couldn't marry you. I remember now! You always wanted to tell me what to do! You never really loved me – it was all words, like a script, without any real feeling at all!'

'Bee! Don't you see? It could be our last chance. The money that might fetch – it could get us both out of trouble. It's not just for myself, don't you see? It's for both of us! Give us a fresh start! Let's have a look at it – see if there's a date on it, eh?' He tried to take it from her while she struggled harder to open the door. 'Let go of me, Seamus! You're hurting me!'

'Give it here!' he shouted.

'No!' she pleaded. 'Let go! Let go!'

Finally she managed to wrench the door open. She

thrust it back against Seamus and hurried down the corridor whimpering in fear. Leaving the theatre quickly, and still clutching the violin-case tightly in her arms, she walked quickly, almost running, desperate to get away. This was a side of Seamus she had never seen before and it frightened her.

Sixteen

When Bianca had gone, Seamus couldn't get her out of his mind. Far from regretting his actions, he was fired by this new challenge and he began scheming. 'A gypsy eh?' he mused to himself. 'Never did like those dirty thieving vermin, always up to no good.' Spurred on by her rebuke, his thoughts turned to revenge. He stood staring out of the window with his hands in his pockets. The rain was pouring down onto the tarmac below. He watched it beating against the glass, running along the top of the rotten window-frame and following its well-worn brown-stained track down the inside of the wall beside him. The weather only served to accentuate his depression. Seamus was a man who often succumbed to feelings of self-pity and deprivation. He was apt to blame everything and everyone for the failure in his own life. Sometimes he would spend hours contemplating his own fate but would never spend a moment studying himself in the mirror or coming-up with anything like self-criticism. But within moments Todd came in, fooling about as usual.

'Bloody rain!' he shouted. 'It's run right down inside my collar. I only nipped out for some fags.'

Seamus turned, noticed Todd was wearing what looked like a pair of purple tights draped about his neck like a scarf, but he said nothing.

His mood didn't go unnoticed however. 'What's eating you this time?' asked Todd. 'We've been turning out the costume department, well, the old broom cupboard to you an' me. You'd be amazed at what's in there. Do you want to come and have a look?' Apparently unfazed by Seamus' blank expression, he continued: 'We could always forget the summer show and put on a pantomime if the worst comes to the worst. There are plenty of old dames' dresses in there!' He paused for a response, and receiving none, carried on undaunted. 'OK, so it's not Christmas for ages, but who cares?'

'Get lost Todd – I'm thinking,' said Seamus.

'Sounds serious, replied Todd. 'I hope it's not catching!'

In a flash, Seamus saw an opportunity and leapt at it. 'Bianca was in here just now,' he said. 'Who does she think she is? A prima-donna or something? Just because her memory's supposed to have come back she's says she can't spare the time. All I did was ask her to come and work for me again and what does she say? She says she's got better things to do! Bloomin' Miss High an' Mighty!'

Todd looked amused. 'Oh well, it would be a fine thing if you had a part to offer her. Had a change of heart about putting on another show then? You haven't exactly got a script to give her, have you? What did you ask her to do this time, scrub the stage?' His sarcasm was never in short supply.

But Seamus had Todd's attention and was loathe to let it go. 'You know that daughter of hers?' he said. 'Bianca flipping worships her, doesn't she? Well, she wouldn't think Colette was so precious if she knew

216

where she'd come from I bet – but then, what do you expect if you go picking up babies off the street?'

'Blimey, that was centuries ago!' remarked Todd. 'I hardly remember now. It was some car accident, wasn't it? Why? Do you know something about her we don't then, boss?'

'No, I'm just saying. People shouldn't go picking up strangers' kids, especially if they've been dumped by gypsies.'

'Gypsies? Who said she was a gypsy's kid? Don't remember that! Is she then?'

Seamus made no reply. A rumble of thunder overhead signalled the beginning of a storm.

Todd scrutinized him and looked genuinely puzzled. 'You're in a right weird mood,' he said. 'There's a touch of Macbeth about you today.'

Todd's attempt at a joke was met with silence but he was reluctant to give up easily and asked again: 'So, what are you on about then? Don't think Colette would like to hear you talking about her like that.' He shifted his feet uneasily. 'What's all this about?'

Seamus didn't answer.

'Hey, are you feeling alright, boss? Want me to fetch you a bottle of something to take the edge off your temper?'

'No, I'm just saying: perhaps people ought to be more careful who or what they pick up off the street, that's all.' As he said this he wrinkled his nose.

'Right! Let's forget it then; it's history.' Then, as he made to leave, he added. 'Anyway, what's so wrong with being a gypsy? At least they're not stuck up snobs like some people I could mention. Take my parents, for instance – they thought themselves so bloody classy, anyone would think they were the aristocracy the way they carried on and look where it got me: a second-rate actor with not a lot going for him.'

Looking genuinely downcast for a moment, Todd waited, perhaps hoping this statement would prompt some sort of compliment, but he was wrong. Seamus ignored him and after a few moments Todd left him to wallow in his black mood alone.

*

It was still raining the next day. Colette was out looking for a job and Bianca was alone in their flat. All too soon, she noticed water trickling steadily though the kitchen ceiling. She placed a bucket underneath but no sooner had she done so than a dark patch spread below the sitting-room window and the wallpaper began to bulge. 'Oh no!' she exclaimed, racing to fetch some newspapers which she placed on the floor. By lunch-time streams of water were flooding down the street and drains were overflowing. She heard the front door slam and footsteps on the stairs. Seconds later Colette burst into the room.

'Hello, darling! Any luck?'

Colette shook her head. 'No, nothing,' she mumbled and began peeling off her wet clothes.

'You look soaked! Are you alright, darling?'

'Mmmn, suppose so,' she replied, easing off her shoes and shaking her wet hair. Bianca, detecting something was wrong, looked at her twice and went to get her a dry towel.

Immediately Colette buried her head in it. Bianca had just begun telling her about the leak in the ceiling

218

when Colette burst into tears.

'Oh, whatever's the matter?'

'Who was that old gypsy man who came here?' she demanded, emerging from the towel with her eyes blazing. 'He seemed to know something I don't. Well, everyone does actually, except me!'

'What on earth do you mean darling? What's happened to start all this?'

'I just met Todd in town, while I was sheltering from the rain. He thinks he's so funny, that man; he really fancies himself – I hate him! He was saying all kinds of things about me! He said I was a gypsy's kid. Honestly, Mum! I don't understand! What's going on?'

Bianca caught her breath and sat down. How brutal people can be! But while she tried to collect her thoughts and decide how best to explain it, Gideon's kind face and gentle manner slipped into her mind like a cooling balm. She straightened her back and took a deep breath. 'Gideon's a very special man, Colette,' she said. 'I haven't told you much about him yet but do you remember the day he was here? It sounds peculiar, but he seemed to know everything about both of us. He helped bring my memory back; and he made me feel well again!'

'So...' said Colette, apparently steeling herself for the worst. 'What you're saying is – Todd was right. I'm one of their kids! So come on Mum! Tell me! Is this Gideon my father?'

Bianca looked incredulous. 'Your father!' She smiled and placed her hand against Colette's tearful face. 'Oh, Colette, my darling, if such a man as that was your father I would be so proud. But no, he's not your father. Of that I'm certain. You know what? We have work to do,' she added, 'and I don't mean clearing up the leaks! Your happiness is more important to me than anything, darling. Rain or shine, we're going to see if we can find Gideon Tremayne and ask him what exactly he knows about you and your natural mother. But one thing I'm sure about – if you are a gypsy's baby, it makes no difference to me – and it shouldn't to you either. People like Todd – they're too ignorant to know any better. I don't know where he got that idea from, but the best thing to do is to take no notice.'

While she went to fill the kettle – hot sweet tea was her usual remedy for any upset – she resolved to tell Colette all she knew.

Ten minutes later she came through carrying a tray laden with tea and toast. 'I've made us a snack, darling,' she said. 'It'll cheer us up.' Casting an inquisitive look she asked: 'How's your friend, Mitzi, by the way?'

'Funny you should ask; when I saw her on Saturday, she didn't look well and wasn't hungry. It's not like her to go off her food.'

Bianca poured the tea and stirred some sugar into it thoughtfully. 'Poor girl, got a tummy-bug probably. Was her boyfriend with her?'

'Finn? Yes, he was there,' replied Colette, spreading a generous amount of butter on her toast. 'They spend a lot of time together now, when he's not working. Well, even when he is actually, she seems to spend a lot of time at the pub. She's looking for another job too, now the theatre's on the brink of closing. Perhaps they'll take her on at the pub. She'd be OK behind the bar I suppose.'

'Have you ever heard Finn talk about a violin?'

she asked.

Colette looked surprised. 'Yes, he was moaning about it on Saturday actually. He's lost it and he's quite worried about it.' Her forehead furrowed. 'He was talking about a gypsy too – sounded like the same one that was here. He said the violin belonged to him.' Suddenly Colette put down her toast and anger flared up in her eyes again. 'Look! I don't get it, Mum! Why does everyone know about that old gypsy except me? Why am I always kept in the dark?'

Bianca rested a hand on her arm. 'Wait there, darling! Don't say another word!' She got up and went into her bedroom.

Colette watched her, suspicion raging in her eyes. 'What? For goodness sake, what now?'

Bianca retrieved the violin from under the bed and carried it through bursting with excitement. 'You see? I've found it! I'd been saving it for him – well, that's not entirely true. Finn accidentally left it on the theatre steps ages ago and I picked it up. I was looking after it for him, but that was the night I had my accident – I lost my memory and forgot all about it.'

Colette was astonished. 'But that's brilliant! He'll be over the moon to get it back!' she exclaimed. 'Where was it?'

'I hid it under the floorboards in my dressing-room. I know that sounds a bit dramatic but at the time I didn't know what else to do with it. I thought it would only be in there until after the performance.'

'And then you fell …! Oh, I'm so pleased you're better Mum! I can't believe it! You're just like your old self again.' Colette jumped up and hugged her. This time her eyes were filled with tears of joy.

221

'Darling,' Bianca began, 'I must explain something. It was only when the old gypsy came to see me that I felt my memory returning. There's something special about him. I don't know what it is.'

'Mum, don't you think you're getting a bit carried away? It's wonderful you've got your memory back, but to say it was all to do with that gypsy, well!'

'Darling, I trust him. I believe he's a good, honest man. It was his kindness which started my recovery, I'm sure of it. My memories came flooding back and I could picture everything! I could remember seeing Finn playing that night. You were there too, remember? It was so cold and I gave him some money. But when I asked him his name he took fright and ran off, leaving this on the pavement. It started raining hard so I picked it up and took it inside. I thought he was bound to come back for it.'

Colette looked confused. 'I vaguely remember you stopping to listen to a busker. I don't know why you even stopped to speak to him actually.'

'I felt sorry for him and he played so beautifully. Didn't you notice how enchanting his playing was?' She paused, 'Colette, darling, I know it sounds silly, but there was something in his eyes which reminded me of you.'

Colette sighed. 'Oh Mum, you're a hopeless romantic! What is it with you about waifs and strays? You're always picking up something!' A smile flickered across her face and reaching out, she took the violin from her mother's arms. 'Well, he'll be relieved to have this back, I know that. Hey!' She began scrutinising the instrument, screwing up her eyes and peering into the hollow interior for a label. 'It looks

222

like an Italian make. It could be worth something you know.'

Bianca went pale. 'Yes, maybe.' she said, recalling the struggle she had with Seamus earlier. Colette turned to her in great concern. 'He might have stolen it from somewhere. How else could he have come by something like this? He's always broke.'

'I'm sorry to say that's exactly what I thought at first. That's partly why I hid it. I didn't want to tell anyone till I'd found out more. I was due on stage and there was no time to think.'

'So what do we do with it now? We ought to take it to the police really.'

'No darling,' replied Bianca. 'I know it's not stolen. Gideon told me it belonged to his grandfather and was handed down to him. It's a family heirloom. Gideon's not what you'd call an educated man, but he's a good man.' She sighed. 'At the time I don't know what else I could have done but I hadn't intended to keep it this long. I must give it back straight away.'

'Well, I think we ought to hear what Finn's got to say about it first. But you know, Mum – never mind about the violin,' she cried, hugging her. 'It's just wonderful you've got your memory back! I was beginning to think I'd lost you forever.'

*

By four o'clock that afternoon the rain was still relentless. It poured down the steep gradient of the hill like a gushing stream. The fast-running water made its escape down steps, through alley-ways and gathered in pools around back-doors. The water carried on down the hill, accumulating in deep swirling puddles round the steps of the Theatre Royale. Gradually the water seeped through the entrance, flooding the thick red carpet within. Feeling particularly miserable, Seamus emerged from backstage intent on going home to immerse his problems in a pint of beer. Instead he found himself stepping onto the soggy floor of the entrance foyer. He looked down in bewilderment and exclaimed: 'What's going on? Hey, George, have you seen this?'

The doorman came up puffing and complaining. 'Of course I've seen it! Never been this bad before, guv'nor. Hope the flipping rain stops soon or we'll all be swimming out of here. Where do you keep the sand-bags?'

Seamus shrugged. 'Have we got any sand-bags? Never had any call for them before.' He stood watching the rain and stared at the wet carpet for several minutes. 'Well, I dare say it'll ease off before too long. Leave it for today and we'll mop up in the morning. I'm off home. Don't stop on too late; not much we can do here till the rain stops. Goodnight then!' Ignoring the doorman's objections, he turned away and left by the side entrance which was on a higher level and still, at that time, dry.

Twenty minutes later, having scattered a few newspapers on the floor in an attempt to soak up the water, the doorman locked-up, switched off the lights, checked his watch and left, like Seamus, by the side door.

Together, Bianca and Colette, struggling under the shelter of a large umbrella, approached the pub where

224

Finn lived and worked. Bianca had the violin-case in one hand and held on to Colette's arm with the other. Deborah was behind the bar and Mitzi was perched on a bar-stool chatting to her and filing her nails. There were several young men sprawled in chairs talking noisily and two gentlemen sitting in the corner window seat, each with a glass of beer, and a sheepdog at their feet. Seeing her friends enter, Mitzi smiled and slipped from her seat to greet them.

'Hello, is Finn around?' asked Colette. 'Mum's got something to give him.' Mitzi glanced at the violin-case and fluttered her eyelashes. 'Coo! Is that his fiddle?' she asked. 'Hey, go an' tell 'im Debs! The lady's found it!'

Deborah rolled her eyes, clearly not sharing Mitzi's delight, and disappeared into the kitchen. She emerged seconds later followed by Finn who looked straight at Mitzi curiously. He had eyes for no-one else.

'Look Finn!' she shrieked. 'It's your fiddle what you keep on about!' She waited, her face a picture of expectation, her little tongue darting between her teeth. 'See?' she squealed, 'It is yours, ain't it? Oh, do say it's yours Finn!'

Bianca stood quietly, waiting. She would have preferred there not to have been so many onlookers. Finn's eyes travelled from Mitzi to Colette to Bianca. When he saw the violin-case in her hand his expression changed to surprise.

'You've found it?' He almost pounced on it, taking it from her and undoing the case in rapture. 'It's here!' he said, almost to himself as though he couldn't quite believe it was true. 'It's come back! I knew it would!' He looked up at Bianca with his eyes shining

225

in gratitude.

'Thanks so much; wait till I tell Gideon!'

'I'm sorry I kept it all this time but I...'

'Mum!' interrupted Colette. 'There's no need to apologise.' To Bianca's dismay she turned on Finn and demanded, 'Why did you leave it out there in the first place?'

'Colette! Shut-up!' cried Mitzi. 'Go on, Finn, play somefin'!'

Finn said nothing. It was as if he hadn't heard. He picked up the violin, checking it and plucking the strings. After tuning it he rested it under his chin and took up the bow, saying, 'I was afeared I'd never get it back.' The honest humility in his voice was in stark contrast to Colette's challenge. Changing his mind about playing it straight away, he stepped towards Bianca and extended his hand to her.

'Thankee kindly,' he said, 'for keepin' it safe for me. It were a stupid thing to do, runnin' off an' leavin' it out in the rain like that.'

Colette was watching him quizzically. She tried a different angle. 'When you see that old gypsy friend of yours, try telling him he needs to get it valued,' she said. 'Tell him it's Italian and he ought to be looking after it. It's probably worth something. Tell him you can't leave a violin lying around like that. It ought to be...'

Finn was quick to interrupt. 'He does care about it! It was his gran'father's an' his dad saved it from a fire. It's his family heirloom an' he gave it to me for safekeepin'.' Turning to Bianca he added gently, 'I'm right grateful to you for bringin' it back.' He smiled as he gazed at the violin again as if he couldn't believe his

226

eyes. 'That night, you know, the night I lost this fiddle,' he confided, 'it were one of the worst days o' my life.'

'Mine too,' replied Bianca softly, catching Colette's eye. 'It was my last night on the stage. If I hadn't had that accident, I would've given it back to you before.'

'But you're getting better now, Mum,' interrupted Colette. 'You'll act again one day, you'll see!'

Bianca smiled. 'Perhaps, but somehow I don't think so. The striking resemblance between Finn and Colette amazed her as she watched the two together, their dark brown eyes hostile, and their spirits on fire.

Mitzi, who was always keen to move things on, urged Finn to play. After tuning it up, he began playing the music he loved the most, *The Star of County Down*. As he played, Bianca and Colette said goodbye, left the pub and walked home through the rain. Bianca slipped an arm through Colette's and said, 'Just listen to him! That lad can certainly play!'

Finn's playing came to an abrupt stop a few minutes later when Fred, the pub landlord, came downstairs to investigate.

'What d'you think you're doin'? Thought I paid you to work in the kitchen, not entertain the customers.'

Finn apologised. He began to explain what happened when there were jovial cheers from the customers, who started banging their beer mugs on the table. 'More! More!' they shouted, laughing and stamping their feet on the floor. 'Come on then! Play somethin' else; somethin' with a bit of spirit to it, lad!'

Fred's miserable expression changed as a new idea appeared to dawn on him. He looked at Finn solemnly and said: 'Well, Finbarr, looks like I'm out-numbered. Are you goin' to play what the customers want or aren't you?'

Hesitating, Finn nodded and struck up a lively Irish jig which had them all applauding, and to Fred's advantage, they all ordered another round of drinks.

Later, Finn was still overjoyed that the fiddle had been returned to him. Now he knew he couldn't rest until he had returned it to Gideon so he decided, that very night after work, he would go and find him and give it back.

*

As soon as they got home, Colette threw herself down in a chair.

'That Finn ought to count himself lucky!' she complained. Bianca went to fill the kettle. The time had come to be honest with her daughter. Seeing her and Finn standing side by side in the pub that night had convinced her; all that the gypsy had told her was true. 'I'm going to make us some tea and then I've got something to tell you,' she said. Colette sighed loudly and reached for a magazine.

'I'm going out soon. Finn's friend's taking me to the pictures.'

'Who's that then? I didn't know you had a boyfriend!'

'He's not my boyfriend! He's got a car an' I've never been in one before so he said he'd take me for a run in it.' She ran her hand through her hair and sighed.

228

'It's not a big deal, Mum.'

Bianca looked doubtful. 'What's his name? Does he work with Finn?'

'No! Danny wouldn't be seen dead working in a pub! He's a dealer. He does a lot of business up country,' she replied proudly.

'What sort of business?'

Colette laughed off the question. 'I don't know! Anyway, I thought you had something important to tell me.'

Bianca brought the tea and poured it thoughtfully. 'Yes, you see darling,' she began. 'I wanted to be sure what the gypsy told me was true. When I met Finn tonight and saw how much the violin meant to him I realized what Gideon was telling me was the truth.' Colette became impatient. 'I'm fed-up with hearing about that stupid gypsy. Is that all you wanted to tell me?'

'No. You see, darling, Gideon told me about you as well.'

Colette sat up with a start. 'Me? How does he know about me?

'Listen darling and I'll try to explain. A long time ago, there was a small boy...' Bianca felt strong now. She had her daughter's attention and the background to her story was at last beginning to make sense. 'His mother had lost her purse in the town,' she explained, 'and she was desperate. She left the boy at home with the baby to go back and look for it. He was only eight years old. Apparently he got worried and set off with his sister in the pram to find her but it was a horrible stormy night. The house was on a steep hill and the boy lost control of the pram. It ran into the road, a car came down and hit the pram and the poor boy thought the baby was dead. He was so afraid of what he'd done and that it was all his own fault, he ran away.'

'You mean, you actually believe that sob story?' cried Colette. 'That gypsy was probably trying to get some money out of you, Mum. Be realistic!'

'Gideon found that little boy a few weeks later. His name was Finn. He was starving and frightened because he'd killed his baby sister.' She paused and looked at her daughter, 'and that baby was you.'

Colette stared at Bianca. 'You mean … the baby wasn't… it was me? You mean Finn's my brother? No! He can't be!'

'I'm certain he is, darling – but be careful what you say. He doesn't know.'

Seventeen

That night, as soon as he had finished work, Finn walked Mitzi back to her lodging. It was still raining and torrents of water were gushing down the cobbled streets. She had a red umbrella which he held over her head, fighting against the wind.

'What do you say to us takin' the fiddle back to Gideon tonight?' he suggested.

'What, in this weather? Are you mad? Where's he camped anyway?' she complained, her coat drawn up tightly under her chin.

'He's parked up near Restormel Castle. I don't mind the rain if you don't.'

Mitzi went strangely quiet. 'I'm so tired though.'

'You'll be alright. Want to get your wellies on an' come with me?' he suggested. 'It's time you got to know him, seein' as he's like a father to me. We'll be alright once we get there. He'll have the fire goin' an' he might even give us supper.'

'No, you go; it's too wet an' I ain't feelin' too good. Anyway you won't want me there when you've got to talk to him about how you lost the fiddle an' how you got it back an' everythin'. Honestly, Finn, I'd be better goin' to bed early than walkin' miles in the pourin' rain.'

'But you never minded a bit o' rain before! Come on, girl, it ain't that far!'

'No Finn!' she cried and just for a moment he detected a tear in her eye. 'I ain't feelin' well, I told you!'

He stepped closer, put his arms around her and kissed her. 'What's wrong? Perhaps you're goin' down with a cold. Have you got a headache?'

'No, but you're givin' me one!'

'Then what's the matter? Why are you bein' like this? Don't you love me anymore, is that it?' he teased, kissing her again.

But she pulled away, refusing to relent. 'Leave me alone, Finn. I'll be alright if you just leave me alone!'

He stared at her in dismay. 'I'm sorry, Mitzi! Are you really ill? Do you need to see the doctor or somethin'?'

She stopped walking and burst into tears.

'What's wrong? Tell me! I ain't never known you like this before.'

'I've already seen the doctor!' she cried, relenting and putting her arms up to be cuddled.

'Look… I weren't gonna tell you, not yet, but Finn. I'm gonna have a baby!' And she collapsed against him in a heap of tears. He held her, feeling the sobs shudder through her body. He loved her more than his own life.

'I dunno what I'm goin' to do, Finn,' she said, sniffing and trying to recover herself. 'I ain't told no-one. I daren't tell anyone, not even Colette 'cos if my boss finds out he's bound to give me the sack an' I won't be able to work, an' anyway I ain't got no money or nuffin' for no baby.'

Finn kissed the top of her head, tilted her face to

232

meet his and kissed her again on the lips. 'I love you, don't I? An' you love me? If there be two of you, then I'll be lovin' you twice as much. You can stay wi' me at the pub an' I'll look after you. I'll ask Fred if he'll let you stay, an' if not we'll think o' somethin'. You an' me, Mitzi, we'll be a family together an' that's how it should be.'

Having said goodnight to her he told her again not to worry and watched her go indoors. Then he pulled up his hood, took the violin and set off in the pitch dark to look for Gideon. It was still pouring but he was too distracted now and hardly noticed the rain. The joy he felt in finding the violin was tempered now by this new responsibility. It seemed such a distant grown-up thing, to become a father. Fears arose when he thought about babies: their crying; their needs; their smallness that stemmed from the fearful memory of his baby sister's fate. These fears had been lurking all those years in the back of his mind and sprang back to fill him with terror. Without realizing it, he had covered the ground quickly and arrived within striking distance of Restormel Castle before even giving his meeting with Gideon a thought. But when he saw the familiar glow of the wood-burning stove shining through the caravan's window, like a beacon flickering in the distance, the confidence he held in Gideon instantly put him at his ease. The sight at once familiar and so dear to him, caused his pulse to quicken in excitement and he stepped forward eagerly.

'Hello there!' he shouted when he saw the silhouette of Gideon move across the window. He climbed the steps and entered, soaking wet and breathless. Gideon was sitting by the wood-stove having his supper. A bowl of soup was perched on his lap. Finn placed the violin before him and opened the case without a word.

'She's a good woman, Bianca Tabora,' said Gideon and sighed, putting down his spoon.

Finn was perplexed at his sombre response. He had so much to tell him – yet now, in the quiet of the caravan, with only the hissing of the kettle on the stove and the pattering of the rain on the roof to break the silence, he found himself casting about for something to say. He wasn't ready to confide in him about Mitzi. 'You're pleased, ain't you, that I brought it back?' he asked, looking at Gideon keenly.

'I am glad you've got it Finn, but yer only need to take it back wi' yer again, seein' as my time ain't yet come. There be no fiddle-playin hands to play it an' nothin' else to do wi' it but look at it, eh son?' He finished his soup and put his bowl down by the hearth.

Finn looked at the kettle; steam was shooting from its spout. 'Makin' tea are you? I could fair do wi' a cup. Shall I brew you a pot?'

'Thankee,' said Gideon. 'Yer came out all this way in the rain just to give it back then?'

'I did,' replied Finn. 'An' to say sorry for losin' it like. Goes to show, I can't promise nothin' to no-one without makin' a mess of it.' He didn't make any move towards making the tea but sat looking downcast, staring at his hands.

Gideon coughed. 'Happen yer best make sure yer can keep a promise in future, lad,' he said. 'There be others now dependin' on yer, so's I believe, an' they needs yer to be strong, besides me. So don't be ready to

234

give up on yerself afore yer be even startin' out on life.'
And having said this, Gideon stood up and began to
pour the hot water into the old enamel teapot that had
been the mainstay of their survival for years. Finn
watched him, and he felt fonder of him than he had
ever done before – the way his old coat hung from his
stooped shoulders, the way his hair curled in grey wisps
straying from under his cap and the pungent horsey
scent of him which had caused Mitzi to wrinkle her
nose. They were both silent as Gideon poured out the
tea and handed him a mug.

'Yer came wi' somethin' else in yer heart I'm
thinkin', didn't yer son?'

Finn glanced up curiously. 'It's what you wanted.
It's more than I dared hope for, since I lost it, to bring it
back to you.'

'Keep it! Keep it by yer, Finbarr. Happen things
may come when yer be needin' to play it. Times'll be
hard for you afore they get better.' He sighed and sat
down again as if to study Finn's face. 'There be a
burden on yer heart that sings louder than birds in the
mornin'. I can fair hear 'em from here an' it ain't nowhere near dawn'. Saying this, he stared harder. 'So
out with it, son. I ain't so old as I can't tell when
summat's wrong. When's the baby due?'

Finn almost dropped his tea. His eyes grew wild
in amazement and fear. 'How did you know about
that?' he demanded. 'Mitzi only told me about it
tonight!'

Gideon was quick to defend himself. 'Are yer
forgettin' me so soon?' he asked sadly. 'Didn't I tell
yer I knows about things? Yer look at the clouds an'
yer see storms a brewin'. Yer look in the shadows an'

235

yer knows it be the sun goin' down. Haven't I told yer often enough, Finbarr, to watch for the signs in the sky? You've been livin' on this earth fair on twenty odd years an' happen times yer be as stupid as a young colt.' Suddenly a smile broke across Gideon's face. 'I knew afore yer even walked in that door, lad,' he said, and offered his outstretched hand. 'I'm proud o' yer, son!'

Eighteen

A few months later

It was a dry but chilly morning when Gideon unharnessed the mare, and leaving the caravan parked by the side of the road, began to lead her to the farrier. The horse had cast a shoe. Slipping a halter over her head, he set off on foot in the direction of the next village. Great Breddenoweth, was about ten miles east of Fowey. There was a smithy in the village who always gave him a good price. Gideon wouldn't let Belle pull the caravan without all her shoes or she would end up lame. It was a gentle walk of about a mile and a half and he hadn't gone far when a Land Rover and trailer tore past him at considerable speed, missing him by inches. While Gideon was still cursing about dangerous drivers, the vehicle screeched to a halt, skidded and reversed back towards them, causing Belle to shy. Gideon struggled to bring her under control.

'Don't worry old girl. Easy now! Easy! he cried. 'Them ain't gonna hurt yer, my beauty. Walk on now, walk on!' When Gideon drew closer to the vehicle a scruffy head was peering at him from the driver's seat.

'Be that you, Rabbiter?' The familiar voice exploded into a hearty laugh as the driver climbed out to greet him. 'Well, I'll be!' roared Albert. 'The very man I've been lookin' for these past three days!'

Before the gypsy reached him, Gideon mumbled, 'Folks'll tell yer castin' a shoe's bad luck,' before hailing his cousin in a friendly tone, 'Yer need to be takin' some more drivin' lessons in that thing.'

Albert ignored this criticism and came up warmly extending his hand. 'How are yer doin' then, brother?'

'Belle here needs shoein' so I just be goin' in to old Harry,' replied Gideon. 'Happen yer still managin' to keep on the straight an' narrow then, are yer?'

'Honest as the day, that's me!' said Albert. 'I'm glad I bumped into you today, brother. That's saved me a gallon or two in petrol tourin' the countryside lookin' for you!'

Gideon scrutinized his cousin with a mixture of affection and suspicion. 'What be so urgent yer got to find me then?' he asked, taking in the traveller's odd assortment of clothing: a satin blue waistcoat, scarlet neckerchief, green checked shirt and pin-striped trousers tucked into leather boots. The whole outfit had seen better days.

Albert set his jaw as though he was about to impart some serious information. 'I saw where you'd left your caravan back there,' he gestured. 'You ought to be more careful, brother, leavin' all your worldly goods unlocked. It were ready for any thievin' gentry to come along and take advantage.'

'Thought I just heard yer say as yer be an honest man, Bert. If any folks have got nothin' better to do than rob an' old caravan what's seen all weathers then they be more worse off than me. That bein' the case they be welcome to what I have, Bert. That's how I look at it.'

'You go on like that, brother and you won't have

238

nothin' left. You won't have a coat left on yer back afore long.'

Gideon studied his face as though wondering if his concern was genuine. 'If one coat goes, I'll get another,' he replied in an off-handed way. 'What were it yer wanted with me that be so urgent?'

The two men were standing together by the side of the road and at this question, Albert took out his tin of Golden Virginia tobacco and began to roll himself a cigarette. He appeared to be enjoying the question but gave no indication that he was going to answer it. The mare grew restless and Gideon gave her a bit of length on the rope so she could move off and graze on the longer grass a few feet away. It was fresh after the rain, glistening with moisture on every blade. Where the sun warmed the wooden gate leading into a nearby field, steam began to waft gently up into the morning air. Beyond them, the light hovered in a mist of lilac and silver.

'I wouldn't let her eat too much o' that fresh grass, brother, or she'll end up with the laminitis.'

Gideon grunted in irritation. 'Think you can tell me anythin' about horses I don't already know?'

Albert heaved a sigh, finished rolling his cigarette and lit it by striking a match on the sole of his boot. Still he didn't answer the question.

'Bad news is it?' ventured Gideon finally.

Albert looked up with eyes of steel. 'No brother. Not unless you think gettin' families back together be a bad thing. Even I know you don't think that. No, what I have to say to you – it be good news. I've had word, that's all.'

'Had word? About what? It ain't my Finn got

239

'imself into trouble is it?'

Albert smiled. 'Thought you told me your Finbarr were in enough trouble? No, it ain't nothin' like that.'

He took a long drag on his cigarette and at last launched into his reply.

'Jack's wife, well, she's been found up Plymouth way. Livin' on her own, she is, an' as poor as a church mouse.'

'Oh?' said Gideon guardedly. 'Who were it found her then?'

'It were our Dulcie recognised her, walkin' round the market up there. Said she looked real poorly: quiverin' and starin' like a mixy rabbit.' He shook his head, dragging on his cigarette which looked in danger of falling to pieces. 'Well, you know my Dulcie, she's a good soul when the mood takes her. She gives her some money and tells her how we don't hold nothin' against her. What with her Jack bein' inside – we can't be arguin' the principle of it – well! We're all family after all.' He smacked his lips as though relishing this new authority.

Gideon was wondering whether to mention he had not long been to see her himself when Albert said: 'Well anyway, she be on her way down.'

'On her way down? What, d'yer mean? On her way down here?'

'To see your Finn, an' her daughter too, I shouldn't wonder. Apparently they both be alive an' kickin' an' there was she all the time believin' they was dead.'

Gideon had no alternative. He had to ask: 'How did she happen by that information then Bert?'

Albert looked at him with a curious frown. 'You

better get your head seen to brother!' he replied. 'Weren't it you told her about it a while ago?' As he said this his face broke into a huge smile and he thumped Gideon hard on the back. 'That got yer worried didn't it!' he cried and roared with laughter. 'Yer don't have to worry about me, brother! Yer do what yer like! Yer please yerself! Take on other folks' kids! Leave yer caravan open so's any passin' thief can help 'emselves!'

His cousin's jokes and riddles were beginning to annoy Gideon. 'Happen I do, Bert,' he said. 'Can't see it be any business o' yours neither.' The delicate character of Finn's mother, Sarah, came back to him and he instantly felt protective towards her. She was so vulnerable and gentle. That feeling of tenderness washed over him again for a moment and he cleared his throat and tried to make it sound as though he didn't care. 'Did yer happen to mention to her that Finbarr's girl be in the family way?' he asked.

'Nope; can't say I did, but our Dulcie, she don't keep quiet about much. Reckon she might have said summat, brother.'

This was, to Gideon's way of thinking, another turn of the Great Wheel but he didn't say so. Instead he asked: 'When be she comin' down then, did yer say?'

Albert looked at his watch, a heavy gold watch that sparkled as he jerked up his sleeve. 'Dare say she'll be arrivin' in Tollwithen station off the train 'bout this time tomorrow, God willin'.'

'Be Dulcie meetin' her then?'

Albert shrugged. 'Who knows what's in that woman's head? Could be she is, but then I've got the motor and I left her pickin' apples so....What I was

241

thinkin' brother, when she's here, we ought to be havin' ourselves a party. We should have a real bash, a family reunion, what do yer say?'

Gideon grunted. A noisy party would be enough to scare the poor woman to death he thought, but he didn't say so. After all, his cousin was only trying to be sociable. 'If yer be of a mind to organize a reunion, Bert, then a grand reunion it'll be. But Bert,' he added and a shadow passed across his face. 'Be careful what yer say to the woman, eh? She ain't of a strong constitution I'm thinkin'.'

'Nah! I leave what talkin' there needs be to Dulcie. I ain't got a lot o' time for women.'

Nothing more was said on the matter and presently Gideon was back on the road leading the mare to the farrier with a little more urgency, and Albert, having returned to his Land Rover, roared past him giving a loud blast on his horn.

Nineteen

Sarah McKinney stepped off the train at Tollwithen. It was a grey morning and raining hard. Sarah had no hat and her throat and legs were bare. She was pencil-thin and the rain would soon soak the thin clothing she wore. In one hand, she carried a hold-all while the other she held up to shield her eyes. She was a woman who had become detached from her own history; she no longer had any sense of 'home' and had no affection for the poor bedsitting-room in Plymouth where she lived. Refusing to allow fears of the past to interfere with her mission, she carried on and blinked as she recognised the streets she had fled from years before. With a pang of anxiety she wondered whether she had done the right thing coming back. It was a gamble to try and put right the misunderstandings of the night which had destroyed her family life. If Finn and Bryony refused to accept her, she would have to return on the train to her lonely room empty-handed. As though this thought exhausted her, she gave a deep sigh and paused to regain her strength. Sarah had no sense of outrage; she placed no blame for her misfortune on anyone but herself. Her guilt was complete.

She waited while the train pulled out of the station and watched the level-crossing gates rise, releasing a single car to carry on over the bridge. There was hardly a soul about but as she looked up the street, she noticed a horse and caravan pulled in by the yard. There was a figure tending to the horse. Sarah stopped, watching in fascination as she realised it was the old gypsy, Gideon. He went to the back of the caravan and pulled out a bag of something which he gave to the horse. She saw him constantly turning towards the station entrance as though waiting for someone. Gradually she saw his attention come to rest on her – he must have recognised her at last. Keen to see a friendly face, she stepped forward eagerly.

Gideon's eyes narrowed thoughtfully as he spotted Sarah's frail figure emerging from the station. Immediately he made his way over to greet her. She looked thinner than ever, he thought, as though the wind would blow her over.

'I had it in my mind to fetch yer,' he said as she grasped hold of his arm by way of a greeting, peering into his face anxiously.

'You've come to meet me?' she asked incredulously. 'How did you know I was coming? Does Finn know I'm here?'

'Happen he's got other things on his mind as more urgent,' replied the gypsy.

'So he doesn't want to see his mother! I knew it would be so!' she cried. 'Let me try and talk to him. I must try to explain!'

'It ain't things o' the past worryin' him just now,' said Gideon. 'He be seein' to his girl, Mitzi. Did Dulcie not tell yer? She be havin' a baby but it be comin' way too early. Finn an' Dulcie be with 'er now. If the baby stands any chance at all o' livin' in this ol' world, it be havin' a fair chance with our Dulcie.'

'Oh!' exclaimed Sarah. 'So Finn's going to be a father? I didn't know!'

'If all be well, dear, an' hopin' it will. I be takin' yer there to see how things be – if yer don't mind ridin' in the old caravan yonder.'

Sarah could only nod as she relinquished her hold on her bag and followed him. After Gideon had loaded it into the back, he helped her pull herself up onto the driver's board and they set off.

*

Children playing near the perimeter of the camp stopped to watch and several dogs barked as Gideon's caravan pulled in off the road. 'Let's be goin' to see how the girl's farin',' he said to Sarah as he helped her down. They approached a group of men sitting huddled on low stools around a fire. They were quiet.

'News?' asked Gideon as he approached them. Sarah stood back shyly, reluctant to be noticed. Albert stood up, took a straw out of his mouth and came over to them. The expression on his face was sombre. He shook his head. 'If it lives another hour, it might last till the end o' the day, brother. I can't say no more than that.' He stared at Gideon and acknowledged Sarah's presence by touching his cap and nodding gravely.

Gideon turned to Sarah. 'Let's go an' see 'em, dear,' he said. As they stepped inside the dark interior of the trailer, they heard a snuffling sound and saw the tiniest fairy face of a baby cradled in Mitzi's arms.

'There yer are dearie,' coaxed Dulcie. 'Hold the little mite closer and try again. See if he won't take a little. Just a drop even – that's it, wet his lips with it! If he'll only suckle a little it'll give him strength.'

Suddenly realizing Gideon was there, Finn looked up. 'He's come too early,' he said, and his voice was low and hollow. It was as though they all knew there was little hope.

Mitzi let out a wail, 'Oh, don't say he's too early again, Finn! I can't bear it! Come on little one, you know you need your mummy's milk to make you strong! Here, come now,' she cried, holding the tiny baby to her breast and guiding her nipple towards the baby's mouth. But the child whimpered without the strength to feed or cry. He was so small, as naked and blue as a skinned rabbit. Without saying anything more, Gideon asked: 'Where's that fiddle, Finbarr?'

'Over there,' replied Finn, nodding towards the back of the caravan.

'Then happen yer better play it, son!' commanded Gideon in a loud voice. 'Play as yer never played afore!'

At his words, Mitzi burst into tears afresh.

'Don't fret, my girl!' said Finn. 'He's right! Could yer reach it for me, Dulcie?'

She did so, complaining. 'Folks believin' these old wives tales!' she grumbled, pulling the violin-case from under the bunk.

As Finn took up the violin and began to play he couldn't help but remember the words Gideon had uttered all that time ago... *'Time'll come Finn, when yer will play that fiddle an' yer heart will burn in yer chest like a raging fire.'* So he played a tune as deep and strong as the sea itself, when the tide is breaking on the

246

rocks. He played like the wind in the trees, when the branches sway and the sky has turned to slate. The music rose and fell in anguish. It was a tune none of them had heard before, a melody that came from the very earth itself. As he played his eyes never left Mitzi's tear-stained face.

Presently, Dulcie nudged Gideon and whispered, 'Look at the baby there. Look, see? He's takin' his milk proper now, bless him! Look dearie!' Then she turned to Sarah with joy. Sure enough, the infant had begun to suckle at last. The relief and happiness on Mitzi's face spread to all of them.

After the baby had been feeding a good while Gideon said, 'Happen that be enough playin' for now, Finn. Let 'em both rest there an' come mornin' he'll be well an' strong, I promise yer!' Finn relaxed and turning to Gideon in gratitude he caught sight of the pale anxious face behind him. He seemed to recognise her and his heart skipped a beat. She stepped forward out of the shadows and unable to utter a word she opened her arms as though to embrace him but almost at once they fell limply by her side again.

'Is it really you?' he asked. She appeared as if in a dream.

Gideon, seeing the confusion on Finn's face, explained without hesitation. 'This be your own dear mother, Finbarr, come all the way from Plymouth to find yer. She's been frettin' and worryin' about seein' yer long enough.' At that, Sarah rushed forward and hugged Finn; he looked astonished. Nodding to him with an encouraging smile, Gideon took the violin from him so he could hold his mother until her tears subsided. Whatever she needed to say, Gideon knew, was expressed in that simple hug. Words, apologies, explanations – all that would come later. She had her boy back and nothing could conceal her joy.

Twenty

The fire was kept burning late into the night. The group around it talked, drank beer, and brewed tea, not wanting to go to bed. They waited respectfully, chewing on their pipes, and rolling their cigarettes in quiet companionship. Sometimes Sarah sat with them; at other times she joined the women and disappeared inside the trailer. No-one around the stick-fire asked who she was – some might have accepted that she was with Gideon – Gideon's woman even – others might have thought she was a relative of Mitzi's – whichever way, the long hours of darkness enveloped all of them as the tiny premature baby clung to life. There was much shaking of heads but now the fate of the child was only a matter of time. They spoke no more about it. Gradually one by one the men turned in, until only Gideon and Albert remained. They sat together for several minutes until Albert, puffing on one of his hand-rolled cigarettes, looked at Gideon with half-closed eyes. But there was a sharp focus in his stare as he said: 'It won't live, y'know. It be half-blood, that's why. They don't thrive proper, none of 'em do.'

At this, Gideon was filled with anger. 'How dare you say that? You be a fool, cousin, to even think such a thing.' Before Albert could utter another word, Gideon lashed out with his fist and landed him a heavy punch on the jaw. It came so suddenly and with such force it sent Albert tumbling backwards off his stool.

'Hey!' he yelled, picking himself up off the ground and complaining. 'Bloody hell! What's up with you, brother?'

But Gideon had already turned and walked away. 'Hey, brother! I didn't mean nothin' by it!'

Gideon didn't even look back. But as he returned to his caravan, a smile flickered across his old face as he recalled with satisfaction the punch he had given Albert. It was well-deserved. It had hit home with the speed of loyalty to his dear sweet Sonya, lying peacefully in her grave with their dead child still in her womb.

*

It must have gone five o'clock in the morning when they all heard the baby cry. Instantly Gideon was on his feet. He rushed from his caravan and went to the door of the trailer, listening intently. That was no feeble whimper – he was crying strongly, choking and crying again. 'OK! It's OK!' came Mitzi's sing-song voice from inside: 'Don't try an' feed quite so fast that's all, little one!'

Gideon went across to the trailer and stepped up into the darkness within where Dulcie, Finn and Sarah were already huddled near the bed. Sarah grasped hold of Gideon's hand and pulled him closer. 'Look at him! It's a miracle!' she whispered. 'He's feeding well at last! He's going to be alright!'

Gideon smiled a broad smile. 'Didn't I tell yer me gran'father wouldn't let us down!'

'Look at 'im!' said Finn. 'He's lookin' pink an'

healthy now; he's even grown a bit during the night, I swear he has!'

Mitzi continued to breast-feed, and her face was a picture of delight. As the baby suckled, a gentle contentment came over all of them. Soon the practical Dulcie declared, 'Well, come on you lot! Show's over! Outside with you! Let the girl see to her baby in private now eh?'

Outside the trailer, Finn's dark, slightly distant, look made his mother feel shy.

'It's been a long night,' she said, 'but it looks as if the baby's doing alright now.' She smiled, hoping he would see something in her that would show him how much she cared. 'He's a little fighter. He'll be fine.'

'Thanks, I hope so,' said Finn. He looked exhausted and moved away towards the fire.

There was no time to delay. She felt she must speak to him but her words caught in her throat. Hugging herself, her nails digging deeply into her upper arms in anguish, she called after him: 'Finn? Can I talk to you a minute? He turned and waited. 'Finn, there's no easy way to tell you this. It's probably not the right time but ... Finn, when you were a little boy, I lost my purse... I...'

Such mounting excitement rose up in her chest and she could hardly breathe. 'I can't expect you to understand now, with the new baby on your mind,' she said, stepping towards him. 'Finn, you see, until Gideon told me about you, I'd always thought you were dead. I thought you and your sister had both been killed in the road. So...well, I came down on the train to find you. I just had to explain – and to say sorry. Gideon met me off the train and brought me here. I hope you'll

251

be able to understand one day, that I didn't mean to abandon you, or little Bryony. I'm so sorry! With your father in … well, it was all too much for me.' These words fell over themselves, broken by sobs as she almost lost control. But when she was able to bring herself to look at Finn again she found he was watching her with a bewildered expression. He looked away from her towards the trailer as though to get his bearings and shook his head. 'I don't know why you're sayin' sorry. It were all my fault, not yours,' he said. 'I'm the one what done wrong. I've hated myself ever since.'

'No, Finn. It wasn't your fault, believe me. I shouldn't have left you that night. You were only little. Even if I had lost my purse – I should have taken you and Bryony with me – I shouldn't have gone back to the shop without you.'

Finn shrugged. 'I didn't know what to do. The baby kept cryin' an' I waited and waited for you to come back and when you didn't I thought I'd go and find you.' He kicked a stone, staring at his shoes. 'When the pram ran down the hill and the car came and hit it, I thought she were dead.'

Sarah couldn't disguise her joy: 'I thought you'd both been killed. But didn't Gideon tell you? He's found her! He said she's called Colette, and she's one of Mitzi's friends.'

'One of Mitzi's… you mean…?' He stared at her in amazement. 'You mean you're sayin' it's Colette – she's my sister?' It took a while for him to absorb this. He looked towards the trailer where Mitzi and the baby provided the reality and security he so needed. 'That's incredible! How can she be my sister?'

'You know Gideon told you she was found alive that night and someone from the theatre took her in…' Now it was all too much and she broke down again.

It was Colette herself who later confronted Finn and challenged him to reveal the truth of Sarah's story. Finn drove the caravan into town to collect Colette and Bianca. Colette appeared tense and reluctant to talk. When they arrived at the camp, Bianca went straight to the trailer to see the baby but Colette walked off on her own. Her face was downcast and she showed none of the joy reflected in the family's happiness at the new birth. This didn't escape Gideon's notice. He was sitting by the fire whittling a stick and he called her over.

'There be some tea here if you've a mind for some,' he said and gestured with his head. She walked back to him reluctantly. 'I be thinkin, dear,' he said. 'Mind yer take good care o' yer mother there,' he said, indicating Bianca who was just disappearing up the steps. 'She be as fond of yer as any natural mother would be.'

'I do take good care of her,' she replied. 'Why wouldn't I?' and she scowled at him. 'What did you tell my mum anyway, that day you turned up at our flat? How come you know so much about us?'

'Look over yonder,' Gideon replied calmly, paring a willow stick with slow firm movements of his pocket-knife. 'That little lady over there,' he said, indicating Sarah who was just emerging from the rod tent with a basket of washing. 'There be yer real birth mother. If yer be wantin' to know more, then yer best go over an' ask her yerself. She's had more shocks in her life than she can handle so go careful now.'

If she was daunted by this, Colette didn't show it. Flashing Gideon a look of contempt, she marched across to Sarah with a defiant stare.

'Excuse me,' she demanded loudly. 'Gideon says you're my natural mother. Have you any idea what right he has to say that exactly?'

Sarah stopped in her tracks. She looked frightened and glanced at Gideon who nodded his head and smiled to give her some encouragement.

'I… I came down on the train to find you…' she began. Her courage almost failed her. 'Gideon said I should speak to you and I was going to,' she said, 'as soon as I'd hung out the…'

'Oh, were you! Well, thanks!' replied Colette. 'Gideon! Gideon! That's all I ever hear! Why does everyone have to take so much notice of that scruffy old gypsy? So! After all these years, you turn up here claiming you're my mother? Well, how do you think that makes me feel? You abandoned me! You left me for dead remember? Supposing no-one had come? If my mum hadn't picked me up and looked after me I wouldn't be here now!' She turned away in disgust only to be met by Gideon's warning stare.

'I know and I'm so grateful to Bianca. But I was at my wits end that night. I didn't know what I was doing. I'd lost my purse – all the money I had left in the world was gone – and when I saw the pram crushed I… I thought you were dead! I couldn't cope. I know it sounds pathetic. I'm sorry, Bryony, I didn't mean to hurt you, or Finn…'

'Bryony?' exploded Colette. That was too much. 'My name's Colette! Colette Tabora! I'm not your poor

254

little Bryony anymore so don't you ever call me that again!'

'That's enough!' shouted Gideon, standing up and making towards them, shaking with anger. 'Folks as don't respect their own kith and kin, they be worse than animals in my opinion.' He paused, waiting to catch his breath. 'Say somethin' comfortin' to her. Happen she's been through bad times; worse than you 'ave ever had to bear yerself.'

There was silence. No-one moved or spoke.

Finally, Colette turned and walked away, declaring bitterly as she went, 'I don't care! She's not my mother!'

'Colette?' Sarah called. 'Please come back! Let me explain!'

But Colette yelled back, 'Get lost, the lot of you!' and bursting into tears she hurried away.

Hearing the commotion, Dulcie came out of the trailer. 'What's all the fuss about?' she complained. 'You've woken the baby.'

Mitzi came behind her with the baby whimpering in her arms. Gideon took off his cap and ran a hand through his thin grey hair, 'That be a wicked ungrateful girl.'

'No, Gideon,' said Sarah softly. 'She's all mixed up, that's all. She'll be alright soon, you'll see.'

Finn, who was coming out of the trailer, met Colette running away in tears. 'I hate her,' she shouted as she passed him. 'She says she's my mother – but she'll never be my mum!' She stopped before Finn, her eyes blazing with anger. 'And she's saying you're my brother! Has everyone gone mad? I hate her... I hate her...' She was about to run on when Finn stopped her.

'Listen! It ain't her fault,' he said quietly. 'It were mine. Don't go blamin' her. It weren't her fault at all so you best shout at me an' get it over with.'

On hearing this, Colette turned to Mitzi in exasperation. 'What the hell's he on about? What's going on? Do you know what they're all talking about?'

Mitzi shrugged, 'No, but I'd shut-up an' wait for 'em to tell you, if I were you. Bianca will tell yer all about it, then perhaps you'll all be quiet an' let this little boy get some kip, eh?' She brought the baby up to her face and chuckled. 'You don't know what all the fuss is about, do you little fella! Families, eh? You've got all this to come you know!'

Dulcie brewed some tea and while Gideon comforted Sarah, they all gathered together to hear the explanation. The argument had upset them all, apart from Mitzi who remained as cheerful as ever as she nursed the baby. Bianca began to tell her version of events from start to finish. 'I must confess,' she said. 'It was wishful thinking on my part – hoping her real mother wouldn't come forward. I loved that baby so much you see.' She looked at Sarah guiltily and bit her lip. 'I'm sorry. I'd never had anyone to love before you see; someone who needed me like that she did!'

Hearing this, Colette visibly softened. She turned and put her arms around Bianca saying, 'You're the only mum I know! You're the perfect mum, the only mum I ever want!'

In spite of this remark, which must have seemed hurtful, Sarah seemed to recover her confidence. She stopped crying and stared at Bianca. 'You said you found a purse in her pram?'

'The police found one, yes,' replied Bianca. 'It was tucked under the mattress inside the pram. No-one came to claim the money and after a few months they told me it was legally mine. It wasn't a lot of money. I started a savings account for her with it, for when she's twenty-one, and I've added to it a bit over the years.' She hugged Colette and added, 'We've had to dip into it lately though, haven't we darling.'

Colette, ever protective, reacted spitefully. 'You can hardly ask for it back now. Not after all this time!'

'No, of course I'm not going to ask for it back!' replied Sarah. 'But how much was in there exactly, do you remember?'

'Sort of, why? Does it matter? My memory still isn't brilliant.'

'Was it twenty-three pounds, seven shillings and tuppence?' asked Sarah, almost smiling.

'Yes, that was it!' cried Bianca. 'I wondered what any poor girl was doing, leaving such an odd amount with the baby, as though it was every penny she had.'

'It was all I had! Every penny! It was all the money I had left in the world.'

Bianca suddenly came to a realisation. 'Then you shall have it all back!' she announced decisively.

'No Mum!' protested Colette. 'We can't afford it!'

Sarah shook her head. 'No, Colette's right. Keep it for her as you planned. I wish it could have been more.' With a shrug of her shoulders she explained, 'It's so sad, it seems such a small amount now and it was so important at the time.' With that, she seemed to fold up her life-sentence of grief and put it away. The mystery was solved. 'So,' she said to herself. 'Of course, I'd forgotten I'd hidden it in the pram! Would you believe it?' She smiled and standing up, went over to hug Bianca. 'Thank you!' she said, 'because all these years I'd been wondering what happened to it. If I'd known it was there all the time I'd never have gone out again that night. I lost my children all for the sake of that money!' And perhaps because it seemed so trivial, she put her hand to her mouth and cried, 'How could I? How could I have risked everything for that?'

Later that evening, when Gideon was damping down the fire, he came across his cousin sitting on the step of his trailer rolling a cigarette. He was expecting Albert to say something derogatory about Sarah, as he rarely kept his opinions to himself. He also wouldn't have been surprised if Albert made some reference to the bruise on his chin.

'I be ready for my bed tonight, Bert,' he said. 'Happen it's been a long day.'

'All days are long if you make 'em. Fine night for a spot o' huntin' brother,' Albert replied and his greeting sounded amicable enough.

'Not for me; time for that tomorrow. G'night to yer, Bert.'

Albert nodded. He put the cigarette to his lips and struck a match. 'By the way, Rabbiter, there be a wanderin' star passin' this way afore long. You might like to watch out for him – he ain't always what he seems. Still, he might stop by here, but then again, he might not.'

'Who be that then?' asked Gideon curiously. 'Should we make him welcome or no?'

258

'Up to you,' replied Albert. 'See what he's got to say for himself first. Goodnight, brother!'

As Gideon left him and climbed the steps to his caravan, he was puzzled. He knew nothing Albert said was ever straightforward, and having considered what the old boy was hinting at, he eventually dismissed it as something to think about for another day. After all, if it was anything important, Dulcie would have told him for sure.

Twenty-One

Two weeks later, Finn returned to work. With the landlord's somewhat amused agreement, he brought Mitzi and the baby back to live with him in his room at the pub. It could only be a temporary arrangement but things had moved on so quickly Finn wasn't sure what he wanted to do – whether to accept Dulcie's invitation to let them move into the trailer with them or accept Danny's suggestion that they do a bit of scrap-metal work together. He felt it would be better to listen to Gideon's advice and keep the security at the pub he had worked so hard to achieve. Gideon had made it quite clear that the option to travel with him in the caravan again was out of the question.

Gideon was sitting with Sarah outside the rod tent or "accommodation" as they called it, which Gideon and the others had erected for her and was where she had been sleeping since her arrival. They looked comfortable together, like an elderly couple who had passed many a day side by side. The tent was made of stout willow and hazel branches which were tied and woven together to form a shape like an upturned boat. Layers of blankets, rugs and a tarpaulin provided warmth and weatherproofing. It was heated by a small wood-stove, which Danny had salvaged from a scrap-metal yard, the flue being rammed up through the roof. The rod-tent gave Sarah a certain amount of privacy. It was set in a sheltered spot between Gideon's caravan and Albert's trailer.

Although the tension of the previous few days had dissipated, Gideon was worried. Nothing had been discussed about Sarah's future and the prospect of letting her go back to her previous lonely existence in Plymouth troubled him deeply. What would happen if she went back to her miserable bedsitting-room and she was lonely or became ill? There would be no way of him knowing. He felt fond of her, moved by her weakness and vulnerability and although he was beginning to feel restless and knew he would have to be moving on soon, he was reluctant to let her go back.

'Have yer got a train-ticket to be goin' home soon then, my dear?' he asked. 'Our Dulcie'll miss yer, givin' her a hand wi' the washin' an' that.'

Sarah smiled. 'I'll miss her too. She's a grand lady.'

Gideon nodded. He couldn't bring himself to say he would miss her too. 'Dulcie's a good woman, in spite o' what some might say.' He paused. The urgency of his question rose up in his blood and he couldn't wait any longer.

'What be yer plans then, Sarah?' he asked 'All these good folks'll get back on the road soon an' I'll be on my way too. There be a country fair I'm headin' for, down Helston way.' He looked at her curiously. 'Finn's stayin' in the town with his girl an' Danny might tally a bit longer. Him an' Colette have hit it off together so I can't see him stayin' away from her too long.'

Sarah shook her head. 'I know – everyone's got

261

their plans apart from me. I don't know. I guess I'll be going back to Plymouth, though I'm not looking forward to it. I feel so at home here with you and all the family. It's more than I could have hoped for, finding my family again, so I know I shouldn't complain.

Gideon patted her on the hand, much as he would to comfort a dog, because he found it difficult to express his feelings in words.

'Danny's been showin' Finn how to drive one o' them motors,' he said. 'Can't see what's wrong with a horse myself. Don't know why things have to be changin' all the time.' Sarah fixed her pale blue eyes on him and bit her lip.

'All good things come to an end,' she said and sighed. 'At least I can go back to Plymouth knowing my children are alive and well, and I've got a bonny little grandson too.' She smiled at him sadly and suddenly she reached out and grasped his hand tightly. 'Thank you for all you've done for us! You've been as good as a father to Finn. I couldn't have wished for anyone better and kinder than you to be a father to him. Oh Gideon! How can I ever repay you?' She was overcome for a moment, took a handkerchief from her sleeve and wiped her eyes.

'I only did what the lad needed. I ain't the kind o' man to turn a poor soul away as what needs food an' shelter.' They were silent for a few minutes but Gideon was thinking hard. In a way he felt he was a little in love with Sarah. It was a feeling he couldn't come to terms with since love, at his age he considered, was a thing of the past. His only true love had been his darling Sonya.

'What about you, Gideon?' she asked, fighting

back the tears. 'Now Finn's settled, will you be alright on your own? I don't suppose you need a woman to take care of you and keep you company?' Her question sounded so simple and yet curiously, he felt his heart pounding. It was unusual for him to feel stirred like this.

'The thing is, dear,' he replied. 'Yer won't be wantin' to be livin' like I do. It be fine in the summer, but when the winter comes...' He paused, finding it hard to put his thoughts into words. 'There be nothin' to wash yerself in but a bucket o' cold water an' nowhere decent to dress yerself that be comfortable an' warm. It's no life for a lady. Why, see how Dulcie an' the others have proper toilets an' cookers in them trailers. I ain't got nothin' modern in my caravan, nothin' nice to offer yer like that.'

She shrugged her shoulders. 'Things like that don't bother me much. God knows, I've had hot baths and a roof over my head but it's not made me happy. Would you be glad of some female company? I wouldn't mind it being a hard life, Gideon, as long as I was with you.' She took a deep breath as though her courage was deserting her so perhaps she blurted out the question more desperately than she had intended. 'Would you mind if I stayed on with you?'

He looked up in surprise and saw she was weeping. 'Don't cry, my dear,' he said. 'The thing is, I'd gladly take yer along wi' me but I can't be givin' yer the things yer deserve. Happen you might regret it afore long. 'I can't be offerin' you much. It be the bare bones of a proper civilised life. As yer see, we 'ave to be eatin' what comes in the hedgerow, wi' the odd rabbit or pheasant for meat. But look my dear: what

263

little I do 'ave, well, yer be more than welcome to share wi' me an' gladly so. If that be enough for yer, well then, we won't think too hard on it no more.'

Sarah gasped, hugged him and buried her tearful face in his chest. 'Thank you!' she cried. 'I don't care how hard it gets. I'd love to stay with you!' Tenderly, he wrapped his arms around her and held her close. He could feel her warm body relaxing and he too felt relieved. Everything was as it should be. 'Then yer can stay,' he said. 'Happen yer will be alright along wi' me.'

Preparations were being made in camp for moving on. Gideon began by checking the wheels, cleaning the horse's harness, securing pots and pans and sorting out his baskets. Sarah was with him, packing the few possessions she had brought with her from Plymouth. There was a sense of excitement and anticipation in the air and the horses were restless, flicking their tails and watching the gypsies' activity with pricked ears.

A taxi pulled up and climbing out, Gideon saw it was Finn and Mitzi, the baby in a shawl, and Colette with Bianca. They explained they had all come to say their final goodbyes. Dulcie was just setting-off to go into town with the others to buy provisions. 'I'll come!' shouted Colette, evidently happy to spend time with Danny, and she ran to join them. Finn and Mitzi agreed to go too, taking the baby with them. Bianca said she would prefer to stay behind. 'See you later!' she called. 'Have fun!'

Albert had no intention of going with them. Complaining about all the fuss women made about shopping, he was impatient to get on the road. Taking his axe he set off into the woods to collect firewood. Gideon invited Bianca to join him and Sarah for some soup.

'No thanks, I'm not hungry and it's such a lovely day I think I'll go for walk,' she replied. Wrapping her long scarf around her head she headed off towards the footpath which joined the field at the far end.

Gideon and Sarah, sitting together inside the caravan, started ladling out the soup. They had been eating for only a few minutes when they heard a shout outside.

'Anyone at home?'

They heard Bianca's voice greeting someone in a familiar, almost flirtatious manner.

'Hello, darlin'! Where is everyone? Ain't nobody gonna be sociable an' offer me a drink?'

'Who be that then?' he asked himself and stood up to look out of the door. Glancing back at Sarah, he saw she was looking very alarmed. The voices came closer. 'Don't be shy!' came Bianca's sing-song voice. 'Come over to the caravan and I'll introduce you!'

Inside the caravan, Sarah whispered, 'Gideon! I seem to recognise that voice, but it can't be him, surely!'

'Who, my dear?' he asked, noticing how pale she had become and how her fingers trembled. 'Don't you fret, there ain't no-one can harm yer here.'

'Hey!' they heard Bianca call. 'Come and meet my friend here!'

The effect the new arrival had had on Sarah was still on Gideon's mind when he stepped out of the caravan and made his way across. He fixed the visitor with a searching stare.

'Come and meet Drew,' said Bianca. 'Drew, this is Gideon!' She turned to Gideon proudly, her eyes shining. 'Drew lives in the flat above us,' she explained. 'He's always helping me out with odd jobs aren't you, darling!'

Drew Caudry,' said the visitor gruffly, stretching out a hand. 'Pleased to make your acquaintance, I'm sure.'

Gideon hesitated. Inexplicably, all the years of his childhood came rushing back to him as he looked into those eyes. He stared at Bianca's friend guardedly and saw a world long since passed by. Like a vision, he saw in his mind's eye the dreadful night when the great fire had spread through the caravans and destroyed the happy Romany community which had sheltered him all through his childhood. A life his parents and grandparents had built up over many years. Generations of his family had been lucky to escape with their lives that night. Suddenly a leaden pain shot up through his chest like a bolt of steel. It winded him, turning under his ribs as though it held him in a vice. He gasped, waiting for the pain to subside.

'You alright mate? Blimey! Havin' a funny turn?'

That voice – there was no mistake. Gideon recovered enough to look the man straight in the eye. 'So,' he said, breathing out heavily, his left arm clamped across his chest as he struggled to steady himself. 'What brings you back here, Jack?'

'Eh?' said Drew, his eyes suddenly meeting Gideon's in an icy stare. A flicker of fear passed across his face. 'What did you just call me, mate?'

'Yer be gone away from these parts near on sixteen years, I'm thinkin'. So what brings yer back if it

266

ain't for more trouble.'

'Bloody hell!' exclaimed Drew, drawing away from him and mumbling a curse to Bianca. 'You never told me *he* was here – of all people!'

'So, you know each other?' she exclaimed, seemingly unaware of the friction. 'Well, I'd never have guessed! Hey, wait till I tell the others!'

'No!' boomed Gideon with all his strength. 'There be things we need to talk about first, him an' me, in private.' The authority in his voice visibly shocked her and she stopped in her tracks.

'Don't say a word to no-one till I say so. Hear me? Not a soul!'

Bianca's smile vanished. Fear drained the colour from her face. Her weakness since the accident crept up on her from time to time and shook her confidence. The two men left her and walked away towards the trees. Drew went first, with clenched fists, swaggering as he walked, and Gideon followed, saying to Bianca as he went: 'Sorry to upset yer dear but go back to the caravan, an' help yerself to some sweet tea. There be the kettle there, on the hob.'

Albert was just returning from collecting wood and he had an armful of logs. He came face to face with them. He looked irritated, stopped abruptly and spat on the ground at Drew's feet.

'Didn't I bloomin' tell yer to make yerself scarce, yer bloody idiot?' he cursed. 'What the flamin' hell are yer doin' comin' here?'

Suddenly Gideon understood. 'So this be that "wanderin' star" you be tellin' me about, Bert?'

Albert ignored that comment. 'I told yer feelin's weren't good for yer here. I told yer, didn't I? I told yer to keep well away.'

'I've served my time,' snarled Drew. 'Get off my flamin' back! I've got as much right to be here as you have! My own wife's stayin' here so I've heard, so get out o' my way.'

Gideon's blood ran cold. Having seen the fear on Sarah's face, he realized now why she was afraid.

But Albert, it seemed, had a grievance of his own. 'You owe me, Jack, remember,' he said. 'Didn't our mother always say we must pay our dues? Ain't that right brother?' he added, turning to Gideon for support. 'He owes me four hundred quid an' I'll make sure I have it off him if it's the last thing I do.'

'Happen that be between you an' him, Bert,' said Gideon. 'There be more urgent matters he has to settle that don't cost nothin'. Family matters that need seein' to.'

Drew stood by with a look of disdain on his face.

'I ain't got nothin' to say to you, Gideon,' he said, flexing his fingers as though at any moment he might let a fist fly.

Albert, close to picking a fight himself, stepped up to Drew and hissed: 'You'll be regrettin' the day yer stepped foot in this camp, Jack! Have yer talk wi' my brother here an' then get out. I'll have my dues off yer soon enough an' don't yer forget it! I ain't seein' my Dulcie goin' short of luxuries all her life just so you can stuff yer face wi' beer an' fags. Reckon the day'll come when you'll get back all the misery what you've caused our family.' And with that, he deliberately dropped the heavy load of wood on Drew's feet and stormed off.

Drew jumped, swore and stumbled back, cursing,

before rubbing his shins and limping after Gideon into the shelter of the trees.

From the safety of the caravan, Bianca and Sarah watched the encounter together. Sarah was anxious and weeping silently into her handkerchief. 'That man,' she said. 'His name's not Drew– it's Jack. He's … he's my husband!'

Bianca turned to her in amazement. 'No, no love, you must be mistaken! He's our neighbour. He lives in the flat above us. Don't upset yourself. His name's Drew Caudry! Of course he's not your husband!' she chuckled, as though the idea was ludicrous. 'Come on now,' she said sympathetically. 'Look – come and take a closer peek at him. See?' she said, patting Sarah's shoulder sympathetically.

But Sarah shrugged her off. 'You don't understand! I haven't set eyes on him for years but I know it's him. I recognised his voice straight away. I'd know him anywhere.' She reached out and grasped Bianca's arm. 'Come and sit down and I'll tell you about him but please, whatever happens, don't let him know I'm here.'

Bianca consented, looking slightly taken aback. Putting a hand to her head as though it was starting to ache, she sat down.

'When Finn was a little boy,' began Sarah, 'Jack was deep-sea fishing. He was away a lot but even when he came home, I never got to see half his wages; he was a drinker. He'd come home drunk and ask me for my housekeeping money… but when I wouldn't give it to him he used to take it out on me.' She steeled herself and continued, 'He got into the wrong crowd – started

269

breaking into houses and picking fights. The police were always after him. Then he went a bit too far.'

Bianca was studying Sarah's face like a child listening to a bedtime story. It was hard to tell if she believed Sarah or not.

'I used to hide what money I could so I had something to buy food with. Soon as he got home the first thing he'd be after was some money to get a drink.'

'Then he got into a fight down the pub that ended up with someone dying in hospital. He was found guilty of manslaughter,' she stopped and sniffed. 'A long sentence, fifteen years... and I was relieved, I'm ashamed to say it, relieved because I knew I was safe at last – even if I didn't have much money. 'Oh, Bianca! I didn't know he was out. What am I going to do?'

A commotion outside stopped whatever Bianca was going to say in reply. They both stood up and looked out. 'The others are back!' Bianca cried. The next minute Colette burst through the caravan door saying, 'What's going on out there, Mum? Gideon's arguing with that ghastly man Drew Caudry. It sounds bad!' The question was directed at Bianca, but it was Sarah who answered. She stood up calmly and somehow regained all her composure. 'There's no easy way of telling you this, Colette,' she said, drying her eyes and taking a deep breath. 'That man over in the woods talking to Gideon – he's your father.'

Gideon, leaving Jack striding about in the woods, made his way back to join the women; his legs felt tired and his steps were laboured. His boots felt unusually heavy as though clogged with mud and his chest ached. 'I be

270

gettin' too old for these troubles,' he said to himself. 'Happen me and Sarah need to get away from here an' get some rest. Them's as hurt us the most, they seem to catch up wi' us in the strangest o' ways.' The pain in his chest reminded him of when the mare had been alarmed at something and stepped back, crushing him against the wall. It had winded him and would have pressed the life out of him if Finn hadn't been there to help. He gasped, stopping to rest for a minute, before walking on.

When he came close, three anxious faces were turned towards him, each with a question on their lips.

Colette was the first to speak. 'It can't be true, can it? Sarah just said that man's my father!'

Bianca corrected her. 'Let Gideon tell us what's been happening first, darling!'

Gideon sat down heavily and rested his arms on his knees before saying anything. Then he took a deep breath and said, 'It be as true as anythin' else, though I'm of a mind to wonder why things be movin' so fast all of a sudden. It be fair makin' me giddy.'

'Please! Just say it's not true!' she pleaded.

'Happen you should go an' ask him yerself,' he replied. 'Finn's back from town, eh? Best ask him to come an' hear what's got to be said too.' It was all too much for him and he looked exhausted.

Sarah's eyes were red and swollen with weeping and she clutched her handkerchief to her mouth. Gideon reached out and squeezed her hand. 'Don't yer worry yer heart about him, my dear. I've had a word with him. He's sayin' he only wants to speak with yer. He says he's done his time inside an' he's come to make his peace with yer an' then he'll be on his way.

271

That's all he wants.'

'Time inside?' shrieked Colette. 'I knew it! I knew there was somethin' dodgy about him!'

'Oh!' Sarah sobbed and wrung her hands. 'I can't face him! What can I say to him?'

'If yer don't want to see 'im, there be no need to trouble yerself. Happen I'll ask Finn to talk to him. Finn can send 'im on his way for yer. It may be for the best.'

'If you want to try, Sarah, I'll come with you,' offered Bianca. 'I don't think he'll hurt you, he's always been so nice to me, hasn't he Colette? I don't understand how he can be – I mean if what you say is true … let's go and talk to him together, shall we? You come with us too, Colette! We'll all go!'

'I hate him,' she replied and scowled. 'I'm not going.'

'Better I go along wi' yer an' all, see he don't try nothin' on wi' yer,' offered Gideon. 'Just wait while I fetch Finn for yer.'

Sarah straightened her back and steeled herself. 'No, thank you, it's alright – I'd rather go alone.'

Gideon nodded. 'Only fair to hear what he's been wantin' to say. Any trouble an' we be just here, my dear. He'll be havin' me to answer to if he harms yer.'

They watched Sarah leave the caravan and walk steadily towards the woods where Jack could be seen sitting on a log. As she approached him, they saw him stand up and light a cigarette.

Colette turned to Gideon. 'What did he really say to you?' she demanded 'I can't imagine that creep saying he's come to make his peace – what did he really come for?'

272

'Happen yer could try thinkin' the best o' folks 'stead o' the worst o' folks all the while. Them's as bad ain't always bad, that's what I believe anyway, though it be hard, I know.'

'You have to learn by your experience!' cried Colette. 'I thought you in particular would know that, since you've been on the road all your life and probably seen more than we have!'

Gideon looked incredibly tired. He gazed at her sadly and sighed. 'Seems to me the more I sees o' life the more I know's I ain't learned nothin' that explains the ways o' the world. There ain't no reason or logic in it – all I know is, if folks want to be happy then they needs other folks to care a bit for 'em 'cos bein' alone – that be the worst of it.' As he spoke, he was thinking that now Jack had turned up, Sarah might not be coming along with him after all. Sadness overcame him for a moment at the thought of heading off alone again. In all his life, ever since he had lost his wife, there wasn't anything he wanted more than to have Sarah by his side.

'That doesn't make sense!' retorted Colette indignantly. 'You have to learn by your experience, and when someone like that man ...' She stabbed a finger in the direction of the woods. 'When someone like that loser ruins his life and everyone else's out of pure selfishness and greed, he doesn't deserve to be happy!'

Gideon was about to reply when Sarah re-appeared at the caravan door. Her face was white and her hands shook but she managed a weak smile. 'It's OK. He's gone,' she said simply.

'Gone?' chorused Colette and Bianca together, 'Why? What happened?'

'I heard what he had to say,' she said and sat down next to Gideon. 'He asked me to take him back – at first. He said he'd got a new job down on the docks, on the east coast. Then he asked me if he could borrow some money. As if I had any!' She shrugged her shoulders. 'I asked him why he had never contacted me or asked about the children.' She raised her eyebrows. 'He seemed to have forgotten he had children!' She gave a little helpless laugh. 'I asked him if he'd heard they were both killed and he said he had and that he was sorry. But when I said it wasn't true and that they were both alive and well, he wasn't really surprised or even interested. He was hardly listening in fact...' She pulled a face, imagining what she said had hurt Colette's feelings very much and she whispered hastily to her, 'I'm sorry, love. That's what he's like though.'

'Didn't he want to see us though?' asked Colette. 'Didn't you tell him we were here? What about Finn?' She looked around. 'Where is Finn by the way? He ought to speak to him!' Sarah shook her head. 'I don't know. I'm afraid that just proves it though – all Jack's interested in is money, that's all he ever wanted – he'll never change.'

'But what will happen now? What about when me and Mum go home to the flat and see him there?' asked Colette. 'What on earth will I say to him?'

Sarah turned to look at her and was genuinely concerned. 'I don't think you'll see him there again. When I said he's gone, I meant he's gone for good. He's not going back to Tollwithen. He said he's hitch-hiking to Dover. He's got a new job in the dockyard, or that's what he told me. He wanted some money to get himself set up there – get himself somewhere to live –

though he wanted to get a drink more likely.'

Colette started crying. Bianca reached across and took her hand. 'Don't cry, darling! You didn't know him and as it turns out perhaps it's best you didn't.'

She caught Sarah's eye and they exchanged glances as though they understood each other.

'But...' she sobbed. 'I thought he would want to see me!' she said. 'And I always wanted *someone* to be my dad.' She sniffed and tried to recover herself. At least he could have asked to see me – and Finn! But he wasn't interested in either of us at all! He didn't even care!' And she broke down and sobbed even louder.

Bianca caught Sarah's eye again and smiled sadly. 'Sometimes, darling, when we finally get what we want, we understand that we didn't want it after all.'

Gideon smiled. The colour had come back to his cheeks and his eyes almost sparkled. He turned and looked at Bianca affectionately and said, 'That be about the best thing I've heard all day. Think on it, an' let's be havin' ourselves a cup o' tea.'

However, when Finn heard what had happened he rushed out, called to Danny to give him a lift and they drove after him. They hadn't gone far when they caught up with Jack hitchhiking by the side of the road. Finn already knew Drew Caudry, a regular at the pub, as a popular but sometimes troublesome character who often drank too much. He had heard only the gist of his mother's story but it was enough to make him realize the truth – that Drew was his father. As soon as Jack saw the car coming he began thumbing a lift. Danny pulled up sharply alongside, skidded to a halt and Finn jumped out. 'Not propping up the bar today then,

Drew?' he said.

Jack eyed him suspiciously, glanced back at the driver in the car and perhaps realized he was in trouble. It was the expression on Finn's face which probably caused him to involuntarily reach for his cigarettes as a gangster might reach for a gun. He took on a blank, guarded expression, put a cigarette between his lips, and squinted at Finn. Exhaling a cloud of smoke in Finn's face, he said, 'Your day off from the kitchen then is it?'

'No. Can't afford to have too many days off. I've got a family to keep now,' he replied, biding his time.

'Congratulations,' said Jack flatly, staring at him coldly. 'Rather you than me. There ain't nothin' like bein' free to do what you want wi' no family ties – you should try it. Free as a bird I am! I'm off to Dover, hitching a lift down there. Want to join me? We'd make a good team you an' me. There's plenty o' work down the docks in Dover, an' when that's done we can hitch-hike up to Felixstowe or cadge a ferry to Calais – plenty o' casual work there if yer don't mind getting your hands dirty – good money too.'

Finn stared at him. 'No thanks. I heard you had a family once,' he said without so much as a quiver of fear.

'Oh yeah? Who told yer that?' A dark shadow swept across Jack's face.

'Word gets around,' Finn replied. 'Y'know what folks are like. When I was a kid, someone started a rumour that my dad had killed someone in a fight down the pub. I never did think it were true. My poor mother told me he were dead – drowned at sea like – an' I believed her. Little boys'll believe anythin' their

276

mother tells 'em.'

'What the bloody hell are you talkin' about?' said Jack, drawing long and hard on his cigarette.

'I'm talkin' about you... Dad.' Finn paused. Memories of the past stole his courage, but only for a moment. 'You are my dad, ain't' yer? Seems some rumours are true after all.'

'Bloody hell! Who are you?' he hissed, spitting his cigarette out and lurching towards him, clenching his teeth. His hands were flexing and tightening up into great clumsy fists.

'You wouldn't hit me, would you – Dad? If it weren't for Gideon takin' care of me I wouldn't be here – I'd be dead more like, after all that's happened to me. An' my poor mum! Why did yer treat her like that? Why did yer leave her with no money for food an' spend it all on drink an' keep getting' into fights?'

'People are always ready to put the blame on other folks. Why did I drink myself stupid an' get into debt an' ruin my life? Because I was a loser, son. Other people could put a tenner on the horses an' win a stack o' cash an' me? I'd lose it wouldn't I? – Every time! The odds were against me Finn, ever since the day I was born. Look at my brother Albert. He could buy a colt for fifty quid an' chances are it would turn out a real winner an' he'd sell it for five hundred! Me? I'd get the runt. Either it would go lame, get the colic, or be too spirited – kick someone in the head an' most likely have to be shot. That's how life is with me – nothin' works out. Count yourself lucky, Finn. You've landed on your feet an' kept yourself out of trouble. So...' He stared at him and said, 'Do you still want to know why I'm like I am?'

'Don't you want to tell my mother? Don't you want to explain to her? Don't you want to see my sister, Colette?'

'Who? Look, Finn. I've done my time in the clink. I've paid my dues, got a job to go to. I don't owe nothin' to nobody.'

'Don't you want to tell my mum you're sorry?'

Jack shook his head. 'I've said all I want to say to her. What's done is done an' I can't help who I am. Too old to change now, eh?' He attempted a smile, and stepping towards Finn he held out his hand. 'I'll be on my way then. No hard feelings?'

Finn looked at his hand which minutes before had been a clenched fist. Years ago he remembered when Gideon had reached out to shake his hand. He had been a stranger then and yet had shown him such sympathy and respect. He remembered the gypsy's kind honest understanding – the quiet compassion he had shown him even though he was only a boy, a frightened runaway boy who thought he had caused the death of his sister by his own immature foolishness. *"Shake old Gideon's hand now, because I be a gentleman, an' you, my young fella, you be a gentleman too in my opinion!"*

He looked at Jack's hand again. He looked up into the steely eyes, and without offering his hand in return he turned away from him and walked back to the motor where Danny was waiting for him. With a loud screech of wheels, Danny reversed the vehicle, did a U-turn and sped back towards the camp. As he drove, Danny glanced across at Finn fleetingly, but neither of them said a word.

Colette saw them arrive back at the camp and hurried to

find out if they had any more news. Perhaps she was hoping her brother had made some impression on their father; her indignation at being ignored by Jack had hurt more than just her pride. Perhaps she vainly hoped he had had a change of heart and expressed a wish to see her after all.

'So what did he say?' she demanded as soon as they emerged from the motor.

Finn bit his lip. He didn't want to tell her how callous and off-hand Jack had been.

'Not much really,' he replied. 'He was goin' off to work an' he was in a hurry so...'

'What are you saying? Are you saying he didn't have time to speak to us? After all these years he couldn't even spare a minute?' She was about to break down but, as she often did, she disguised it with a flaring temper. 'He always had plenty of time before, when he was hanging around us in that stinking flat, smoking his cigarettes and strutting about as if he was God's gift to women. I hate him! Oh, how I hate him!' The tears came at last, putting an end to her torrent of words and releasing all the pain and sense of injustice she felt. She cried in despair as though nothing could comfort her.

Danny, who had been standing by watching with dark soulful eyes, nodded to Finn and stepped towards her. He put an arm around her and as naturally as horses respond to each other, she turned and rested her head on his shoulder. Danny winked at Finn and brought his other arm round her, enclosing her in a circle of security. 'It's not fair!' she sobbed. 'It's just not fair!'

'Shouldn't go cryin' over a bastard like that,' said

Danny. 'Better off without 'im from what I've seen of 'im.'

Colette didn't reply but she buried her face in Danny's chest as the new sensation of manly strength aroused her. Her senses were raw. She kept weeping, but her sobs quietened. His leather jacket pressed against her cheek; the new scent of masculinity, of motor oil, horses and tobacco entered her world for the first time. Soon her tears subsided but she remained enclosed in Danny's arms. Finn, evidently respecting their new found privacy, mumbled something about seeing to the horse and wandered off back to the caravan.

'Want to come for a ride then?' Danny asked her, releasing her and jangling his keys. Colette's face emerged from his jacket, blotched and tear stained. 'I don't know,' she said. 'Mum might be ready to go home. '

'It's OK, I'll run you both back when you're feeling better. Come on, girl, blow a few cobwebs away. That bloke ain't worth cryin' over. Ready?'

As though entranced, Colette followed him to the motor, drying her eyes as though suddenly the landscape had transformed itself into somewhere magical.

'Oh, I'd better just tell Mum where I'm going!' she exclaimed.

'Nah!' he said. 'Don't bother, we won't be long, girl. Jump in!'

He turned the ignition, the engine started up and they were off. As soon as they had picked up speed, all thoughts of telling her mother where she was were forgotten.

Twenty-Two

At dawn, having been woken by a lot of noise, Gideon pulled on his boots, climbed out of the caravan and was just in time to see Albert's trailer pulling out onto the road.

'Hey Bert!' he called. 'You be headin' north or where?'

'Land's End, brother!' shouted Albert, stopping the trailer at an angle on the grass verge and climbing out to speak to him. He came back across the grass and reaching Gideon, looked at him curiously. 'What's goin' on wi' yer lady friend then?' he asked. 'She be going wi' yer or what?'

Gideon nodded and his face crinkled into a smile. 'No-one's forcin' her! She be goin' to tag along o' me for a while, see how the land lies yonder.'

Albert nodded. 'Good man,' he said. 'But don't let her boss yer about like my woman do me, eh?'

'I won't,' replied Gideon, smiling. 'Reckon some folks need to be together, an' I ain't complainin'.'

'Right then,' said Albert, turning back to the trailer. But having taken only a few steps, he stopped again. 'Danny's gone into town – apparently he needs some spare parts from the garage.' He raised his eyebrows. 'Spare parts indeed! I've heard that before!' Reaching the trailer he climbed up laboriously, since his old arthritic frame appeared to struggle at the

281

sudden exertion. Re-starting the engine, he called from the window, 'I'll be seein' yer, brother! Hope you're in a better temper next time,' he added knowingly, rubbing the bruise on his chin in an exaggerated fashion and grinning. They both knew what he meant.

Gideon waved. 'Won't be long afore our paths cross again, I don't doubt,' he replied, but he was unable to make himself heard above the noise and chuckled to himself as he watched Albert drive off. Returning to the caravan he found Sarah emerging from her tent with a shawl wrapped around her shoulders. 'What was all that commotion about?' she asked.

'They all be goin' on their way, my dear. Reckon Danny might catch 'em up later; Bert said he's gone into town. Finn an' Mitzi will be goin' back home today. Finn's got it in 'is head to be learnin' to drive a motor. Happen Danny'll soon be back in town to show 'im how.' He smiled wearily. 'Yer needn't be a worryin' over Finn, he's a sensible lad. Seems Danny's taken a shine to Colette though...'

'Colette was looking a bit starry eyed last night, wasn't she! Well, if Danny teaches Finn to drive, it might be a good thing – now he's got a family.'

Gideon disagreed. 'Nothin' wrong with an old 'orse, so far as I can see.'

Sarah shook her head. 'It's different for the youngsters though, Gideon. Times are changing. They'll all move on, you'll see.' She looked at him steadily. 'Then it'll be just you, me and the old horse.'

'Happen so,' he replied. 'Have us some peace and quiet again, eh my dear?'

But Finn didn't go back to town that day. Seeing Albert

282

leave, he told Mitzi it would be good for them to stop the night and spend some more time with Sarah. He set about making them a tent out of branches and tarpaulin, as they had for Sarah when she arrived. He was as skilled as Gideon now in the craft of weaving willow. When it was finished he made a fire and they sat down to reflect on their future.

'I hope it's the right thing I'm doing, agreein' to stay at the pub. But I couldn't be leavin' a good job like that now we've got our baby to look after. If I wasn't workin'…'

Mitzi glanced at him. 'But we don't want to stop in the pub forever, Finn. Your room ain't big enough for kiddies, you said so yourself.'

'No, but if I keep workin' we'll save up an' get us a bigger place to live. Durin' the day I can find us some fruit-pickin' an' potato pickin', an' then work for Fred in the evenin'. Now he's hired me to play the fiddle on Saturday nights as well I'm earning a bit more. He might give me more time playin' if the customers like it. We'll have to mind our pennies though Mitzi, now we're a family. '

Mitzi lifted her face up towards him, a little frown creasing her brow. 'I could earn a bit too. I liked makin' them paper flowers Dulcie showed me, Finn. Reckon I could sell some o' them door to door like a proper gypsy? If I can sell chocolate an' ice-creams I don't see why I couldn't do that.' But Finn was lost in thought. She tried again, gently stroking the baby's head as he lay sleeping peacefully in the wicker cot Finn had made. 'I love it here, sleepin' in the tent in the open-air an' eatin' round the fire. Them other gypsy kids seem real healthy, well, they would be wouldn't

283

they, wiv all the fresh air an' that. Reckon he'll be healthy too if we could live like this,' she reasoned, 'an' we wouldn't have no rent to pay an' no stupid landlord breathin' down our necks. We wouldn't need too much money then eh?'

'We can't live like Gideon has all his life. He's told me – he wants me to have a family an' settle down an' that's what we're goin' to do ain't it? The gypsy blood ain't got into you, has it, my girl?'

'Perhaps it has, Finn,' she replied, looking away from him wistfully. 'I hope we'll be OK. Our son's got the gypsy blood in him though, ain't he? That means he'll like livin' in the caravan, playin' in the fresh air an' sleepin' under the stars. You liked it too, when you was a boy. You told me you loved it, bein' wiv Gideon an' bein' free.'

Finn smiled. 'Yeh, but one day, y'know, when I've saved up a bit o' money, I could buy us a motor an' a posh trailer wi' showers an' a kitchen an' that. Danny's fair taught me a bit about motors already – how the engine works, an' reckons I'll soon be able to drive one. Would you like that, my girl? Drivin' along in a motor-car like a real lady?' He kissed her lightly on the lips and she giggled.

Musing for a bit, he sat back as though the possibilities were almost within his reach. He was paring a stick with his pocket-knife but eventually he put down the stick and turned to her. 'I ain't gonna give up my job. I've got to take care o' you an' the baby an' earn enough money to find us a real home of our own wi' a nice fireplace an' a garden for him to play in an' a nice kitchen for you to do some cookin'.' He stopped talking and looked at her. 'Yer trust me, don't yer, to

284

work hard and get us a proper place? We don't want to be wanderin' around the lanes not knowin' where our next meal's comin' from – not when we've got our little one to think of, eh?'

'But you said you loved it Finn, when you was with Gideon an' goin' huntin' an' catchin' rabbits an' all that stuff.'

'I did but I can't be goin' back to that life. I've grown to like livin' in a house an' I want to do what Gideon wants me to do, not what Albert wants 'cos Albert can't see no other way. Gideon wants me to make a life for myself – for us – an' put down some roots. I owe it to him for takin' care o' me and I owe it to you and our baby there to make sure you're safe an' got a proper home to go to at night when it's cold an' dark.'

'Yeh, but you said...' Mitzi began but Finn silenced her with a kiss. 'We'll be a real family. You'd like a nice house an' a motor one day wouldn't yer?' he asked, smiling, and taking up the violin, he smoothed its burnished body, tuned it and took up the bow. Mitzi, sighing contentedly, picked up the sleeping child and settled back nursing him while Finn began to play. The first strains of a lullaby escaped into the fresh Cornish air. The baby stirred and threw one tight little fist up, arched his back and stretched, and then, as if sleepiness had won him over, he relaxed and lay quietly in her arms again.

Gideon was sitting with Sarah by the fire drinking tea. 'Do yer hear that boy play now!' he said. 'I've been missin' the sound o' that fiddle since young Finn left. Tis good to have him here again for a bit.'

'I'd never have known he could play like that!' replied Sarah. 'That night, when the baby was so poorly, I was afraid he was going to die. It's incredible how he started to come to life when Finn began to play the fiddle!'

Gideon was pleased. 'Sometimes it stirs the soul, good music,' he replied. 'Gives us hope an' makes the heart beat a little faster, eh? When he were a boy, as soon as he touched it he could play it. There be no explainin' it. Some folks 'ave the gift, my dear, yer can tell.'

Sarah took a deep breath and launched into something which must have been on her mind.

'You're a good man, Gideon. Tell me, what happened to your young wife? Albert said it had been hard.'

'It were hard, an' some say it were on account o' me fallin' for the wrong girl. When I met Sonya, my parents, God bless 'em, they wouldn't have it. She weren't a Romany yer see, but I loved her more than my own life. Happen they didn't understand that. They said I'd be dead in their eyes if I were to marry her. They didn't want no more o' me. It weren't easy, but I had to make the choice between Sonya and my parents.'

'So you went and married her anyway?'

'No, my dear. We were like any man an' wife should be, but no, we had no ceremony. We had no money for all that. Even so, she were a good wife to me while she were alive.'

'What happened to her?'

'She died tryin' to bring our baby into the world.'

Sarah put a hand on his arm. 'I'm sorry.'

286

'Poor Sonya! She were a good gal, an' she'll be up there waitin' for me when I return. Her an' our own lost baby, an' my ma an' pa, an' my gran'father – they'll all be there. There's comfort to be had from that.' He sighed as though contemplating a long awaited dream. 'It won't be too long now – my returnin',' he said. 'I can feel it in my bones.'

'Not yet awhile, I hope,' she said, casting a curious eye at him. But Gideon said nothing more.

For a long time she sat mute, mixed emotions flickering across her face as wave after wave of sadness and excitement seemed to wash over her. This whole world, of Gideon and the Romany gypsies, it all seemed somehow to justify her own suffering – as if their struggles were all wrapped up in her own. It was as if they had shared their lives after all.

'Why did Sonya die,' asked Sarah, 'when she was in labour? She must have suffered so much, the poor girl!'

'The baby were all wrong inside of her, just like some lambs be either growin' the wrong way or tangled up inside. No, my dear, there weren't no way of savin' her.'

'But didn't you fetch a doctor?' demanded Sarah in dismay.

Gideon raised his head and looked straight at her realizing she was criticising him. 'I'd already been for the doctor. I galloped all the way till the 'orse were in a sweat. They come out to her alright – the doctor an' the midwife wi' their strong smellin' stuff, givin' their orders and tellin' her how to breathe.' He stopped speaking for a moment as the vivid memory of that night came back to him. His eyes watered and he choked a little and shifted on his seat before continuing. 'They was goin' to operate but it were all too much for my Sonya an' afore they could do anythin' more she squeezed my hand an' she sort o' smiled at me an' just fell asleep. So gentle she went – like she were sort o' happy to let go.' He shuddered, the grief catching him for a moment. 'Peace an' rest. It were what she needed.'

Sarah gasped. 'Oh, but no! The baby!' she cried. 'Didn't they manage to save the baby?'

He shook his head. 'They tried to get 'im out it were too late – it were how things had to be. He sniffed and wiped his nose on his sleeve. 'Who knows the way o' things? It's nature what tells us what to do an' how to live. Like the sea, when the storm be lashin' and tearin' at the shore one minute an' the next it turns an' licks our feet like a kitten. Happen we don't understand the way o' the world an' how some things just 'ave to be.'

'I'm sorry! I'm so sorry! I didn't mean to upset you.'

'It all comes right in the end, my dear. We all be goin' back to the soil, an' the leaves'll cover us over. One day the sun'll go down on the name o' Rabbiter, an' that'll be the start an' finish of it all.'

'No, don't say that, please!' she protested.

'There ain't no stoppin' it, Sarah. The wheel be turnin', always turnin', but nothin' as needs to worry about. That's the way of it.'

Perplexed, she stood up and set about making their breakfast. She took some bread from the tin and said. 'I'll make some toast when the fire gets going but we'll need some more wood,' she said.

'I'll fetch some,' he replied. 'Won't be long. You hungry?'

Sarah shook her head. 'Not really.'

'Yer need to eat. There be a good day ahead of us, to get packed up an' ready for the morrow.'

'What's tomorrow?' she asked.

'Finn and Mitzi, they'll be goin' back to town in the mornin'. Then we'll be off on the road too, eh?' He smiled at her. 'Yer still want to come along wi' me?'

'Of course I do.'

While Gideon went to fetch the wood, a thought struck him. It was the sudden realization that he wasn't quite as comfortable with his destiny as he once was. Even though he had told Sarah that his returning was going to be soon – and he firmly believed it was – for the first time in years, he really wanted to go on living for a while longer. Sarah and her companionship had given him new hope for the future. He wanted to care for her, to see that she wasn't left alone any more. And there was something else. He had never been a man who doubted his own decisions, but circumstances recently had made him think and question his own wisdom. When he came back carrying an armful of wood, he saw her sitting there waiting for him expectantly and his heart skipped. He was growing so fond of her with her quiet ways and her gentle companionship.

'I must be goin' soft in my old age,' he said as he set about starting the fire.

'Oh why? Have you forgotten something?' She seemed relieved that practical things had to be attended to and she put the pans out ready to start cooking.

'There be somethin' on my mind what I can't get

round,' he began.

She looked up. 'What is it?'

'I promised my pa I'd take that fiddle to the grave wi' me.'

'Yes, I remember.'

'I told Finbarr he'd best burn it in the fire when I'm gone, along with the caravan an' all my other… '

'Yes, Gideon, you told me,' she replied. 'You'll feel better when we've had some supper. I'll warm the soup so we can…'

'I shouldn't have!'

He sat down and stared at the ground for a while. When he raised his head, his eyes were filled with tears. 'I'm sorry my dear.'

'What's the matter?' she asked in dismay. 'You mean you wish you hadn't told me, is that it?'

He shook his head. 'No, no, happen I shouldn't have made Finn promise. Fact is, he needs that fiddle to keep playin'. It's part of him now an' he can earn money with it for his family. It'll be summat to fall back on, summat to carry 'im through storms an' troubles ahead for when I ain't here. If he has that fiddle, well, be like I were still here with 'im, lookin' after 'im like.' Gideon's shoulders sagged and his tears fell like melting ice on his dry weathered face.

Sarah, so moved by his honesty, reached out and took hold of his hand. 'You mustn't worry,' she said. 'If you gave your father your word you must stand by it. Finn will respect that. He'll be alright, you'll see. He can get himself another fiddle to play.'

Gideon recovered a little and smiled sadly. 'Yeh, but another one – it won't be the same. It won't have my gran'father's spirit, nor his history in it. I tell yer,

290

Sarah, my dear, I wish I'd never made the lad promise. It were wrong o' me.'

'Well then,' she replied. 'If you've changed your mind, why don't you tell him? Tell him tomorrow before he leaves. That'll put your mind at rest won't it?'

He nodded and felt his mood lifting. 'Happen I will then. We're all family in the end, my dear, an' he should keep it by him after all. That's only right an' natural, eh?'

The caravan was packed, the harness waxed and polished, and the horse well-groomed and fed. All was ready for an early start. Finn and Mitzi would share breakfast with them before they too would say their goodbyes and be on their way, back to town for Finn to start work again.

That night, when Sarah was asleep and all was quiet in the camp, Gideon awoke in a sweat. He had dreamt that his grandfather had gone back into the fire. But as he lay in bed recovering from the fright, he began to feel unwell. He got up, drank thirstily from the cold water casket by the caravan door, and went quietly over to the tent to reassure himself that Sarah was still there. The grass was wet with dew and soaked his feet but he saw she was sleeping peacefully so he returned to the caravan and tried to settle down. Far away, an owl hooted and close-by, the sudden bark of a fox sounded raw. It filled him with dread. Again his mind wandered in a fever and he tossed and turned in his trestle-bed. Drifting off to sleep, he heard the jangle of fairground music. It was as though he was back working on the carousel with his father. 'Come on an' get yourselves a ride!' he mumbled in his sleep.

'Sixpence a ride! Come on now!' Then an image of Sonya, young and dark and defiant, suddenly stood before him. She was laughing, teasing him with her hands on her hips and her dark hair falling about her face. He called out to her, 'Sonya!' Sonya!' and she threw her sixpence at him, giggling.

He came to with a start and shook his head, feeling hot and dizzy. Sweat stood on his brow and his chest felt tight and heavy. He rose from his bed unsteadily, went to drink the cool water again and climbed back into his bed. Then the heavy pain came, as though something was pressing down on him. 'Sonya!' he cried. This time she was with child, moaning with pain in the strong throes of labour. He must run for the doctor... he must... But he couldn't breathe...

Suddenly Dulcie appeared and he sighed and lay back with relief.

'Don't you be grieved,' she said. 'Sonya's at her peace now. Her pain's gone an' she's sleepin' in a better place, dearie.' She patted his hand as though the quick little pats were somehow conveying a message. 'What I'm sayin' is, she's passed over. Your Sonya's gone to her rest.'

'Gone?' He tried to sit up but his chest was so heavy he could barely move with the weight of it. 'No, Dulcie, no, she ain't gone I'm tellin' yer!'

'There was nothin' more we could do, love,' she said. 'She's gone an' taken the little one with her. God bless their little hearts, the pair o' them. They'll be company for each other on the way.'

Gasping, Gideon tried to sit up. He needed to get some air. But the fairground carousel ride kept going round and round in his head making him dizzy... the music grew louder and louder... the children were squealing, the lights were blinding...

'Sonya!' he roared into the darkness. A sudden piercing pain in the chest caught him like a stab wound and he cried out: 'Sonya! Sonya, where are you?'

A woman appeared. Her face was pale in the moonlight. She had a shawl drawn tightly around her thin body. 'Gideon! What on earth's the matter?

'Oh, Sonya, my dear, I knew you'd come!' he muttered, falling back on the pillow with a sigh.

'No Gideon! It's me, Sarah! You've been dreaming, that's all,' she cried, bending down to him and bringing her face close to his. 'See? It's me! Do you have a pain?' she asked, placing a hand on his forehead. His lips quivered and trembled as he tried to speak and he turned to look at her with wild tormented eyes.

'Would you like some water?' she asked and went to fill his cup. When she helped him sit up, he drank clumsily, 'Ah, that's good, Sonya! That's very good!'

Perplexed, Sarah said, 'It's me, it's Sarah here, Gideon, not Sonya. You've had a nasty dream, that's all. Do you feel any better now?'

'Ah, Sarah, yes, of course. I'm sorry.' Shivering now he wrapped himself in the blanket and settled down again. Her presence made him feel better and he reached for her hand and said:

'Goodnight my dear, sleep well and don't yer go worryin' yerself no more.'

'Are you sure you're alright?' she asked.

'I be as well as any old fool could be, see if I

293

can't find myself a bit o' camomile tomorrow – always swore by a bit o' camomile, my gran'father did.'

'Goodnight then,' she said. 'Call me if you need anything.'

With an anxious glance across her shoulder, she went back to her tent, but on returning to her bed, she found the happiness that had flooded through her the previous day had been so quickly driven away. The fact that Gideon wasn't well robbed her of any sleep. She lay awake for hours worrying and listening for him. She heard the strange sounds of the night, an occasional passing car, the rustle of a hedgehog, the hoot of an owl. Presently she rose from her bed, draped her shawl about her and went to take a look at him again. To her relief he was quiet and sleeping peacefully. She went back to her bed yet still she lay awake, longing for the first glimpse of light, for the first note of a bird-call heralding the dawn. More than anything she longed for when she would hear him up and about early, collecting dry wood from under the hedges, the clank of the water-can as he filled the kettle for their tea, the crackle of sticks as he set the fire. Eventually she must have drifted off because when she awoke again it was broad daylight and sunshine was streaming in through the tent. So relieved that at last it was a new day, she climbed out of bed and went outside. There was no sign that anyone was up and the blackened charcoal patch on the grass remained from the night before. Climbing the steps to Gideon's caravan, she found him still wrapped in his blanket and fast asleep. Of course he was tired, she thought, he had been up half the night. She smiled to herself and crept over to him quietly. She was almost upon him, her heart bursting with affection when she saw that his sleeping face was bluish white, as though it was cast in wax.

'Gideon?' she whispered. A cold shudder ran through her. 'Gideon?' she cried, louder now, her heart pounding. She touched his cheek. He was as cold as iron. A cry rose from her throat; a desperate haunting cry, like a wild bird breaking cover when the shots are fired. 'No!' she cried. 'No, it can't be! Tell me it's not true!' But he didn't move. She shook him, calling his name again and again. But the only answer came from far away across the fields: the eerie cry of a curlew calling. And then silence.

Finn was awake, with Mitzi in his arms and the baby sleeping in the wicker cot he had made for him. Suddenly he heard a woman scream. 'What was that?' he cried. 'Something's wrong!' He scrambled out of bed and pulled on his jeans. Diving out of their tent, he stopped and listened – nothing. There was no-one about. 'Hello?' he shouted. No response. He stood looking around, sniffing the air much as a hound would do. Mystified, he drew near Gideon's caravan, and then he heard the sound of a woman sobbing. It was a sound at once familiar and strange. So many years ago he had heard his mother crying in the kitchen. It was a desolate, lonely sound and it made the hairs stand up on the back of his neck. When he climbed the steps and entered the dim interior, it was difficult for him to see.

'Are you alright?' he asked, blinking, trying to see.

But before Sarah even had time to turn round, he

saw the humped, blanket bound shape of Gideon on the trestle-bed. He moved closer, and as he did so, Mitzi came up the steps behind him, holding the baby. She stopped at the open door, and the morning sun sent a shaft of light, as sharp as a sword, across Sarah's shoulder and directly onto the gypsy's face. Finn caught his breath. 'No!' he said quietly under his breath, 'No! You can't go now! You can't!'

Mitzi went to his side and tried to speak. Her voice was broken and husky and tears overwhelmed her. Finn's strong arms enveloped her and the baby, in a huddle of comfort.

'Bless 'im,' said Mitzi, beginning to weep. 'He's gone, ain't he? He looks just as peaceful as anyone could do, don't he?' She reached out for Sarah and hugged her too. After a while, overcoming her own tears, she took Sarah outside.

Alone with Gideon, Finn stood motionless. He couldn't comprehend what had happened. He had found his mother, discovered his sister was alive, and he had a new baby son. He felt he should have been ready for this, that he should be stronger and yet – Gideon was the key to unlocking all the wrongs of the past. Gideon was his future – he wanted to prove to him that he could work hard and make him proud of him. Sadness and despair welled up inside him – that Gideon should leave them now! He felt like shouting: Why now? But instead he turned away, remembering his promise. It was the last thing Gideon had trusted him to do. So he left the caravan to fetch what he knew Gideon needed for the final time. Passing the two women, both weeping, he saw his baby son was awake; his blue innocent eyes were scanning the morning sky in curiosity and wonder.

Within minutes he returned to the caravan carrying the violin. He raised the bow and began to play. Louder and louder, more and more desperately he played, all the while watching the dark shape of Gideon's body as though somehow expecting the music to bring him back to life. The two women joined him as he played, sitting together by the bedside. When Mitzi gave Sarah the baby to hold, her tears subsided. Finn played on and on, but the old gypsy's face remained motionless, as smooth and white as marble. Finn knew Gideon's soul was returning to the place he had longed for; the place Sonya had been keeping for him, the place beside his grandfather. So he kept playing to accompany him on that final stretch of open road.

The golden days of Romany were over. While Finn played, Gideon's soul sank back into the earth. The time had come for him to return to the land of his ancestors. Before him had gone generations of gypsies who were pure in heart and simple in their beliefs. They were at one with nature and at odds with the engulfing tide of modern life. Never again would Gideon rise from his bed at dawn, collect dry sticks to make a fire. But even so, his spirit would hover in the shadows under the trees forever. His feet would tread gently, causing no more than a flurry of fallen leaves in the breeze.

Twenty-Three

News spread fast among the gypsy community of old Gideon's passing. Within three days, Albert and a convoy of vehicles arrived for the funeral. That evening there was a solemn gathering of the family round the fire. As it grew late, stories were told in hushed tones, the flames lapping at the shoreline of their memories. Finn sat with them and he felt at one with them, as if he had been a gypsy all his life. Beside him, Mitzi was breastfeeding their baby son. Nearby his mother Sarah was helping Dulcie with plans for the funeral. Romany tradition required that the gypsy's caravan should be set on fire and burnt. The arrangements were made as follows: Gideon would be buried in the churchyard of St. Bartholomew's Parish Church in Tollwithen. Afterwards, some refreshment would be provided at the camp and when the time was right, Gideon's caravan, along with his possessions, would be burned.

However, while the discussion was going on, Finn was worrying about something else. The women were planning the great fire and were busy sorting through Gideon's things. Finn knew the fiddle should be burnt too, but nothing was said about it. Suddenly he stood up and went to fetch it. He knew it was his responsibility to send it on its way, to its final resting place. Without saying a word, he tuned up and began to play *Amazing Grace*. He played with such sadness they all stopped talking and listened. When he finally stopped and sat down, it was Albert who broke the silence.

'Well now Finn!' he said. 'We have to take regard o' my cousin's wishes but I'll be honest with yer. That fiddle might be worth summat an' I ain't got the resources I once had. I'm thinkin' that it be criminal to burn it. That's all I'm sayin'. I don't mean nothin' by it, I'm just sayin'.'

Dulcie, as though already anticipating his remark, shook her head in disgust. 'If you're meanin' what I think you're meanin', my husband, well, you ought to be ashamed of yourself.'

'I'm not sayin' anythin' as what you ain't thinkin' already woman and don't try tellin' me different. We ain't so dumb as to think that musical instrument necessarily needs to be burned in the fire. All that superstitious stuff, bah! We've got responsibilities. Gideon will soon to be lying there in the good earth. He were a man who never turned his back on his responsibilities. So what I'm sayin' is – it would be ridiculous to burn it. Sacrilege, that's what it would be! We should sell it in a rightful an' proper manner and share what it fetches, seein' as we've got extra mouths to feed now, with him passin' on an' leavin' his family behind.' He waited now, to let his meaning sink in. He was, in fact, looking quite proud of himself for having put it so eloquently.

Dulcie exploded. 'You thieving pitiful, disrespectful, artless, little man!' she yelled. 'What you're really saying is you're goin' to nick that fiddle from under our noses an' fill your dirty pockets wi' the profits, you greedy little man. Is that how you're goin' to honour our dead cousin's memory? Poor Gideon who ain't even able to defend himself! You make me sick!' she bawled, and gathering up her full black skirt, she stormed off.

Finn was a bit taken aback. He decided to give Albert a chance to explain. 'Perhaps what you were gettin' at was you're thinkin' you'll have to take on the responsibility of me and Mitzi and the baby there, an' my mother too. But we ain't askin' you to look after us, Bert. I've got a job an' I'll be earnin' enough to keep us. You've no need to worry about us.'

Albert stood up and paced about in an agitated manner with his hands thrust in his pockets. He made a gesture with his head as though he had something to say in private. Finn, understanding him, followed him and they stopped a good distance away from the others.

'Well, who's goin' to take care o' that woman then?' demanded Albert when they were out of earshot. 'She were sort o' like his woman weren't she? Least that's what folks were sayin'.'

Finn thought quickly. 'I know he cared about my mother,' he replied. 'He wouldn't want her left alone wi' nowhere to go.' The proposal he had thought of putting to Albert was an important one. 'I don't mind lookin' after her. Mitzi an' me, we'll manage somehow. We're used to hard times an' my mother is too. But I can't let you sell Gideon's fiddle. I've got to put it in the fire. It were a promise I made to him an' I gave 'im my word.'

Albert was staring at him as though he was mad, but undeterred, Finn launched into what he had to say. 'That fiddle's goin in the fire, it's got to. But what

300

would you say if Mitzi an' me kept some o' Gideon's things? Them rugs an' blankets, we could use 'em for when we get ourselves a proper home. An' I'd be right proud to have his pocket-knife.' He paused, always unsure of Albert. 'Just a few bits to help out? We ain't' got much, startin' out with the new baby an' that.'

Albert scoffed. 'I don't know, Finbarr,' he replied, shaking his head, and sitting down on a tree-stump he began rolling a cigarette. 'Dulcie,' he shouted, 'Come here, woman!' She came across haughtily; her great bulk was swathed in black. 'Young Finn here,' said Albert, evidently believing he had gained an accomplice. 'He still says we got to burn that fiddle there, but thinks we might leave off burnin' some of our cousin's other things so he can have 'em for his family.' He hesitated, wondering if this new angle would direct the argument in his favour. 'If we don't burn everythin' though, we're goin' to burn in hell, ain't that what you say?'

'Burn in hell?' cried Dulcie, her chin wobbling. 'Why, you got enough cause to burn in hell already, my husband, even if you was to give up the tobacco and join a monastery this very night!' She laughed, a rippling laugh that quickly dissipated the brooding tension that had built up between them. She shook out her full skirts and wobbled her bosom back into shape. 'Look here, young Finn,' she said. 'If you want to take what you need for your family to start a new life, you take it. The burnin' of Gideon's fiddle an' his caravan will go ahead alright, but you see that your girl has what she needs first. Old Gideon won't mind partin' with a few odds an' ends, I knows him well enough for that.' She smiled as Mitzi came across with the baby.

301

'But as for that fiddle,' she said and suddenly gave her husband her full attention. 'That fiddle burns, right, Bert?'

'Huh! Suppose so,' he grumbled. 'Decent money goin' up in smoke. You're all bloody mad!'

'What's going on, Dulcie?' asked Mitzi.

Dulcie took hold of her arm. 'Finn's an honest fella. He's got his head screwed on. He ain't even tempted to take the easy way out, not like some I could mention. You stand by him, my dear, an' he'll take good care of you.'

Sarah came over and joined them, looking anxious and rather lost.

'And you, my dear,' said Dulcie, turning to her. 'Seems you've found your family again. Been a long time comin' but you'll be fine now, no need to fret no more! If Gideon do trust a person, then we all know that person's goin' be to alright. An' as for you, Albert – you can shut your face an' start doin' a bit o' work.'

Twenty-Four

Romanies gathered from miles around for Gideon's funeral. They crowded down the narrow streets of Tollwithen and packed the footpath through the churchyard leading to St. Bartholomew's Church. Finn stood firm with the violin tucked under one arm and the other arm around Mitzi's shoulders. The funeral directors wore black and carried the coffin slowly, with dignity. Sarah threw a posy of wild flowers in their path and the bearers responded by bowing their heads to her as a measure of respect.

As the coffin bearers came nearer, Mitzi whispered: 'You goin' to bury that fiddle with 'im then, Finn? You'll 'ave to go an' put it in his grave quick then, won't you, before they see you?'

'No, it's goin' in the fire tonight,' he replied, but even saying this, he was filled with trepidation. He couldn't bear the thought of burning it, even though he knew it had to be done.

Colette, who was standing nearby with Bianca, must have overheard because she came up and said in Finn's ear, 'You're not really going to put that in the fire are you? It might be valuable! Are you stupid or something?'

Finn glared at her. 'I'm not stupid, Colette. Gideon always said it's to go with him when he passes on an' I promised him I'd put it in the fire. Some things are worth more than money to some folks, an' you're the one who's stupid if you don't know no better.'

Astonished by his reply, she pulled a face. 'Why though? It doesn't make any sense! He won't know!'

Finn turned to her, his eyes blazing. 'Because I gave him my word, that's why.' At that moment he heard Gideon's voice in his head as clearly as though he was standing next to him. *"Sometimes yer 'ave to believe there's more to this old life than you can understand what's logical. Don't yer think so, lad?"*

Mitzi chimed in. 'Yeh! Colette's right, y'know Finn! You don't have to do it! We could sell it! Gideon wouldn't want us to go hungry!'

But Finn's confidence returned. He looked at them both sadly. 'Didn't I always tell you it's got to be done. I promised him! Now leave me alone!'

Stepping forward he followed the procession towards the church. But when the coffin bearers reached the door he stepped back and watched until the coffin disappeared into the dark recesses beyond. He couldn't bring himself to go in. He heard the organ music and the hymns being sung but overhead the raucous cries of rooks in the trees told him that his path lay elsewhere. It was time to say goodbye.

That evening, there was a large gathering of Romany family and friends. Colette appeared to have found solace in the company of Danny who made much of doting on her and paid little attention to Finn or anyone else. The occasion led to much eating, drinking and telling of stories. Even in grief, love and laughter eventually creeps in. The coming together of those souls left behind forges a new bond as the dead are allowed to slip away into the past. The future beckons the living, even as the sun rises on a new day.

Bianca noticed that Sarah was sitting alone. She went over to her and said, 'I'm sorry the way things have turned out. You were going to stay on with poor old Gideon weren't you?'

Sarah nodded and smiled sadly. 'There won't ever be another man like Gideon.'

'He was a bit of a dark horse,' replied Bianca. 'You couldn't help but trust him. Mind you,' she added, 'Colette took a while to take to him.'

'That girl's got a mind of her own,' Sarah replied and turning, looked Bianca straight in the eye. 'I'm so grateful to you, you know. You've brought her up to be a proper young lady. You can be proud of her – and I'm proud of her; thank you.' Sarah smiled and gave Bianca a hug. 'If she'd stayed with me, who knows how she would have turned out.'

'She would have been fine, I'm sure. Colette's strong you know. She would have coped with good times and bad. But you, Sarah darling, what are you planning to do now?'

'Oh, I'll go back to Plymouth I suppose. But I won't be the same person as when I left. My children are safe and happy, leading lives of their own. I've got nothing to fear now. I'll come back to Tollwithen and see them now and again. I'll be fine. You've no need to worry about me.'

'Then you'll come back and see us too? Come and stay with us, promise?'

'I promise.'

Bianca hugged her, kissed her on the cheek and left her to go in search of Colette.

Her daughter's fondness for Danny hadn't escaped her notice. She saw them together now, arms around each other, their presence merely shadows under the trees. They weren't joining the group by the fire, eating or drinking with the others. Their new found love had isolated them; they had eyes only for each other. Tears streamed down Bianca's cheeks, but they weren't tears for Gideon, they weren't for Colette or even for Sarah. They were for herself. She was so lonely. Without meaning to, she found herself wondering what Seamus was doing. Would he be lonely too, left in his flat with more time on his hands than he ever needed? Her thoughts were leaping ahead of her. So many times she had rekindled her memories of the night at rehearsals that ended when some crazy motorist ploughed into a pram. She remembered the evening he had come to dinner and proposed to her and she had been so off handed with him, so dismissive. Poor old Seamus! He'll never change I suppose. But then she stopped herself and wondered – but should I change?

*

After midnight, the festivities gave way to a more sombre task: the burning of Gideon's caravan. Finn put old Belle between the shafts of the caravan for the final time. He drove down the lane, accompanied by a few gypsies on foot, to a wooded clearing nearby. It was dark but there was a clear sky and the moon lit their way. There he unharnessed Belle, Gideon's old mare, and tethered her to a fence a safe distance away. The horse neighed and shifted, as though sensing the dramatic end to her working-life. 'Easy, easy,' said Finn, stroking her velvety nose and scratching behind her ears. 'You'll be goin' along with Bert old girl, so don't you fret.'

Leaving the mare he went back to find Mitzi who was standing under some trees with the baby wrapped in a shawl. He caught Albert's eye. As they had agreed, he took up the violin and began to play the Irish ballad: *Danny Boy*. Some of the gypsies joined in by singing. Then, with a heavy heart, he began playing Gideon's favourite hymn, *Abide With me*.

Albert struck a match, lit a taper of screwed up newspaper, and threw the flaming torch through the caravan door. A murmur of approval, like a salute to the great gypsy, rose up from the small crowd who had gathered there. A few applauded briefly. Almost immediately a roaring fire grew from within, flames licking up the sides hungrily as a crackling and roaring took up the old wood and turned the whole caravan into a furnace. The spectacle was reflected in all their eyes. Gideon's years of travelling the quiet leafy lanes became nothing more than pictures in the fire. Finn played on, driven by a desperate need to reach out to the old gypsy who had become not only his dearest friend but his father. Within minutes he knew he would have to sacrifice the violin and give it back to the history of his ancestors...

Suddenly he felt a hand on his arm.

'Finn?' said his mother. 'I know how you must be feeling; that fiddle's a part of you now. It must be so hard to let it go.'

He nodded. 'It has to be done though,' he said

and smiled sadly. 'Reckon old Gideon'll be watchin' me even now, makin' sure I put it in the fire, like I said I would.'

'You know what?' said Sarah. 'Just before he died, he told me he wished he'd never made you promise – because you need it. So…'

He looked at her intently. 'He was ill though; maybe he wasn't thinkin' straight. What would you do, if you were me?'

'I think it's your decision, Finn. You knew him better than anyone. He loved you; you were the son he never had.'

Finn turned towards the fire, choking with emotion. The heat scorched his face. With a rush of energy and grief raised his arm and shouted at the top of his voice, 'Gideon! Here it is! I've kept my promise!' and he hurled the violin into the flames.

As he watched it burn, his emotion subsided and a feeling of completion replaced his sorrow. Taking the bow and case, he threw them also into the fire and then turning to embrace his mother, he murmured, 'It's all over!'

For several minutes they stood watching the fire together in silence. Blades of grass around it took flame and kindled a few tiny fires which spread a few inches before fizzling out. Smoke billowed up into the star-lit sky. Gradually the whole structure was consumed. Soon the heat died away, bringing a darkening chill to that empty place. The caravan, just a blackened skeletal frame now, stood smouldering. Small clinking sounds were heard as the charred wood fell away from the steel rivets and the cold night air permeated the weak structure. The baby started to cry and Sarah turned to

Mitzi. 'I'll take him for you,' she said. 'You look after Finn.'

'Thanks,' she replied, handing the infant over to her.

Finn had walked away and was standing by the dying embers alone. Mitzi went up to him and put her arms around him. 'You did what he asked you, Finn,' she whispered, peering up into his face. 'He'll be happy, knowin' that.'

He didn't respond.

'I know how much Gideon meant to you,' she persevered. 'But I love you.'

He looked down at her and took her in his arms. 'I love you too,' he whispered. 'Mitzi? We'll be alright, won't we? Old Gideon, he'll be glad of us bein' together an' startin' our new life won't he... it's just that I...'

She nodded and kissed him. 'We'll be fine,' she whispered. 'Don't worry no more!'

As the fire died down, Finn returned to his mother's side. 'It'll seem funny, not havin' the fiddle to play. But he kept tellin' me how important it was, to look after it so he could return it to his gran'father. I gave him my word. It was the only thing he really cared about...'

'I think the only thing he really cared about was you,' replied Sarah.

'It was special, that fiddle, I don't know if I'll play another. But do you know what? I feel as though I've done the right thing. Something's changed. I feel that everythin's goin' to be alright now.'

In the glow of the dying fire, Finn saw his mother

smile; her face became transformed; her skin became smooth and her hair became tinged with gold. As tears of happiness wetted her cheeks, she looked young again, just as he remembered her.

'All those years ago,' she said. 'I left you alone with the baby and went to search for my purse – I've regretted doing that ever since. What was in it anyway? A few pounds! In going off to find that silly purse I lost everything I loved and cared for. I'd nothing left. All these years I've lived by myself, believing you and your sister were dead. But Gideon understood why I had to go back to find it. He understood why I was so desperate. He said it was just like when a horse has picked up a sharp stone. It can't think of anything else but the stone and the pain in its foot. My purse was like that stone. I'm sorry, Finn.'

'He was always kind an' forgivin'. He learned me lots o' things an' I ain't blamin' yer either for leavin' me to go an' find yer purse. I shouldn't have taken the pram out in the storm, but it's all in the past now. Put them memories away for old Gideon to look after eh?'

*

By the next morning, all the gypsies were quickly dispersing. Finn felt he had to go back one last time and take a look at where Gideon's journey had finally come to an end. Mitzi went with him.

The pungent smell of wood smoke still hung in the air as the clearing opened out before them revealing the remains of the steel frame, the scorched grass, and the patch of blackened earth left after the big fire. Finn could sense Gideon's spirit was there as clearly as if he were to emerge from the trees at any moment, bearing his old basket of mushrooms for breakfast.

'Just think,' Finn admitted, 'last night I almost thought Gideon was goin' to come walkin' out that fire! Him an' that fiddle of his!' he chuckled. 'Just can't believe he's really gone. Shows yer how daft I can get.'

'You ain't so stupid,' Mitzi replied, looking up at him with her usual innocent stare. 'I was half-expectin' to see him too.' She glanced into the woods. 'Do you think he's here somewhere, watchin' over us?'

Finn was just about to answer when he heard the leaves rustle in the undergrowth and some birds flew up in alarm. 'Sssh,' he said and nodded towards the shadows under the trees.

Glancing down he saw Mitzi was watching the space intently, with a little frown on her forehead. Suddenly he was overcome with love for her. 'Don't worry, he's not really comin'!'

She lifted her face to look at him. 'Do you think he can hear us though?' she whispered.

'Of course he can,' he replied, and sweeping her up in his arms he kissed her. 'Come on, let's go home; we're all done here.'

Twenty-Five

A few weeks had passed by when Finn, having just finished work in the kitchen, stepped outside for some fresh air. He saw his friend, Danny, leaning against the wall of the pub, smoking.

'Alright Danny? Phew! Don't ever get a job in a hot kitchen,' he said, pausing to take some deep breaths in the cool evening breeze.

'I won't mate, don't you worry,' replied Danny, tossing his cigarette-end away and straightening-up.

'Waitin' for Colette? Gettin' a bit late to be takin' her out now, ain't it?'

Danny shrugged. 'Could be.' He was unusually serious. 'How's the family doing?' he asked.

'Both fine, thanks. Colette an' Mitzi are probably up there in the room, gossipin' as usual. Want to go on up?'

Danny glanced at him uncertainly. 'Colette ain't up there, mate, she's at home, packing her bags.' He stared at Finn meaningfully. 'I've been waiting to talk to you, as it happens.'

'Packin'? What do you mean? Is she goin' away then? She never said anythin' to us.'

Danny stared at him. 'Look, mate. I'll tell you it straight. Colette's comin' away with me. She's leaving for good, tonight. We're heading up to North Wales. There's a farm up for auction;. there's a lot of machinery for sale. There'll be plenty o' scrap goin' beggin' if I'm right. Driving overnight's better. The roads are clear an' there ain't so many people about bein' nosy.'

'Why would Colette want to be goin' to an auction?'

Danny ignored the question. 'Thought I'd best let you know. She'll be OK, don't fret, I'll look after her.' He held out his hand as though it was to say farewell. 'Be seein' you, mate; don't let 'em work you too hard, eh? It ain't worth it.'

Finn took his hand but slowly, saying, 'So you mean Colette's goin' away to live with you? You mean you an' Colette are…? Why didn't she tell anyone? She would've told Mitzi at least, if that was true. How long have you been plannin' this?'

'Planning? I don't plan, mate. Life's too short. I told Colette I was movin' on tonight an' asked if she wanted to come along. She started on at me – like women do – so I say to her she can either come with me or stop if she wants. Sounds simple enough don't it? Well it is. She's decided she's comin' with me.'

The hairs stood up on Finn's neck. He took a step towards him, clenching his fists.

Danny's eyes narrowed. 'Let it go, Finn,' he growled. 'It's up to her what she does. She's all grown up now. I ain't forcin' her. It's a free country.'

'I know you an' her were gettin' it together a bit but I never knew it were that serious,' replied Finn. 'D'you love her then?'

'Serious? I don't know about serious! Love? Who knows. We get on OK, her an' me. She's a bit of a free spirit, like me. She'll be alright, don't worry. I'll feed

313

her when she wants feedin' and buy her a few pretty things. Women are easy enough to keep, like horses. Treat 'em gentle an' they'll follow you an' work hard – sure footed an' faithful, that's women.'

'You're wrong Danny. She wouldn't want to live like that. She won't want to leave Bianca on her own either. I'll go an' talk to her; make sure she knows what she's doin'. She can't go with you tonight.'

'Better hurry up then, mate. While you're at it, remind her I ain't forcin' her to come wi' me, but I bet she does.' He started to walk away, putting his hands in his pockets and whistling as though he hadn't a care in the world.

Finn ran up the stairs to tell Mitzi. He knew too well the string of girls who had been hurt by Danny in the past. Perhaps what attracted them was his cool detachment. Danny's quiet knowledge about things had impressed him too when he was younger. He had learned so much from him, tried to copy his ways, admired his skill with motor-cars and engines and envied him his experience with women. But taking his sister away without warning? That was different.

When Finn reached their flat, Mitzi was busy washing nappies. The room was full of steam and smelled of bleach. He found her with her sleeves rolled up revealing her plump little arms. Greeting him, she stopped her work for a minute, dabbed her rosy cheeks with her apron and kissed him. Her hair was wrapped in a towel and the spin drier was rattling and vibrating so much that she rushed back to it and stood holding it steady and giggling.

He went to her, cuddled her, but couldn't bring himself to tell her about Colette and Danny; it was

314

hopeless above the noise of the machine. He threw himself down in an armchair to think. After a few seconds he couldn't wait any longer and jumped up, and lifted the lid to stop the drier. 'I've just seen Danny outside. Did yer know him an' Colette were goin' away together? He's takin' Colette away with him tonight.'

Mitzi's shocked expression told him everything. 'You're kiddin'! I know she's crazy about him – everyone knows that – but I can't believe she'd run off with him! Are you sure?'

In all her innocence she seemed more excited than worried for Colette. 'That's what he said. I'm not sure I trust what Danny says anymore. I'll go and talk to her – make her change her mind.'

'Can you stop her going though?' asked Mitzi. 'I wonder what's come over her! She used to be so sensible! Much more sensible than me!' A mischievous giggle escaped her. 'That's what love does for yer I suppose!'

'I've got to stop her,' Finn said. 'I'll go now.'

'Tell her to come an' say goodbye before she goes!' Mitzi called as he went.

*

Colette was in her bedroom with the door closed. Bianca, assuming she was in one of her moods, knocked and called out:

'Have you got a minute darling? I've had an idea.'

Colette emerged looking flustered. 'What is it, Mum?'

'I was just thinking: we should decorate -

315

brighten up this old flat and drive away the cobwebs. White would be best, don't you agree, darling? White paint everywhere! We should be able to afford it; it's the cheapest paint going. We can start tomorrow by giving the whole place a spring-clean!' Her enthusiasm shone in her face. 'We can make some new curtains too, a nice buttercup yellow. What do you think? It'll cheer us up!'

Colette wasn't interested. She sighed impatiently. 'Why spend money on someone else's property? If the landlord sees it he'll only think the place is worth more and put the rent up.'

'Oh, don't be so pessimistic! Why should we put up with this tatty old wallpaper? Half of it is stained or peeling off and just look at the doors! They're all chipped and peppered with drawing-pin holes. Come on, darling, what do you say?'

Colette slumped down on the sofa and stared at the floor. 'Mum,' she said and turned to her decisively. 'The thing is: I won't be living here much longer.'

'Not living here? Of course we will!' Bianca replied with a laugh. 'We've got no choice. We can't afford anything better so we might as well make the most of it. It's comfortable and at least we've got a bathroom. It's more than some people have got.'

There was an awkward silence. 'Mum?' Colette lifted her face and revealed the tears in her eyes. 'What I mean is, I won't be living here anymore. I'm going away with Danny.'

'Going away? What do you mean darling?'

'If I don't go with him, he said we'll have to split up. He won't stay in one place for long, Mum, he can't stand it. Last night he said he's been in Tollwithen too long already.' A surge of tears descended on her and she buried her face in her hands and wept.

Bianca turned pale. 'But why? You're going away with him – you mean for good? But where?'

'Oh, Wales or somewhere! Anywhere! I don't know Mum! He just travels. He's always on the move. He's got the Land Rover and trailer. He just parks up where he feels like it, does a bit of scrap-metal trading and then moves on. It's how he's always lived, it's what he's used to and he can't change.'

'But you can't mean it! You're not like them, darling. You're not a gypsy. You can't live like that!' she cried. 'Danny can't be expecting you to live like he does, with nowhere to call home. Travelling round the country, living in a trailer and... No darling, you can't possibly! I don't believe you'd even consider it!'

'I love him, Mum! He said he would look after me. I could wash and cook for him and help out with...'

'But you deserve better than that! Washing and cooking for some man you hardly know! He won't appreciate who you really are! Does he love you? Does he want to marry you? I expect he hasn't even mentioned that! You've got a life ahead of you. You've had a good education; you could do well for yourself given half the chance.' She paused, 'I know it hasn't been easy since my accident, but I'm getting better now. We can...'

'If I don't leave with Danny tonight I might never see him again.'

The word struck Bianca like a bullet. 'Tonight? But think, Colette! This is your home!' She broke down.

'I know Mum. I don't want to leave you, but what else can I do?' And her tears broke out afresh.

'Oh, my poor darling.' Bianca rushed to her and hugged her. 'We'll talk to him. We'll go together and explain that you can't go. We'll tell him you're not used to travelling on the road all the time; you're too sensitive! He'll understand when we explain. He can come back here and visit you whenever he likes. He can even stay here; he'll be more than welcome...' She bit her lip.

'No!' said Colette. 'I feel so restless here. I feel caged in – in this tiny miserable flat. I want to do something with my life, see the world, meet people. And I want to be with Danny, I just have to.' She looked up into her mother's eyes. 'What else can I do, Mum? I'll lose him otherwise.'

'If he cares enough for you he'll come back. Believe me he will, darling!'

Colette shook her head. 'Mum, you know that man who lived upstairs, Drew or Jack or whatever he called himself? You know they said he was my father. I can hardly bear to think of it – I hate him so much – but it must be true. You see, I think it's the gypsy blood in my veins that's making me like this. I can't deny my birth right, can I? Even if I didn't ask for it, I can feel it! I've made up my mind, Mum. I'll go and pack. I'm going to leave with Danny tonight.'

Saying this she fled back to her room. Bianca heard her opening and slamming drawers. The noise interspersed by the sound of her crying. Her heart felt raw with pain. She sat thinking about how she had lived and breathed for Colette - her precious daughter, her best friend. She had had so many ambitions for her;

so many hopes for her future. How could she carry on living without her? How could she let her go away with that man? Could she bring herself to wish her well, bless them both with happiness? They were after all, she told herself, just two young people in love. But what is Love? Is Love simply that elusive thing that sweeps away reason and practicalities? How can she stop her, and should she?

A knock on the door interrupted her thoughts and a smile broke through the tears as she recognised who it was.

'Is she still here?' asked Finn. 'I had to come! I have to talk her out of it.'

Bianca frowned. 'So you've heard? Yes, she's in her bedroom, packing her bags.'

Finn nodded. 'I just saw Danny.' He sat down and put his head in his hands. His action reminded Bianca of when the old gypsy first came to see her. That easy, homely way Gideon had about him. Finn possessed that same quiet brooding masculinity that made her feel so trusting and hopeful.

'Can I get you a cup of tea or something?' she asked, steadying her voice and making an effort.

Finn shook his head. 'Thanks, no. I was hopin' I weren't too late to catch her, that's all.'

'But it's no use, Finn. I've tried talking to her. She won't listen.'

He breathed slowly, watching Bianca. His dark eyes scanned the room, waiting. In a moment the bedroom door was flung open and Colette emerged carrying a large suitcase.

Finn stood up. 'So you're really goin' with him?'

She nodded. 'If I don't...'

'If you don't, you think you won't see him again – is that it?'

'He's a gypsy; he has to keep travelling on. It's in his blood and... and it's in mine!' she added defiantly.

'And mine,' he replied calmly. 'But it ain't no different to other folks' blood. Them that say it's different are only sayin' it so they can shut us out in the cold an' turn their backs on us.' Suddenly he was thrown back into the past when the dying fire had cast shadows across Gideon's face when he told him he had to leave and strike out on his own. It filled him with fear when he remembered his words:

"The road I travel on, it's a long aimless road, Finn. The nights are dark an' cold an' the caravan's damp as yer well know. If yer stick along wi' me much longer yer feet'll grow like mine, like twisted old tree roots wi' no soil around 'em."

'Gideon showed me another way,' said Finn. 'He brought me back here to Tollwithen where it all went wrong wi' my life so's I could put things right again an' settle down.' Looking away, he saw Bianca was listening intently. 'Gideon said it ain't good to keep travellin' all the time an' he were right. That's why I'm stayin' here with Mitzi and settlin' down. Why don't yer ask Danny to stay too?'

'He won't!' she cried and stamped her foot impatiently.

'Ask him.'

She shook her head. 'No! I've got to go.' She went over to Bianca and enveloped her in her arms. 'Try to understand. I've got to go with Danny. He's waiting for me. I'm sorry, Mum!' She kissed her and hugged her before picking up her suitcase and making

320

for the door.

'No wait!' shouted Finn, rising swiftly from the chair. 'Stop!' But she was off down the stairs, banging her suitcase mercilessly on every step as she went. 'Colette!' he shouted.

She didn't even look back.

Turning to Bianca, he said, 'I'll go after her.'

Pausing half-way down, he saw she had followed and was standing at the top of the stairs. 'Don't worry,' he called. 'I'll bring her back, whatever 'appens. I won't let go of her again, I promise.'

Bianca went to the window and saw Colette hurrying away down the street with her suitcase and Finn running after her; he soon caught her up. She stopped and they seemed to be arguing. But Bianca couldn't bear to watch any longer and, as tears filled her eyes, she turned away. When she looked again, her heart leapt with joy. Finn was carrying the suitcase and they were coming back! Colette and her brother were on their way home.

The End

Acknowledgements

My thanks and love to my husband Graham, for his enthusiasm, proof-reading, IT skills and wide-ranging support for my writing. While the hours ticked by as I sat at my desk, his patience and endurance never failed to impress me.

Thank you also to my sister, the writer and artist Bernie Ross, for her encouragement, and author/tutor Gill Vickery for that morning in her Creative Writing class when the seeds of an idea for this novel were first sown.

I am also grateful to my friends for their support including authors Madalyn Morgan and Kate Harris; to Brenda Griffiths for proof-reading and to my daughter-in-law, Julie Wood, for her help with the title - I had so many title options at one point I didn't know where to turn! Finally I would like to thank the Society of Authors and especially fellow members of the Romantic Novelists' Association, who never failed to advise and give me a boost when I was flagging.

I hope you enjoyed reading THE GYPSY'S SON. My heart goes out to all the Romany gypsy folk who travelled the highways and byways of the British Isles in their horse-drawn caravans, facing a harsh and unpredictable future. In writing this novel, I wanted to capture their affinity with nature and their restless spirit. Their simple way of life was bound to change when the modern world encroached on their Romany traditions. Change isn't necessarily a bad thing, but we can still remember the old ways with affection.

45623360R00199

Made in the USA
Charleston, SC
29 August 2015